15 GRAVES

Chris Thorndyke

~

Content compiled for publication by Richard Mayers of Burton Mayers Books.

Cover artwork designed by Martellia Design

First published by Burton Mayers Books 2023.

ISBN: 9781739630959

Typeset in Garamond

www.BurtonMayersBooks.com

DEDICATION

For my three sons, with love.

ACKNOWLEDGMENTS

My thanks to Sofie Wikander for introducing me to the Swedish island of Hanö and giving me the initial inspiration to write this novel. Also, to the kind and helpful assistance shown to me by the helpers of Hanö's tiny museum, whose information and guidance helped me in my research and allowed me to step back in time to follow in the footsteps of the crew of an early nineteenth century Royal Navy frigate based on the island. To the group of fishermen, I met on the quay in Nogersund, who furnished me with their tales of the sea, particularly the two fishermen brothers whom I have borrowed to play the parts of Erik and Olof in my story. My thanks to the Royal Navy for their diligence and support of the island's "English Cemetery" and their yearly visits to pay tribute to the fifteen English sailors buried there. Finally, not forgetting a big thank you to my wife, Anki, whose never-ending patience saw me through to the last chapter of my tale.

AUTHOR'S NOTE

A small cemetery located on the small island of Hanö, off the southern coast of Sweden and overlooking the waters of the Baltic Sea, is home to fifteen graves. A wooden cross, erected by the Royal Navy in 1973, marks the spot where the graves are located. In each of these graves lie the remains of a British Royal Navy sailor laid to rest after making the supreme sacrifice in service to his country and selfless fealty towards comrades. Today, British warships still visit the cemetery to pay tribute to the sailors, who in 1812 gave their lives in defending the island against the might of Napoleon's navy.

The characters in my story are fictitious, but through my research bear a great resemblance to the crew of a certain British frigate based on the island in 1812. I have gratefully borrowed Clifford Williams and Richard Davis to play a part in my story, two actual members of the crew whose names are still legible on the few gravestones that have weathered time to overlook the Baltic Sea from their resting place high up on Hanö's uppermost point.

Although most of its records have been lost in the annals of history, I have managed to resurrect these naval heroes to play their part yet again, in one of the many tales of valour that helped stop Napoleon's relentless surge through the Baltic Sea and his ruthless appetite to conquer everything within his grasp.

1

March 1812
Danzig (Gdansk) Poland

The sound of heavy riding boots hastening up a flight of marble stairs echoed around the ornately decorated walls of the prestigious medieval Artus Court building in the old city of Danzig. Two men dressed in the uniforms of French naval officers stopped at the top of the stairway. Not saying a word, they looked at each other and with a smile turned into a long passageway that led past rows of imposing wooden doors.

General Jean-Luc Bonard, appointed by Napoleon as First Secretary General to the semi-autonomous city-state of Danzig, traced a finger down the long scar that began under his right eye and finished in the deep cleft of his chin, a scar incurred from a Prussian cavalry officer's sabre six years before at the battle of Jena-Auerstedt on the plateau west of the River Saale in Prussia. From his office window he looked down on the horse drawn carriages pulling up on the wide forecourt below. Sombre individuals paid off their drivers, then hurried into the building to offload whatever claims or private business they needed to impart to the officials managing what was now Napoleon's self-governing city-state.

A resounding knock on his door broke the silence. Turning away from the window he made his way towards a grandiose oak desk and, seating himself, he reached for a folded map of the Baltic.

"Enter," he commanded.

The two naval officers walked briskly into the room. Jean-Luc, his eyes cast down on the map he had spread across the top of his desk, smiled as the two naval officers stood stiffly to attention before him.

"At ease gentlemen," he said, looking up. "My meeting with Commandant Joubert, your commanding officer, finished a short time ago and was most informative, hence your summons to my office. Our plans for the attack on Hanö Island, about which you have already been briefed, will go into effect on the completion of your mission. Commandant Joubert assures me you're both now well-prepared and will leave tonight."

Jean-Luc studied the two men standing before him, wondering whether they were completely aware of the seriousness of their mission.

"I want to emphasise the urgency of the mission on which you're about to embark. Without information regarding the island's defences and the British ships moored in their harbour, our task of taking the island will be considerable. His Excellency, The Emperor, insists that Hanö Island be taken and the British Royal Navy ships that hide away in the protection of that small harbour, destroyed once and for all. I need not tell you that the British presence on this island is a major obstacle to His Excellency's plans for our future invasion of Russia which will require an unhindered passage through the Baltic. Gentlemen, Hanö Island must be ours. "You," he said, looking at one of the officers, "your name and rank?"

"Jacques Petit, Lieutenant sir."

"And you?" asked Jean-Luc, nodding to the other one.

"Pierre Renaud, Lieutenant sir."

"As you know, we've arranged for you to be met in the port here on the hour of nine tonight by a Swedish fishing vessel. The master of the vessel is a Swedish fisherman and merchant operating in Nogersund, a small harbour on the mainland coast of Blekinge, four kilometres off Hanö. His name is Erik Gunnarsson and although he supplies the British base with essential victuals, he and his crew have a hatred for the British. Aboard the vessel will be Erik's brother Olof, Erik's son Lars, and two brothers Nils and Gustav Lundberg, who work as part of Erik's fishing crew. You will be disguised as Swedish fishermen working for Erik, as your false identity papers will confirm. Should the vessel be stopped by a British frigate, leave the talking to Gunnarsson, act as though you do not understand

English. When you arrive in Nogersund, he will arrange for you to be part of the crew of his boat that takes victuals to the island once a week. Once you are on the island, you will meet up with your contact there, then it is up to you. Gunnarsson and his family speak excellent English, as do you both. Good luck. You have two weeks - no more – before he returns you here. Again, I stress the importance of your mission. That is all gentlemen. I wish you God speed."

Jacques and Pierre hurried along the windswept embankment of the old port of Danzig. Hands thrust deep inside their trouser pockets, they shivered with the night-time cold as an icy wind blowing off the Motlawa river cut through the coarse woollen peasant clothing meant to disguise them as Swedish fishermen. A full moon lit up the two solitary figures hastening along the deserted riverbank towards the location of The Great Medieval Crane and the steps down the side of the embankment where Erik and his crew would be waiting to ferry them out of Danzig. The sound of a distant church clock chiming the hour of nine made them stop to peer over the side of the embankment at the dark waters below.

"No sign of the fishing boat here," said Pierre, blowing on his freezing fingers.

"Could be round the bend," replied Jacques. "We were told to head for The Medieval Crane on the side of the embankment and that's not far, round that bend. Come on."

The dark shape of Danzig's most famous waterfront crane loomed before them as they rounded the bend, their breath steaming out of their mouths like clouds of discarded tobacco smoke. The huge crane towered before them, dominating the sheds and warehouses around it. Designed in 1442 as a riverside working crane to offload ships' cargoes and manage the winching up of ships' fore and main masts, it was rated the biggest crane in the world. Jacques and Pierre stood with their backs to it searching for the flight of steps that would lead them down to a river jetty, where hopefully Erik's fishing boat would be waiting. Squinting through the darkness, Jacques nudged Pierre, "There're the steps, over there. I can just make out the first one cut into the embankment."

They were about to make a move when out of the shadows a tall figure appeared on the top step holding up a lantern.

"You two," he called, softly beckoning them, "come this way, the boat's waiting and we want to make use of the wind. Hurry."

On board the fishing vessel the two French spies watched as two of the crew unhitched the mooring ropes, the vessel drifting clear of the embankment.

With the wind filling the fishing boat's broad sail, Jacques and Pierre felt the vessel glide out into the centre of the river, the imposing shape of the crane casting a deep shadow across the moonlit water.

"My name's Lars Gunnarsson," said the crew member who had met them at the top of the steps.

"Up there at the helm is my father. Next to him is my uncle Olof and the two deckhands are Nils and Gustav, two brothers."

"How long before we reach Nogersund?" asked Pierre, looking out over the stern at a row of dark warehouses on the embankment above.

"About an hour along the Motlawa river, then out into the open sea. Weather and wind permitting, I would say we will be there about midday tomorrow. Hopefully, we will avoid the British frigates patrolling the sea lanes, but should we be stopped then leave the talking to my father. We've already loaded the hold with fish, they're down there on ice just in case the British search the vessel."

Jacques looked up as Erik came strolling towards them, a huge Viking of a man with a long grey beard to match. Expressionless, he regarded the two spies while Lars looked on.

"When we reach Nogersund you two will be my guests until I arrange for you to join my crew for our trip over to Hanö, probably only a night at the most. So, as Lars has told you we've a long way to go. My brother Olof will be at the helm for the next six hours, then Lars will take over until dawn. The rest of us need to get some sleep. Down in the hold is a bit cramped and stinking of fish but there are five bunks, so I suggest you both get your heads down."

Erik, a good head, and shoulders taller than the two Frenchmen, looked down at them studying each in turn.

"Your papers are in order I assume?"

Jacques pulled a crumpled document from his pocket.

"Perfect," uttered Erik, looking it over. "From now on you'll be known by the name on the document, Per Carlsson."

Looking at Pierre's false paper he smiled, "and you Magnus Andersson need to get some sleep. Down those steps there, gentlemen. Find any bunk in the hold, I'll be down as soon as I've briefed Olof."

Jacques and Pierre followed Lars down the vertical flight of wooden steps to the hold below, recoiling at the pungent smell of fish that engulfed the whole area. Three compact bunk beds rising on one side of the hold gave little room to move between two compact bunks on the opposite side.

"You two take the two bunks over there," said Lars, his English singing the melodious accent of the Swedes. "Gustav and I can take two of the others on the other side as we'll be up in six hours to take over from Olof and Nils."

Lying on the top bunk, Jacques felt the change in the movement of the boat as it approached the end of its journey down the Motlawa river. The smooth passage through the water quickly changed to a to-ing and fro-ing as the vessel fought its way through the rolling waves of the open sea. He pulled the rough blanket covering him further over his head, listening to the gentle snores of his partner coming from the lower bunk.

Sleep seemed a long way away for Jacques. His mind was racing ahead, picturing their course of action after their arrival on the island. Once they had deposited whatever supplies they would be helping to take to the British, they would vanish into the forest that covered two thirds of the small island. They would plan their itinerary with the French agent already based there - spying on the movement and times of British ships departing and entering the harbour, the defensive strength of the small naval garrison and the most suitable point to land a detachment of their marines. Erik would ferry them off the island two weeks from this date, returning them to Danzig where they would give their report to General Bonard. Jacques smiled knowing that promotion and decoration awaited the two of them on the success of their mission.

The fishing boat continued to rock its way further north into the Baltic Sea compelling Jacques to relax to the swaying movement of the vessel. Sleep soon came to him, blocking out the tall dark shape standing at the side of the two bunks. With a serious look at the two Frenchmen slumbering peacefully, Erik slid into the lower berth of the other three compact bunks and, with the sound of his son Lars snoring in the bunk above him, he pulled the coarse blanket around him giving way to the long-awaited sleep he had been longing so much for.

2

Dawn was breaking over the choppy waters of the Baltic Sea, marking out a lone British warship slicing its way through the white crested swells that surged and crashed against its bow. A gusty wind billowed out its sails, driving it across the broiling expanse while an orange sun climbing slowly above the horizon silhouetted the dark outline of the rocky island of Hanö several leagues away.

James Carey, captain of the thirty-six gun fully rigged frigate HMS Hector, stood on its quarterdeck focusing on the distant speck of rock that was home to a handful of British Royal Navy warships. Knitting his brow over the vulnerability of the island to an attack by the French, he turned to watch the sharp efficiency of his crew. Brushing off feelings of apprehension, he sucked in the salty air whipping before him, relishing the open sea and the thrill it presented. HMS Hector was on patrol, searching for French vessels or anything unfriendly that could threaten Britain's operations.

Turning his gaze, he scanned the frigate's deck, pleased with the efficiency of his crew's detail to duty his eyes roaming aloft to the precise crisscrossing of the ship's rigging. He scrutinized the lofty foremast accommodating the big square sail known as the fore course, appreciating the skillful work that had gone into its making.

His eyes combed the foretopsail yard that crossed it seeking out the foretopsail that swelled as it caught the wind. From the foretop gallant sail his eyes flicked over to the maintop sails seeing them bulge in the salty gusts, while below them the ample main sail ballooned majestically in the strengthening wind.

The bold mainmast, set between the foremast and the smaller mizzen mast, stood a hundred and twenty feet high, proud like an eminent overlord regarding his territory. Two finely polished crosstrees at the upper ends of the top mast and holding thick ropes known as shrouds, smiled down haughtily as Hector rode the white caps that reluctantly gave way before it.

The ship's cannons, positioned on each side of the upper deck and resembling a pack of black mastiffs pointed out to sea through their open gun ports, ready to savage anything unwelcome that dared approach. Twenty-six eighteen pounder cannons secured on carriage mountings jutted out contentiously, thirteen on portside and thirteen on starboard side, while ten carronades peered indifferently out to sea from positions on the quarterdeck and forecastle.

James smiled in satisfaction, his eyes seeking out the lonesome figure of the look-out perched high on the top sail yard, scouring the vacant sea for any sign of sail that would give the British frigate cause for concern.

A complement of two hundred and ten men comprising able and ordinary seamen, commissioned and non-commissioned officers made up HMS Hector's crew.

James turned afore to breathe in the salty brine and savour the salt-kissed air that surged around him. The youngest son of Nathaniel Carey, a successful Plymouth importer of sugar and tobacco, James was commissioned a lieutenant in the Royal Navy in the summer of 1805 at the age of twenty-one. A posting as Third Lieutenant to HMS Leviathan quickly followed where he was soon recognized as a most able junior officer. Within several months HMS Leviathan was part of Admiral Nelson's windward column at the battle of Trafalgar where James distinguished himself in being part of a boarding party in the attack and capture of the Spanish ship San Augustin. Mentioned in dispatches for his courage and skill as a junior officer, he was appointed First Lieutenant to the frigate HMS Volage in 1808. Seeing action against the French in the Mediterranean, he again distinguished himself in the capture of a French brig just north of Corsica. Further gallant exploits aboard HMS Volage quickly brought his name to the attention of the admiralty, and in the new year of 1812 he was assigned the position of captain to the Royal Navy frigate HMS Hector, part of Admiral Sir James Saumarez's fleet stationed on the Swedish island of Hanö.

"Seems all quiet out there, captain," said Hector's first

Lieutenant, Daniel Sutherland, joining James on the quarterdeck.

"One can never tell Dan," James said, opening his telescope and squinting through its lens in a sweeping movement of the sea.

"May see a Frenchie today. Prepare the ship for battle drill, officers to the quarterdeck with me."

"Aye, aye, sir," replied Dan, turning towards the ship's boatswain. "Mr. Nark, prepare the crew for action stations drill and be sharp about it. Captain wants to see seconds shorn off the last drill. Set to Mr. Nark."

Shrill whistles from the boatswain's small pipe stirred the crew into action as Nark bellowed out his commands. James watched as able seamen clambered up the shrouds and ratlines to their battle positions while others, including ordinary seamen and those unfortunate to have been pressed ganged, raced to their appointed stations around the deck.

The sharp clanging of the ship's bell ringing out a command to action stations brought the remaining ship's officers hurrying to the quarterdeck.

"Mr. Piper," Dan called to the Master Gunner, "prepare all guns for action."

"Aye, aye, Mr. Sutherland," replied Thomas Piper springing into action and yelling towards his gun crew.

James nodded at the precision and speed of his crew, pleased that if put into real practice his ship would be ready in an instant for any action that presented itself.

"Bring her round, Mr. Sturrock," he shouted to the coxswain. "Three points to starboard."

"Aye, aye, sir," replied Davey Sturrock, coxswain of HMS Hector, "three points to starboard, captain."

"Give fire Mr. Sutherland, guns seven, eight and nine starboard side" James commanded.

"Seven, eight and nine guns, starboard side fire, Mr. Piper," yelled Dan.

As the three guns roared in their gun ports, James grinned.

"Now Mr. Sutherland, guns ten, eleven and twelve, portside give fire."

Dan's command to Thomas Piper was drowned in the thunderous noise of the portside guns booming.

Telescopes firmly set against their right eye, James and his officers watched three wide splashes far out to sea as the three cannon balls found their invisible targets.

"Bring her back on course Mr. Sturrock," commanded James. "A good drill Mr. Sutherland, instruct Mr. Nark to return the crew to normal duties. We'll shave a few more minutes off the next drill."

"Aye, aye, sir," replied Dan.

James turned to his second lieutenant Richard Devonshire, who stood studying the gun crew in their routine of cleaning and preparing the cannons just fired for future action.

"Well, Mr. Devonshire. Your thoughts on the exercise?"

"Speed to action stations seemed to be up on the last drill sir, and the gun crew were quicker off the mark on your order to give fire."

"Reflections?" asked James raising an eyebrow.

"If the gun crew are as quick in reloading once guns have fired, then I think they'll have reached near perfection sir."

"That'll be seen in our next drill Mr. Devonshire. Thank you for your observations."

James turned to the ship's chaplain, Sebastian Pomeroy. "Mr. Pomeroy, care to join me in my cabin for sherry. You too Mr. Kirkland and Mr. Basset."

Edmund Kirkland, surgeon to the crew and Jeremiah Basset ship's purser nodded to their captain following him and the chaplain off the quarterdeck towards James' cabin, a deck down in the stern of the ship.

"Mr. Sutherland," shouted James, stopping, "you have the quarterdeck. Who's at watch?"

"Able seamen Richard Davis and Clifford Williams sir."

"Very well, carry on Mr. Sutherland."

"Well Gentlemen," said James, raising his glass. "A good exercise and a much speedier delivery of the guns. To the King."

"To the King," the three echoed draining their glasses with one swift mouthful.

"Please be seated gentlemen," said James, indicating to the cook's mate to replenish their glasses.

"I'd like your thoughts on the state of our defenses on the island."

"Seems we've got the Frenchies bottled up safely enough by our rigorous patrolling captain," suggested Edmund Kirkland. "They've come off worse in every action we've engaged them in."

"Apart from the occasional ship that breaks through our line, I'd say that Frenchie's happier staying in his own port than having a go at us," said Jeremiah Basset.

"But are they lying low in pretense? We only have a handful of ships engaged in patrolling the major sea lanes," suggested the veteran chaplain of Trafalgar, Sebastian Pomeroy.

"That's exactly what's on my mind," said James. "With most of our small fleet out of harbour, Hanö's wide open for attack. Should the French be planning a big push through the Baltic, then our base will be first on their list. We obviously need to be reinforced."

"The navy's stretched at the moment gentlemen," said Jeremiah.

"As it always seems to be," interrupted the ship's surgeon.

"Troubles brewing again across the Atlantic with the newly formed United States," continued Jeremiah. "There's talk of war again and the French will undoubtedly give those ex rebels their immediate support. To ask for reinforcements here, is nigh on impossible captain."

"Then we'll have to think of something," said James.

"I've a feeling the French are planning something big, a possible attack on the Swedish mainland or even Hanö itself. I ask you for your support gentlemen when I take this up with Commodore Percival back at base. I believe the southern-most part of the island is where the French will try to land a detachment of their marines, while their main fleet attacks the harbour on its northern side."

The unexpected clanging of the ship's bell ringing out an alarm around the ship suddenly jolted the four of them from their seats. Jumping to their feet they rushed out in the direction of the upper deck.

"Sail, sail on the starboard side," hollered the lookout, high up on the main topsail yard. "Sailing northerly on our starboard side bow."

"Report Mr. Sutherland," demanded James, taking the telescope handed to him by his first lieutenant.

"Looks like an average-sized Swedish fishing vessel captain, about a mile off our starboard side."

James swept the telescope in an arc, focusing on the vessel.

"That it does," he said, viewing the Swedish flag flying from the stern of the fishing boat. "Nevertheless, we'll investigate. Mr. Sturrock bring her round, two points to starboard."

"Aye, aye, captain, two points to starboard."

"Mr. Nark," yelled James, "full sail, now."

"Aye, aye, sir," called Bill Nark.

"We'll intercept her Dan. You and a boarding party search her, never know who or what might be on board, prepare to fire a warning shot across her bow.

HMS Hector closed in on Erik's fishing vessel, a longboat holding a boarding party waiting to be winched down its side. Jacques and Pierre stood rigidly still, nervously watching, and wondering whether their mission would end before it had even begun.

3

All eyes aboard Erik's fishing boat watched the British longboat approach, its officer standing erect in the bow while two of the crew raised their oars as the boat brushed up against the side of the Swedish vessel. Dan Sutherland grasped the rough rope ladder at the side of Erik's boat and clambered up onto the deck followed by four of his armed search party, the two rowers remaining behind in the longboat. HMS Hector, towering above the fishing boat, looked on as Erik's vessel rocked to and fro in the choppy swell.

"Who is in charge of this vessel?" asked Dan.

"I'm the skipper lieutenant. My name's Erik Gunnarsson."

"Where are you headed?" asked Dan, his eyes scouring the deck.

"To Nogersund," replied Erik. "We have a haul of fish to get to my warehouse on the quay. You may know me as your supplier of fish and vegetables. Once a week I come over to the harbour on Hanö Island with supplies."

"That I do Mr. Gunnarsson, forgive me for not recognizing you. But my orders are to search your vessel and to inspect your crew. I'm sorry if this is an inconvenience."

"Please, be my guest lieutenant. We have been at sea for the last three days. The hold is full of fish." said Erik smiling at Dan.

"You four," said Dan, pointing at the four able seamen, "two of you check the hold and two of you search the deck for anything you think maybe suspicious. Mr. Gunnarsson please ask your crew to line up in front of me with their papers ready. Thank you, sir."

Erik spoke to his crew in Swedish although they all understood

Dan's instruction. Jacques and Pierre joined them at the end of the line, their hands thrust deep inside their jacket pockets as Dan checked Erik's papers first. Coming down to the end of the line, Dan stopped directly in front of Jacques and Pierre.

"Your papers please gentlemen?" he asked.

Instinct told the two Frenchmen to keep quiet although Pierre nearly followed Dan's request.

"Visa honom dina identitetshandlingar," Erik shouted earnestly, towards the two spies.

Acting the part, Jacques nodded and whipped out his crumpled identity document offering it over to Dan. Pierre watched Dan scrutinize the paper then hand it back to Jacques with a nod.

"What's your name?" asked Dan, looking seriously at Pierre.

Holding his tongue although he very well understood Dan's question, Pierre played his part looking questioningly towards Erik.

"Vad heter du?" shouted back Erik, playing his part equally well.

"Ah ja," said Pierre, thinking quickly, "Magnus Andersson."

Erik breathed a sigh of relief as Dan scanned Pierre's false identity paper, handing it back to him with a smile.

"All clear in the hold sir," said the returning seamen from below. "Only a load of fish on ice and five empty bunk beds."

"Anything around the deck you two?" asked Dan, looking over at the two seamen who had searched the deck area.

"No sir, nothing unusual," came the reply.

"Very well Mr. Gunnarsson. You are free to continue your journey on to Nogersund. I expect we'll see you on the island with the fish you're carrying down in the hold. Good day to you sir."

"Fucking bastards!" uttered Olof, as they watched the British search party return to their ship.

"Second that!" frowned Erik, turning towards Jacques and Pierre, "well-played you two. Full sail Lars, my old sea legs are wanting dry land. Take the helm Olof, we're heading back on course and home. The rest of you look lively, they may still be watching us from their frigate."

James watched the sail on Erik's fishing boat take the wind as it spurred away on course for the Swedish mainland, something was nagging him something in his mind telling him there was something not quite right about the Swedish vessel.

"Mr. Sutherland," he called over to Dan, "to the quarterdeck please."

Dan made his way over to the quarterdeck where James was following the wake of Erik's fishing boat.

"Well?" asked James, turning towards Dan.

James listened carefully to Dan's description of the search, raising his eyebrow when Dan related the inspection of the crew's identity papers. A curious thought crossed his mind although Dan assured his captain there was nothing out of the ordinary with their identities.

"Apart from the skipper, what number of crew were there?" asked James.

"Six, captain," replied Dan.

"Six crew members and a skipper for that size of fishing boat?" queried James. "Doesn't it seem a bit overcrowded Dan? With all the fishing vessels we've pulled up over in the last few months, there's never been more than four and a skipper for that size of vessel. Strike you a bit odd?"

"Now you mention it captain, it does. Seven crewing a five-berth vessel doesn't seem right, although everything was in order on board. The skipper's name is Erik Gunnarsson, he's the supplier of fish and vegetables to our quartermaster. His English was fluent when I questioned him."

"I know of him," said James. "It's his daughter who comes over mostly with our supplies. I've seen her commandeering some of our men to help carry boxes of fish to our cookhouse. Seems a bossy shrew, but she gets away with it as she's a good looker. Long auburn hair and tall, couldn't be more than twenty - she's turned my head a few times!"

"Yes sir, she's certainly a beauty," agreed Dan.

"After two days Dan we have liberty. We can take a boat over to Nogersund, to Erik Gunnarsson's warehouse. I want to know more about his crew members and how long they've been in his service."

"Yes captain," replied Dan. "We may be in for a bit of a surprise!"

Erik's boat coasted into the small harbour of Nogersund where a small number of helpers waited on the quay alongside its docking site. Dozens of ice-filled wooden boxes lay stacked around them, the ice glistening like a horde of cut diamonds in the midday sun. An attractive auburn-haired young woman stood next to a mooring post shading her eyes from the sun as the fishing vessel glided up to its berth. Grabbing the mooring rope that Nils cast onto the quay she quickly dropped the looped end over the post, wrapping a further length of the rope tightly around it.

"When the ramp drops onto the quay," she shouted to the line of helpers standing ready with their wooden boxes, "board the boat. You know where the fish is kept in the hold below. Fill your boxes with the fish and hurry over to the warehouse. Stack the boxes in the cold area and be quick, I don't want the ice to melt."

As she finished her instruction, the wooden ramp crashed down onto the quay allowing the helpers to hurry onto the vessel, the ice in their boxes beginning to succumb to the warmth of the early spring sunshine.

"Papa," she called out to Erik who stood watching the procedure with a smile. "We need to hurry, the ice in the boxes won't keep for long, can you all help? There are more boxes here on the quay."

"Lars," yelled Erik, "take Nils and Gustav with you and go and help your sister. Take the two Frenchmen as well."

"You four come with me quickly," instructed Lars, looking at the two brothers then at Jacques and Pierre. Grab one of those boxes of ice, fill it with fish from the hold and take it to that warehouse at the end of the quay, the one with the double doors wide open. My sister Anna is in there, she'll show you where to put them. Come on, hurry!"

The two spies struggled up the steps that led from the hold, the ice in their boxes slowly beginning to melt as the fish they'd managed to scoop up slithered around in their death throes, some already dead others wriggling and slapping against the sides of the boxes. The inside of Erik's warehouse was dark and cool as they followed Lars through the open double doors. Helpers were stacking their boxes on a stone floor at the end of the building while others gutted the fish with razor sharp knives, the whole area holding the fish being surrounded by thick blocks of ice.

"Hurry it up," shouted Anna, glaring at the two Frenchmen.

"Stack your boxes on top of the others and then move out as fast as you can. Too many bodies around the stacks can melt the ice."

"Come on, let's get back to the boat," said Lars, "my father's ready to take you to our house."

Erik and Olof were watching several of the harbour workers carrying the last boxes of fish off the boat as Lars and the two Frenchmen joined them on the quay.

"Well, if you're ready gentlemen we can go up to the house, lunch is calling. Olof will wait until all the fish has been unloaded and then join us later. Nils and Gustav have already gone up. This way gentlemen."

They followed Erik past rows of long wooden sheds, some empty and closed, others with their doors wide open showing off various crab pots and fishing nets hanging from dusty rafters. Erik waved a hand in a friendly response to two fishermen busily scraping the underside of an old rowing boat, then turning a corner they came upon a steep hillside peppered with thick rows of pine trees overlooking a coastline of scattered beaches and tiny inlets.

Wooden houses set between the trees peeped out curiously at the two spies following Erik and Lars up a winding path that zigzagged its way towards a solidly built house at the top of the track. Spectacular views across the expanse of sea met them at the top of the stony pathway. Wedged in a tight corner beneath them the modest harbour of Nogersund looked lazily out to sea, its long quay jutting out like a finger pointing towards something lost on the distant horizon. The sound of a door opening behind them quickly drew their attention and turning they watched an attractive middle-aged woman come hurrying down the front steps.

"Christina," said Erik, turning towards his wife, "these are the two gentlemen I spoke of. They'll be staying with us for the rest of the day and overnight. Our supplies for the British base on Hanö will be ready tomorrow, so they'll be accompanying us there. Now, as you know the two gentlemen are from the French garrison-port in Danzig and they do not speak any Swedish. So, as their English is far better than our little smattering of French, we will speak only in English."

"Absolutely," said Christina in English. "Welcome gentlemen, my husband has explained the purpose of your, let us say, visit to us. I hope you will be comfortable in our home. Come, lunch is now ready, Nils and Gustav have already arrived, and I guess Olof and Anna will be here shortly."

Jacques and Pierre gave a short bow to Erik's wife, smiling their appreciation at her warm welcome to them. Lars quickly followed his mother up the steps and as they were about to follow him Erik put a hand on Pierre's shoulder indicating them to wait.

"If you look very carefully out to the open sea," he said, pointing out over the treetops below them, "you can see the outline of Hanö Island over there, to the left of the harbour below us."

Jacques and Pierre squinted in the direction Erik was pointing, gradually making out the small dark pencil-line shape of the island. For a moment, the two spies fixed their eyes on the silhouette dotted far out to sea, knowing that their future and the future of their beloved Emperor must be sealed the moment they set foot onto its shoreline, the words of General Jean-Luc Bonard ringing clearly in their ears, *The island must be taken. Hanö Island must be ours.*

Realising what each other was thinking they nodded in their recognition, and then looking back at Erik waiting for them at the top of the steps, they hastened up after him eager to get their mission underway.

4

Early next morning, with a blustery wind filling the fishing boat's sail, Erik guided his vessel out of the harbour of Nogersund and out into the open sea. Boxes of fish lying on beds of ice filled the hold below while sacks of freshly packed vegetables lay in neat rows along the vessel's deck. Jacques and Pierre watched the mouth of the harbour become a distant speck as the fishing boat ploughed its way through the choppy swells towards the British garrison harbour on Hanö Island.

With her long auburn hair billowing out behind her, Anna sat on one of the water barrels checking the tally sheets of the supplies they were carrying.

Erik's attention was suddenly aroused by the distant sight of a naval vessel heading towards them. Squinting in its direction he yelled an instruction to the two brothers Nils and Gustav, "Reef the sail, and quick about it."

As the fishing vessel slowed its pace, the fully rigged British warship cruised ever closer towards them.

"It's that bastard that stopped us yesterday," said Nils to his brother, as the imposing sight of HMS Hector loomed into sight.

"All of you to portside," yelled Erik. "Give them a wave as they pass us. We don't want to arouse their suspicions. They'll recognise us and know we're taking supplies to the island. Come on now, she'll soon be passing."

Nils and Gustav rushed to portside where Anna sat watching the approaching frigate. Jacques and Pierre joined them as Hector's bow came closer into sight.

The Royal Navy frigate was not at full sail and moving gently at only a few knots through the water, so creating a minimum swell. Looking over its portside at the approaching fishing boat, James nodded, knowing that at such a slow speed the swell from the frigate would only slightly rock the fishing vessel as it passed and not present it with any great danger.

"That's the fishing boat we stopped yesterday Dan. Must be making for our base with the fish they'd caught. We'll have a good look at them as we pass."

"Indeed captain," replied Dan. "I recognise those crew members waving to us. Looks like Gunnarsson's daughter is on board."

James did not hear his lieutenant's reply. His eyes were fixed on the figure seated on the water barrel, her long hair streaming out in the wind.

As the two vessels came abreast, Anna looked up at the two men staring down at the fishing boat, her eyes locking onto the frigate's captain. She felt herself stir as he held her gaze. Something was triggering a well of excitement deep within her. Perhaps it was the warm smile he directed towards her as the two vessels passed. Gazing into the wake of the British frigate, she breathed in deeply, unable to dislodge the picture of him and the smile he had given her.

Erik guided his vessel closer to the mouth of the harbour. As they sailed through, Jacques and Pierre scanned its layout, scouring the tracks and paths that led away from its quay.

Coasting up to a mooring, Jacques' eyes widened at the sight of a warship berthed in a deep-water section of the harbour. Pointing it out to Pierre they nodded in unison recognising it as a third-rate ship of the British Navy, its two continuous gun decks having near on seventy closed gun ports. They knew immediately that the warship was a ship of the line and had probably been retired out to Hanö's harbour, but nevertheless capable of affording great destruction in a maritime arena of action.

Nils jumped onto the quay to secure the mooring ropes. Anna raised herself off the water barrel, her thoughts still captivated by the passing of the British frigate and the image of the British captain. Turning, she looked back at the entrance to the harbour wondering if she would ever see him again; something inside her told her she would.

A shout from Erik broke her spell and with a smile and a nod to her father she picked up the document itemising the supplies they were carrying and waited for the British harbour official to come aboard. No-one was permitted to leave the vessel until the harbour master had checked and tallied what they were bringing in. Following that, an inspection of the crew's identity papers would be carried out before the unloading of the supplies could begin.

Jacques and Pierre watched an overweight British harbour master and his assistant come aboard, taking their time in tallying the list of items on Anna's dispatch sheet. She stood on the deck looking increasingly agitated at the sluggish time the procedure was taking. After checking the crew's identity documents, the two officials left the boat leaving Anna to begin organising the offloading of the supplies.

Erik led the two French spies along the wharf passing a row of three securely locked wooden warehouses, each of their side windows encased in thick metal bars. Jacques and Pierre were quick to note such security when their attention was suddenly drawn to an adjacent building where a gang of carpenters were busily working on what looked like a sloop-of-war. The vessel was obviously undergoing certain repairs and by the urgency in which the carpenters were going about their work it seemed that completion of the war ship was of the utmost priority.

The sudden sound of men's voices, raised in agitation from inside a warehouse at the end of the quay, made the three of them look over to where a group of soldiers were trying to lead two huge looking cart horses out of its double doors. The animals' turbulent whinnying made Erik and the two spies move closer. Harnessed to a huge cannon, the two horses were becoming ever more distressed by the constant hollering from the soldiers and the frequent crack of a whip. By pushing the cannon from the back, they finally cleared the warehouse and with a few soothing actions calmed the horses into hauling the great gun to a stony track that led up a steep hillside.

"Seems they're taking that cannon up to the island's highest point," said Erik.

Jacques and Pierre watched the group spurring the horses on as the heavy gun was slowly dragged up the hill, the sound of its metal wheels grating over the loose stones lining the track until it finally disappeared round a corner.

"That's the third one this week," said a wiry looking middle-aged man, relaxing on a rocking chair outside a fisherman's hut. He sat puffing away at a clay pipe squinting towards them in the mid-morning sunshine. Steel-blue eyes set deep within his weather-worn leathery features gazed impudently up at them, a shock of white hair falling untidily over his shoulders.

"Jacob," said Erik, his eyes darting around the quay nervously, "the two you're expecting. Speak to them in English, they can't speak our language and I know you only have a smattering of uncouth French."

Jacob looked at the two French spies. "Do you know this island?" he asked them, taking the pipe from his mouth.

"No, we don't," replied Jacques turning towards Erik. "Is he our contact here?"

"That he is," replied Erik, looking around to make sure they could not be overheard.

"Jacob Forsberg. An old seadog and as much a hater of the British as I am. You can trust him with your lives. He knows every inch of this island as he was born here."

"The second part's true but I'm not sure of the old seadog!" came the reply.

Jacob looked up at Erik with a smile, deep lines of crow's feet stretching the corners of his eyes. "That I do gentlemen," he said, "and time is getting on, so best be up and away to my shack in the forest. You've got fish and vegetables to see to Erik Gunnarsson, with that pretty daughter of yours."

"That you're right about, Jacob Forsberg," said Erik, smiling. "Quickly," he said to Jacques and Pierre. "Pick up those nets hanging next to Jacob. Pretend to be checking them over. Two marine officers will be passing any second, don't want to arouse their suspicions."

The two Frenchmen wasted no time in grabbing the fishing nets hanging from the side of the shed next to Jacob. Looking away from the two passing soldiers, Pierre held one side of the net while Jacques pretended to closely examine a hole in it. Paying no attention to the two fishermen inspecting their nets, the two British officers walked past unconcerned. Jacob raised himself from his rocking chair, frowning at the backs of the two marines; then, hawking up a wad of phlegm, he spat onto the path they had just left behind.

Erik bade them farewell, wishing them luck in their mission and reassuring them he would be back to collect them in two weeks from a point on the island that Jacob would show them. With a slight wave he walked back casually towards his fishing boat where Nils and Gustav were making the boat ready to leave. Anna was on board after having organised the transfer of the supplies to the garrison cookhouse.

Erik grinned at the thought of his daughter's vigour in everything she put her mind to, reminding him of what he had been like at her age. He was pleased to see her waiting patiently on the boat. Nils slipped the mooring rope from its quayside post and jumping back on board grabbed one of the thick poles used to propel the boat away from the quay. Both brothers leant heavily on their poles, the fishing boat gliding smoothly away into the middle of the harbour where a gusty breeze quickly filled its sails driving it out into the open sea. Looking at the island creeping away behind him, Erik was suddenly overcome by a dark feeling of impending disaster. The war between Europe's two super-powers was about to explode over the occupancy of the island. Nogersund would surely be affected, but he owed it to his alliance and loyalty to the French to take their side. What they would expect of him would soon become clear. With a glance over at his daughter he gripped the ship's wheel and with a frown set his sights on the mainland ahead.

Jacob guided the two agents up a steep hillside track that led to the highest points of the island. Two deep rivets in the stony track, caused by the wheels of the heavy cannon, stretched half-way up the hilly pathway until they disappeared into a narrow lane. Far beneath them an expanse of sea glistened under the early spring sunshine. Stopping, Jacob turned, pointing down to the scene below, "There goes Erik," he said, "he has a fair wind up. Should be home in no time."

Jacques and Pierre looked down onto Erik's boat ploughing its way towards the mainland thinking of the toy boats they had often played with as young boys.

"Come on, we've a bit more climbing to do," said Jacob. "I want to take you to the highest part of the island where there's no forest. We need to be careful up there as that's where those marines were taking the big cannon. There're two more big guns already placed up there."

Huge grey boulders lay scattered around a landscape of windswept grass and bracken as the three spies stood on the highest point of the island, the white capped swells of the Baltic Sea surging far below them.

"Duck down quickly, behind that bush over there," hissed Jacob making a dive for a thicket of brambles.

"Redcoats, about a hundred yards away."

Peering around the bush they saw the group of marines manoeuvring the heavy gun to within distance of two other great cannons facing directly out to sea.

"That's the cannon you saw shackled to the two horses down in the warehouse," he said. "They've positioned each cannon within about twenty yards of each other to defend the harbour below."

"They're obviously expecting an attack at some time," mulled Jacques.

"What do you think their range is?"

Jacob squinted out to sea then looking back towards the three heavy guns.

"Probably over a mile from where they're fired," he said. "From up here they'll have a great advantage of anything approaching the harbour. I wouldn't fancy being part of an attacking fleet with those big guns aiming at me."

"What about the southern end of the island?" asked Jacques. "How well defended would that be?"

"Not at all," replied Jacob, "down over there," he said, pointing in the opposite direction from where the cannons had been placed, "is where the forest begins. It's quite dense and covers the rest of the island down to its rocky shoreline. Apart from the odd fisherman's hut it's uninhabited. Anyone landing there would have to traipse up through its rough stony trails to get up here - it's not that easy."

"What about anchoring a ship off its shore?" asked Jacques, "and then relaying its crew in longboats to the rocky shoreline?"

"Could be done," said Jacob smoothing his chin, "but only at night. There's a British sloop that patrols around the island at various times during the day."

"But not at night?" asked Pierre anxiously.

"Not sure about that one," replied Jacob, "you'd best scout around the shore at night, see what goes past."

"Looks like they're leaving," said Pierre, nodding over at the two horses being led away from the cannon.

"So they are," said Jacob, "but they've left two of their group to guard it as they had with the other two guns. Look, over there you can just make out two guards sitting next to each cannon. There'll be four gunners to each cannon and two marines to guard them. They'll change the guards at dusk."

Jacques and Pierre peered around the bush searching the heather covered ground until their eyes rested on the two other cannons. Sitting next to the wheels of the great guns, the bayonets on their muskets glinting in the afternoon sunshine, two marine guards from each cannon gazed out across the sea far below them, oblivious to the three spies watching their every movement.

"Come on, time to leave," whispered Jacob, "to my shack in the forest. I want to know your plans and how you intend to go about them in preparation for the oncoming invasion."

5

James grasped the sides of his table as a choppy swell rocked HMS Hector from side to side. Two upright chairs slid across his cabin as the ship lurched to one side, the map spread across his desk threatening to follow suit. Steadying the chart that held new coordinates for a fresh course, he smoothed it down and stood gazing out of his cabin window. Hector would sail further south searching the Baltic for more enemy shipping to engage, and if luck would have it the boarding and capturing of one as a well-earned prize for his crew.

His thoughts quickly changed to the memory of Erik Gunnarsson's daughter and the way she had looked up at him from the deck of her father's fishing vessel. The smile she had given him deeply engraved in his mind.

The whole scene, he thought, had been a kind of serendipitous encounter, where fate was now pointing towards something that he would be unable to avoid. He vowed to find her again. Strong emotions about her had begun to occupy his thoughts; maybe she would be at Gunnarsson's warehouse when he and Dan went to question her father. Something told him she would. Gathering up the map, he left his cabin for the quarterdeck to set the new course with Davey Sturrock and a briefing with his two lieutenants.

The strong wind that had rocked the frigate for the past two hours had now abated, allowing members of the crew to scale the riggings to check the shrouds holding the fore and main sails.

"Sail, on our portside. Sail on the portside bow," came a

hollering from the lookout.

Arriving on the quarterdeck, James turned to face his second lieutenant, "Your observations, Mr. Devonshire?"

"She's a Frenchie captain," replied Richard squinting through his telescope. "About two miles off our port bow sailing in a northerly direction. Two rigged square masts, a brig sir. A two-mast square rigger."

"Cargo or warship Mr. Sutherland?"

"By the looks of the guns she's carrying on her single deck, I'd say she's equipped for battle captain," replied Dan.

"She's coming about sir," said Richard. "She's seen us and intends action."

"Fancies her chances against us!" exclaimed James, closing his telescope. "Prepare for battle stations Mr. Sutherland. Inform Mr. Nark to strike full sail. Two points to our port bow, Mr. Sturrock."

"Aye, aye, captain. Two points to our port bow," yelled Davey Sturrock.

James flicked open his telescope as the call to battle stations sounded around the ship. Shrill whistles from the boatswain's pipe saw several sharp shooters scramble up the shrouds and ratlines to their positions high up on the yard arms while the clanging of the ship's bell saw the rest of Hector's crew racing to their action stations. Hector's senior officers quickly joined James and his two lieutenants.

"Mr. Kirkland," said James, closing his scope and turning to face the ship's surgeon, "prepare for possible casualties."

"Aye captain," he replied, hurrying away to the ship's sick bay one deck below.

James smiled at the sight of the French brig, the thrill of the forthcoming action beginning to pump adrenaline through his veins.

"Keep her straight Mr. Sturrock. I want to bear down on the Frenchie from our bow."

"Aye, aye, sir," replied the coxswain.

"Mr. Sutherland," shouted James, "prepare all guns. If we can, we'll disable her, I want her as a prize. If not, we'll sink her."

"Mr. Piper, prepare all guns ready for firing," yelled Dan. "Fire on my order. Captain prefers her as a prize."

HMS Hector leapt forward as the wind caught its full sails, the French brig directly in its onward path. The sudden sound of a whoosh of air over their masts told them the French had their range as a cannon ball fired from one of the brig's carronades whizzed above Hector's main mast.

"Hold her steady Mr. Sturrock," yelled James.

"She's turning sir," said Dan, his telescope pointing firmly towards the French brig. "Showing broadside captain on her port side. Her guns ready to fire."

"This is where our drilling will win us the day. Reduce sails when I order."

One hundred yards from the brig, James yelled the order,

"Now Mr. Nark, reduce sails."

James smiled at the celerity in which his order was carried out, their speed lessening as they bore down on the French brig.

"Two points to port Mr. Sturrock and hold her steady. Steady as she goes."

Three of the brig's cannons fired as Hector made her turn to come broadside onto the French ship. A deafening roar followed by the whizzing sound of cannon balls zinging through the air made every hand on Hector's deck automatically duck. Two twelve-pounder cannon balls tore directly over Hector's masts, the third cutting a neat hole through its mizzen sail but fortunately missing its mast.

"A little too quick, I think," mused James, looking over at the mizzen as Hector drew broadside onto the French brig. "She's firing too high gentlemen. Trying for our masts. Now Mr. Sutherland, starboard guns one, two, three and four fire."

As the frigate sailed past the French brig, the thunderous sound of the four starboard guns echoing across the sea brought a cheer from Hector's crew. Turning gracefully through the smoke-filled scene, its portside cannons primed and ready to fire into the brig's port side, Hector's crew braced itself for an onslaught of cannon fire from the French ship. Nothing happened.

Seconds ticked by without any retaliation from the brig.

Flicking open his telescope James trained it on the doomed ship.

"I believe they've struck gentlemen. They've struck their colours. Mr. Sutherland, your observation?"

"They have indeed sir," replied Dan, "they're surrendering. Looks like we've crippled them seriously captain. Half her foremast is down and her main sail's hanging, most of her rigging is in disarray. There's a breach in her upper portside and no sign of any guns remaining on her deck."

"Bring To, Mr. Sturrock, directly alongside her," ordered James.

"Mr. Nark," yelled Dan, "Captain's ordered Bring To, adjust the sails."

"Aye, aye, sir" replied the boatswain.

Davey Sturrock quickly responded to James' order, the frigate slowly gliding alongside the crippled French brig.

"Prepare a boarding party Mr. Sutherland, with ship's carpenter and mate. Mr. Devonshire the quarterdeck is yours."

Grappling hooks on the ends of thick ropes were thrown over the French brig's portside to attach to its bulwarks. Strong arms on HMS Hector pulled on the ropes until the vessel was brought up close to the frigate for two ramps to drop between the two ships. James led the first of the boarding party across one of the ramps while Dan followed with a dozen men on the other.

The brig's deck was in turmoil with no sign of any officers on the quarterdeck. Hector's cannons had struck the French ship with pinpoint precision, its foremast lying in a tangle of rigging across its deck. Tattered sails dangled wistfully over a gaping hole on its upper portside while many of the brig's crew lay where they had fallen. Some were missing an arm or a leg while others lay in pools of blood that swirled around the deck like spilled wine.

"In the name of King George III, King of the United Kingdom of Great Britain and Ireland," shouted James, his voice carrying over the shattered deck. "I commandeer this vessel and accept your surrender. Where is the officer commanding this ship?"

"Our captain is dead," a voice uttered in perfect English from midships. "Killed by a flying splinter from the foremast. I am lieutenant Andre Pascale acting commander of this ship and permitted to offer our surrender. Now, perhaps you would inform me to whom I am addressing?"

"I am Captain James Carey of the British Royal Navy's frigate HMS Hector," replied James. "You Lieutenant Pascale, and those of your crew who are still alive are my prisoners. You will be held aboard this ship until my ship's carpenters have made it reasonably seaworthy for us to tow it back to our garrison on Hanö Island. You and your crew will then be incarcerated there until preparation can be made to transfer you as prisoners of war to England. I hope that is clear."

Looking around the stricken deck, James regarded the number of wounded in need of urgent medical attention.

"Lieutenant Pascale," he said, turning again towards the French officer. "Is your ship's surgeon alive?"

"That he is captain," replied Pascale.

"Then perhaps you'd get him up here to attend to these wounded men. My men will take a few of your wounded to our ship's quarters where our ship's surgeon will attend to them. Is your sick bay still functioning?"

"To a certain extent," replied the lieutenant, issuing an order to one of his crew to find their surgeon.

"Mr. Sutherland, delegate a party to organise the transfer of those most seriously wounded to their sick bay. Make sure their surgeon attends to them. I want a heavy guard on those prisoners able to be held below these decks. See to it Dan."

"Aye, aye, captain," replied Hector's first lieutenant.

"Mr. Austin, your presence please," called James, turning to look for Hector's carpenter.

"Captain?" replied George Austin, coming alongside James.

"Six hours at the most George. I can't afford any longer. It will be a patch up job. Just enable her to keep afloat for her to be towed back to Hanö. It seems her main is stable enough and it looks as though her sails will hold. Check her rudder and any damage that may have been done to her hull. There's no room on Hector for their wounded should we have to sink her. Six hours George."

George Austin looked at his captain as if he had asked him to sail around the world in a day, then with a shrug of his shoulders he nodded. "Very well captain, six hours!"

"Lieutenant Pascale," James called to the French officer. "Accompany me to my cabin if you please, I have a number of questions."

Andre Pascale stood motionless in James' cabin, his eyes staring straight ahead.

"Please be seated Lieutenant," said James, indicating a chair at the captain's table. "Although you are my prisoner, you as acting commanding officer of the brig we have just commandeered, will be treated according to your station.

Pascale nodded.

"What is the name of the vessel you have just surrendered?"

"La Marie Louise."

"From which port did you last sail?"

"From Danzig, captain."

"And the purpose of your sailing in these waters?"

Looking directly at James, Pascale smiled and said nothing.

"And the purpose of your sailing in these waters?" demanded James.

"Ah, come captain!" replied Pascale loudly. "We are at war sir. You can't expect me to reveal the orders we were sailing under."

"May I remind you lieutenant," said James, looking seriously into the face of the French lieutenant, "that you were several miles off the coast of Southern Sweden and our garrison on the island of Hanö when we engaged you. You were also sailing in a northerly direction. Where were you headed lieutenant?"

"That, captain, I refuse to answer. And I will add that all written information you may seek on board La Marie Louise has been destroyed. Our dead captain and I burnt every document that would have been of interest to you before we engaged. A matter of security captain."

"As you wish lieutenant," said James, dissatisfied with Pascale's answer.

"You'll be escorted back to the brig and confined to your cabin until we reach Hanö. You have my word that your crew will be treated fairly as prisoners of war. Guards will be posted to watch over you and your crew. That'll be all, lieutenant."

Pascale rose slowly from his chair.

"Mr. Hatchett," called James, moving quickly towards the door.

The door was opened by a giant of a man, thick set and tanned by years of being at sea. A grubby bandana tied tightly around his head emphasised a black eye patch covering his left eye.

"Lieutenant Pascale, this is Ned Hatchett our ship's master-at-arms and now in charge of the guard detail over you and your crew. He'll escort you back to your cabin."

As Pascale left the cabin, James nodded towards his master-at-arms. "Keep a tight watch over him Ned, I've a feeling he's a slippery one."

Ned smiled at his captain, tapping his right eye, "This one won't let him out of sight captain, that's for sure!"

6

Jacob led the two French spies across a sloping field where long grass grew waist high yet yielded striking views across the open sea and harbour below. A few goats in a top corner stretched their necks to peep over the long green shoots, curious to know who was intruding their turf. Jacques could see that the high grass would present perfect cover for them to monitor the movement of British ships arriving and departing from the harbour far beneath them. The field led away from the stony track they had ascended previously, the picture of the three British cannons pointing out to sea still fresh in their minds. Half-way across, Jacques and Pierre halted to gaze down at the sight of the harbour and open sea below. Ahead, Jacob had stopped at the edge of a dense forest, the near proximity of the trees blotting out all but a few rays of sunlight. Beckoning the two spies to follow, he turned and - leaping over a few scattered boulders - disappeared into the forest's dark confines. Hurrying after him, the two Frenchmen followed suit, chasing him along a beaten track that snaked its way further into the heart of the forest and on towards the cabin deep inside the thicket of forest pines.

Standing in the dusky light of Jacob's shack, Jacques and Pierre regarded what was to be home for the next two weeks. In the centre of the room, a roughly made table from what looked like lengths of salvaged wood stood proudly to attention, while an old seaman's chest peeped out timidly from under a set of rickety bunk beds. Nestling contentedly beneath a dirty glass window, a wooden cot hugged the wall, its wooden slats partially viewable beneath a sorry-looking mattress. At the far end of the room a well-used cauldron attached to a chain hovered over a blackened grate, its stone fireplace staring out suspiciously at the two strangers.

"Over in that chest are a couple of wire snares," said Jacob, "go and get them while I fetch some firewood, and by the way, the cot's mine."

Pierre opened the chest seeing two lengths of wire with nooses fashioned at their tops. Next to the two snares, two bottles of brandy stood proudly alongside various maps, fishing tackle, and a telescope.

"Those bottles are for later," said Jacob, coming back in and stacking the firewood in front of the fireplace. "Before you make yourselves too comfortable, I'll show you the track that'll take you down to the rocky shoreline. From there you can have a good look to see if there's anywhere suitable to land a craft. On the way down I'll set the snares, so hopefully we'll be dining on Hanö hare or squirrel later. If you're not sure of how to set a snare watch me carefully. When I am not around, I'll be down in my hut on the harbour checking to see what's going on and how often the sentries patrol along the quayside. While I'm there you can hide up in the field of long grass, keeping track of the movement of British ships coming and going.

"After we've eaten you can tell me your plans before we go down to the shoreline again to see if the British are patrolling there at night. We may have a long wait, so you can bring one of those bottles you saw in the chest. Come on, give me those snares, and follow me."

They followed Jacob over the layers of heavy stones that seemed to cover the entire forest floor. Every now and then they glimpsed rays of sunbeams stabbing their way through the densely packed trees, highlighting clusters of blue bells scattered over the forest floor. Tiny butter-coloured violets lying reverently at the feet of giant conifers peeped over at them, whilst all around them the pervading odour of earth loam and damp vegetation filled the area.

Jacob moved over the rough forest ground with the agility of an experienced woodsman stopping at various turnings to enable the two spies to catch up.

At last, he took them on a twisting track that descended through a tunnel of foliage. All three had to bend their heads to avoid a backlash of leaf covered branches that drooped across their pathway. Half-way down the track he stopped.

"Look," he said, pointing to a length of flattened grass to one side of the track they were on. "That's a run. A small track made by rabbits and squirrels. They use them mostly in the early mornings and evenings as routes to where they can find food. It's like our roads and carriageways that enable us to get to the shops and markets to buy food. Now watch carefully."

Moving quietly into the bushes, he dropped to his knees at the side of the run. Jacques and Pierre joined him kneeling quietly and watching every movement he made in placing the snares along the run at two discreet intervals.

"Ok," he whispered, "that's done. On our way back as evening is setting in, our dinner should be waiting. Come on, follow me."

Glimpses of the closeness of the sea between the trees told them they were nearing the end of the downhill track when a sudden turning brought them out of the forest and onto a grassy bank overlooking the rocky shoreline.

A huge grey rock, its surface flat and smooth, rose majestically before them whilst round black stones the size of cannon balls lay scattered alongside rows of craggy rocks and boulders.

As far as they looked there was no sign of any inlet or cove, just a progression of rocks that occasionally gave way to narrow shingly gaps.

"Around that bend the shoreline continues but is still quite stony," shouted Jacob, pointing ahead along the coastline. "There's hardly any activity there, just the occasional fisherman setting his nets and a few fishing boats dropping their pots close to the shore. This is not a good landing point but around that bend there's a small pebbly cove worth looking at. I'd say it could accommodate a couple of longboats quite comfortably."

"Sounds good," said Jacques, turning to where Jacob stood next to the grassy bank, "lead on."

They followed the bank along the stretch of coastline coming once again into the shade of the forest. Passing a gap in the trees, Jacob pointed out to sea at a lone fishing boat bobbing up and down on the sea's swell.

"Checking his pots for crab," he said. "Seafood's quite abundant round this part of the island. Come on, the cove's not far from here."

Through the cover of trees, they made out a shingly inlet stretching down between jagged rocks and boulders to the waterline. Jumping down onto its crunchy surface they stood studying the lie of the small cove, picturing the possibility of several longboats coasting up to its shoreline.

"Look, over there," said Pierre, pointing. "Looks like an entrance to a cave beneath those cliffs."

"Think you're right," said Jacob. "I've never noticed that before, come on let's take a look."

They traipsed across the cove to where the rocks ran alongside columns of granite cliffs rising steeply to meet the forest above. Scores of seabirds nesting in their nooks and crannies screeched and squawked at the intruders tramping around below them, while out at sea the shrieks and cries of multitudes of gulls circling and diving for food, smothered any chance of conversation.

Ignoring the screams of the gulls, the three spies gingerly manoeuvred along the top of the rocks until they came to a gaping hole cut into the face of the cliff.

"Pretty dark in there," said Jacques, peering into the mouth of the cave. "Hello," he bellowed, his call echoing around the dark interior.

"There must be a chamber in there," said Jacob, "or you wouldn't have heard the echo."

"Let's go in and see," suggested Pierre, moving further inside.

A little light filtered into the cave showing a wide chamber stretching away from the entrance. They stood marvelling at its natural formation, peering at the niches and alcoves that had formed over thousands of years.

"I wonder who used this cave before," whispered Jacob. "I'm sure it's seen human activity over the years, but I would guess the British have no idea of its existence. You can only see its entrance from the cove or if you're approaching it from the sea."

"But coming from the sea," said Pierre, "you'd only see it if you knew it was there. I doubt if the entrance is that easy to locate from the sea with all these gulls flying around it."

"It was probably used by the Vikings hundreds of years ago," said Jacob. "As a hideaway or treasure trove, who knows?"

"Look, down there," interrupted Jacques, pointing to the floor of the chamber. Jacob and Pierre stared down at the grit covered ground. Streaks of light from the mouth of the cave showed the remnants of what had once been a narrow path leading away from the chamber and disappearing into a dark void at its far end.

"There must be a passageway there," said Jacob, squinting into the darkness and moving closer towards it, "I wonder how far it goes?"

The three of them groped their way further into the cavern's surroundings following the pathway until it vanished into the pitch blackness of the cave.

"We can't go on," said Jacob, "who knows what's up ahead? Without any light we'd be lost in there."

"I think it's a tunnel, leading to somewhere on the island," said Jacques.

"We'll come back tomorrow at first light," said Jacob. "I've got birch-wick torches back in the shack."

They walked back along the bank following the coastline to the track that wound its way back up through the forest to where Jacob had concealed the two snares on the animal run. As the track led them up towards the overhang of drooping branches, Jacob raised his hand bringing them to a halt.

"Shush," he whispered, "can you hear that shuffling - it's dinner!"

The three of them dropped to their knees inching their way forward to the animal run where the sound of a desperate scraping could be heard from within the bushes. Jacob pulled back a bush and there with their heads tightly caught in the nooses of the snares, two fully grown hares wriggled and squirmed frantically in their forlorn efforts to escape.

"Move aside," said Jacob, springing to his feet. As quick as a flash he bent down and grabbing the back legs of one of the hares he stamped on its head whilst quickly jerking it upwards. Dropping the dead hare to the ground he swiftly dispatched the other in the same way.

"Quick and painless," he said. "Now, back to the shack and get the pot ready."

Later that evening, having supped well, the two spies sat around the table telling Jacob the importance of their mission and how their report would affect the planned invasion of the island. Listening intently, he threw a few more logs onto the glowing embers watching as the flames gyrated vigorously upwards to the sound of the dried wood hissing and crackling. Sitting back, he regarded the two Frenchmen closely.

"Along with Erik Gunnarsson and his brother Olof, I have a great hatred for the British navy, and want to see them destroyed and off this island forever."

"Why do you and Erik hate the British so much?" asked Pierre, looking at him seriously.

"The mother of Erik and Olof was Danish," he began, staring at the flames greedily licking their way around the blackening logs. "Five years ago, in August 1807, she went back to her family home in Copenhagen to visit her sister and family. I suppose it was a bad time for her to go there then as The Danish Government had just agreed to be part of Napoleon's Continental System and join his trade embargo against Great Britain.

"Denmark, ostensibly, was not at war with Britain at the time, although the French were pressing for the Danish fleet to begin action against Britain and to declare war. Well, before any decision was made by the Danish Government a British fleet blockaded the port of Copenhagen, two days after Erik's and Olof's mother had arrived there. She was stuck, with no way of getting out. In no time the British started a bombardment, their heavy guns pounding the city and destroying many of the buildings near the harbour. The house their mother was in with her sister and family took direct hits from the British cannon fire. All were killed and the house destroyed. Erik and Olof were devastated as were their families, but there was nothing they could do except fester a deep hatred towards the British for killing their mother. The Danish fleet was subsequently destroyed and after the British fleet had departed, the Danish Government naturally declared war on Great Britain and hence joined forces with Napoleon."

Jacques and Pierre nodded slowly as Jacob came to the end of his explanation. It was now clear to them why Erik and Olof took the risk of assisting the French in their clandestine operations of transporting French agents by sea and acting as carriers of information between Jacob and the French.

"Now we understand," said Jacques, watching Jacob staring into the fire. "But what of you Jacob, what happened to you to cause you to hate the British so much?"

Jacob turned his attention away from the fire, and looking intently at the two French spies shook his head dispiritedly,

"Not now," he said, "it's time to see if any patrol boats are sailing around the island at night. Come on, the fire's nearly out. We can take a lantern each and one of the bottles of brandy from the chest."

Holding their lanterns out in front of them, they followed closely behind Jacob as he led them through the darkness of the forest.

Pierre looked fearfully over his shoulder as an owl hooted from somewhere far away, the sound of a forest animal scuttling away into the undergrowth urging him to keep up behind Jacques.

It wasn't long before they felt their path descending, the smell of the sea suddenly drifting up through the darkness. A whispered command from Jacob to duck their heads, told them they were approaching the overhang of drooping branches and the animal run where they had caught the two hares. As the track dropped down to the coastline, shades of moonlight lit up the surface of the huge grey rock they had seen previously, a gap in the trees affording them a view of a full moon lighting up the rocky shoreline. Picking their way carefully along the forest path it was not long before the moonlight showed up the shingly cove where they had found the entrance to the cave.

"Over there, between those rocks," whispered Jacob, "that's where we'll wait. There's a good view of the sea from there and if a patrol boat passes that's where we'll see it."

They settled themselves between the rocks feeling the cold and dampness of the cove seeping through the coarse material of their clothes.

"Here," said Jacob, offering Pierre the bottle of brandy, "have a long swig. It'll keep out the cold."

Pierre pulled the cork on the bottle, knocking back a good measure then handing the bottle to Jacques.

"Strange isn't it," he said, "that the birds here aren't making a sound. When we were here earlier you could hardly hear yourself speak for the squawking they were making."

"Well," said Jacob, looking at Pierre, "do you squawk and make loud noises when you're sleeping?"

"Ha," said Jacques, springing to his feet and rubbing his backside, "of course he does! Quiet, look! There're lights bobbing about out there."

Jacob and Pierre jumped to their feet looking out over the rocks and out to sea where two dim lights were wobbling to and fro in the darkness.

"Get down behind the rocks," whispered Jacob. "With this full moon it's easy to see what's ashore from the sea."

They squatted down behind the rocks listening to the dull splash of oars dipping in and out of the water. A gap between the rocks gave them a good view towards the waterline. Squinting through the darkness, they watched as the shape of a longboat suddenly appeared out of the darkness. Two lanterns swung steadily from its bow and stern.

"Hold it here," a voice boomed from the bow of the boat, "stop rowing."

The three spies held their breath as they watched a red-coated marine officer snatch off his black bicorn and bend his ear towards the cove.

"I'm sure I heard someone talking," he said to a sergeant next to him. From out here, sound travels from the shoreline clearly. Sergeant, can you see or hear anything?"

"Nothing sir," replied the sergeant, squinting towards the pebbly cove and listening to the stillness around them. "Could be worth going ashore and having a look around," he suggested.

Making no response to the sergeant's suggestion the marine officer stood peering intently towards the cove, searching its moonlit nooks and crannies and listening for any unusual sound.

"Not now," he replied. "Time's getting on, but we'll pass here again on our way back in another couple of hours, if there's anything suspicious, we'll go ashore then. Carry on now sergeant."

Crouching behind the rocks, the three spies listened earnestly as the longboat moved steadily away, the sound of its oars dipping in and out of the water dwindling as it disappeared into the darkness.

"Now we know," whispered Jacob, "a British longboat comes by twice at night. Come on, back to the shack, I'm getting cold."

7

HMS Hector dropped anchor outside the walls of Hanö's harbour. The crippled French brig followed suit while the thick ropes used for towing her snaked up Hector's stern as powerful hands hauled them aboard the British frigate. All hands waited to attention on the main deck. Dan Sutherland, appointed to oversee the captured brig's journey back to the harbour at Hanö, looked up from its quarterdeck at the Royal Navy's white ensign flying above the French navy's colour, a sign of a captured ship. Towing the brig behind the British ship had hindered the frigate's speed but a strong wind throughout the night had seen Hector plough its way through the rough sea, the thick towing rope stretched to its limit but holding firm as it pulled La Marie Louise several lengths behind it.

"Mr. Devonshire," said James, turning towards his second lieutenant. "Take a longboat with six men and inform Lieutenant Sutherland to await transporters. Then, make haste and report to the harbour master. Tell him I'll present myself to Commodore Percival as soon as we alight on the quay.

"Aye, aye sir," said Richard, saluting his captain.

James watched the longboat go alongside the French brig, Richard clambering up a rough rope ladder hanging from its side. It was not long before he was back in the longboat and on his way through the mouth of the harbour.

Commodore John Percival, Commanding Officer of the harbour of Hanö, gently touched each side of his mouth with a white linen napkin before rising from his breakfast table.

"All quiet down in the harbour, Stanley?" he shouted to his orderly.

"Yes sir, all quiet," replied able seaman Stanley Bradshaw, hurrying into the dining room with the commodore's cloak and tricorn.

"Splendid," said the commander in chief. "I'll be off now. No need to accompany me as it is only a short walk to the wharf, but I'll expect you later, on board.

"Sir," replied Bradshaw.

Commodore Percival made the short walk from his residence overlooking the harbour to the quay where his flag ship lay anchored, his mind busy with plans of strengthening the defences of the island. Making his way up the gang plank, he stopped to observe a longboat being hastily rowed through the mouth of the harbour, six able seamen and a Royal Navy second-lieutenant looking intent on getting to the quay as fast as possible.

He watched as the young officer scrambled up a rusty ladder to disappear into a quayside cabin housing the harbour master and officers of the guard.

The British harbour master sat listening to Richard's report, then rising from his chair he beckoned Richard to follow him out of the cabin and away in the direction of the commodore's flag ship.

Standing to attention opposite the commodore, Richard gave his report.

"A French brig, splendid!" said Percival, his thick bushy eyebrows raised in pleasure at Richard's report. "Now," he said, turning towards the harbour master, "start the process of taking those prisoners off the brig and locking them up in the empty warehouses on the other side of the harbour, then get Captain Carey and his crew ferried into harbour immediately. When everything is done, and those prisoners are safely locked away, send Captain Carey to my cabin."

Saluting the commodore, the harbour master hurried away to commence his task.

"You have done well lieutenant," said the commodore, smiling at Richard. "I'd like you to assist the harbour master in making sure all the prisoners are locked away safely, then as an officer of the ship that captured the French brig, you together with HMS Hector's first lieutenant will attend my cabin after I've spoken with your captain. My orderly will fetch you both. So, for now that'll be all, lieutenant."

James entered his commanding officer's cabin with the customary naval salute, his eyes taking in everything before him. Commodore Percival rising from his chair, duly saluted his captain.

"Captain Carey, please be at ease," said the commodore, looking up from the papers arranged over his desk. "Please be seated," he said gesturing for James to make his way over to one of the two elegant two-seater settees placed opposite each other on the far side of the cabin. James took the one facing the commodore's desk with a clear view of the cabin's large bay window.

"A sherry, captain," said the commodore, offering James a cut crystal glass brimming with a fine pale sherry. "Now," he continued seating himself on the opposite settee. "First, my congratulations on your prize, your capturing of that French brig. I will recommend a reward for its capture. As to the amount, that will be decided after it has been thoroughly inspected. Any serious damage will, of course, be noted. Now if you please, I'm ready to listen to your report of the action that took place."

James cleared his throat as the commodore took a large sip of his sherry, then as his commander settled back on his settee, he began.

"It was early yesterday morning, sir. We were only about two hours out of harbour when our lookout raised the alarm of a distant sail on our portside bow."

Commodore Percival listened attentively to James' account, pausing only to refill their glasses. James summed up his report emphasising his unease as to the French brig being in waters close to the British base while sailing in a northerly direction close to the Swedish coast. He raised the commodore's curiosity even further when he told him of his suspicions as to the true nature of the French naval lieutenant, suggesting that Lieutenant Pascale was hiding something, something that had probably been in his orders but had been completely scuppered due to HMS Hector's intervention.

"How many prisoners in all have you brought here, captain?" asked Percival.

"The brig's record show it had a complement of one hundred and five sir. That included warrant officers and three commissioned officers as well as her captain who was killed in the action. After our engagement with the brig, forty crew were accounted either killed or lost overboard. We've brought back sixty-five prisoners sir."

"I'll have them transported to a prison in England, likely

Dartmoor, as soon as one of our ships can be fitted out," said the commodore." I cannot release any frigate but there's a sloop that could do the job with a minimum crew. A good bosun aboard will make the prisoners work as crew. The sloop should be ready soon, took a twelve pounder through her stern engaging a Frenchie a couple of months back, you may remember it." James nodded.

"I want you to question the French lieutenant further. If what you think about him is true, then we will need to find out what his ship was doing in waters close to us and where she was heading. They came out of the port of Danzig you say. Frenchie could be building up his fleet there and if so, we need to find out. Now, I believe your two lieutenants are waiting outside."

Sir, I have something to say more before you admit them," said James, looking the commodore directly in the eye.

Looking a little astonished, Percival answered, "Yes of course captain, go ahead."

"It concerns the security of the harbour sir, and the island itself."

"Well, and what of it, captain?" replied the commodore.

"For some time now I've been uneasy about its vulnerability to attack from the French. Our frigates are out most of the time patrolling the sea for enemy shipping, leaving the island seriously undefended. I know there's a detachment of marines stationed here sir with heavy cannon directed out to sea, but the south part of the island remains open to attack as it's completely undefended. Should the French plan an attack on the island then the southern part would be where they would hit, landing a detachment of their marines to come up behind us while their fleet attacks the harbour. All our fire power would be directed at their fleet, we would be unaware of what was coming at us from behind."

"Captain," said John Percival, looking rather agitated at James' discernment. "I doubt very much the French would bother about the southern part of this island, the rocky shoreline prohibits any vessel landing there. Should they achieve this, they'd have a damned difficult job getting up through the dense forest that leads from there to here. No, I am sure that they've already discounted any means of attacking us from that location. They're more than likely going to throw everything they've got at us in a frontal attack on the harbour, and that is where we will concentrate our defences. The three heavy artillery guns up on the northern most height will give us a great advantage in pounding their fleet. Our frigates will then move in amongst them with lethal fire. I've already sent for reinforcements captain, which I expect will be forthcoming."

"But sir," interrupted James. "I doubt those reinforcements will materialise as they've probably already been seconded to the Americas. War is again imminent there and the French will seize the opportunity to weaken us with their assisting the new United States government. While that is going on and they can see that no reinforcements have arrived here, they will strike. They need this island to take control of the Baltic, and with us defeated they will soon occupy every country with coastlines along it. The south part of this island needs protecting sir, with two of our frigates lying off its coastline and a detachment of marines located there."

"No captain," Percival replied, curtly. "I've already told you that we'll have all our fire power here, at the island's northern end which is where the French will hit us. But, on the other hand if you can convince me further that the southern tip needs strengthening with a frigate and a company of our marines then I may concede to your request. Now, I have promised your two lieutenants a formal welcoming from me, and to congratulate them on their ship's successful action against the French brig. As officers of HMS Hector I'm pleased to welcome them, and as you are their ship's commanding officer, you will join us. After that, I expect you to question your captured French lieutenant and see if you can find out more from him. I note that you are at liberty tomorrow. Find the time in between your ship's duties to increase the questioning of him. If you believe him to be a spy then we must discover more about his mission, and quickly."

"Sir," replied James, with a frown.

A sharp knock on the commodore's door saw Stanley Bradshaw enter with HMS Hector's two lieutenants. With a deep sigh and a quick change of facial expression, James rose from the settee to join the commodore in welcoming his two grinning officers.

8

Early next morning Jacob and the two French spies, each carrying two birch- wick torches, crunched across the shingly cove towards the mouth of the cave. Flocks of seabirds euphoric over the arrival of the new dawn, soared high over the sea, gliding gracefully on the ascending air currents then spiralling down to disappear under the surface to feed off the shoals of fish that frequented the island's rocky seabed.

At the mouth of the cave, Jacob lit three of the slow burning torches from the tinder box he always carried with him. As the chamber flooded with light, they made their way towards the dark void at its far end.

"It's pitch-black in there," said Pierre, peering into the dark gap.

"Can't you feel the cold air wafting out from in there?" said Jacob. "It's a tunnel and it must lead to an open exit somewhere on the island."

With Jacob leading they stepped into the darkness stretching their torches out in front of them. Shuffling forward in single file they soon became aware of an overwhelming dank smell heightened by the clammy moisture-covered walls around them. With every step they took, a feeling of timelessness seemed to prevail as though something or someone from long ago had just passed before them. Keeping close behind each other they moved further along the dark passageway, the light from their torches casting eerie shadows along the walls beside them. Coming to a bend, Jacob held up his hand for them to halt.

"What is it, Jacob?" whispered Jacques.

"Shush, can you hear it? It's coming from just around the bend up there."

A deep humming sound like the heavy breathing of scores of sleeping sailors, vibrated steadily in the darkness ahead.

"Sounds like a crew's sleeping quarters at midnight!" said Jacques.

"But what the hell is it, Jacob?" asked Pierre, nervously.

"Listen again," said Jacob, his eyes as wide as saucers. "Bats, hundreds of them, just round the bend and they're all sleeping."

"How are we going to get past them without waking them? We'll have to go back, the one thing I can't bear are bats. They terrify me!"

"We're not going back," said Jacques. "We must see where this tunnel leads."

"We'll walk right under them," whispered Jacob. "You know that bats sleep hanging upside down. The roof of this cavern's just about high enough for us to walk under them, lucky we're not any taller than we are. If they wake it won't be good for us, so control your breathing and not a sound until we're well clear. We can pass them in the dark, so extinguish your torches. Whatever happens just keep right behind me. My night vision's good, so hopefully it'll get us past. Put the torches out now and remember - not a sound."

They rolled their torches along the gritty pathway until they were out, total darkness suddenly enveloping them. Pierre listened anxiously to the growing murmur of the bats, clamping his eyes shut as Jacob led them slowly forward around the bend. Clutching onto the back of Jacques' jacket, he sensed the first of the upturned little creatures getting nearer. Walking very slowly, the three spies inched their way forward.

Gradually, Pierre opened his eyes squinting through the darkness as he shuffled along behind Jacques. Above their heads scores of dark bundles, their specially evolved feet locked onto the tunnel's granite roof, hung huddled together unaware of the three spies creeping silently beneath them.

Half-way along, Jacques and Pierre felt Jacob stop, suddenly side stepping and moving sharply to his left.

Moving with him in the darkness they felt their way to the side of the wall. Night vision had kicked in with the two Frenchmen enabling them to distinguish various dark shapes around them. Looking up, Jacques noticed the hanging forms of the sleeping bats, now little more than a finger's length from the tops of their heads.

Pierre suddenly cringed, making out a bunch of dark shapes hanging low over the middle of the pathway. He realised that had Jacob not moved close to the wall they would have walked straight into the dangling mass, waking them and subsequently the whole roost. With a cold shudder, he tightened his grip on the end of Jacques' jacket. He couldn't remember how his fear of bats had started. He'd been able to block it from his mind at an early age, but the terror of coming across one, let alone a roost of them was something he'd never dared contemplate. His horror of bats, and even more so the terror he knew he would feel at being touched by one, was bringing on a compelling urge to break away from the other two and run forward into the darkness beyond. Gritting his teeth, he took a deep breath and shuffled on.

Turning a bend, the humming noise of the bats grew louder and, looking up through the darkness, Pierre suddenly recoiled in horror. Multitudes of dark shapes hung from the roof of the tunnel like overgrown bunches of black grapes, their single humming tones pulsating far into the dark passageway ahead.

And then it happened. Something hairy and fury suddenly brushed against the right side of Pierre's face, the prick of a claw digging into the side of his cheek. His ear-splitting scream, like the keening wail of a banshee, ripped through the darkness shattering the silence around them. For a moment nothing moved.

"Down, hit the ground flat, now," yelled Jacob at the top of his voice, his command echoing far down the passageways of the tunnel.

Pulling Pierre with him Jacques fell to the ground lying flat on his stomach, his hands covering the back of his head. Pierre, shaking uncontrollably, followed suit. A tremendous sound like a gale force wind bellowing the sails of a galleon, reverberated off the walls of the tunnel as hundreds of bats dropped from their upturned positions, flapping their wings rapaciously in their efforts to take flight from such a severe awakening. From where they lay, the three spies winced at the high-pitched squeals of the bats finding their way through the narrow passageway, the wind rush from hundreds of flapping wings blasting over the three prostrate bodies.

The noise of the bats fleeing their refuge seemed endless until an abrupt silence settled around them. Jacques and Pierre lay where they had dropped, hands covering the backs of their heads. Pierre still shook with the terror he had experienced, his face buried into the grit and sand beneath him.

"Get up, they've gone," said Jacob, lighting one of the torches. Light from his torch slowly flooded the passageway as Jacques pulled himself up. Dusting himself down he looked up at the roof and the surrounding walls, coughing and spitting out the grimy dirt he had sucked in from the tunnel's floor.

"They've all gone," he said, "not one remaining bat. Come on Pierre, up you get it's safe now."

Pierre forced himself up, dirt and grit covering his face.

"I'm sorry," he said, softly, "I just hate the little demons, I can't bear them - they terrify me."

"Here," said Jacob, looking at Pierre. "Light your torch from my tinder box, then give it to Per. The tunnel's empty of them now and I guess there's not much further to go before we come to the exit. Those bats won't be back for a while so come on, follow me."

They followed Jacob in single file, Pierre looking nervously at the roof above lest there still be a few sleeping bats, but there was nothing to worry him.

The passageway took them around two more bends where they cautiously braced themselves for whatever new danger or horror may be lurking, but they passed quietly through, the light from their torches showing the ground ahead beginning to incline in an upward direction.

"Look, daylight," said Jacob, pointing to the far end of the tunnel where a circle of light glinted before them. "It's the end of the tunnel, come on."

They hurried onwards feeling the gradient of the ground beneath them rising in a steep slope, the circle of light in front of them becoming larger. Rays of bright sunlight burst through the gaping hole at the tunnel's end as they scrambled through the exit, greedily sucking in the fresh air that greeted them.

Rows of tall conifers and birch trees spanned the area before them, sunshine glinting through their foliage. From where they stood on an open stretch of clifftop, a narrow pathway littered with small round stones and boulders twisted its way deep into the shadows of the forest. High up in a pale blue sky a handful of sea birds circled the surrounding cliffs, their squawking reminding the three spies of the cave's entrance far below.

"We're on the edge of the forest," said Jacob, staring into the trees stretching endlessly before them. "That's the path we'll take, straight through the forest.

It's an easier path than the one down there below us."

"Yes, exactly," said Pierre, joining Jacques at the cliff's edge and looking out to the sea far below them. "Are you thinking what I'm thinking?"

Jacques smiled, his eyes searching the vast area of sea below and then at the thick forest of trees behind them.

"It's perfect," he said, "and, it's undefended. This is where our invasion will come. We'll send a decoy fleet to attack the harbour while our marines are landing on the shingly cove in longboats. This path through the forest will be far better for them than the narrow coastal one down there, especially as it will be the dead of night. We'll bring them up through the tunnel and then through the forest this way. They'll be better concealed in the tunnel than marching along the coastal path down there. Jacob, show us the route from here through the forest to the field that overlooks the harbour, the field where the long grass grows."

"Before that though," said Jacob, looking at the two of them, "we'll need to know how often that longboat passes the cove at night. We'll take it in turns to hide down on the cove and record the time the boat passes. Then you can make your plans. Per, you'll take the first watch tonight."

With a nod towards Jacob, Jacques looked out across the bluey-grey waters of the Baltic Sea, seeing in his imagination part of the French fleet discharging several longboats filled with Napoleon's marines. He would wait on the island after Pierre had returned to General Bonard with the plan that the main part of the French fleet should attack the harbour, while two ships from the fleet would sail here, to the south of the island, unloading a detachment of marines who would land on the shingly cove in longboats. He and Jacob would light beacons on the cove and then guide the marines up through the tunnel. After making their way through the forest and taking over the heavy cannons on the heights, they'd attack the British from their rear. But first, they would have to find a way to take out the British longboat that patrolled this part of the island at night. Only then, he knew his plan would succeed.

9

James was no nearer discovering the truth as to why the French brig, La Marie Louise, was on a heading towards the Swedish mainland and in waters close to Hanö Island. Throughout his questioning of Lieutenant Pascale, he was becoming more convinced that the Frenchman was avoiding certain questions and hiding facts that would have given the British captain a clear picture as to the objective of the French brig and her crew. The more evasive Pascale had become throughout the questioning, the more certain James had been that La Marie Louise had been on a secret mission to the Swedish mainland.

No other members of the crew had volunteered any information and a wall of silence had met Dan Sutherland when he had questioned the ship's surgeon and purser. Something was not quite right. Pascale was obviously lying in protecting the true nature of the French brig's mission. James was determined to find out before Pascale and his crew were transported to Britain and incarceration in Dartmoor prison. The work on the sloop-of-war that would take the French prisoners to England was near completion and it would only be a matter of days before Commodore Percival gave his order for the ship to sail. He would have to convince the Commodore to delay the sailing if the truth of the French brig's mission could not be determined, or to let the sloop sail without the French lieutenant. A task he knew would not be easy.

A fresh wind caught the sail of the small skiff, bouncing it over the choppy swell of water that lay between the Swedish mainland

and Hanö Island. James snatched at his tricorn, pulling it off lest it be blown away while Dan adjusted the skiff's single sail as the wind whisked the little boat on towards the harbour of Nogersund.

Looking back over the stern as they began to distance themselves from the island, Dan pointed vigorously at a low dark cloud clipping the tops of the trees.

"What on earth?" yelled James, squinting at the cloud.

"Bats, captain," shouted Dan, "hundreds of them. They're nocturnal, sleeping in caves during the day and hunting for food at night. Can't imagine why they're out at this time in the morning."

"Something must've spooked them from their cave," shouted James.

"Undoubtedly sir," said Dan. "Wonder what it could've been?"

James turned his attention back to the sight of the Swedish mainland and their approach to the harbour of Nogersund. Today the crew of HMS Hector were at liberty and as arranged he and his first lieutenant were heading towards the small harbour to find out more about Erik Gunnarsson's crew and how many were registered to sail with him. Something had not seemed quite right about the fishing vessel they had stopped and boarded, its crew showing no sign of disgruntlement or protest when Dan had asked them to line up and present their papers.

As the mouth of Nogersund harbour drew closer, he smiled at the thought of the ulterior motive for the visit. Anna, the magic of their brief encounter still in the forefront of his mind. He would find her of that he was certain.

There was little activity taking place around the harbour as James stood on the quay surveying the scene around him. Dan hastily fastened the skiff's mooring rope to a wooden docking post, then joined his captain in inspecting the area.

Several fishing vessels bobbed up and down at their berths, one making ready to leave harbour, but as close as they looked there was no sign of Erik Gunnarsson's boat. At the end of the quay, a large sign nailed to the side of a spacious looking warehouse caught their attention – "*Gunnarsson Bröder. Fiskhandlare.*"

"Looks empty, captain!" said Dan, seeing James' attention focused on the warehouse. "They're probably out at sea."

"We'll take a look," said James.

The warehouse doors looked firmly shut as they approached the wooden building. Several fishermen busily mending nets and crab pots ignored the two Englishmen walking along the quay dressed in ordinary civilian clothes. Sweden, under threat from Napoleon, was participating in a proxy war against Britain, the two countries however resisting any armed conflict that the French tried to encourage between them. Nevertheless, James had decided that for them to dress as civilians would be a safer option than being dressed in the uniforms of officers of the Royal Navy.

"Captain, there's a light showing through that small window at the side of the warehouse," said Dan, pointing to where a dim light flickered.

"Well, someone's in there," said James, stopping outside a pair of heavy wooden doors. "Let's see who's in!"

The handle on one of the doors turned easily, allowing James to pull the door a fraction towards them. Peering into the dimly lit space they could see no sign of anyone.

"Come on," he said, looking at Dan.

A pile of fishing pots and nets closely stacked up against a wall took up one side of the warehouse, while a couple of old barnacle-covered rowing boats in much need of repair lay forlornly on the opposite side. At the far end, what looked like a wall of ice running about three yards in front of the warehouse's end wall glinted through the dull light, a fishy aroma oozing from its glistening sides.

The sound of someone moving around above them broke the silence.

"Who's there?" a female voice called in Swedish.

It was impossible for them to see who had called out, the dim light pervading throughout the warehouse making it difficult to distinguish where the voice had come from.

"State your business and then leave."

A window on the opposite wall from where they were standing, shed a little light on a wooden staircase tucked away to its right-hand side. The staircase rose to a darkened gallery above where the voice had come from.

"Do you speak English?" James called.

"Of course," the voice replied in English, "what do you want here?"

"We've come to speak to Erik Gunnarsson on an important matter," James shouted.

"He's not here," the voice replied, "he's out fishing with his crew until sundown. "Can I help you?"

It suddenly occurred to James who the voice might be. His heart quickened a pace as a picture of Anna looking up at him from her father's fishing vessel, flashed before him.

"Yes, I think you can," he heard himself say.

"Wait there, I'll be down in a minute," the voice called.

James felt the blood rushing through his veins, his throat drying up with every second passing. He wondered if she would recognise him, remember him from when their eyes had first met. Since he had seen her sitting on the water barrel on her father's boat, her long auburn hair flowing behind her in the wind, he had secretly longed for this moment.

A clatter of feet descending the staircase caused the two officers to hastily discard their tricorns.

Stepping off the last stair Anna looked at the two men standing before her, her mouth opening slightly in surprise. Her lips quivered gently as her eyes rested on James.

"Miss Anna Gunnarsson, I gather," said Dan, with a courteous bow.

"Yes, that's correct," said Anna, still gazing at James.

"May I introduce you to Captain James Carey of His Majesty's Royal Navy frigate HMS Hector. I am Lieutenant Dan Sutherland, first officer."

James took Anna's hand, and looking into her eyes, touched it gently to his lips, feeling that fate had finally trapped him.

"I'm honoured, Miss Gunnarsson," he said.

"Captain," replied Anna, curtseying politely.

"Miss Gunnarsson, we're here," said James, forcing himself to think levelly, "to ask your father about his crew."

"His crew are not really my concern," replied Anna, "only that my uncle Olof and my brother Lars together with our two deck hands Nils and Gustav, are the only crew my father has registered."

James looked at Dan, his eyebrows raised.

He did not want to involve Anna in his suspicions about her father, nor of the two extra deck hands that had been aboard the fishing vessel when Dan had searched it. He and Dan would find out later when they had an opportunity to question Erik and Olof and maybe Lars. How they'd do this, he would have to think of a way. The question was, who were the two extra deck hands and what had they been doing on Erik Gunnarsson's boat.

"Captain," said Anna, looking at James. "I'm afraid I must leave you now. I have two heavy bags of vegetables to take up to our house. My mother's making a big soup for dinner. If we leave together then I can lock the doors to the warehouse."

"Why of course, Miss Gunnarsson," said James. "Can I help you carry one of the bags?"

Anna grinned at James as if she'd been waiting for him to find a way to prolong their moment together.

James looked at his first officer, "wait for me by the skiff Dan."

Dan nodded with a smile, "Of course, captain."

At the bottom of the hillside track that led up to the Gunnarsson's house, Anna pointed to a wooden bench nestling peacefully under the shade of a pine tree.

"Come and sit," she said, directing James to the seat.

They sat under the tree not speaking, aware that the moment they had both been secretly longing for had now arrived. Drawing a deep breath Anna played with a length of her auburn hair, not sure of what to say.

"I understand that it's you who regularly brings our supplies across to the island," said James.

"Yes, that's right," said Anna, with a smile. "It's usually my father who takes me over. It's my job to keep your quartermaster happy with our supplies of fish and vegetables. We were making a delivery when your ship passed us the other day. I think you noticed me then."

"That I did, Miss. Gunnarsson," said James, wanting to take her in his arms. "As I feel you did with me!"

Anna blushed, her hand rising to cover her mouth.

"It was unavoidable, captain," she said, looking directly into James' eyes.

For a moment they gazed at each other, both feeling something drawing them closer together.

"You wanted to know something about my father's crew. Is there a problem, captain?"

"Not at all Miss Gunnarsson," said James, not wanting his investigation to ruin this moment. "It's just that we routinely stopped your father's fishing boat at sea several days ago and on checking his crew we noticed he had, what we think, were two extra hands on board. We're only checking to see if they are registered as his crew. There is no cause for concern."

"I know nothing of these two extra crew members," said Anna.

"I really do not concern myself with whom my father and Uncle Olof have working for them.

My job, as I have told you, is to keep your garrison supplied with our fish and vegetables. That is all."

"Of course. I'm sorry to have brought this up with you," said James, determined to change the course of the conversation.

"Have you been stationed on the island long, captain? I haven't seen you around the harbour."

"Since the New Year," said James, "when I took over my present ship, HMS Hector. But please, call me James. It's nice to hear my name instead of my rank all the time. It sounds even better when spoken by you."

Anna smiled reaching down for her two bags, "I will James, and please call me by my first name. But now I really must be going."

"May I," said James, holding out his two hands.

"Thank you," replied Anna, smiling. "Our house is at the top of this hill. Our next delivery to your garrison on the island is a week to this day, would you be at sea then, or maybe ashore in the harbour?"

"A week to this day is liberty for my ship," said James, his heart skipping a beat. "Yes, I will be ashore Anna. If you will be in the harbour then, perhaps we can meet."

"I would like that, James. We deliver to your garrison early in the morning. My brother Lars will be skippering our boat, perhaps mid-morning on the quay?"

"Perfect, I'll wait for you there," said James. "Now let me carry those two heavy bags up that hill."

At the top of the track that led down to her house, Anna stopped. Taking James' arm, she pointed towards the dark silhouette of Hanö island far out to sea.

"That's where I shall look, every time I leave my house," she said, smiling at him. "It will remind me of you James."

Looking into her eyes, he took her hand and gently pressed it to his lips, then with a courteous bow he turned to make his way back down the stony track.

"Until next week on the quay," he called, turning to give her a radiant smile.

She watched him make his way back down the hill and the path that led back to the harbour where Dan would be waiting with the skiff. Her heart lifted as she saw him turn at the corner and with a wave look back up to where she stood.

"I knew you would come to me James," she whispered, waving back at him. "But how will I be able to tell this to my family?"

Picking up her two bags, she stole one last look towards the bottom of the hill and the now empty corner where he had stopped to wave goodbye. Then, with a joyous smile, she hurried up the steps to her front door and to her mother, who unknown to Anna, had been watching everything from behind the curtain of their front window.

10

Early evening had settled in around the island's small harbour, transforming the sun into a flaming orange ball above the horizon. Jacob sat outside his hut on the quay noting everything going on around him. That afternoon, several Royal Navy officers had hurried onto the flagship berthed in the deep-water end of the opposite quay to attend, what he assumed, was a meeting with the commodore. What they had discussed, he would love to have known but he guessed it involved the defence of the harbour. The British were obviously expecting an attack and would soon begin their preparations with the few ships they had. The three great cannons mounted on the highest points of the island continuing to be their greatest asset.

He sucked on his clay pipe taking interest in the sight of a small skiff coasting up to a docking post at the end of the quay. He watched a figure in civilian dress lower the sail while his colleague leapt up onto the wharf to wrap a mooring rope around a wooden post.

"Strange," he thought, "wonder what a couple of civilians are doing here?"

Sitting back in his rocking chair his eyes followed the two men until they disappeared inside a long wooden building, part of which he knew acted as the officers' mess. He had already noted two Royal Navy frigates lying at anchor outside the harbour, their crew enjoying a day of liberty.

Enquiries around the quay had informed him three more frigates were out at sea patrolling the shipping lanes, two of them due to return later that evening while the third would return at midnight. A sloop-of-war would soon be returning after its daily exercise of patrolling the island's coast, giving leave for three manned longboats to begin their nightly patrols of the islands' coast. At the far end of the opposite quay his eyes picked out the doors of a spacious boat house lying wide open where a dozen carpenters were working tirelessly in repairing a damaged naval sloop, the restoration looking near to completion.

His thoughts switched to the tunnel they had discovered in the cave on the shingly cove at the southern part of the island. He'd bring a detachment of French marines through it and then lead them to the highest point of the island where they would take over the three heavy guns overlooking the sea. The plan should work, of that he felt certain. But first, they would have to establish the times the longboat passed the cove at night.

His eyes travelled over to the far end of the quay resting on three of the old warehouses where two heavily armed Royal Marines stood guard outside each one. He'd been surprised to see this when he'd arrived at the harbour earlier but had managed to find out that each warehouse held about twenty French prisoners that had been brought in two days before, the wreck of their ship anchored just beyond the mouth of the harbour. The ship had obviously been seriously damaged in its action with the British. He had to find out why the prisoners were being held there. He knew the guards would be changing soon, it would be the best time to approach them. There was always one who would succumb to a drink after having been standing on his feet for most of the day, especially when out of sight of an officer. With the bottle of strong brandy tucked away in his jacket pocket he was sure he would get the information he wanted. It was the look of the two guards lolling up against the side of the furthest warehouse that caught his attention.

Those are the two, he decided, getting up from his rocking chair.

Tapping the bottle of brandy in his inside pocket, he closed the door to his shed and strolled off nonchalantly down the quay in the direction of the three temporary jails. A few yards from the first warehouse he paused, studying the two marines standing guard. Seeing Jacob standing opposite them they quickly brought up their muskets as a warning for him not to come any nearer. With a slight wave of his hand to let the guards know he had no intention of approaching them he moved on. Coming to within earshot of the third warehouse he stopped. The two guards lolling up against the front side did not pay him much attention, the looks on their faces showing they were tired and fed up. He stood studying them for a moment, looking carefully from one to the other, checking for the one whom he thought would be the easiest to dupe.

His eyes settled on a thick-looking face staring blankly across the quay.

"Excuse me," he shouted. "I wonder if you could help?"

"Fuck orf and be on your way," came the reply.

"I'm looking for one of your colleagues," shouted Jacob, accentuating his Swedish accent, and speaking very slowly.

"Who d'ya want?" asked the guard.

"His name's Harry Smith," said Jacob, quickly conjuring up a name from nowhere.

"Never heard of 'im," shouted the guard, turning to confront Jacob.

"I can describe him to you," yelled Jacob.

"Go on then," said the guard, "but come closer as I can't really 'ear ya."

Jacob noticed a bunch of keys hanging from the guard's leather belt as he strode over towards them, his eyes expertly flicking over the front of the warehouse. The doors looked firmly shut with strong metal bars solidly set behind each of the two windows cut into the building's wooden sides.

"I've got something for Harry," he said, looking into the faces of the two guards.

"Look I've already told ya, I don't know any Harry Smith now piss orf."

"He's tall with a drooping moustache and has a tattoo of a naked Creole woman on his left arm," persisted Jacob, grinning at his bizarre imagination.

"You know of anyone fits that description?" said the guard, turning to his partner.

"Naw, never 'eard of no Harry Smith 'ere, nor of anyone with that kind of tattoo. It's bollocks, tell 'im to bugger orf, Alf. Sarge will be 'ere soon with Sid and Wilf to relieve us."

"You 'eard him," said Alf, looking at Jacob threateningly.

"Shame, I've got this bottle for him," said Jacob, lifting half of the bottle from his inside jacket pocket in full view of the two guards. They watched him slide the bottle back into the pocket, their eyes lighting up greedily over its contents. Jacob noticed their eagerness to get their hands on the bottle.

"Well, that aint no problem squire," said Alf, licking his lips. "Give us the bottle and we'll find Harry and give it 'im."

"I've a better idea," said Jacob, grinning. "Let's open it up here and have a drink. Don't suppose Harry would mind if we did."

"What 'ere?" said Alf, looking up and down the track that led away from the warehouse.

"There's no-one around Alf," said his partner, coming closer. "Could murder a drink after standing outside 'ere all day guarding those fuckin' French bastards inside. Come on Alf, couple of slurps won't do us no 'arm!"

"Yeah, go on then squire. Open it up."

Jacob drew the cork, forcing himself not to laugh at the looks on their faces, their eyes glued to the bottle as they greedily licked their lips.

A few swigs and they'll tell me everything, he thought.

"Here," he said, handing the bottle to Alf.

Grabbing the bottle, Alf thrust it to his lips tilting his head back as he gulped down a good measure.

"Cor, proper good that. Bliddy strong brandy!" he said, taking another long swig.

Alf's partner, drooling at the sound of the brandy sluicing out of the bottle, scratched crudely at his crotch before snatching the bottle from Alf and guzzling more than a fair share.

"Who's in there?" said Jacob, snatching the bottle back from Alf's partner.

"Bunch of Frenchies," said Alf. "Prisoners of a brig one of our frigates captured couple of days back. They'll be goin' to England as prisoners of war, soon as that sloop over there's ready. Couple of days they reckon."

"How many prisoners are in the warehouse?" asked Jacob, holding the bottle tauntingly towards Alf."

"'bout twenty or so," said Alf, his eyes transfixed on the bottle. "There's an officer in there with 'em too. A Frenchie lieutenant from the brig. Seems to be an important fucker, as the captain of our frigate what captured them came in early this mornin' and took 'im out for questionin'. Supposed to be comin' back again, tomorrow early."

Jacob let Alf have a hearty swig before handing the bottle over to his partner, smiling at the blissful murmurs emanating from him as he gulped at the powerful spirit.

"Are you two on guard here every day?" asked Jacob.

"Yeah, till they be shipped out, probably in a couple of days," replied Alf, beginning to slur slightly.

"The night guards," said Jacob. "When do they come on?"

"When we're relieved, in 'bout an hour."

"Do you hand over the keys to the new guards when they relieve you?" asked Jacob, thinking this had better be his last question.

"Yeah, fucking right," said Alf aggressively. "Now give us 'nother swig of that brandy."

"Yeah, come on squire. Give it me, first," slurred Alf's partner.

"Gentlemen, you've been most helpful," said Jacob. "Please have what's left of the bottle, I must be away."

"That we will squire," garbled Alf, grabbing the bottle from Jacob.

With one arm held out to keep his partner at bay, Alf guzzled several mouthfuls of the powerful liquor, finally handing it over. Swaying on his feet, he watched resentfully as his partner greedily gulped at the strong spirit. Unable to stand it any longer, he jealously snatched it back ignoring his partners protests. Staggering over to the warehouse, Alf clutched the bottle closely to his chest while his partner, careering drunkenly after him, tripped and fell flat on his back. Wolfing down the rest of the strong brandy and seeming to grab at nothing but thin air, Alf slumped down sniggering at his partner's lewd gibbering about ravishing a naked Creole woman behind the warehouse.

Then, flinging his head back, and with the dregs of the brandy trickling down his chin, he bellowed out a bawdy barrack room ditty, its crude verses reverberating loudly around every corner of the harbour.

A deep-throated roar exploded over the wharf as Alf reached the final verse of his ditty. A giant of a marine warrant officer, his eyes bulging with fury, stood pointing at the two drunken guards lying wasted in front of the warehouse. Pounding along the quay towards the two floundering idiots, he hollered out in his rage for the night-duty guards to follow him and to bring with them a length of strong rope.

Tears of laughter filled Jacob's eyes at the sight of the Royal Marine sergeant, red in the face with streams of sweat pouring from beneath his cap, berating the two drunken boneheads staggering before him. The scene became even more farcical as four burly marine guards trying to hoist up the blabbering dimwits slipped and fell to the ground in the ensuing struggles. Chuckling, he decided it was time to depart.

As the evening drew in, Jacob made his way to the hillside track that would lead him up to the field of long grass and into the forest where the two French spies would be waiting in the shack for his return. He would share the information he had got from Alf, suggesting they think of a plan to free the French lieutenant.

Pausing to look back over his shoulder towards the harbour, he grinned at the sight of Alf and his partner being roughly escorted along the quay towards the building that housed the officers of the guard. Stumbling along with his head thrown back, Alf continued to belt out his raucous lyric while his partner, smirking from ear to ear, prattled on to his guards about a naked Creole woman he was going to roger behind one of the warehouses.

11

General Jean-Luc Bonard stubbed out the cheroot he had been smoking into a deep ashtray at the side of his desk. His mind was working overtime at the disastrous news he had received that morning. Pushing back his chair, he stood and walked across to the French windows that looked down onto the cobbled courtyard below. Staring down at the figures hurrying in and out of the Artus Court Building, his eyes picked out the familiar sight of a high-ranking French naval officer striding towards the entrance doors.

"Must give it to him," thought Jean-Luc, "he's never late, always on time."

Returning to his desk, he sat back counting the seconds before two demanding knocks signalled the arrival of the man he was expecting.

"Come," he called.

Commandant Henri Joubert, commanding officer of all French naval personnel in the port of Danzig, gently closed the door behind him.

"Henri, I'm pleased to see you, come on in," said Jean-Luc, getting up to welcome the commandant. "Take off your cloak and join me for a glass of cognac before we begin."

Smiling, Commandant Joubert hung his cloak on the peg next to the door extending his hand as he walked towards Napoleon's First Secretary General of the city-state of Danzig.

"General Bonard, a pleasure," said Henri, firmly shaking Jean-Luc's outstretched hand.

"Enough of the formalities Henri, please address me as Jean-Luc, we are after all friends as well as colleagues, are we not?"

"Absolutely Jean-Luc," replied Henri, wondering why he had been summoned so urgently.

"This fine cognac also graces the table of His Excellency himself," said Jean-Luc, pouring Henri a good measure from a crystal decanter.

"To the Emperor," said Jean-Luc, raising his glass.

"To the Emperor," reiterated Henri.

"Sit Henri," said Jean-Luc, smiling.

"The two officers you recommended to infiltrate Hanö Island have been there for five days now. We know they're with our agent on the island, but so far there's been no further news of them. They have another nine days to fulfil their mission before we bring them out. What's your knowledge of them to date?"

"I have nothing to add to what you've just told me," Henri said, taking a sip of his cognac. "Our build up for an invasion of the island is now complete. Our fleet, with several detachments of marines, will be launched three days after our two spies have returned, that is twelve days from now. There must be no delay Jean-Luc, no delay."

"Absolutely," said Jean-Luc.

"The report they bring back will be crucial to our launching the invasion, this they know. I'm confident they'll succeed in giving us the information of every defensive position the British have, together with the routine of their ships out on patrol. We will also need their advice on where we can land our marines on the island and the strength of the British Marines there. Before we launch the invasion, we must have this information."

Henri nodded in agreement staring at his empty glass.

"Now," said Jean-Luc, refilling their glasses, "the main reason I've asked you here concerns a matter of urgency you need to know. Several days ago, I approved a secret mission to depart from our base here in Danzig. The instruction for this mission came from the highest level. Yes, from His Excellency himself, who also wrote in a personal message to me, if I may quote: "General Bonard, deliver that island to me."

Now, there are certain members of the Swedish hierarchy together with high-ranking officers in their armed forces, who are let us say, leaning to our side in our war with the British. They do not like or agree with their government's decision to allow a British base on their island. They have also become very anxious, if not paranoid, about Sweden being invaded. His Excellency has put a letter together with a demand they collaborate with us in our invasion of the Island. Should they not oblige, then His Excellency will have no alternative but to invade their mainland. The letter was to be delivered personally to a high-ranking Swedish admiral by the name of Carl von Krassow based in the port of Karlskrona. The letter was entrusted to an agent of ours, a lieutenant in our navy, who would wait for their reply and then return here.

"I had no knowledge of this!" said Henri, indignantly.

"The lieutenant was made aware of its contents," continued Lean-Luc, "and ordered to memorize it in case of him having to destroy it, should he be captured by the British."

"What's the name of the agent?" asked Henri.

"I'm coming to that," answered Jean-Luc. "He was assigned to one of our brigs here in Danzig, La Marie Louise. If engaged by the British at sea, they were to take appropriate action or make a run for it. Under no circumstance was the letter to fall into the hands of the British. If the situation looked dire then they were to destroy the letter and engage the British while our agent slipped away in one of the brig's small skiffs. Information reached me early this morning that La Marie Louise had been attacked and disabled by a British frigate. Its captain killed, and our lieutenant and the remainder of her crew taken prisoner to the British base on the island. They will remain there until a ship becomes available to transport them to England as prisoners of war. His Excellency will be furious when he has news that the mission has failed.

What is more, the British now have the possibility of discovering our plans for the invasion.

Our agent could very likely be persuaded to tell them everything. The letter to Admiral von Krassow included confidential information on our invasion plans, the date and time of the invasion, the number of ships in our fleet and coordinates where we are to link up with the Swedish force. These plans have now been placed into serious jeopardy."

"Who is this agent?" said Henri, looking concerned.

"Andre Pascale," replied Jean-Luc, "a navy lieutenant based here in Danzig.

I'll send an immediate order for Erik Gunnarsson, the Swedish fisherman loyal to us, to meet us here. We'll brief him and send him to the island immediately to instruct our spy master there, Jacob Forsberg, to find a way to rescue Pascale. Once they have freed him, Gunnarsson will ferry him to Karlskrona to deliver the contents of His Excellency's letter."

"I just hope you'll be able to get to him in time," said Henri. "But surely, Jacob Forsberg will be aware that a large group of prisoners were brought onto the island and have been locked up. When they find out they're French and there are officers in the group I'm sure they'll attempt a rescue."

"I just hope you're right Henri, before Pascale's made to talk."

Jacques was skinning two plump rabbits when Jacob opened the door of the shack. Looking surprised at the two Frenchmen busily preparing supper, he pulled up a chair and sat studying them.

"Well, looks like you've turned into a couple of good trappers," he said, smiling.

"Those two rabbits look about ready for the pot! As dinner seems a while away come and have a drink, I have a bottle of wine I found in my hut down on the quay. I've got some news from the harbour that you'll want to hear, but don't forget Per that it's your watch for the longboat tonight."

Jacques nodded towards Jacob, then throwing a few more logs onto the fire he cut up the rabbits into small pieces dropping them into the bubbling pot before joining his two comrades and the mug of wine that waited patiently for him.

Pierre scribbled notes in a notebook as Jacob described, in detail, everything he'd observed in the harbour that afternoon, highlighting the positions of the British frigates anchored outside the mouth of the harbour and the schedules of those out on patrol.

Jacob paused, replenishing his and Pierre's mugs before coming to the news concerning the French captives, and the keen interest in a certain French lieutenant the captain of a British frigate was showing.

Coming to the end of his report and regarding the two French spies seriously, he let the information he had just given sink in.

"You said that the British captain was going to question the lieutenant early tomorrow, Jacob," said Pierre, chuckling at the picture Jacob had painted of the two imbecilic guards.

Jacob nodded, raising an eyebrow at Pierre's comment.

"Yes, that's what the guard with the keys said," he replied.

"Then I think we'd better be down there to see when they escort the lieutenant out of the warehouse and where they take him for questioning. The number of guards they use and when they return him to the warehouse."

"I'm sure they'll be questioning him regularly," added Jacob. "They seem to consider him an important catch. They'll be moving them to England soon, now that the sloop-of-war is virtually fit to sail. So, we haven't much time."

"Per will be down on the cove tonight watching for the British longboat," said Pierre. "He won't be back till late. So, Jacob, you and I can go down to the harbour before dawn and wait for the French lieutenant to be taken out for questioning. Per can sleep until we return."

"Yes, that's good," said Jacob, looking at Jacques. "Ok with you Per?"

Jacques nodded towards them.

"Take this with you," said Jacob, handing Jacques a brass pocket watch. "It keeps good time, and you'll need it to record the times the longboat passes and returns. Magnus will take tomorrow night's watch and then it'll be me the following night. If the times of the longboat passing and returning match with each of our recordings, we'll then be ready to plan to disable it before the invasion begins. But before that, freeing the French lieutenant is our priority.

We should be back here by mid-morning. The British captain will have finished his questioning of the French lieutenant by then and will have left the harbour aboard his frigate on his daily patrol. The three of us can then think of a plan to free the lieutenant. Now, is supper ready? My stomach's starting to rumble!"

Jacques made his way through the darkness holding up the lantern Jacob had given him. Several times he stumbled over jutting tree roots but managed to get onto the path that led down to where Jacob had snared the hares on their first day in the forest. He was pleased when the path levelled out, and through gaps in the trees he was able to make out the full moon lighting up parts of the rocky shoreline. He stopped where an opening between the trees gave him a clear view across a stony inlet to the open sea.

Jagged rocks rearing up over beds of blackened stones and boulders reminded him of a painting of a dark and desolate scene of hell he had once been terrified to look at as a child. Moon beams piercing the murky water cast pale bands of silver far across its dark surface, but as much as he craned his neck to peer for signs of a longboat, nothing came within sight. Holding up the lantern he continued along the path towards the shingly cove, the hooting of an owl sounding somewhere faraway in the forest.

The path narrowed as the gaps in the trees became less frequent and then, through the rays of moonlight, the image of towering cliffs soaring above the trees loomed before him. The sound of waves breaking over shingle told him he had reached the cove. Jumping down from the pathway, he crunched his way over to the nest of rocks where they had previously spied on the British longboat.

Holding the pocket watch up into the light of the lantern he noted it was five minutes before the hour of ten, then settling down between the rocks he shuffled himself into a comfortable position and waited, hoping the longboat hadn't already passed by.

He shivered as the night chill cut through the course material of his jacket and pulling up its collar he concentrated on the quietness surrounding the cove. Looking up, he gazed at the stars spread across the night's sky, then blowing out the candle he shoved his hands deep inside his pockets and sat back listening to the gentle lapping of the waves. Beams of moonlight lit up the sea between the rocks in front of him, so providing him with a clear view of any approaching craft.

He smiled as visions of French marines coming ashore on the cove flashed before his eyes. His plan of guiding them up through the tunnel to the forest pathway and taking over the British heavy guns looking ever more likely to succeed.

Suddenly he was alert. The sound of oars dipping through water broke the stillness around him. The longboat was approaching.

Peering through the gap, he saw the shadowy shape slowly coast into sight, the light from the full moon showing up a red-coated marine officer standing erect in the bow.

"Stop rowing," the command rang out.

Jacques watched the rowers bring their oars up out of the water, the British officer standing with his head bent towards the cove, listening for any sound that would prompt them to beach the craft and come ashore. The longboat rocked gently up and down as all eyes scanned the dark shadows between the rocks. Jacques held his breath, not daring to move. It seemed an age for the British officer and his crew to take in everything around the cove. Jacques followed their every movement as they listened and peered into the dark nooks and crannies that furnished the silent inlet.

Then, without warning, he suddenly froze; something was climbing slowly up the inside of his left leg. Needle-like pricks dug into his skin as he felt a little demon crawling sluggishly up past his knee cap. He could feel the upward march of whatever creature it was, pitting its way upwards towards his groin.

The longboat had not moved, the British officer now joined by a sergeant, stood silently studying the dark scene before them. Jacques wanted to scream, to jump up and shake the creature out of his trouser leg, but to do that would be the end of his mission and likely of him. He clamped his eyes shut, biting anxiously into his lip as little claws buried themselves further into the top part of his leg as they felt their way slowly upwards to the warm area around his crotch.

Perspiration poured from him, the claws of the little creature pushing into the soft fleshy part of his groin. Very slowly he began to move his hand towards the front buttons of his breeches, he couldn't let whatever was attempting to nest there take any more advantage.

Gently opening the buttons, he inserted his hand feeling around for the obnoxious little intruder when a loud command rang out across the cove, "Carry on sergeant, let us be away further on down the coast. There's nothing here."

With his hand clamped firmly over his privates, Jacques watched the longboat pull away from the cove, the sound of its oars dipping in and out of the water becoming fainter as it disappeared into the darkness.

In a flash he jumped to his feet dropping his breeches and underwear, his righthand scraping frantically at the area of his crotch where he had last felt the creature. With a sigh of relief, he sensed something fall from between his legs and looking down he watched as a little spider crab, that only moments before had nearly cost him his mission and probably his life, scuttle away in the moonlight to find sanctuary under the row of rocks.

Shaking his head, he forced himself to forget the trauma and with the longboat now safely out of sight he set his mind on the purpose of his mission. With a deep sigh he ducked down behind the rocks pulling out the pocket watch and lighting the candle inside the lantern from the tinder box Jacob had loaned him. Twenty minutes past the hour of eleven.

Now he'd wait for the longboat to return and no matter how long it took he'd remain standing. He'd stay upright, standing behind the very rocks that had ironically given refuge to the little tormenting trespasser who had very nearly cost him everything.

Erik listened with a serious frown as Christina told him of the stranger who had sat on the bench with Anna and then accompanied her up the hill to their house. His frown deepened when she described how close they had been with each other, and how Anna would regularly stand at the long picture window in their front room scanning the wide expanse of sea.

"Something's got into her Erik," she said with a sigh, "and I'm sure it's all to do with the stranger. I'm certain he's an English navy man, probably based over on Hanö Island. Erik, I think she's falling in love with him."

"Christina, our daughter will never associate with an Englishman," said Erik, furiously, "We will never accept an Englishman into our family, never. Tomorrow, I have a meeting with the General Secretary in Danzig, so I'll leave at first light. When I return, I'll find out what's going on and I'll remind her of what they did to her grandmother. Never Christina, never, never!"

12

Pierre and Jacob rose just before dawn. Dying embers from the previous night's fire cast a soft red glow around the cabin revealing the sleeping form of Jacques stretched out on the top bunk. Picking up their tricorns they let themselves out of the cabin.

Wet droplets from a heavy dew splashed against Pierre as he followed Jacob through the field of long grass. Far below them the lanterns of the British compound twinkled around the harbour, letting the two spies know the British were about their early morning business, while far out to sea the dim light of a new day rose slowly above the horizon.

The view from Jacob's hut at the end of the quay gave a good aspect of the three warehouses where the French prisoners were being held. Jacob pointed out the furthest one where two marine guards lolled nonchalantly up against its front side. Seeing the two guards were not Alf and his partner, he smiled, wondering whether they were still locked up in the garrison's guardhouse.

"That's the one where the French lieutenant's being held," he said. "If the guards I spoke to yesterday were telling me the truth, then it won't be long before the British captain comes to question him."

No sooner had he finished his sentence, when through the faint light of the early dawn, they saw the British captain in the company of two of his crew.

Keeping well out of sight, the two spies watched the captain address one of the marine guards then stand back to allow him to open the warehouse door. With a look over his shoulder and a nod to his escort, Captain James Carey hurried into the dark confines of the island's temporary jail.

It was not long before he reappeared, a marine guard holding the arm of a dishevelled looking individual whose hands were firmly tied in front of him.

"Thank you, corporal," they heard the British captain say to the guard, "we'll have him back to you before the end of your shift."

The guard saluted, then turning he locked the warehouse door.

The two spies watched the ship's captain and his escort lead the French prisoner in the direction of a row of wooden sheds, stopping at the last one in the row, the two seamen remaining outside on guard while the captain led his prisoner inside.

"Come on," said Jacob, "there's a pathway behind those sheds, we'll scout around the back and see if someone has left a window open."

All was quiet as they crept through the shadows towards the last shack in the row, stopping occasionally to listen for a sound that would warn them of anyone approaching. Nearing the last shed, Jacob grabbed Pierre's arm.

"There in that shed," he whispered. "It's vital we know what's going on in there. Look, someone must be smiling down at us, there's a window half open."

Pierre looked up at the small semi-open window half-way up the back of the wooden building. Jacob gently tugged at his arm pointing to a water barrel at the side of the shed, perfect for one of them to stand on. It didn't take long for them to manoeuvre the barrel into a position under the window.

"Up you go Magnus," Jacob said, softly, "I'll keep watch here. If the captain and the prisoner are in sight, you should be able to hear what's being said. It's not a large area inside. Don't attract their attention, whatever you do."

Pierre hoisted himself up onto the barrel and, stretching himself up to the level of the window, he squinted through the dirty glass. Peering closely, he made out the figures of the British captain and his prisoner seated at a table only a few feet from the window. He immediately recognised the uniform the prisoner was wearing. Albeit torn and dirty it was the uniform of a French navy lieutenant. The two drunken guards had been right about a French officer being held by the British. Turning his ear to the window he listened carefully.

"I'll ask you once again Lieutenant Pascale," came the voice of the British captain, "where exactly was your ship heading when we engaged you? Your course was set towards the Swedish coast, not far from our garrison here on Hanö Island. We need to find out why you were there. I've calculated that from the position where we first sighted your ship and the course you were on from your departure port of Danzig, your destination would have been to a point on the eastern part of the Blekinge archipelago, very likely the naval port of Karlskrona. Now why should you be going there?"

"Very clever of you Captain Carey!" said Pascale, looking up at his interrogator, "but of that you will never ascertain, never."

"I'll put it to you lieutenant," said the British captain, leaning over the table and looking directly into the face of the French prisoner, "that you were engaged in a secret mission to involve certain Swedish nationals in some clandestine plot concerning our base here on Hanö Island. You are a spy lieutenant, and I will prove it. I am sure you were in possession of secret instructions. You will talk lieutenant, or be made talk, and when we find out there will be no option but to have you shot. You are however a prisoner of war and will remain so. The day after tomorrow at midday, a sloop will transfer your crew to a prison in England. You shall remain here for further questioning until you submit to the truth of your mission."

Pierre had heard enough, carefully letting himself down from the water barrel he bent his head towards Jacob whispering in his ear, "They're moving the prisoners to England at midday in two days but keeping the French officer here for further questioning. Seems like he's part of an important mission that the British captain thinks may threaten this island."

"We've got to get him out and with us," said Jacob, "but it might be best we wait until they start transporting the prisoners. Come on, let's get back to the cabin and start the planning."

Jacques was awake and breakfasting at the table when Jacob and Pierre returned to the cabin. Dipping a crust of bread into a mug of ale, he watched his two comrades settle themselves at the table beside him, the looks on their faces showing they had something important to tell him.

"Looks like you've got some news for me," he said, chewing the soggy mass he had just popped into his mouth.

"We certainly have," said Jacob, "but first, tell us about what you found out last night."

"Well, something happened that very nearly would have cost us the entire mission here," said Jacques, noticing the sudden looks of concern spreading across the faces of his two confidantes. "I reached the cove at five minutes before the hour of ten, settled myself down behind the rocks where we'd spied on the longboat before, and waited. It wasn't long before I heard it approaching. From the gap in front of me I watched as its crew upped their oars. Beams of moonlight lit up a British officer and his sergeant standing in the bow peering at the cove and scrutinizing everything around me. With their heads bent they listened for any sound that would have caused them to come ashore. Time seemed to drag by as I watched them and then I froze. Something was crawling up the inside of my leg."

Jacob and Pierre listened quietly, a smile stretching across Jacob's face as Jacques described how the little crab had finally scuttled away under a rock.

"Well Per," said Jacob, "You've certainly got self-control. Waiting for that longboat to leave must have been agony for you."

"What else could I have done?" said Jacques, "If I'd screamed out, that would've been the end of our mission and of me. Damn little crab, he got away before I could stamp on him. You'd better look out for him Magnus, if you do see him or any other little demons crawling out from under a rock keep your trouser legs tightly secured."

"Yes, be very careful!" said Jacob, concealing his smile. "Now, what time did the longboat return?"

"Ten minutes before the hour of one," said Jacques. "It passed without stopping. It looked as though the crew were intent on getting back to base, not one of them looked over at the cove."

"Right, let's recap," said Jacob. "You arrived at the cove at five minutes before the hour of ten and it wasn't long before the longboat arrived. Then, when the longboat left you looked at the pocket watch again, and it was twenty minutes past the hour of eleven. So, let us say it must have been about forty or forty-five minutes past the hour of ten that you saw the longboat approach the cove?"

"Yes, I'd say so," agreed Jacques.

"I think it's safe to say then, that the longboat will approach the cove after ten but before the hour of eleven. Magnus, be down there before ten tonight. Take the pocket watch I loaned to Per and the lantern. If the arrival and departure of that longboat including its return, corresponds to Per's timings, it means it's likely keeping to a schedule. If it's the same when I am down there tomorrow night, then we'll know for sure."

Pierre nodded towards Jacob.

"Now Per," continued Jacob, "listen carefully to what we're going to tell you about what we found out on our visit to the harbour early this morning. Magnus, you begin."

Jacques listened attentively to Pierre's account of the questioning of the French lieutenant, not interrupting his partner until he came to the point of the British keeping the French officer on the island for further questioning.

"If you're right about the British not sending him to England with the others," said Jacques, "then I think the best chance of us springing him, would be when they're emptying the warehouses of the prisoners and loading them onto the sloop. He'll be left virtually alone in that warehouse whilst the attention of the guards will be on getting all the prisoners safely embarked. I could start a minor disruption while you two deal with the guard with the keys. If we plan it well it could work."

"Yes, it could," said Jacob, thoughtfully. "We've got the rest of today and tomorrow to plan it out before the sloop sails for England with the prisoners.

Once we have the lieutenant with us and we've found out the purpose of his mission, I'm sure he'll be able to help in some way with more ideas for the invasion. We'll hide him here until Erik returns with his fishing boat, then he'll return to Danzig with you two."

"Well," said Jacques, looking seriously at his two comrades, "I have another idea that will better fulfil our task of being here. Listen carefully, this is what I think. When we've sprung the lieutenant, we're going to have to include him in our plan for the invasion of the island. We'll show him the tunnel through the cave and the route through the forest to attack the British from the rear. When Erik Gunnarsson returns to pick us up, the lieutenant will go with Pierre while I stay here on the island with you Jacob. Pierre, you, and the lieutenant must convince General Bonard of using the main invasion fleet as a decoy while a detachment of Marines land on the shingly cove. Explain that Jacob and I will have lit beacons to guide them in. Once you and the Marines have landed on the cove, we'll take them up through the tunnel in the cave and then on through the forest to take over their heavy guns and then attack them from their rear. When we have those heavy cannons in our possession, we'll fire them down onto the British below, wiping them out completely together with their ships." Jacques paused, looking at his comrades, then continued.

"Give General Bonard the information that Jacob gathered concerning the British frigates at anchor and their patrol schedules, the British strength within the harbour and stress the position of their three heavy guns on the island's heights. You must emphasise the case for a night-time invasion, as Jacob and I will have disabled the British longboat by the time the fleet gets within sight of the harbour. A night-time attack will intensify the element of surprise and what is more, being the dead of night will give us the freedom to get through the tunnel faster as the bats will have left their daytime habitat. Finally, the timing of the invasion. We must know it before the fleet sails."

"Yes, a good plan Per," said Jacob, "I agree with everything you've suggested and by the smiles and nods of Magnus he obviously agrees too. But first we're going to have to spring the French lieutenant and find out from him why the British suspect him of being a spy, then we can put your plan into action. Now, let us talk more about your idea of creating a diversion on the day they move the prisoners and how we're going to snatch this spy from under their very noses.

The light from the lantern helped Pierre check the time on the pocket watch as he settled himself behind one of the craggy rocks on the cove. Five minutes before the hour of ten. Pulling up the collar of his jacket he listened to the sound of the waves breaking on the shoreline. Mindful of the warning Jacques had given him about a certain little crab's likeness for the warmth of the human crotch, he tucked the bottoms of his trouser legs firmly into his boots then, blowing out the candle in the lantern, he concentrated on the darkened coastline ahead and waited.

13

Commodore Percival listened without interrupting as James recounted his recent questioning of Lieutenant Pascale.

"I believe he's a spy sir, and I believe he was on a mission to the Swedish mainland, likely to the port of Karlskrona. The big question is why. I have a theory he was carrying a secret message from his superiors to some high- ranking Swedish military officials concerning a possible invasion, either of the mainland itself or our base here on Hanö. We know there's a group of aristocratic Swedish military commanders who favour the French, and who are ready to collude and provide military assistance whenever Bonaparte snaps his fingers. I'm certain Lieutenant Pascale was carrying confidential material bound for this group, probably proposals and requests for them to organise sections of their military in assisting the French in a forthcoming invasion. It's imperative, sir, that we find out what this French lieutenant was carrying. The sloop-of-war is ready to sail with the French prisoners tomorrow, but Lieutenant Pascale should not sail with them, we must detain him here for further questioning."

Commodore Percival looked gravely across his desk at James, "If what you are saying captain is correct, then it would seem more likely there will be an invasion attempt of the island. Bonaparte will need to make sure, this part of the Baltic is free of the British if he plans to invade the Swedish mainland from the south. With us destroyed and out of his way he will have free rein to send an armada to wherever he desires. He knows his alliance with the Swedes is paper thin, apart from this small group of high-ranking Swedish fraternizers. He'll therefore be in a stronger position if he takes over their country. Should that happen captain, our war with him would drag on and on. Yes, permission to detain the French Lieutenant here for further questioning is granted. He will not sail with the rest of the prisoners. Use whatever means to get the information from him, whatever means, captain. Should he be a spy, then you have my permission to have him shot."

"Aye, aye, we will sir, thank you sir," replied James, getting up from his chair.

HMS Hector lay at anchor outside the mouth of the harbour, ready and waiting for its captain to come aboard. Dan Sutherland had orders from James to meet him on the quay opposite the gang plank that led down from the warship where Commodore Percival had his working quarters. On seeing his captain descending he stood to attention,

"Captain," he said, saluting James.

"At ease, Dan," James replied, casually. "Commodore Percival has approved the detaining of Lieutenant Pascale for more rigorous questioning. Pascale will not be leaving with the other prisoners tomorrow. I've been given the go ahead to use whatever means to get the information we need.

I won't approve of any physical torture, so we must find another way of making him talk, something that may frighten him enough to confirm my theory of why he was on this mission and his plans of where he was going and whom he was to meet."

"That'll be a tall order captain," said Dan, looking out across the harbour. "From what you've said about your questioning of him he seems adamant not to reveal anything. Also, time's getting on and if Frenchie's planning an attack on our base it may come at any time soon."

"Exactly," said James. "But it won't be just our base here at the harbour, I'm sure they'll be planning to take the whole island. I've warned about the lack of defence on the southern part. The commodore dismissed it as my being over- cautious, believing the French will concentrate on destroying as many of our ships as they can by aiming their attack solely at the harbour. Come on, we can discuss it later as Hector's waiting for us. We'll sail down to the southern part of the island and look for an inlet that could serve as a landing place for their longboats."

Davey Sturrock brought HMS Hector as close to the southern part of the island as would allow. James stared out at the rocky coastline, his two lieutenants running their eyes along the jagged rocks that dominated the entire shoreline.

"Gentlemen, I want you to search for a cove or inlet that could serve as a landing point for longboats launched from ships from around this area.

We're expecting Frenchie to land their marines somewhere along this coast."

Scanning every inch of the craggy terrain, James was unable to pinpoint any likely spot where longboats could land. Through his lens he picked out tall cliffs rising to meet the forest above, but as close as he looked, his view was constantly blocked by flocks of sea birds swirling around the face of the cliffs.

"Captain," said his second lieutenant, "those cliffs at the end of the coastline, from what I can see they're sheer and would be impossible to scale. There's no sign of any cove or possible landing place either."

James nodded, his telescope ranging over the cliff's face and the rugged shoreline below. A swirling mass of seabirds filled the view of his lens, allowing only brief glimpses of the rocky coast.

"Mr. Sturrock, take us around to the other side of the island," instructed James. "We'll have a look there, although I doubt if it'd be any better than here."

James watched the flocks of seabirds circling the face of the towering cliffs. Opening his telescope, he trained it once again onto the sheer walls of the cliff's face. His heart suddenly jumped as something caught his eye. What looked like an opening at the bottom of the cliff zoomed up in front of his lens.

"A cave!" he murmured.

It had been impossible to see it from where they had been looking previously owing to the mass of seabirds, but now, it was clearly in his sights.

With the wind swelling her sails Hector gently cruised around the island's southern-most point.

"Only rocks stretching along the coast as far as the eye can see, captain," shouted Dan, sweeping his telescope along the shoreline.

"Mr. Sturrock," yelled James. "Turn us about. Back to the position we held a moment ago on the other side of the island. Be quick about it."

"Aye, aye, captain, turning about now."

As Hector turned, James focused his telescope on the cliff face where he had seen the entrance to the cave. Colonies of seabirds still swooped and circled in front of it, but he had seen it and he knew what it meant. Slowly, he moved his telescope over the towering walls until the dark aperture of the cave's entrance came briefly into sight. A score of birds suddenly blocked his view causing him to lower the scope and sweep it along the jagged coastline. He knew there had to be an inlet or cove somewhere nearby.

"Did you see it, Dan?" asked James, turning to his first lieutenant.

"I did, captain. It's a cave, cut into the cliff face."

"But there should be a cove nearby," said James. "Wherever there's a cave there's a cove."

"It's impossible to see from here captain," said Dan.

"Precisely Dan," said James. "So, we're going to find it. We'll make our way down there by foot after we've questioned the French lieutenant at dawn tomorrow. We'll check out the cave entrance and search for a cove or inlet nearby. That's the place where the French will land their marines. How they will get them up to the forest above I have no idea, but with luck we may find the answer to that. God-forbid if they've managed to find a route, but with this part of the island being undefended you never know! Mr. Sturrock, follow a setting four degrees south by southeast, full sail Mr. Nark. Dan, you have the quarterdeck, I'll be in my cabin."

Late afternoon saw HMS Hector skipping over white- tipped rollers that swelled before her bow as a brisk wind drove her ever closer to her home base on the island of Hanö. James watched the distant speck of the island drawing closer, his thoughts conjuring up images of a cave entrance guarded by colonies of squawking seabirds. After leaving the southern tip of the island they had encountered nothing but miles of empty sea. Engrossed in his thoughts he was suddenly interrupted by the sound of a gentle cough,

"Captain, if I may?" asked Dan, coming onto the quarterdeck.

"Yes of course Dan," replied James.

"I've thought of a way of how we might get the French lieutenant to talk. Torture, I know, is out of the question. But what if we made him think that unless he tells us everything about his mission when we interrogate him later this evening, he'll be taken to an execution site in the morning and shot as a spy."

"Yes, could work Dan," said James, thoughtfully. "The commodore has given permission to have him shot as a spy, but that would be after we have firmly established his guilt Nevertheless, it would ultimately be up to me to decide his fate. However, please elaborate a bit more."

"At the back of the shed where you've been questioning him," continued Dan, "there's a cliff wall that rises to meet a bank of grass and bushes. Before we take him to the shed for questioning this evening, have two of our men insert a thick post in front of the cliff wall with an open grave dug next to it. We'll take the path at the back of the sheds and walk slowly past the cliff wall where the post and open grave are. We won't say anything, just let him look at the sinister sight and ponder on what he sees. When he's in the shed for questioning he's bound to ask what it's for. You tell him it's an execution site that has recently been used for spies we've caught. Tell him that in his absence he's been sentenced to death by firing squad which will be carried out at dawn. I'll be watching with a sombre look to make him believe he's going to be shot. No questioning about his mission, just let the horror of execution sink in. After a few minutes we'll take him out of the shed and back to the warehouse. If he has any fear, he'll make a plea for his life. He'll have the night to think about it and if he values his life he'll talk. He won't want to die as an unknown failure, never to be recognised or heard of again. I'm sure he'll talk, captain."

"Think you could be right Dan," said James, nodding. "There's nothing more we can do to get him to talk. This could work, I like the plan. You arrange it. Once we've anchored and gone ashore, arrange for the post to be inserted and the hole dug. The six crew members will have to be briefed about the plan and then issued with muskets before dawn tomorrow. Yes, the more I think of it the more I think it will work."

14

Long shadows stretched behind the row of sheds that led away from the warehouses holding the French prisoners as dusk settled over the harbour of Hanö. Lieutenant Pascale looked contemptuously at James and Dan as he was frog marched between two of HMS Hector's crew towards the path that ran directly behind the line of sheds.

"Where are you taking me captain?" he asked, "this is not the normal route we take to the place of questioning."

"I thought we'd give you a change of scenery lieutenant," said James, "and by the way, my first officer Lieutenant Sutherland, will be with us this evening."

Pascale made no reply. Turning, he looked at Dan and - giving a scornful sneer - he pulled himself upright flexing his shoulders and holding his head high.

The path at the rear of the sheds was covered in shadow, apart from a beam of moonlight shimmering over the high wall at the end. Dan nodded towards his captain letting him know everything was ready. James smiled, feeling that what Pascale was about to see would shake him into revealing everything.

Nearing the wall, the Frenchman's facial expression suddenly changed. His mouth dropped open in shock and his eyes widened in a look of utter horror. Stopping in his tracks, he looked over at the lurid picture he was passing.

A high stone wall pitted with small round holes loomed up at the back of an area of rough patchy grass. A thick wooden post showing signs of congealed blood trailing down its shaft, rose a few feet in front of the wall whilst a freshly dug open grave, its black interior wide and open, climaxed the entire grisly setting. At that moment a cloud passing over the moon threw the whole spectacle into a dark scene of death. Shaken, Pascale shuffled into the shed.

James looked over at Dan and raising an eyebrow nodded in the direction of the execution area, smiling at its authenticity.

Seated at the table, Pascale looked ashen.

"What is the meaning of that out there?" he stammered, looking up at James.

James looked away with a sombre look catching Dan's eye.

"I asked you what the meaning of that is?" asked Pascale, raising his voice shakily.

Very slowly, James moved over to the table, drawing back a chair. Without speaking he looked at his prisoner, his eyes projecting a heavy-hearted look. Pascale looked from James to Dan and then back to James, his face creasing with an understanding of the horror that James was about to confirm.

"I remind you captain," he stuttered, looking desperately at James, "that I am an officer in the French navy and a prisoner of war."

"You are a spy, Andre Pascale," replied James. "I have been ordered to inform you that, in your absence, a Royal Naval tribunal has found you guilty of espionage. By your silence and refusal to reveal the content of your mission, you have been sentenced to death by firing squad. The sentence to be carried out at dawn tomorrow."

"But this is outrageous," cried Pascale. "I must be treated according to my rank. This is war, and I surrendered to you, I must be treated as a prisoner of war along with the crew of La Marie Louise."

"That is all, lieutenant," said James, sternly. "Now come with us, the matter is over."

Outside the door of the warehouse, Pascal looked at James despairingly, disbelief stamped all over his face. They were going to execute him without any proof he was a spy. He shuddered at the thought of what lay ahead of him the following morning.

"Untie him," James instructed his two crew members. "Lieutenant Sutherland and I will see him into his quarters. Wait here until we return."

Taking Pascale's arm Dan led him into the building.

A small box room built as a storeroom next to the spacious interior of the warehouse served to hold Pascale. As acting commander of the French brig, he had been shown the courtesy of his rank and allocated a room to himself. A narrow bed, lounging despondently along a brown painted wall, shared the tiny room with a sorry-looking table and chair wedged tightly into a dusty corner. Dan lit the solitary candle on the table and watched as Pascale sat forlornly on the bed.

"We'll come for you at dawn," said James, sedately. "There's nothing more to say lieutenant except my advice for you: to make your peace with God."

They watched him look pleadingly towards them. With a sigh, James turned to Dan, indicating for him to leave the room, then pulling up the chair he sat motionless until he heard the door close behind him.

"We believe that the mission you have failed to accomplish will prove to be a minor hiccup in whatever plans your superiors may have been expecting you to fulfil," said James, speaking softly. "They will quickly adapt to a change of plan owing to your failure, and you will be forgotten lieutenant. You are expendable to them as was another spy we caught and shot a short time ago."

James paused, taking in the disconsolate look spreading over Pascale's features. "You are going to die at dawn lieutenant, unrecognised and a failure. There will be no memory of you, no posthumous medal, just your body lying in that freshly dug grave at the back of the fish hut where we questioned you. No-one will remember you, except for a few of your family members who live far from here. But you will soon be forgotten to them while your body lies here under foreign soil, at the back of a shed in a harbour that no-one has heard of."

Pascale stared at James, his face creased in anxiety, a picture of the execution site forming before his eyes. He frowned at the thought of his superiors, warm and safe back in Danzig, not caring about him and all the others they had lost on various secret missions. But then he was an officer in Napoleon's Republic, a navy man and proud of it. His duty was to do and die for his Emperor and the glory of France. He would hold his head high as they tied him to that blood-soaked post. This British captain was wrong, he was a hero and would die as one for the greater glory of the Republic he served. But then, who would know? Who would tell his story?

"There is a way lieutenant for you to elude the execution at dawn tomorrow," said James, softly.

For a moment Pascale seemed to recover himself, his look suddenly changing into one that saw hope and his life to live.

"I am authorised to offer you a deal," said James, looking compassionately at his prisoner. "You will evade execution on the condition you tell me everything about your mission to the Swedish coast. I want to know its purpose, the offer from your government to whomever you are proposing and the names and ranks of your collaborators in Sweden. I believe you were carrying a secret document for the eyes of certain Swedish military chiefs. When we attacked your ship, you destroyed it and committed it all to memory. It is simple lieutenant, tell me everything and sail with your crew to England tomorrow or die tied to that post in the execution yard, forgotten and lost on this island."

Pascale remained quiet, his eyes resting on the quivering shadows dancing above the only candle in the room.

James waited, watching the expression on Pascale's face as he struggled with the dilemma of making a choice. Slowly shaking his head, he raised himself off the bed and looking painfully around the room muttered a short phrase in French.

"In English, please lieutenant," said James.

"I will die for the Republic," said Pascale, mournfully.

"Your Republic will not thank you, lieutenant. They will just forget you."

"We shall see, captain. We shall see."

"Very well lieutenant. We will come for you at dawn," said James, getting up and walking to the door. "But tonight, think of the offer of life I have offered. Our war will not last forever and when it is over you will have a life to live, release from the prison in England and a new start. There is still time, it is your choice lieutenant."

James walked quickly away from the warehouse, Dan at his side.

"He didn't buckle, Dan. I really thought he would, but he has tonight to ponder his fate, we will see when we come to fetch him at dawn. Now, the place of execution at the back of the shed was brilliant. How did you get that blood on the post?"

"It's rose-red paint sir," said Dan, chuckling. "We found it when we picked up the post from that boat shed where they've repaired the sloop that's taking the prisoners to England. Phillip Power, one of our crew, is a dab hand with a paint brush."

"Well, he certainly made it look like someone lost a lot of blood tied to that post!" said James, grinning.

"I've selected six men for the firing squad tomorrow captain," said Dan. "We'll issue the muskets when we meet up with them here on the quay just before dawn. As Ned Hatchet's one of them I know he'll organise them well.

"But what happens when we tie Pascale to the post, blindfold him and he still refuses to talk?"

"Let's hope he talks, Dan, because if he doesn't, you will deliver the final shot to his head with your pistol, on my order."

Pierre had returned to Jacob's cabin in the early hours of the morning, with news of the British longboat arriving at the cove at twenty minutes before the hour of eleven. As Jacques had reported the previous day, the British officer had spent around thirty minutes standing in the bow of the boat listening and peering at the nooks and crannies that covered the shingly inlet. Satisfied there was no need to come ashore, the officer had issued the order to move on further down the coast. Two hours and fifteen minutes later Pierre had noted the longboat returning past the cove without stopping.

"The times of the longboat arriving and returning past the cove correspond with Per's report," said Jacob, getting ready to leave the cabin for his turn down at the cove. "We'll see if it's the same for me."

"We won't disturb you tomorrow morning," said Pierre. "You won't get back here until the early hours, and you'll need your sleep before we leave here. The sloop will sail at midday with the prisoners, that means they'll be loading them around the hour of eleven. As we have planned the break in to free the French lieutenant an hour before that, we should leave here around the hour of nine."

"Yes, I agree," said Jacob. "Now, before I leave, let's go over the plan again. When we get to the harbour, you two, busy yourselves with something in my shed, look as though you're checking a net or something. This will give me time to snoop around and see if everything is normal around the quay where the warehouses are located. I'll have a good look around the back of the warehouses for anything untoward that may hinder our plans. Per, start the fire in the back of the warehouse next to where they're holding the lieutenant. Take one of the birch-wick torches I made up earlier and a handful of the silver birch bark chippings I've cut up. These chippings will make excellent kindling. Spread the chippings under the main back wooden panel, then light the torch using my tinder box. Once it's alight set fire to the chippings. There's a lot of dry grass and bracken under that warehouse so it shouldn't take long before the back panel starts to burn. When it looks as though the fire's going to take off, get rid of the torch and run around to the front bellowing - "FIRE". The prisoners inside will smell smoke and it won't be long before they see the flames and start yelling for the guards. Magnus and I will wait for the commotion to start. When the guards' attention is focused on getting those prisoners out of the warehouse, we'll move. I'm sure that the soldiers guarding the warehouse where the lieutenant is, will rush over to help their comrades. If not, then we'll have to disable them. We'll move fast and slip in through the main entrance shouting out for the lieutenant.

"Once we've got him, we get out quickly and then away up the track, through the forest and back here. Per, it will be up to you to keep the commotion going but keep an eye on the entrance to the warehouse. When you see us, make sure no-one recognises the escaping prisoner, if someone does then silence him before he can raise the alarm."

"Yes Jacob, that's fine." said Pierre, nodding.

"It should work," added Jacques, "But there's one thing troubling me and that's the hue and cry that'll follow. The British are bound to send out search parties to try and find him. The first place they'll look will be where he can best hide away, and that's here in the forest."

"I know," said Jacob, "but the shack here is well hidden and its position is well away from the various pathways and tracks used by those making their way through the forest, it's really very difficult to find."

"All very well," said Jacques, " but we'll have to keep a very careful look out for anyone snooping around."

"Absolutely Per, you're right," said Jacob, turning towards the door, "but believe me, no-one will find their way here. Now, I am off to the cove. Don't wake me too early in the morning."

15

Ned Hatchet, and five of Hector's crewmen selected to form the firing squad, waited patiently at the end of the quay as dawn came stealing over the harbour. Seeing his captain and first lieutenant approaching with what looked like six muskets wrapped in blankets, Ned quickly brought the five sailors to attention.

"At ease," said James, unravelling three of the muskets. Dan followed suit, cradling the muskets he had uncovered from his blanket.

"Mr. Hatchet, issue these muskets to each of the crew including yourself. Lieutenant Sutherland has briefed you all about what's going to take place shortly and the part you're all going to play. I must emphasise that what we are about to do is vital to the security of this island and our garrison here. The prisoner we are about to bring out has crucial information we need to know. Up to now he has refused to cooperate with us, believing he'll die as a hero for his republic. This is our final chance to get him to talk, and I'm relying on him to crack at the last moment. I ask you all to play your part convincingly. Lieutenant Sutherland will act as the officer in charge of the execution. It may well go to the very end when you hear the order to present muskets and to take aim. If he still refuses to talk at that point, remain with your muskets levelled while I attempt one last plea for him to reveal the information.

Lieutenant Sutherland has orders to finish him with a pistol shot to his head if he refuses to talk. Now, if there are no questions, we'll march at a slow pace to where he's being held."

James and Dan walked ahead of the group listening to the crunch of boots on the quay's surface as the six seamen marched in twos behind them.

"Squad halt," bellowed Ned on arriving at the warehouse.

"Keep them at attention Mr. Hatchet," ordered James, as he and Dan followed the marine guard into the warehouse.

The sound of a key opening his door brought a deep sigh from the French lieutenant as he hoisted himself off the bed.

"Are you ready?" asked James, noticing the dark shadows embedded around Pascale's eyes.

"Ready for a killing, captain. The killing of me?"

"Remember my words of last night lieutenant," said James, softly. "Reveal everything and live to see the end of this war. The crew of La Marie Louise will know nothing of what you tell me. Your fellow officers have no idea of what your mission was. As far as they know you were acting as First Officer of the ship, and when your captain was killed you rightly surrendered to save more casualties among the crew. I doubt they know anything of your mission. You can go to England with them as prisoners of war, knowing they know nothing of what transpired between us."

"You are assuming too much captain!" muttered Pascale.

"Corporal," said James to the marine guard standing in the doorway, "bind him and escort him outside."

"Sir," responded the guard, slipping a length of rope around Pascale's wrists.

Ned Hatchet detached himself from his group striding over to the door of the warehouse where the marine guard had appeared with the French lieutenant. Following behind, James nodded towards his master-at-arms. With a look of derision, Pascale raised his head defiantly as he was led away towards the group of five crewmen, cursing to himself as Ned bundled him in between the two front sailors.

"When you're ready Mr. Hatchet," called out James.

"Squad, about turn," barked Ned. "One two, one two, one two."

The group marched along the path behind the row of sheds, Ned having to pull Pascale to his feet at times as the true horror of what was about to take place caused him to lose his footing and stumble.

The early morning sun had risen, but not high enough to quash the lingering shadows that still shrouded parts of the harbour and the square of rough ground flaunting the blood-stained execution stake and the open grave.

Pascale shuddered as Ned marched him over to the thick post, crying out as his arms were wrenched back behind the pole and his hands roughly tied together.

As Ned was about to drop a black hood over the prisoner's head, James came forward placing a hand on Ned's arm.

"Wait. Stand back a moment, Mr. Hatchet," he ordered.

Tears of hopelessness filled Pascale's eyes as he stared at the resolute expression on the British captain's face.

"You only have to tell me to stop, lieutenant, and I will know that you're ready to talk," said James. "This nightmare will then end, and we'll prepare you for the journey to England along with the rest of your crew. What is it to be for you, to live, or to die here alone and forgotten?"

Pascale dropped his head. "I can't," he muttered.

"But you can live," whispered James into his ear.

Raising his head, the Frenchman looked around the barren execution site, the men of the firing squad looking expressionless and playing their part in waiting for the order that he knew would end his life. James stood motionless, the distant cries of seagulls circling the harbour, the only sound.

"So be it. Carry on Mr. Hatchet."

Ned dropped the black hood over Pascale's head. Deep gasps for breath and a pleading sigh came from beneath the cowl. With a quick turn about, Ned returned to the line of crewmen, taking up his musket and readying himself for the order that was about to come. James fixed his eyes on the hooded figure tied to the post. He waited, then turning towards Dan he nodded.

"Squad, make ready," commanded Dan. "Present."

The sound of six heavy muskets being presented echoed around the square.

"Take aim."

All eyes focused on Pascale. The hooded figure flexed his neck, his chin jutting rigidly out in front of him, waiting for the six musket balls to rip through his body. His hood wavered as his head shook and trembled in his torment. James closed his eyes, the passing seconds seeming like minutes.

Just then, the sweet aria of a lonely blackbird singing out its joy at the start of a new day suddenly broke the doleful silence around them. Beneath the hood Pascale heard the joyful call of the bird's mate. Closing his eyes, he pictured his own loved ones far away.

James looked over at Dan indicating for him to draw his pistol. Seconds ticked by and then a muffled cry came from beneath the hood.

"Stop. Stop captain. I'll tell you everything."

James raised his hand indicating to Dan to lower the pistol. Turning towards his crewmen he bellowed an order to his master-at-arms.

"Mr. Hatchet, untie the prisoner."

Ned Hatchet strode over to the trembling figure, catching him as he crumpled to the ground.

"Escort the prisoner back to the warehouse, Mr. Hatchet," commanded James.

"Lieutenant Sutherland, allocate one of the crew to assist the master-at-arms."

James and Dan walked away towards the path that led back to the warehouses, Pascale shuffling painfully along between Ned and a member of the crew.

Now I'll know when we can expect an attack, thought James, *and who in the port of Karlskrona is waiting for a dispatch that will never arrive.*

James led Pascale back into the tiny box room that served as his cell while Dan dismissed his squad of crewmen. Drawing up the chair from the corner of the room he sat opposite the bed where Pascale was nervously staring at the bare walls around him. Outside, the sound of a flurry of activity had begun as preparations were underway for the transporting of the French prisoners. Unconcerned, Pascale sat on the edge of his bed, his mind reliving the horror he'd only just experienced. Dan entered the room, closing the door behind him.

"You've made the right decision lieutenant," James said, calmly. "Give me the information that was in your communique, and for whom it was intended. You can then board the sloop with the rest of your crew members. You'll be sailing for England at midday."

Pascale sat in silence, not taking his eyes away from the walls around him.

"Lieutenant, I am waiting," said James, sternly.

"I will tell you everything captain," Pascale croaked, turning to face James.

"But, in God's name and in all humanity, please let me get over the ordeal I've just experienced. I am in shock, captain, and need a little time to recover."

James looked away from the agonised look creasing Pascale's features.

"Dan, what do you think?" he asked.

"The sloop's not sailing for another three hours," said Dan. "I think we should give him a little time to recover, and then return."

"Very well," said James, turning to look at his prisoner. "We'll return in an hour when I expect you to tell me everything I want to know."

Pascale's eyes followed James and Dan as they left the room,

"Thank you, captain," he muttered.

Jacob awoke to the tones of Jacques and Pierre going over the plan to rescue the French lieutenant. The two spies looked over to where he was pulling himself up from his cot, a smile spreading across his features.

"It's time for us to be getting ready," he said. Over there in my chest, Per, are a few birch-wick torches. Take out one of them and then if you look next to the grate, you'll see a pile of chippings. Grab a good handful, they're best for starting a fire. Now, the British longboat turned up fifteen minutes before the hour of eleven but didn't hang around for long and disappeared after about ten minutes. I was frozen down there and was pleased to see it reappear at twenty minutes before the hour of two. It didn't stop but carried on into the darkness. By the way, Per, nothing seemed to want to settle in my crotch, not a sign of any little creatures wishing to explore up my trouser leg!"

"Ha," chortled Per, with a grin. "I'm not surprised at that!"

"We'll have to think of a way of disabling that longboat before the attack," suggested Pierre, smiling at Jacques' comment.

"That's been on my mind too," said Jacob, "but let's sort that later. I think the three of us should go through today's plan one more time before we leave."

With the birch-wick torch tucked safely under his jacket and with his pockets filled with silver birch chippings, Jacques followed his two comrades along the now familiar trail that twisted its way towards the field of long grass, and hence on towards the track that led down to the harbour.

Turning to the two Frenchmen, Jacob raised a thick cudgel he was carrying, "Look down there," he said, pointing it down at the harbour far below them.

Peering down they made out the shape of a sloop-of-war berthed in the deep- water section behind the ship of the line. A whirl of activity was taking place as sailors hurried up and down the gangplank with sacks of victuals for the voyage. Squinting closer they made out sections of the crew scurrying around the deck busying themselves with preparations for the vessel's departure. High up on the yardarms, the dark outlines of sailors checking the shrouds and rolled up sheets of sail affirmed the sight of a ship getting ready to sail.

The harbour was a nest of activity, exactly as the three of them wanted it to be. Looking down on the whole scenario they were reminded of its likeness to a hard-working colony of ants.

"Come on you two," said Jacob, "we've got a French lieutenant to rescue."

16

From Jacob's hut on the quay, they had a good view of the comings and goings around the warehouses holding the French prisoners. Jacob's eyes focused on the warehouse next to where the French lieutenant was being held. Two marine guards lolled impassively against the front panel of the wooden building, the looks on their faces showing the monotony of their lengthy time on guard duty.

A sudden movement at the warehouse door quickly caught his attention.

"Psst, over there by the door, someone's leaving the building," he whispered.

"It's the British captain I saw questioning the lieutenant," said Pierre, peering towards the warehouse, "and that's the first officer of the frigate that stopped and searched Erik's boat on our journey to Nogersund."

"They must've been questioning the prisoner again," said Jacob, his eyes following the two British officers walking to the end of the quay.

Jacques looked over at the middle of the three warehouses, the two marine guards outside casually chatting to each other.

"It seems that all the action is taking place over on the other quay," he said, in a low voice. "It might be a good idea for me to start the fire now?"

"Yes, before they finish preparing the sloop," replied Jacob, watching James and Dan enter the long wooden shed that acted as the officer's mess. "Those two are obviously going for breakfast.

Here, Per, take my tinder box. Give me a few minutes to walk over to the guards. I'll distract them while you make your way around to the back of the warehouse."

Jacques watched Jacob making his way over to the two guards, the area around the three warehouses looking quiet and deserted. All the activity around the harbour seemed to be centred on finalising the preparations for the sloop's journey to England. It would not be long before the first of the prisoners were led out to begin embarkation.

Jacques waited until Jacob had engaged the guards in conversation and then with a nod towards Pierre he slipped away, stealing himself in behind the row of vacant sheds that neighboured the three warehouses. Moving silently along he came to a gap between the last shed and the first warehouse. Peering through the gap he saw no cause for alarm, everything along this part of the harbour was still and quiet, apart from Jacob's voice chattering away to the two guards. Inching himself on, he bent down to pick up handfuls of dry wood and bracken lying scattered around, they would be excellent to add to the chippings inside his jacket pocket. Coming up to the rear of the second warehouse, he stopped. Looking over his shoulder to make sure there was no-one around, he stretched flat out on the ground, peering under the raised wooden floor.

Seeing an old empty fish box, he dragged it over and, piling the dried wood and bracken into neat stacks, covered them with the box. Next, he fumbled inside his pocket pulling out handfuls of chippings which he spread liberally under the box. Satisfied he now had a good deck of kindling, he crawled back out and, taking the birch-wick torch from under his jacket, he lit the top of the oily bark, a gentle offshore breeze helping to fan the flame. Carefully holding the blazing torch out in front of him, he wriggled back under the wooden floor gently lifting the box with his spare hand while letting the flame touch the stacks of kindling.

Seconds turned into minutes without any sign of fire from under the box. Thinking he would have to repeat the operation again, a stream of smoke suddenly wafted up, a soft palpitating orange glow forming around the sides of the box. It was time to get out. Flames suddenly leapt from the box as it caught fire, leaping and spiralling upwards in their effort to reach the bone-dry wood of the warehouse floor. Throwing the torch onto the burning stack he quickly slid back out and waited. It wasn't long before smoke began to seep through the rear wooden panel, a phosphorescent glow spreading along its lower timbers.

"Fire," he yelled at the top of his voice, starting his frantic run from behind the warehouse. "Fire, Fire," he shouted as he ran to the front of the building, "get them out, the place is on fire."

The two guards chatting to Jacob suddenly spun around on hearing the alarm.

Jacob stepped back looking over his shoulder beckoning Pierre to hurry over and join him.

"Fire, Fire," bellowed Jacques, "get those prisoners out quickly."

The guard with the keys ran to the warehouse door unlocking it and flinging the door wide open. What had been a quiet scene only moments before, was now one of chaos as a score of prisoners tumbled out, desperate to get away from the fierce flames now blazing at the back of the warehouse.

"Get those prisoners corralled over there, away from the fire," yelled the marine warrant officer striding over to where the prisoners were milling around. "You lot," he shouted to a group of marines running towards him, "guard them with your life. Shoot any that try to run. I'll organise a water chain."

"Shall we let ours out sergeant major?" yelled one of the guards outside the warehouse holding the French lieutenant. "There's a risk our building will catch fire too. Those flames are getting out of control."

"Yes, but wait until we've got this lot sorted, shouldn't take long. I could do with you over there giving the guards a hand to get those prisoners straightened up. Let your partner stay where he is and when you've finished get back to your post and then let your prisoners out."

"Did you hear that?" said Jacob. "Come on, the one with the keys is still over there. Per, wait here and make sure no-one comes near us."

Jacob and Pierre slipped quietly away to where the guard with the keys stood staring at the ongoing commotion. Certain that no-one was watching them, they crept up silently behind him.

He never knew what hit him, just a blinding flash before his eyes and then darkness as Jacob's thick cudgel smashed over the back of his head.

"Pull him under the front panel, Magnus," said Jacob, "I'll get the keys."

Grabbing the keys from the guard's thick leather belt, he fumbled along its ring feeling for the right key. Finding it he quickly inserted it into the lock and with Pierre close behind him they burst into the dark confines of the temporary gaol.

"Lieutenant, lieutenant," yelled Jacob. "This is a break-out, we're here to rescue you. Where are you?"

"Answer us lieutenant," Pierre screamed in French, "we're here to get you out."

"I'm here, in the small storeroom. Listen I'll bang on the door," came the reply in French.

A frantic banging on the door in front of them made Jacob search for the key.

Seconds ticked away, the chance of the other guard returning becoming ever more probable.

"It has to be this one," he sighed, gritting his teeth, and holding the key up before his eyes. Thrusting it into the keyhole he turned it. Nothing happened. Sweat pouring from his forehead, he yanked the key out, spat on it and inserted it one more time. The lock clicked and the door flew open. Pascale stood before them with a confused look stamped over his face.

"Come on lieutenant, follow us quickly," yelled Pierre in French.

Not waiting to ask any questions, Pascale bolted out of the door after them. Jacob stood with his hand raised at the front entrance, a quick glance around the corner of the door at the commotion still going on told him all was clear for them to move.

"Come on," he said, "there's no sign of the other guard yet, but he'll be coming back at any moment."

With Pascale following closely behind they tore out of the warehouse unseen. Pierre thrust a woollen fisherman's hat into Pascale's hand and, pulling it tightly over his head and a fraction above his eyes, the Frenchman hurried after his two liberators as they blended into the milling crowd. A chain of hollering marines passing buckets of water along a line made them pick their way discreetly past them. No-one paid any attention to the three hunched figures hurrying away from the chaotic scene.

At the end of the quay the three spies stopped to catch their breath. Pascale glanced over at the sloop-of-war moored behind a prestigious-looking ship of the line.

Looks like I won't be sailing to England after all, he thought.

"They'll have found the guard I knocked unconscious by now," said Jacob, looking back at the pandemonium going on further up the quay. "It won't be long before the hue and cry is on for you lieutenant. Come on, we'd better get well clear of here before they establish some form of control."

With a final look at the chaos engulfing the scene, and the thought of the British captain's face on discovering his prisoner had escaped, Pascale finally managed a brief smile.

Looking up at the dark outline of a forest stretching far across the higher part of the island, he pictured himself shrouded in the dark hood, his arms strapped behind the wooden stake waiting for his life to end. In his mind he heard it again, the sweet aria of the blackbird singing out its message of hope at the start of a new day. With a deep sigh, he turned and hurried on after his two rescuers.

"What!" yelled James, into the face of one of the guards ushering the French prisoners out of the warehouse. "Gone. What d'you mean gone! How the hell did it happen?"

"Sergeant-major ordered me to help organise the other prisoners from the burning warehouse sir and when I got back here my partner was lying over there unconscious. He'd been knocked senseless, his keys taken, and the lieutenant, gone."

James looked around at the chaotic scene on the quay. The French prisoners had been evacuated from the three warehouses and were being assembled into three long lines along the lower part of the quay. The fire in the middle warehouse was now under control as a constant soaking from buckets of water had stopped it from turning into a blazing mass. Thick grey smoke billowed up from its smouldering remains.

"Looks like we've got some foreign agents on the island who knew he was here," said James, turning towards his first lieutenant. "They couldn't be that far ahead of us. They've either got a boat waiting somewhere in the harbour or they've made tracks into the forest up there."

"Whoever they are captain, they must be French, or local Swedes loyal to the French."

"You and Lieutenant Devonshire round up our crew and make two search parties," instructed James. "One to try and hunt them down around the harbour, and the other to comb the forest for any sign. I'll inform Commodore Percival of what's happened. You'll find me in the officers' mess or on board the ship of the line. And

Dan, don't forget we were going to check on the entrance to that cave we saw near the southern tip of the island. We can arrange to do that later, finding Pascale and his accomplices is the priority now."

"Aye, aye sir" replied Dan.

17

Jacob threw open the door of his shack, a ray of sunlight from between the forest trees piercing the dimness inside.

"Pull the cover over that window," he shouted, pointing to the window over his cot.

Pierre quickly drew the length of rough sacking hanging at the side of the window across its dirty pane, securing it to a nail in the wall.

"There'll be a search party heading up here right now, if I'm not mistaken," said Jacob. "They'll not find us here, but the paths through the forest will soon be full of marines. We can lie low in here, the three of us taking turns to keep watch outside. Out there is a rough shelter I built to keep the firewood dry, behind the stacks is a good place to keep watch as there's an excellent view of the approach to the shack. It's nearly noon now so over the next eight hours one of us will be out there, eyes wide open and listening for anything that could cause alarm. When night falls, they're bound to call off the search. Magnus, you take the first watch, then you Per, and then me. By the look of you lieutenant, I think you need a long rest, but first you can tell us why you were singled out as a priority prisoner. Magnus, you get going. Per will relieve you in just over two and a half hours."

With a nod, Pierre left the shack.

"Come, lieutenant, take a seat," said Jacob, ushering Pascale over to the table.

"Per, over in the corner is some food and a bottle of ale. Just enough to last us till dusk, so one of us will have to go down to the harbour later and get some more. Whoever goes can see what's going on down there and whether the hue and cry has been called off."

Jacob sat opposite Pascale noticing the dark shadows of exhaustion lodged around his eyes. Pascale watched Jacques set the food down on the table and without waiting for the other two he reached out, snatching up a large crust of bread and breaking off a similar sized portion of the cheese which he hungrily devoured, gulping down the ale in several long mouthfuls.

"I must thank you for getting me out," he said, wiping his mouth with the back of his hand. "But with all due respect to you, I don't know who you are or why you did it. So, before I tell you everything you want to know about me, I'd appreciate knowing something about you and the other two."

"That's reasonable," replied Jacob.

"I'll start lieutenant, and then Per can tell you more as to why he and his partner Magnus are here."

Pascale sat back listening intently, his eyes flicking back and forth from his two rescuers as Jacob outlined their mission on the island.

When Jacques suggested Pascale return to Danzig with Pierre on Erik Gunnarsson's fishing boat, Jacob was quick to notice the sudden look of uncertainty that flashed across Pascale's features. Jacob read this as a sign he was withholding something important. He'd find out.

"And now lieutenant, we're waiting to hear from you," said Jacob, his eyes focusing on Pascale. "Start from the beginning and don't leave anything out. We need to know everything."

Pascale cleared his throat and in a weak voice began. "My name is Andre Pascale and I hold the rank of naval lieutenant within our Secret Service. I was recently assigned to Danzig to complete a secret mission by order of our Emperor."

Jacob and Jacques listened attentively without interrupting as he recounted everything, from his mission to deliver the communique to Admiral von Krassow, to the attack on the ship La Marie Louise. He paused after giving them an account of the rigorous questioning he had undergone.

"You said that your communique to the Swedish Admiral was a direct order from your emperor, and that their fleet was to join up with yours at a certain co-ordinate to begin the attack on the island," said Jacob.

"That's correct," replied Pascale, "or they'd face invasion themselves."

"And you know the date and time of the planned invasion," added Jacob.

"I do," said Pascale.

"Are you going to tell us?" asked Jacques.

"No," answered Pascale. "If I tell you, and by some unfortunate circumstance you are captured by the British, they'll have means of extracting the information from you. It is better that this confidential information remains with me. I was prepared to tell the British when I was tied to the execution stake, I wanted to live and at that moment nothing was more important to me than life. Now the situation has changed, and I must try to get to Karlskrona and Admiral von Krassow. I trust you to help me do this."

"I understand," said Jacob. "How we will do this I have no idea but give me some time and maybe something will turn up."

"There is no time," said Pascale. "In a few days Admiral von Krassow will believe there will be no invasion as no communique has reached him. He will withdraw his fleet and stand down his attack force. We also believe there are British reinforcements on its way. The attack on Hanö must go ahead according to the date and time set by our Emperor."

"I'll see what I can do when I'm down at the harbour," said Jacob, "there maybe someone who can be bribed to get you to Karlskrona."

"Get me on a boat, Jacob," said Pascale, "and as I embark, I'll whisper the date and time of the invasion for your ears only. Should anything happen to me, then it'll be up to you to deliver this dispatch to the Swedish Admiral."

Jacob nodded, understanding the necessity of Pascale's mission.

Dan led a detachment of his crew through the field of long grass and into the forest, searching for signs that the prisoner had fled into the cover of the densely packed trees. In single file they picked their way along a narrow pathway pitted with stones and small boulders that twisted its way further into the dark thicket. Seeing a fork on the pathway ahead he raised his hand for the troop behind him to stop. Dark shadowy gaps between the trees showed signs of various animal tracks disappearing deep into the undergrowth.

"Mr. Hatchet," he called, turning to beckon the ship's master-at-arms to join him.

"I'll take half of the detachment and proceed along the right-hand split of that fork up there. You continue up the path with the rest. If you come across Pascale and his accomplices fire a musket shot as a signal for us. Should we come across them we'll do the same. Is that clear?"

"Aye sir, it's clear."

"I want him taken alive, Mr. Hatchet. Bound and brought back to the harbour."

The path Dan had chosen descended through a thick growth of trees, at one point the branches of several trees forming a tunnel of foliage across the track they were on. There was no sign of anyone having recently passed that way.

The pathway eventually levelled out and between gaps in the trees they were able to catch glimpses of the sea shimmering in the early afternoon sunshine.

Dan turned to the able seaman walking behind him, "What's your name, sailor?" he asked.

"Clifford Williams, able seaman sir," came the reply.

"We're going to take a good look down here, Williams," said Dan. "There's good scope for us to scan the shoreline. While we're there I want you to scout up ahead, look for a cove or small beach that could act as a landing place for several longboats. If you find one get back here straightaway. Don't forget to keep a lookout for signs of anyone who may have passed by. Take another crew member with you. We'll be here for no more than half the hour."

"Yes sir, I'll take able seaman Richard Davis with me sir."

"Splendid, carry on," replied Dan.

Dan watched his two crewmen sprint away up the path until they disappeared round a bend in the trees.

"Follow me down to the shoreline, men" he ordered to those waiting behind him. "I want you to spread out over those rocks and look for signs that someone has been here. Holler, if you find anything."

One by one they jumped down onto a small patch of shingle, some beginning to search between the scattered rocks while others climbed to the top of various boulders to scour the shoreline.

Looking up and down the rocky coastline, Dan searched for an area of beach that might act as a landing place for several longboats. As far as he was able to see there was nothing that could accommodate any boat, the closeness of the rocks stretching for miles. He realised the cliffs they had sailed past a few days before had to be further on down the coast, probably out of reach now, but if they came across them, he would certainly look for the cave entrance he and his captain had glimpsed from their telescopes. Should they find it, then there was also the likelihood of a cove or inlet nearby.

Flocks of seabirds, hovering high in the sky and drifting effortlessly on the rising air currents suddenly caught his attention, his eyes following them as they arrowed away towards a bend at the end of the shoreline.

Suddenly he was alert. Bending his ear towards the line of flight the birds had taken he listened as the unmistakeable sound of the squawking of hungry young chicks floated towards him. *The cliffs are there,* he thought. *Ha, and the birds have shown me.*

Turning towards his men, he cupped his hands around his mouth bellowing out an order, "Assemble back on the pathway, men. On the double now. Make sure you don't leave anything behind."

The search party quickly assembled back on the pathway. "Nothing there, sir," said a young sailor. "Looks like no-one's ever been there."

Dan nodded towards his crewman, "Fine, but keep your eyes peeled."

"Well, would I be right in saying there are a range of cliffs around that bend?" asked Dan, seeing Clifford Williams waiting alongside his crewmate.

"You would sir," replied Williams. "There were no signs of any inlets along this shoreline, but around the bend there's a shingly cove lying beneath a row of steep granite cliffs.

"Then lead on Williams, we'll be right behind you," said Dan.

Williams and Davis led them along the path that twisted its way over stones and fallen tree trunks until finally stopping at the edge of a line of sheer cliffs that overlooked a small pebbly cove.

"There's a cave somewhere over there in those cliffs," shouted Dan. We won't have long before we resume the search, so let's set to and find it."

Dropping down onto the cove, Dan watched his men scrambling over the rocks, his eyes focussing on the layout of the shingly inlet.

"Lieutenant, it's here!" came a shout.

Ignoring the incessant squawking from flocks of seabirds, Dan and his men clambered up over the slippery rocks following the hollering shout of the crewman who had found the entrance to the cave. Stopping at the cave's entrance Dan pointed to two of his crew, "Stand guard out here, the rest of you follow me into the cave."

Inside, Dan looked up at the chamber that faced him. Three of his men lit candles they took from their kit bags, bolstering the light that crept in from outside.

"There doesn't seem to be any sign of this place being used as a hideaway," said Clifford Williams.

"No," said Dan, "but I expect it was, hundreds if not thousands of years ago."

"Look lieutenant," cried one of his men, "seems like footprints leading over to that dark niche in the corner."

"Lower the candle to the ground," said Dan, "let me see."

From the light of the candle, they saw faded footprints embedded in the gritty sand leading over to a dark corner of the cave. Following the footprints, they stopped at what looked like a narrow alcove cut into the cave wall.

"Let me have your candle," said Dan to one of the crew.

"You two with the other candles, follow me."

Dan stepped into the dark recess holding the candle out in front of him, the other two crew members gingerly following him.

Holding up their candles, they walked a few paces into the darkness, the stench of damp mould and the pitch blackness around them bringing on an uneasy feeling of anxiety. Dan led them forward, the light of his candle showing their way suddenly narrowing as the cave walls closed in around them.

"It's a tunnel," he said, stopping and holding his candle far out in front of him.

"Look at the flame on the candle, it's flickering with the draft of air coming towards us. We'll have to see how far it goes."

They were stopped by a sudden shout echoing loudly behind them.

"Lieutenant, come back, quickly."

"Looks like there could be a problem back there," said Dan, turning to his two crewmen. "Come on, we'll go back."

Clifford Williams stood peering into the entrance to the tunnel as Dan and the two sailors emerged from the darkness.

"Lieutenant, a musket just fired from up there in the forest. It must have been from Mr. Hatchet's group, they must've found something."

"Only one shot, Williams?" he asked, moving towards the cave's exit.

"Only one sir, then silence."

"Let's hope they've found them," said Dan. "Come on, back up to the forest."

They clambered back over the rocks, crossing the shingly cove and onto the path that would lead them back up through the trees to the fork on the main forest pathway. Thoughts of the cove and tunnel they had just discovered played on Dan's mind. *Should the French marines invade this part of the island,* he thought, *then this inlet will be the one they'll use to make their landing. But the question is, when will they come?*

18

Jacob looked up as Pierre entered the shack. Holding a finger to his lips he indicated the sleeping form of Andre Pascal stretched out on a thin mattress in the far corner.

"Per's taken over from me," Pierre whispered. "It's all quiet out there, no sign of the British. Makes me wonder whether they've sent out a search party at all."

"Oh, you can be sure they have," said Jacob. "They're probably over on the other side of the forest by now, keeping to the tracks that lead to the end of the island."

"Well, there was no sign of them out there," said Pierre.

"That's because my shack's well-hidden and off the beaten track. They won't find it, of that I'm certain."

"I hope you're right," said Pierre.

"I'm going out there," said Jacob, jumping up and fastening his jacket. "I've got an idea where they might be. If I'm right, I'll steal up behind them and set a false trail for them to follow. That'll keep them well-away from us, and away from any track they may stumble on that could lead them here. All in all, it's best to be sure. Stay with our guest. Should he wake, make sure he doesn't wander off outside. You and Per take care of my vigil if I'm not back in time."

Pierre nodded, watching him make his way to the door and then quietly leave the shack.

Outside, Jacob stood listening for anything unusual that would give him cause for alarm. Satisfied with the quietness around him he walked away towards the shadows in the trees, acknowledging

Jacques with a quick wave.

Wonder what he's up to? thought Jacques.

Jacob moved stealthily through the forest, stopping occasionally to listen for any sounds that would indicate the nearness of a search party. He followed a track close to the main pathway staying under cover of the drooping foliage but keeping sight of the path below him, the path he knew the British would follow in the hunt for their escaped prisoner.

Rounding a bend, he suddenly halted. Voices could be heard speaking in English from somewhere along the main pathway. Inching forward, he stopped at a gap between two conifers. His eyes scanned everything before him until finally settling on a group of about fifteen armed British sailors assembled at a fork along the track. He watched a navy lieutenant beckon a giant of a man wearing a grubby bandana with a black eye patch over his left eye, to come forward and join him.

Controlling his breathing and craning his neck further between the gap, he watched the lieutenant point in the direction of the right-hand fork and then lead half of the search party down a narrow track into the dimness of the overhanging foliage.

The rest of the group led by the giant, moved off up the path picking their way over the loose stones and boulders that lay scattered over its surface. Jacob followed, edging his way through the trees until the track he was on suddenly took a dramatic turn and began to peter out. Turning, he made his way down onto the main pathway quickly ducking behind a thick bush at the side of the path. He knew the pathway led to an open stretch of grass above the clifftops, the place where he and the two French spies had exited from the tunnel of bats only a few days before, it was there he'd start the chase. Not moving from the cover of the bush he listened to the chattering of the group ahead, knowing they would soon be upon a sharp bend as the path widened in its approach to the clifftops.

Satisfied they had all passed the bend, he left his cover and, creeping cautiously up to the turning - he peered around the corner. Several of the search party were taking a rest on the open stretch above the cliffs, lolling about on the grass while the giant and two of his men gazed down at the wide expanse of sea far below them.

Thick shrubbery growing between a line of conifers on the far edge of the clifftop concealed the only track leading down to the rocky shoreline. He would take them there. Taking a deep breath and with his head down he took off. Breathing heavily, he raced up the path looking around nervously as if being chased by a pack of vicious hounds. Various shouts of alarm rang out from the group of sailors as he came into sight, the giant turning to see him running hell for leather across the open stretch of clifftop towards thick shrubbery on the far side.

"That must be one of them," yelled Ned Hatchet, "quickly, after him! Don't let him get away!"

Half-way across, Jacob looked over his shoulder at the pursuing band of sailors. If he kept up this pace, he would reach the track leading down to the rocky shoreline well before them. He'd lead them up the coastline on the opposite part of the island, well-away from any track that could result in them stumbling across his cabin. He knew of a trail halfway along the shoreline that led back up the cliffs to a dense part of the forest where they would certainly find themselves hopelessly lost.

Looking up, he saw the thicket of shrubbery getting nearer. The sudden crack of a musket being fired from behind caused him to duck his head fearfully. The hissing sound of the musket ball whizzing past his right ear urged him on, and with the ever-closer yells of his pursuers ringing in his ears, he crashed through the shrubbery, mindlessly tripping over a thick bush root and tumbling head over heels down the rough track.

Twenty paces behind, Ned Hatchet heard a sudden yell ring out from the other side of the shrubbery. Bringing the search party to a halt, he listened for a cry for help that would suggest their fugitive had been hit by the single shot. There was nothing, only the persistent cries of the seabirds circling the clifftops.

"Can't hear nuthin' on the other side," said Ned. "he's either dead or managed to get away somehow. He'll have gone over the edge 'less there be a track leadin' down to the shoreline on the other side of that bush. Come on lads, after me."

One by one, Ned and the search party squeezed their way through the thick shrubbery wary of the steep drop down to the rocks below. A few spindly pine trees, growing precariously near the edge of a precipitous drop, met them on the other side.

"Mr Hatchet, a track, look!" one of his men called.

Ned turned and, casting his eyes over the edge of the clifftop, he saw a rough track littered with hawthorn bushes dropping away down the cliffside. It twisted and turned, dropping out of sight in places, but by squinting carefully he managed to see the end of it dropping away onto the pebbly shoreline below. Looking around, he searched for any signs of their fugitive: there was nothing.

"Look, down there at the bottom of the cliff," a voice yelled, "looks like it's 'im and he don't look too good!"

Gingerly looking over the edge, Ned made out the shape of someone dragging himself slowly over the rocks.

"That's 'im!" he yelled. "Come on lads, he looks injured. He won't be goin' far. Take it easy goin' down this pathway. Follow me."

A long way down from where Ned and his search party were just starting their descent, Jacob looked up from the rock he was pulling himself over and grinned.

I was lucky not to have gone over the edge, he thought. *If it hadn't been for that hawthorn bush, I crashed into, I wouldn't be here now. Ha, they think I'm injured but I'll wait like this until they're down, then I'll lead them a merry dance!"*

Looking over his shoulder, he saw the search party had made it down to the rocky shoreline. He watched them clambering over the rocks towards him, pointing their muskets and hollering for him to give himself up. As they got closer, he jumped up and with a cheeky wave in their direction he leapt away over the encircling rocks, chuckling at the howls of anger trailing after him.

Dan led his men up to the fork on the forest pathway, stopping to look closely in the direction Ned Hatchet and his men had taken.

"I'm pretty sure the shot came from further along," said Clifford Williams, pointing up the trail. "From where we were, it sounded as though it had come from the clifftops."

"One way to find out," said Dan, turning towards his men. "Those of you carrying firearms, prime and load, then follow me."

Rounding a bend, they found themselves staring across an open grassy stretch at the end of which seemed to be nothing but a sheer drop.

"The shot must've come from here, lieutenant," said Clifford Williams, walking over to the cliff's edge. "That's where we were sir, down there. If you look closely, you'll see where the forest path exits from the trees. You can just about see the beginnings of the shingly cove where we found the cave at the bottom of these cliffs."

Dan looked over the edge, seeing the outline of the forest path beneath the trees, the sunlight glistening off a stretch of shiny shingle between a row of jagged rocks.

"Lieutenant sir, over here," a call rang out.

Looking around, Dan saw one of his men holding up a round water canister, the initials HMSH clearly etched on its side.

"That's one of ours," shouted Richard Davis, "HMS Hector. Mr. Hatchet's party must have been resting up here."

"But where are they now?" asked one of the sailors.

"Spread out men," said Dan. "The shot we heard doubtless came from up here. Probably fired at our escapee or an accomplice. Ned Hatchet must have given chase. Look for a track leading away from this clifftop that drops down to the rocky shoreline below. I didn't notice any sign of a trail leading up from the cliffs below here, so there must be one at the far end of this clifftop or somewhere over there on the other side."

It didn't take long for a shout to go up on the opposite side,

"Lieutenant sir, over here. We've found a track behind thick shrubbery."

Dan and the rest of his men hurried over to where one of the crew was pointing to a row of thick green bushes.

"It's behind those bushes, sir. My mate found it and he's waiting there."

"Come on then," said Dan to the rest of his men, "ease your way through the shrubbery but be careful, there's a big drop on the other side."

Careful not to go too close to the cliff's edge, Dan studied a narrow track snaking down its precipitous side. His eyes travelled down the dusty trail stopping at one of the many hawthorn bushes balanced precariously on the edge of the track. The sudden hollering of his men and their pointing down at the rocky shoreline below made him look cautiously over the side. What he saw made him abruptly holler out an order, "Williams," he roared. "Fire a shot into the air to let Mr. Hatchet and his men know we're here."

"Sir," replied Clifford Williams, presenting his musket.

Far below on one of the rocks, Ned Hatchet squinted up the cliff face at the sound of the musket shot. Grinning, he said, "Looks like the lieutenant and his boys have decided to join us. "Let them know we've seen them, men. Come on, up on your feet, wave at them but don't lose sight of that bastard we're chasing, and don't let 'im get away."

Jacob stopped at the sound of a musket being fired. Looking

back, he smiled at the sight of the giant and his men looking up and waving towards a line of figures making their way down the cliffside track.

Perfect, he thought. *They'll find it hard to get out of the place where I'm taking them.*

19

A narrow goat's trail, overgrown with bracken and thorny bushes, rose steeply from behind a group of jagged rocks. Jacob stood watching Dan and his search party clambering over the crusty boulders that littered the island's entire southern coastline.

That's the path that leads into the densest part of the forest, he thought. *I'll get them to follow me up there and then lose them.*

"Williams," shouted Dan, "he's over there on that rock, can you get a shot in before he disappears. Looks like there's a trail running up the cliff behind him, that's the way he's planning to go."

Clifford Williams raised himself. Levelling his flintlock musket, he sighted the runaway at a range of about a hundred yards. Squinting along the barrel he gently pulled the trigger.

The sound of the cock hammer hitting the priming pan lid on the musket echoed along the shoreline, warning Jacob he had only a matter of seconds before the musket discharged. As the gun roared, he threw himself from the rock, the whizzing sound of the lead ball tearing into the now empty space.

A loud cheer went up amongst the sailors.

"Looks like you may have got him Williams," said Dan.

Unscathed, Jacob had fallen onto the start of the goat's trail, a thick covering of bracken and coarse grass breaking his fall. He knew the British search party would soon be upon him if he stayed in one place. Checking nothing was broken, he scrambled to his feet, quickly ducking back down as the face of the English lieutenant peered over the top of the rock.

"No sign of him, Williams. I was sure you'd got him," said Dan. "That narrow path down there is the start of the trail that leads back up to the forest. He might be making his way up there. You may have winged him and slowed him down. Come on, back to Mr. Hatchet and the others. I'm sure we'll find him struggling up that track."

Pulling himself up, Jacob made sure the two sailors were out of sight before he began the steep climb up the narrow trail. Half-way up he heard a shout behind him. *Now,* he thought, *better let them see me.*

Turning round, he saw the search party slowly picking their way up in single file, the English lieutenant leading with the giant closely following.

"There he is," yelled a voice. "You were right sir, Williams missed him, but we'll get him now."

"Come on men," urged Dan, "the forest's thickening at the end of this trail. Put on a spurt and we'll get him before he loses us in those trees up there."

The view from the top of the trail spanned a large area of sea stretching far away from the island. Jacob stood looking at the vast expanse, breathing heavily after sprinting up the last steep part of the track. The trail now levelled out behind him, disappearing into the dark confines of the forest, the tightly grouped conifers allowing little light to filter through their growth. No-one entered this part of the forest unless they were sure of a way out. Lines of animal runs led into thick vegetation, shielding the vertical drops that promptly fell away from the clifftop. Mistaking one of these for a path, would lead to a quick end. Grinning, Jacob made sure he was in full view of the sailors scrambling up the narrow track, then turning, he disappeared into the trees.

Dan and the search party stood at the top of the cliff looking at the trail receding into the dark forest undergrowth. To their right, the cliff fell away in a precipitous drop to the craggy coastline below.

"There must be a way through those trees," he said, squinting into the darkness. "He's in there somewhere. Come on, keep to this trail, and stay together."

Jacob stood in a darkened gap between the tress regarding an animal run that led into a thick set of bushes. On the other side was a vertical drop over the clifftop. He'd set a trap for them.

Pulling off the short neck-scarf he was wearing, he dropped it on the animal run in front of the middle part of the thicket. Then moving away, he continued down the trail, dropping an empty tobacco pouch onto the track that twisted its way through the closely grouped trees.

They'll never find their way back from here, he thought.

With a smile, he leapt over a fallen tree trunk, carelessly catching the pocket of his jacket on a sharp twig. Wrenching it loose, he sprinted on towards the sound of a little stream bubbling its way through the trees. He knew that by following the stream in the opposite direction it was flowing, he'd eventually come back to the main forest pathway, and then on to his shack. Stopping to look back over his shoulder, he listened for any sound that would warn him of the British search party. There was nothing, except for the sound of a gentle breeze whispering through the pine needles of the closely knitted trees.

"Lieutenant, there's something over here," called Ned Hatchet, "looks like he went through one of these bushes. Dropped his neck scarf in his hurry to get away!"

Dan looked up as Ned and a crewman pushed their way through the thicket in their eagerness to find out. Dan froze, suddenly realising the bluff.

"Wait, no don't, it's a trick," he yelled.

Too late, a chortling scream rang out from behind the bush. Two of the crew hearing the frantic yell rushed over to help, but were stopped by Dan.

"Hold it," he shouted, "there's a vertical drop right on the other side of those bushes. You're not going the same way as the other two. Keep close to me."

Warning the rest of the crew to stay back, Dan pointed to the two sailors. "You two, after me, but slowly."

A shout from Ned on the other side rang out as Dan and the two crewmen eased their way through the thick foliage.

"I can't hold him much longer. Someone, help me, quickly."

Ned, straining, and panting with one arm clinging to a thick branch while the other stretched over the side of the cliff, looked desperately over at Dan as he held onto the fallen crewman.

"Hold him Ned, we're nearly with you," shouted Dan.

"Hurry, sir. Please," urged Ned.

"With your left hand," shouted Dan, to the sailor moving along the ledge behind him, "anchor yourself onto that thick branch we're approaching. Then grab my left hand as I reach down to grab your mate with my right hand."

Dan and his crewman inched themselves along the ledge towards Ned.

"Now," yelled Dan, "grab that branch."

Locking himself onto the thicket's stout branch, the crewman thrust out his right arm as Dan knelt beside Ned. Grasping the sailor's right hand, Dan stretched over the side of the cliff and with his free hand grabbed the dangling crewman's arm just below Ned's shaking grip.

"Sir, the ledge, it's beginning to crumble," shouted the crewman clasping Dan's left hand, "we must hurry."

Pieces of granite began to slip over the side of the cliff, crashing down onto the rocks below. As Dan tightened his grip, a large piece of the ledge to the left of where they stood gave way, hurtling down the side of the cliff.

"Ned, we've only got one chance before the whole of this ledge gives way," shouted Dan. "One big pull, now."

With their arm muscles taught, they heaved in unison until a contorted looking crewman showed above the side of the cliff. With one last effort they pulled him up, his legs scrambling to find the narrow ledge beneath him.

"Get off the ledge now," screamed one of the crewmen, "it's giving way!"

Pulling the injured sailor with them, Dan and Ned crashed through the thicket of bushes hearing an almighty crack as the ledge they had been standing on broke away, the sound of it plummeting down to the jagged rocks below echoing around them.

Dusting himself down, Dan looked at the ashen faces before him. "Come on men," he said, shakily. "The trail's twisting away through those trees. It's bound to lead us out of here eventually. Our runaway could've only gone down that way, he must know of a trail out of here. Look out for signs that he passed this way."

The group moved off down the ever-darkening trail, the trees around them bunching so close together that it was impossible for them to see any sign of a track leading out.

Rounding a bend, a shout went up from two of the crew leading the group.

"Lieutenant, there's something lying on the trail."

"That's it," said Dan, picking up the empty tobacco pouch. "It must be his."

"Could it be some sort of decoy sir?" said Ned looking at the pouch.

"There's nothing to indicate any trap," replied Dan, "and there's no other trail here. He must be getting careless, thinking that some of us blundered through those bushes and plunged off the side of the cliff. This trail will lead us in the direction he took. Come on, time's getting on and evening will soon be on us."

The trail took them further into the denseness of the trees, when to their dismay it abruptly stopped.

Peering closely at the ground they looked for signs of the track, but there was nothing. They had come to a dead end. Long straight trees shot up around them like rigid bars of a cage. There was no trail, just the stillness of the forest and an overwhelming stench of damp forest vegetation.

"We couldn't be lost sir, surely?" said Ned, looking around with a confused look.

"That tobacco pouch was a bluff Ned," said Dan. "He knew we'd keep to the trail we were on, knowing it would lead us here. Looks like we're trapped!"

"But, lieutenant," said Ned, "he obviously came this way so there must be a way out. He had to know of an exit that would lead him out of here."

"You're right Ned," said Dan, turning towards his men and cupping his hands to his mouth. "Listen up," he called, "there must be a trail leading away from here. Search your hardest for it, but don't venture too far, it's easy to get lost in here."

The group spread out, kicking away the forest debris and peering down at the ground for some indication of a track leading away from where they were. It wasn't long before a shout went up.

"Hey, I've got something," a voice yelled, "come quickly, over here. It must be his."

Dan looked at the small metal tinderbox the crewman was holding up.

"He must've dropped it," said Dan, "he wouldn't have discarded something like that so easily. Best let me have it, sailor."

"Look sir, a piece of cloth," said another crewman, pointing at a piece of ripped cloth hanging off the end of a sharp twig.

Dan pulled the piece of cloth away from the twig looking at it carefully.

"Listen sir," said one of the men, "I can hear water running."

"It's coming from up there, through those trees," said Ned, "sounds like a stream."

"Directly in line with this fallen tree trunk," said Dan, "come on, it could be the way out of here. He must have gone the same way."

The search party trudged off through the undergrowth making for the tinkling sound of a stream somewhere within the darkness of the trees.

"There it is, sir," said Ned, peering through a gap, "looks like a small brook making its way down towards the sea."

Dan and Ned stood back, studying the course of the stream while the rest of the crew refreshed themselves.

"We'll follow the stream up that way," said Dan, "and with a bit of luck, we may even stumble back onto the main pathway. Catching that runaway will have to wait. Our priority now is to find our way back before nightfall. Round up the men, Ned. Let's be on our way."

Taking the tinderbox from his pocket, Dan studied it carefully. *This is not Pascale's*, he thought. *So, who was it we were chasing? He obviously wanted to trap us here and lead us away from Pascale. So, that's it, Pascale's hiding away somewhere in this forest and whoever we were chasing doesn't want us to find him.*

20

Evening was drawing in as Jacques stood outside Jacob's quayside hut watching the activity going on around the harbour. There was no sign of the sloop moored behind the ship of the line, so it had surely sailed for England with the French prisoners from the three warehouses. The middle warehouse where he had started the fire, was now a crumpled black mass of burned rubble, the two warehouses either side of it having survived but looking as though they would collapse at any moment.

Their supply of victuals in the cabin was now desperately low and owing to the British search party roaming the forest it had not been wise to try and snare any forest game. Jacob had not returned, and as nightfall would soon be upon them, Jacques had made the decision to visit the harbour to try and procure some supplies. Jacob would never have agreed to him venturing down to the harbour alone, but the need for food was now urgent. With the last bottle of brandy from Jacob's chest tucked away inside his jacket pocket, he hoped to bribe someone in the quartermaster's storehouse to part with some bread and bacon. At the far end of the opposite quay, a candle flickered in the front window of a long wooden building that held the garrison's food supply. Whoever was there might be tempted. Pulling up the collar of his jacket, he gently tapped the bottle in his pocket and made his way towards the light.

A long wooden table displaying several sheets of paper stared at him as he opened the door to the storehouse. Two empty chairs stood at either end, a soldier's red coat hanging from the back of one of them. The whole area reeked of a mixture of meat and fish, reminding him of a food market he often used to visit back home. This part of the storehouse was obviously the clerical area. His eyes flicked over everything around him. A long hessian curtain hanging across a narrow aperture at the end of the room told him that the stockroom lay beyond. Mentally, Jacques was rehearsing what he would say. He would speak in faulting English, putting on a Swedish accent akin to Jacob's, and hope that whoever he was addressing would take him for one of the island's locals.

A series of murmurings suddenly sounded from behind the curtain followed by an incomprehensible mumbling, and as Jacques strained to understand what he was hearing, the curtain was suddenly thrown aside and a corpulent individual holding a feathered quill hurried over to the table to snatch up one of the sheets of paper. Hurriedly, he scanned its contents, then with a satisfied grunt he dipped the quill into an ink pot and - with it slightly dripping over the page - he ticked off various items of stock on the sheet. Turning, he looked at Jacques over a pair of pince-nez spectacles balanced at the end of his nose.

"Yes?" he asked.

Jacques took a deep breath and was about to speak when they were interrupted by the door to the storehouse suddenly flying open as an overweight harbour official blundered in breathing heavily.

"What is it, Quigley?" asked the storeroom clerk, frowning at the interruption.

"Come on Smithers," said Quigley, gasping for breath. "An unexpected supply has just arrived. I had no idea you had ordered extra to what arrived a few days ago. Come now, we must check it before I allow it to be unloaded. Bring a tally sheet with you, together with your quill and ink. Hurry, make haste before it gets dark."

"But I know nothing of this," stuttered Smithers, raising his eyebrows.

"No matter, someone has obviously authorised it," said the harbour official, still panting. "Come on, I don't want to miss out on dinner."

"Very well," replied Smithers, reaching for the red coat hanging on the back of the chair.

Grabbing a sheet of paper, he picked up the quill and a pot of ink and, adjusting his pince-nez, turned to Jacques. "If it's something very urgent you wanted then you can come back in an hour when we should be finished. Until then I bid you a good evening, sir."

Smoothing down his wig, he hurried off after the harbour official who repeatedly faltered along the quay to wipe the sweat from his brow before waddling off in the direction of a newly arrived fishing boat at the end of the quay.

Standing outside the storehouse and chuckling at the comical sight of the two military officials, Jacques' smile quickly faded as his eyes settled on the bearded fisherman tying a rope around a mooring post at the end of the quay. Erik was back on the island.

Smithers and Quigley hurried through the itemising of the supplies on Erik's boat, taking a fraction of the time it had taken when Jacques had first arrived in the harbour on Erik's vessel. Dinner was on the mind of the corpulent harbour official and as Jacques looked on, he saw him hurriedly sign the paper Smithers offered him, and with a wave of his hand indicated Erik was free to move what supplies he had brought into the storehouse. With that he tottered down the wooden plank onto the quay, shuffling off towards the garrison's dining area, leaving Smithers to look around for someone to help Erik unload the supplies. In an instant, Jacques presented himself before the storehouse clerk with a polite offer to help. Looking relieved at not having to carry anything himself, Smithers hurried back to the stockroom to make room for the arrival of the new rations.

Erik had seen Jacques approach his boat. Waiting until Smithers was well out of sight, he clasped Jacques' hand in a friendly greeting.

"No questions yet," whispered Erik, "just carry half of these boxes up to the storehouse, I'll carry the other half. When we're done, I'll explain why I'm here alone. There are only six boxes of fish, so we can get it done quickly."

Smithers was pleased at the small quantity of fish he had to make room for in the stockroom and giving Erik a receipt for the items, he quickly ushered them out with a friendly smile. Hurrying away towards the garrison's canteen, he wondered who had given the order for an extra supply of fish as it certainly wasn't needed.

"This is unexpected Erik," said Jacques, "what brings you here at this time of the evening. It will be dark soon."

Erik looked at Jacques with surprise. "I'm here with important instructions from your superiors in Danzig. But why are you here alone on the quay, shouldn't you be up in Jacob's cabin? It's far too dangerous down here. You could be caught."

"We needed food and Jacob's out somewhere in the forest and hasn't returned," said Jacques. "A lot has happened since you left us here. Come to the cabin with me and I'll tell you everything. You can give your message to us there. Jacob should be back by now. I was going to try and bribe that quartermaster's clerk with a bottle of Jacob's brandy for some bread and bacon."

"Good job you didn't," said Erik, smiling. "He would've rumbled you straight away and called the guard. There's fish and bread onboard you can have. By the way, no-one here ordered the fish we've just carried in, it was just a ploy to get into the harbour. They recognized me as their supplier and let me in without asking any questions.

Erik followed Jacques along the hidden track to Jacob's cabin, anxious to give the three of them the news he was carrying.

Seeing Erik suddenly walk through the door, Pierre jumped up in dismay.

"Ah Magnus," said Erik, grinning, "Glad to see you've settled in so nicely."

"It'll do for the time being," said Pierre, looking curiously at Erik.

"I'm here to give the three of you an urgent message from Danzig," said Erik, putting the fish and bread onto the table.

"Jacob's not here," replied Pierre. "He went out into the forest over seven hours ago to look for a British search party. But what's the message?"

"I've only just returned from Danzig after a secret meeting with your superiors," Erik replied. "It's known to them that one of their agents was taken prisoner after the ship he was on was attacked and crippled by a British frigate. He's being held prisoner here on the island. This agent was bound for the port of Karlskrona where he was to meet a Swedish admiral collaborating with your navy. The agent's instructions were to give the admiral precise information regarding the invasion of the island, as the admiral has agreed with your Emperor to assist in this attack. Information on the exact co-ordinates to join the French fleet for the invasion were included in this agent's dispatch. Should he not complete his mission, the planned invasion of the island will be in serious jeopardy. My job is to ferry him to Karlskrona first thing in the morning and when he's delivered his dispatch take him to General Bonard in Danzig. But first, you must free him."

"Would this agent's name be Andre Pascale?" asked Pierre,

smiling.

"Yes, but how did you know, and why are you smiling?"

A voice behind Erik made him spin round in surprise.

"Because he is here," said Pascale, coming out of the shadows.

"Erik," said Jacques, "you'd better sit down. This is Andre Pascale and yes, we rescued him from the British, so while Magnus and I cook the fish, Andre will brief you."

Astounded at the sudden turn of events, Erik sat down at the table indicating to Jacques to open the bottle of brandy he had taken to bribe the quartermaster's clerk. Taking a large gulp, he sat back listening to Pascale's opening lines of what was going to be a long rendering of his seizure by the British.

Coming to the end of his account, Pascale reached for the brandy and - pouring himself a good measure - knocked it back in one mouthful.

"So, you see gentlemen, it's important for me to get to Karlskrona first thing tomorrow. Admiral von Krassow will not wait forever and the success of the invasion of this island greatly depends on our collaboration with a section of the Swedish navy. My meeting him is therefore crucial to our plans."

"What about us, Erik?" asked Jacques. "Were there any instructions for us? We had planned that Andre would go back to Danzig with Magnus when you picked us up at the end of our mission here on the island. I was to stay here with Jacob to carry out a plan we had made when the attack began. But now, it seems everything will change!"

"No. Andre comes with me to Karlskrona tomorrow, without fail," said Erik. "But let me know your plan, and I'll take it to General Bonard when I return Andre to Danzig. I'll come back here with his answer the day we bring the supplies over to the British, that will be in three days' time as from tomorrow. My son Lars was due to skipper the boat, but I'll be doing it now. While my daughter Anna's organising the unloading, I'll meet you here in Jacob's cabin. Until then, you are both to continue the excellent job you're doing."

Leaving the fish simmering in a pot, Jacques and Pierre sat opposite Erik and - helping themselves to a generous measure of the brandy - told him of the cave they had found and their plan of how they thought the attack on the island should now proceed."

Nodding, Erik turned to Pascale,

"We'll leave at first light tomorrow. There'll be a different watch on the harbour than there was when I came in this evening, so they won't know that I came in alone. Two of us leaving shouldn't cause any alarm. All being well and with a good wind, my mission with Andre will go to plan and I'll be back here with the supplies, and your answer."

The fish smelt good as Pierre placed the pot on the table and as they dipped slices of bread into the rich juice, they suddenly looked up startled as the cabin door flew open. Standing in the doorway, Jacob stared at the group sitting around his table. "My God," he said. "That smells good!"

21

James listened to Dan's account of the previous day's pursuit through the forest, and the wild goose chase the stranger had led them on across the rocky shoreline.

The course of the little brook had led Dan and his men through a row of thick undergrowth, eventually running parallel to a section of the main forest path where they had found their way back to the harbour. It was past the hour of midnight when they had returned to their ship.

"And you failed to find out where in the forest he was hiding?" asked James.

"Yes unfortunately, sir," said Dan. "But I think you'll be pleased to know that we found the cove, together with the cave and a tunnel that we think runs through the cliffs. Four of us entered the tunnel but we didn't manage to get that far as we were called back by one of the crew."

"The commodore has agreed for us to explore the southern part of the island on foot today," said James. "Show me where the cave is, Dan, and the trail that leads to it. If the cove is wide enough to accommodate at least two longboats, then that is where the French will land their marines. Inform Ned Hatchet and two of the crew we'll be leaving on the hour of nine. Tell them to bring two lanterns, we'll need them inside the cave and the tunnel.

"And the rest of the crew sir?"

"I've already instructed Mr. Devonshire for the crew to carry out a full cleaning of the decks and berths, ready for inspection when we return. Mr. Piper knows his routine concerning Hector's cannons, and the ship's officers will be responsible for their own quarters."

"Very well captain," said Dan.

"As the crew have liberty in three days," said James, "they'll do an excellent job, I'm sure. None of them will want to miss out on that, by having to do again what they might dodge while Lieutenant Devonshire's back is turned. Meet me at the end of the quay with the other three on the hour of nine."

"Sir," said Dan, saluting his captain.

Dan stood with Ned Hatchet, Clifford Williams, and Richard Davis, watching their captain being rowed from their ship towards the end of the quay where they stood waiting.

"At ease," said James, acknowledging them with a nod. "No need for strict regularity. We are on a fact-finding mission today exploring the cave and tunnel you found yesterday. What also interests me is the size of the cove lying near the cave. Williams and Davis, you carry the lanterns that we'll need inside the cave. I trust they're in order and will be sufficient for us once we're inside the tunnel. Lieutenant Sutherland will lead us down the track that drops down to the shoreline. Mr. Hatchet, you will be our back marker. If we're all ready, we can go."

Visions of a detachment of French marines stealthily advancing out of the forest played on James' mind as they crossed the field of long grass.

Suddenly he froze at the horrific thought of the French turning the three heavy cannons down onto the British sailors and marines defending the harbour. *It would be all over in no time,* he thought, *and Napoleon would have no problem in grabbing the Eastern Russian Governorates before taking Sweden as his final prize. My God, what are we in for?*

Bright sunlight pierced through the trees as the group made their way silently through the forest, the fork on the pathway suddenly coming into view as they turned a bend. Dan led them down the narrow track, stopping occasionally as James studied the lie of the stony ground. Thick branches drooped low over the pathway and in parts dense undergrowth spilled over the rough ground, impeding a clear route through.

Such obstacles would surely restrict a fast-moving detachment of men, pondered James, *and should it rain then the wet stones would be a slippery handicap to face.* He would recommend the felling of some trees across the pathway to act as an added barrier.

"Lead on Dan," he said.

Gaps in the trees allowed them to glimpse the mounds of black craggy rocks and boulders lining the coastline. These, James had seen through his scope only a few days before as HMS Hector had cruised along the coastline looking for a cove or inlet. *There's no way any landing craft can come ashore here,* he thought.

Turning a corner Dan brought them to a sudden halt, the path they were on abruptly coming to an end. A range of towering granite-faced cliffs stared out to sea before them while colonies of squawking seabirds swooped and dived over the water, their young hungrily screeching out from the nooks and crannies in the cliff's face.

"Over there, captain," said Dan, pointing to the cove on his right.

James jumped off the path onto the cove, his eyes scanning the surrounding rocks and gauging how far apart they were from this possible landing point. Then, moving down to the shoreline, he stopped at the water's edge. Dan watched him as he slowly turned to his left and then to his right, studying the distance of the rocks from where he stood and picturing the actuality of the French coming ashore in their longboats. Wading a few paces out into the sea he peered down at the seabed through the crystal-clear water, his eyes searching for any submerged jagged rocks that would rip out the bottom of a fast-moving longboat. Frowning, he turned back to the shoreline.

"Between the rocks on each side of the water's edge," he said, looking at Dan, "there are no rocks on the seabed. Landing craft can beach here without danger of ripping themselves apart on any rocks below. It's an ideal place for the French to land their marines.

"The pathway we came on seems to be the only route to and from this cove captain," said Dan, looking back to where the path suddenly stopped. "Those cliffs are sheer, and with all those seabirds swirling around them I doubt very much if anyone would attempt scaling them."

"You're right Dan," said James. "We know there are French agents on the island, and you can be sure they've already scouted around down here. If they're serious about landing their marines on this cove, then they must have found another way out from here. They could use the path we came on, but it's open for ambush and laden with obstacles. No, I doubt they'll consider using that as their main exit path from the cove. There must be another way they've managed to find."

"The tunnel, captain," said Dan, looking across at the entrance to the cave. "That could be the answer."

"Yes, you could be right Dan," said James. "Come on, show me."

Ignoring the din of the squawking gulls, the five men from HMS Hector clambered over the rocks towards the mouth of the cave. Standing in the darkened chamber, Dan produced the tinderbox his crewman had found in the forest and lit the two lanterns.

"The entrance to the tunnel is over there, captain. That dark cranny in the far corner."

"You lead Dan with one of the lanterns," said James. "Mr. Hatchet, take one of the lanterns and follow in the rear. I'll follow behind Lieutenant Sutherland. Williams, and Davis behind me."

Holding the lantern at arm's length, Dan stepped into the pitch blackness, the others keeping close behind. An eerie silence merging with the stench of damp mould enveloped the dark passageway, the light from their two lanterns conjuring up darkened images that danced creepily along the walls beside them.

"Bloody spooky in 'ere," whispered Richard Davis.

"Bloody right," answered Clifford Williams, "keep thinking something's following us."

"Mr. Hatchet," said Davis, stopping and turning to the ship's master-at-arms. "Can you feel it? Like something's following us."

Ned Hatchet stretched his arm out fully, so allowing the light from the lantern he was carrying to flicker over the ground behind them.

"Nuthin' there," he said, "can't see any further down there. Better keep quiet Davis, before Captain sends you back there to investigate."

With a shiver, Richard Davis turned back around, hastening up the passageway after the others.

Dan continued to lead them forward into the darkness, the light from his lantern giving some idea of the condition of the passageway. The ground seemed clear to walk on, the dim light showing there were no unforeseen obstacles impeding the way.

This is the way the invading French marines are likely to come, thought James.

"I can see that the tunnel bends to the right here," whispered Dan, holding the lantern forward. "But there's a strange sound coming from up there. Listen, can you hear it?"

The five of them bent their heads towards the darkness beyond, listening intently for anything unusual.

"Can't hear nuthin'," said Richard Davis, his eyes as wide as saucers.

"Listen," whispered Dan, "it's coming from around the bend, a low humming sound."

Concentrating, they all listened again until they began to nod in agreement.

"Yes, said James. I can just about make it out. What on earth could it be?"

"Well, we're about to find out," said Dan, moving forward.

Gingerly, the others followed, keeping close to each other as the humming intensified. Through the darkness it was impossible for them to make out anything to explain the unusual sound, then by the light of Dan's lantern they suddenly saw the tunnel widening into a small dark chamber, the roof abruptly dropping to a few feet above their heads. Dark blobs seemed to hang from the roof in front of them and as Dan raised the lantern, they gasped in horror at the sight of hundreds of furry little black creatures dangling upside down, their sleep-filled humming echoing around the chamber and far along the tunnel.

"What the hell are those things?" shrieked Richard Davis.

A shocked wail went up from Ned Hatchet, who being several feet taller than the rest, was too late to avoid his head scraping through the dark clusters.

"Duck," screamed Clifford Williams, "they're waking!"

"Bats," yelled Dan, "everyone down, now."

Four bodies hit the ground in an instant, except for Ned Hatchet who stood shaking in shock as hundreds of the hairy little fiends covered him from head to foot, flapping their wings frenziedly and screeching hysterically in distress after being woken in such a way. Screams of horror filled the tunnel as Ned shook with terror, his face and body becoming blanketed with scores of the little demons.

Lying face down in the grit, James listened to the agonising screams coming from his master-at-arms, the rush of hundreds of wings beating feverishly around him reminding him of a ship's sails flapping violently in a gale force wind. And then it was suddenly over as silence settled over the chamber. Raising themselves they looked at the bleeding figure of Ned, still standing but shaking uncontrollably.

"Quickly," shouted James. "Anything you've got to act as bandages, tear off strips of clothing if necessary."

They tore at their long shirts, producing strips of material which James bound around Ned's cuts.

"Thank you, captain," he said, wheezing for air. "I'm too tough to go down to a bunch of those little fuckers. I'll be alright."

"You're in shock, Ned. Just take it easy," said Dan.

"Do you want to rest up for a while?" said James.

"No captain, just get us out of here."

"Very well," said James. "Davis, take the lantern and take over Mr. Hatchet's position at the rear, he can move up behind me. The bats have left the cave now so we should be able to continue unhindered. Come on, we should be coming to an exit soon. Lead on Mr. Sutherland."

Dan led the way out of the chamber, the light from his lantern showing they were back in the narrow passageway.

"Sir," cried out Clifford Williams in surprise, "the ground below seems to be going uphill."

"You're right Williams," replied James. "We seem to be going up the cliff, believe it or not."

The ground below them began to rise in a steep incline, each of them conscious that they were walking up what seemed like a hill inside the cliff.

"Look, daylight ahead," said Dan, increasing his pace. "Looks like we're coming to the end of the tunnel."

The end of the tunnel loomed into sight, the darkness of the passageway giving way to the daylight that streamed through its exit. Scrambling through, they breathed in deeply, drinking in the fresh salty air that rose from the sea below. Ned Hatchet breathed a sigh of relief, grateful to be out of the darkness and the horrific trauma he had experienced.

"This is where we were yesterday," said Clifford Williams, "here on the clifftop. One of the crew found a water canister left by one of your men, Mr. Hatchet. Over there are the rows of thick bushes we went through to get to the path that leads down to the rocky shoreline below."

"Yes, and that's where the fugitive we were chasing nearly went over the top," said Ned, squinting towards the bushes. "The shot you heard lieutenant was fired from up here."

"That's the main pathway that leads through the forest," said Dan, pointing to a wide track disappearing into the trees. Looking away from the path and over the side of the cliff to the trees below, James nodded.

"I can just about make out the trail we took along the coastline down there," he said. "The path up here is ideal for the invaders, far better than down there. Yes, this is where they'll come, up through the tunnel and then along this path. They'll make it a night-time attack as the tunnel will be free of bats."

"If you please, captain," said Dan. "I think you ought to suggest to Commodore Percival that he should order a complete military search of the forest. I'm now sure, the fugitive we were chasing deliberately took us into the dense part of the forest to take us away from where they're hiding Pascale. I've a feeling we may have been close to their hiding place at some point."

"Yes, when we get back to the harbour I most certainly will," agreed James.

Early that same morning as the sun peeped up over the horizon, Jacob led Erik and Andre Pascale across the field of long grass towards the path that descended to the harbour below. The three spies walked nonchalantly towards the quay where Erik had moored his boat, ignoring the garrison's militia who were busying themselves with the usual mundane preparations of a new day. Erik jumped onboard to ready the vessel for their departure.

"Godspeed Andre," said Jacob, looking seriously at the French lieutenant.

"Aren't you forgetting something?"

"Have I left something behind?" answered Andre looking confused.

Moving in close to the French spy, Jacob whispered in his ear. "Get me on a boat Jacob, and as I embark, I'll whisper the date and time of the invasion for your ears only. Have you forgotten what you said to me?"

Andre's eyes widened in surprise as he looked at Jacob's stern expression.

"Those were your exact words," said Jacob, "meaning, that should anything happen to you, then I would be able to prepare for the invasion."

With a nod, Andre leant forward and shielding one side of his mouth he whispered into Jacob's ear.

"Everything depends on Per's and Magnus' report to General Bonard regarding the size of the attack force the French will send. My instruction to Admiral von Krassow is for his flotilla to be at a rendezvous coordinate two miles off the island and ready to join up with the French fleet. Now, as Per will be staying on the island with you, it will be up to Magnus to convince General Bonard of Per's plan of how the attack on the island should proceed. It's a good plan and I'm sure the General will agree with it. Whatever happens, the invasion will take place on the 31st day of March at midnight."

"Andre, come aboard, the boat's ready to sail. A good wind is up," shouted Erik. "Jacob, untie the mooring rope. See you three days from now at your cabin. I'll bring the General's answer."

Jacob unhitched the mooring rope and tossing it onto the fishing vessel, watched Erik guide the fishing boat out of the harbour until it rounded the harbour wall and disappeared into the early morning sea mist.

Walking away from the quay, he stopped at the door of a long wooden cabin a short walk away from the harbour. Lifting its latch, he closed his eyes savouring the heavenly smell of freshly baked bread.

"I'll take four of those tasty smelling loaves, Ulf," he called to the owner. "Add on a side of bacon, a flagon of ale and two bottles of brandy."

Packing Jacob's items into a wooden box, Ulf tallied up the amount, holding out his hand for payment. With a smile, Jacob dropped him a few coins and with a friendly farewell he left the cabin.

The weather that morning promised to be good. Seeing the mist lifting, he decided to spend the morning at his hut on the quay, going over the information Pascale had given him.

Settling down in his rocking chair outside the hut, he filled a mug with the ale he had purchased and fumbling for his pipe suddenly realised he had no tinderbox. Cursing his bad luck for losing it in the forest, he decided to buy another before the day was out.

His eyes scanned the area before him, settling on a group of four men standing together watching a longboat being rowed across the harbour towards the quay where they were waiting. Something about the men seemed familiar, especially a tall one, a giant of a man with an eye patch over his left eye. Pictures of himself running across the grassy open area above the cliff tops where the English sailors had given chase, flashed through his mind. He remembered hearing a musket shot and as he ducked, he had looked around to see a giant of a man with an eye patch and wearing a bandana wrapped tightly around his head racing after him. This was the man, no doubt.

By the friendly way the others were chatting and their obvious comradery, they had to be part of the search party that had chased him across the rocky shoreline and up the goats' trail into the forest. He watched as the longboat stopped by a ladder attached to the quay, a familiar figure climbing up to join them. And then the penny dropped as the figure turned his head in his direction. Quickly he looked away, turning his back as the group made their way towards his hut.

With them safely passed, he looked back over his shoulder, curious to know why they had taken the steep stony track leading up towards the field of long grass. He'd recognised the familiar figure as the captain of a British frigate who'd taken Andre Pascale into one of the fishing huts on the quay for questioning only a few days before.

What are they up to? he thought.

He considered following them, but the chance of being caught tailing them made him decide to keep up his vigil over the harbour and get back to the cabin with his newly purchased supplies. With a reassuring grunt, he sat back with another mug of ale, letting his eyes soak up the bustling activity going on around him.

Towards midday he closed his quayside hut and, taking the bread, bacon, and bottles of brandy, he walked nonchalantly around the quay, noting how many British frigates were at anchor before making his way up to the field of long grass.

As he approached the field, a dull humming noise from above made him stop and look up, his mouth dropping open in utter horror.

"Bats!" he cried. "No, it can't be. But how?"

Racing along the forest track towards his cabin, he cursed the prospect of their plans being thwarted.

"They've found it," he yelled, bursting through the door of the cabin.

"Found what Jacob?" said Pierre, jumping up in shock.

"The cave," screamed Jacob. "I saw a group of the British search party down on the quay with lanterns. I watched them go up the steep stony path and enter the field of long grass that leads into the forest. They must have been on their way to the cove where the cave is and, on my way back here, I saw a thick cloud of bats flying over the treetops. They obviously disturbed the bats when they found the tunnel."

"Merde," swore Jacques. "What can we do? We can't change our plans now."

"No, it won't be necessary to change anything," said Jacob, thinking.

"Assume the British now know of the tunnel and are expecting an attack at some time. They cannot be totally sure we will use the tunnel in our invasion or that your marines will land on the south part of the island. They'll be expecting a frontal attack on their harbour garrison from the sea. Should they suspect a rear action coming from the south, they haven't the manpower to keep up a forceful surveillance around the exit of the tunnel day and night. All their might will be concentrated in and around the harbour. What is more, they do not know when the invasion will start. I have the trump card in knowing the exact time and date."

Jacques and Pierre looked at him in surprise.

"Yes, Andre told me before they sailed this morning."

Opening one of the bottles of brandy, he poured himself a large measure, knocking it back in one gulp. Then leaning over the table, he looked directly into the faces of the two spies, "Now listen carefully," he said.

22

A strong wind caught the sail of Erik's fishing vessel, driving it further towards the port of Danzig. Midnight over the Baltic saw the fishing boat well on course and over half-way towards its destination. At the helm, Erik looked up at a myriad of twinkling stars spread far across the dark expanse of a night sky. Yawning, he looked around at the sound of Pascale approaching.

"Beautiful, isn't it?" said Pascale, looking up at the stars. "It's like they've all been strung together with lengths of invisible string. That's the brightest star in the night sky. Its name is Sirius and it's one of the closest stars to earth. Now, time for you to get your head down. My turn at the helm."

Erik nodded, pleased to be relieved for a much-needed sleep.

"Wake me in four hours, we'll be nearing land then. You should have no problems tonight, weather's set fine and calm and this wind will be with us all the way. You're a sailor Andre, so you'll soon get to know this lady. She won't give you any trouble. Keep your eyes peeled for any British frigates. If you see one kill the lanterns, then wake me immediately."

Pascale stood at the helm, his eyes scouring the dark waters as he recalled his meeting with Admiral von Krassow. They had sailed without incident and reached Karlskrona at midday. Leaving the fisherman at the port, he'd hired a carriage to take him to an address where the admiral could be found.

Under a cloak of secrecy, he had been ushered into a grand room where the admiral and five other prominent high-ranking officers of the Swedish navy had listened to him reciting the emperor's dispatch in English. Serious faces had stared at him as he came to the end of his communique. Quoting Napoleon's words, he had warned them that should they not comply with the conditions set out in the dispatch, then there would be no alternative but for the French to invade the Swedish mainland. They had acquiesced, asking for guarantees that the island of Hanö revert unconditionally to Swedish control once it had been seized. Pascale promised to relay their request. He had departed with a letter of compliance that promised a Swedish flotilla to link up with the French attack force at the proposed coordinates at midnight on 31st March. It would consist of two squadrons of rated warships, under the command of rear-admiral Frederik Hastfer. This information was now vital for him to deliver to his superiors in Danzig and arriving back at the harbour he had been pleased to see that Erik had readied the fishing boat for departure. In a strengthening wind, Erik had guided the fishing boat out of the harbour while he had sat back breathing a long sigh of relief.

Erik tossed and turned in his sleep. He dreamt of chasing after Anna through a forest, calling out her name and begging her not to run away with the English sailor whose bulbous peasant features peeped out at him from behind the surrounding trees. He could not let his daughter run away with someone who resembled a pig, and an English one at that. In his dream he saw Anna stop and come running back towards him. Opening his arms to her he felt his body shuddering, something was causing his right shoulder to tremble.

Pascale was gently shaking him. "Erik, it has just passed the hour of four. You asked me to wake you."

"Yes, thank you," muttered Erik. "All quiet out there?"

"Yes, all quiet. Nothing to report. The wind has strengthened, and there's a stronger swell out at sea."

"Ok, you go up on deck. I'll be up when I get myself sorted."

A dim light was beginning to steal across the sky as Erik took over the helm. The dream he'd had played on his mind, causing him to make the decision to change the plans for the next delivery of supplies to Hanö. He would accompany Anna over to Hanö island, and while on the crossing he'd speak to her about the Englishman her mother had seen her with outside their house. He'd stress the seriousness of how her feelings for this Englishman could destroy their family. Lars would have a free day and Olof would skipper the vessel. This would also give him the chance of delivering General Bonard's answer to the new plan of invasion entrusted to him by the two French spies.

Pascale appeared with some bread and cheese he had found in the hold, and while they breakfasted the pale light of dawn began to spread over the murky waters. Erik scanned the horizon, his eyes settling on a dark silhouette of land.

"Look, straight ahead," he said, pointing out to sea. "The Polish coast and the mouth of The Motlawa River, no more than an hour away from where we are now. Once we enter the river, it'll take us just over an hour to reach the port of Danzig. We can moor up at the bottom of the steps where The Great Medieval Crane is. From there it's a short walk to The Artus Court building where we'll find General Bonard. Let me speak first about Per's and Magnus' plan concerning what they've discovered and how they think the attack on the island should begin. Once I have his answer and his fresh instructions, I can start the journey back. With a fair wind I should reach Nogersund in the early hours of tomorrow."

A harbourside clock, not far from the Great Medieval Crane, struck the half hour of six as Erik coasted the fishing boat up to the jetty at the bottom of the embankment steps. Leaping off the vessel, he secured the boat's mooring rope to a thick wooden post on the small pier.

Jean-Luc Bonard stared into an oval mirror conveniently positioned on the wall behind his desk admiring the waxed ends of his ample moustache.

A gentle knock on his door told him his secretary had his agenda for the day.

"Come," he called, picking up a clean napkin from the side of his desk.

A bespectacled middle-aged clerk, in the uniform of the French navy, opened the door. "If I'm not disturbing you sir," he said, standing rigidly to attention. "There are two men waiting to see you urgently. They say it is of the utmost importance that they see you."

"Did they say what it was about?" asked Jean-Luc.

"No sir," replied the clerk, "but they said you would recognize their names."

"Yes, well what are their names?" said Jean-Luc, impatiently.

"Lieutenant Andre Pascale and Erik Gunnarsson," said the clerk.

"Mon Dieu!" exclaimed Jean-Luc, leaping out of his chair. "Show them in immediately and inform Commandant Joubert to join us directly."

"Gentlemen, please be seated," said Jean-Luc, eagerly welcoming his new guests.

Pascale and Erik sat opposite Jean-Luc, the sound of a clock ticking rhythmically on the opposite wall.

"I hope you've something good for me Lieutenant," said Jean-Luc, looking sternly at Pascale. "News that will offset the disaster of your being captured by the English and losing not only the entire crew of the ship you were on, but the brig as well."

"Sir, may I say," said Pascale, looking seriously at Jean-Luc, "that Captain Masien was tragically killed during the action. With the number of dead and wounded I had no alternative but to surrender to the British. The only longboat attached to the brig was fatally damaged in the action. As instructed, I had memorised your instructions to Admiral von Krassow and was able to burn the written dispatch. The British have no idea of the purpose of my mission."

"But you were taken prisoner by the British," interrupted Jean-Luc, "and held in their harbour on Hanö Island. Did they not make you talk, and how did you escape? We sent Erik Gunnarsson here, to instruct Jacob Forsberg along with our two agents on the island to break you out and then to bring you back here."

A loud single knock suddenly broke the discussion.

"Come," called Jean-Luc, looking over at the door.

The door was opened by a perspiring Henri Joubert, anxious to know why he'd been summoned so urgently.

Jean-Luc signalled him to seat himself on the remaining empty chair at the end of the desk.

"Sir," said Pascale, looking back at Jean-Luc. "Erik Gunnarsson has some vital information to give you from your two agents on the island. As he must return to Nogersund by tomorrow morning, would you allow him to give you his report first?"

"By all means," said Jean-Luc, indicating Erik to go ahead.

The two commanders listened without interrupting as Erik told them of Jacques' and Pierre's new plan for the invasion. He omitted nothing of what Jacques and Pierre had instructed him to say. When he had finished, Jean-Luc looked over at Henri, his eyebrows raised questioningly.

"I like it," said Jean-Luc, nodding. "Henri?"

"Yes, it could certainly work," said Henri, looking interested. "As long as our marines can take over their big guns on the highest point of the island."

"Sir," said Pascale, "once we've taken over their heavy cannons, we'll sight them down onto the British positions around the harbour. With their almighty fire power and the bombardment from our fleet, the island will soon be ours."

"Yes, I can see that will work," said Henri. "But I can't make a decision yet until I've heard your report, Lieutenant Pascale."

"I'm afraid you're going to have to stay a while longer, Monsieur Gunnarsson," instructed Jean-Luc.

Erik groaned inwardly, knowing his sleep time once back in Nogersund would be cut short. "As you wish," he said, smiling gracefully at Jean-Luc.

The clock on the wall opposite Jean-Luc's desk pointed to the hour of nine. He would have to wait until Pascale finished his account and then for the two French commanders to come to a decision.

Clutching the sealed document from Admiral von Krassow, Pascale began his report by describing the British frigate's attack on La Marie Louise and the subsequent capture of himself and the brig's crew. Step by step he gave his account, pausing after recounting each incident. He was careful to omit the episode of his near execution, not wanting his superiors to know that he'd capitulated the moment he was certain he would be shot. He described his meeting with Admiral von Krassow in detail, then paused before continuing.

"Sir," he said, looking at Jean-Luc. "The admiral requested one major inclusion to the agreement."

"Yes, and what was that?" asked Jean-Luc, frowning.

"After we have taken and secured the island, it reverts back to Swedish control."

"Bah!" said Jean-Luc, looking across at Henri. "And what did you tell him, lieutenant?"

"That I could only pass this request onto you, sir," replied Pascale.

With a serious look, Jean-Luc stood up and - pouring two glasses of cognac - he passed one to Henri, then taking a large mouthful from his glass he walked across to the large window that looked down onto the courtyard below.

Staring down at the passers-by, he suddenly raised his voice.

"That is out of the question. Hanö island must be ours and will be ours. Let the Swedes think they will have it back, but I can tell you now that His Excellency will never agree to surrendering the island. So, that is an end to that. Now, can I assume that what you've been holding throughout your report is a document from Admiral von Krassow?"

"It is sir," said Pascale. "Their letter of compliance."

Jean-Luc held out his hand for the document.

"I can see Monsieur Gunnarsson is anxious to leave with our answer, so join me Henri while we consider its contents."

The clock ticked away monotonously, each minute passing an added delay for Erik. Looking over at Jean-Luc and Henri deep in conversation, his eyes wandered over the décor of Jean-Luc's ample office. The large map of the Baltic stretching across the wall behind the general's desk caught his eye, but the hands on the clock showing it was approaching the hour of eleven distracted his attention; he needed to be away by midday at the latest. A slight cough from Henri indicated they were ready with their answer.

"We have gone over our two agents' plan most thoroughly," said Jean-Luc, looking at each of them, "and together with the information provided by Lieutenant Pascale, we agree to the suggestions put forward by them."

"You, Lieutenant Pascale, will join Lieutenant Pierre Renaud after his return to Danzig. The two of you will be part of the detachment of marines that will land on the cove and then pass up through the tunnel to attack the British from their rear. You will also assist Jacob Forsberg in the attack on the big cannons the British have mounted on the highest point of the island.

Monsieur Gunnarsson, you will be at the arranged point in five days to pick up Lieutenant Renaud and return him here to Danzig when he will give us a complete breakdown of the strength of the British garrison. Inform Jacob Forsberg and Lieutenant Petit that they must light the beacons around the cove, one hour before our bombardment of the harbour commences at midnight. So, I suggest you depart forthwith, Monsieur Gunnarsson. I wish you a safe and fast journey. Good luck and thank you for all your sincere efforts in helping us with our war against the British."

Erik hurried away towards the embankment steps on the opposite side of the Medieval Crane. His fishing boat lay bobbing up and down on a slight swell and wasting no time he unfurled the sail and cast off, a fair wind blowing down the Motlawa River allowing the boat the speed Erik wanted. Setting his course for the harbour of Nogersund he smiled at the sound of a clock somewhere along the riverbank chiming out the hour of midday.

23

The sun was rising over the harbour of Nogersund as Anna made her way towards the warehouse. Smiling, she was pleased to see that Nils and Gustav had started loading Erik's fishing vessel. There was no sign of her brother Lars and thinking he might be busy onboard she called out to the two fishermen.

"Is my brother onboard?"

Shaking their heads, Nils called back, "No sign of him yet. Perhaps he's waiting for instructions from your father. Looks like your father arrived back in the early hours. Can you check what boxes of fish need to be loaded, we've already brought the vegetables onboard."

"Yes of course," replied Anna, hurrying over to the warehouse.

Excitement surged through her as she marked the boxes of fish to be loaded, it was today she would meet James. All week she had been longing for this moment. Not a morning had passed, without her looking through her father's telescope from the large window in the front of their house for a glimpse of what might have been James' frigate setting out on an early morning patrol. She was pleased that Lars would be skippering the vessel, knowing he wouldn't ask any questions when she announced she would leave them for a few hours to walk around the island alone. She would not mention anything about James to Lars, not yet anyway.

The weather looked fine for the day, a stiff breeze giving the water outside the harbour a slight swell. She could not wait to get the business with the supplies over and done with, and for midmorning to come, knowing James would be waiting for her on the quay. She would act normally, so as not to cause her brother to suspect anything.

Gustav had gone on board to prepare the fishing boat for departure, leaving Nils to carry the last boxes of fish down to the vessel. Anna checked that the tally documents were all in order and, placing them in a deep pocket of her gown, she closed the warehouse doors. Humming the tune of a love song that had been playing in her head all morning, she casually followed Nils along the quay. The sight of two shadowy figures approaching the fishing boat caused her to shield her eyes from the strong rays of sunlight streaming over the harbour. Quickening her pace, she suddenly stopped short as a wave of disappointment surged over her. Crestfallen, she gazed at the figures of her father and her uncle Olof hastening up the vessel's ramp. Seeing his daughter standing on the quay, Erik beckoned her to hurry up on board. Trying hard to hide her disheartenment at the prospect of her date with James being quashed, she followed him up the ramp.

"I assume everything's been loaded and ready for the garrison, Anna?" said Erik, looking at her questioningly.

"Yes papa," replied Anna. "I thought Lars would be taking us over today."

"No, I gave him the day off, Olof is skipper today. I had a long and tiring journey back from Danzig yesterday, not getting back here until the early hours of this morning, so I'm taking it easy onboard today. I also want a serious talk with you when we're under way."

Anna wondered what the serious talk would be about and what he had been doing in Danzig to cause him such a late and tiring journey.

"When everything's unloaded," he said, "Olof and I have an important meeting on the other side of the island. You'll have to busy yourself with something until we return to the boat, it won't be until later in the afternoon."

Anna's heart jumped with joy.

"Is it with the British?" she asked, cautiously.

"No. We've arranged to meet some of the island's fishermen who want to do some business with us," he said, hating the lie.

Anna watched the harbour disappear as the fishing boat coasted round the harbour wall and out to sea, the stiff breeze suddenly catching its sail and propelling it forward. With the wind blowing through her long hair, she sat in the stern, anxious about the serious talk that was coming her way. She hoped he hadn't found out about her meeting with James, as she was very aware of his hatred for the English.

Leaving Olof at the helm, Erik looked around the vessel for his daughter and seeing her in the stern he made his way over to where she was seated.

Anna looked up at him nervously.

"Your mother mentioned that she happened to see you in company with a stranger outside our house a week ago," he began. "As your father, I'd like to know who he was, Anna."

Anna went cold, her mind searching for an answer that would satisfy him.

"I was coming home last week with two heavy bags of vegetables for mama when a gentleman stopped and offered to carry them up the hill for me. That is all papa," she said, digging her nails into the palm of her hand.

"Well, your mother reckons there was something more in the way you regarded each other, and the way you watched him walk away until he stopped and waved to you from the corner. She is also certain that he is English and most probably a sailor based on the island of Hanö. Your mother is rarely wrong about such things."

Anna looked away from her father's gaze, focusing on the choppy swell out to sea. She felt herself welling up, her eyes beginning to fill with tears. How could she explain her feelings for James to her father who harboured such a hatred towards anyone who was English.

"I'm shocked to know that mama was spying on me," she said. "I never knew she was doing that."

"Oh no," said Erik. "She wasn't spying on you Anna, she just happened to look out of the front window and there you were with this stranger. Looking into each other's eyes, like love - struck teenagers! And your early morning vigils at the front window with my telescope, searching the sea lanes for a sign of a British frigate out on an early morning patrol. Every morning for the past week, Anna. Now you cannot deny that! This is the reason why your mother's sure he's a British sailor."

Her eyes filled with tears. "Papa," she said, gently. "I am twenty-one years of age, and I respect you and mama, and I love my home. So, I will tell you exactly what happened, but you must realise that I am a woman with feelings, and they have happened to me. This stranger is an English captain of a frigate based on the island of Hanö. He and his lieutenant came to the warehouse a week ago looking for you. They wanted to know how many crew members you have registered for the fishing boat. Something wonderful happened between us as we talked, things like that do happen papa, I only wish you could understand that. It is the first time such a feeling has happened to me. I was beginning to think that it had avoided me and would never happen. But it has happened, and I don't want to lose it."

Erik stared at his daughter, her words about the English captain coming to the warehouse and asking about his crew ringing warning bells. He would have to find out more.

"I do understand that attraction can lead to strong feelings, Anna," he said. "But you know how I feel about the English. They killed your grandmother: my mother."

"James didn't kill grandma, papa," said Anna, looking into her father's eyes. "He was nowhere near Copenhagen when she was killed."

"Ah, now he has a name," said Erik, wanting to know more.

"Yes, Captain James Carey," she said, smiling.

"Now Anna," said her father, sternly, "I want you to be truthful. Have you and this English captain arranged to see each other again?"

Anna looked away from her father, her mind wrestling with how she would answer. The thought of lying to him while she secretly met James seemed her only option, but she had never lied to her father and knew he would see through her if she did. Her eyes settled on the rocky coastline of Hanö Island as Olof brought the fishing vessel closer to the mouth of the harbour.

"Yes papa," she said. "Today, when I have completed the unloading of the supplies."

Erik was silent, feeling the anger of his daughter falling in love with an Englishman. This man was more of a personal foe than an enemy of war. What on earth would his brother Olof say? As the fishing vessel glided through the mouth of the harbour, Erik nodded to himself. He would play along with Anna and get to know more about the English captain and why he had come to his warehouse asking questions about his crew. He could very well be the captain of the frigate who had stopped his vessel over a week ago.

And on the other hand, conceding to Anna's desire to meet her Englishman would strengthen the bond between father and daughter and allow him to pick up on any information about the captain and his movements she may innocently drop his way. Pleased that she had chosen not to lie to him, he looked empathetically towards her. "Very well," he said.

Nils jumped onto the quay, wrapping the boat's docking rope around a wooden mooring. "Drop the ramp, Gustav," he called, "General Quigley's waiting here!"

Chuckling, Erik nodded to the harbour official who had checked the bogus order of fish he had brought over the evening Jacques had appeared on the quay. Sweating profusely, the obese administrator waddled aboard, shouting out pompously that as his time was very precious, they should begin the tallying. Anna was pleased to oblige, wanting to get the job done as quickly as possible. Finalising his inspection, he signed the tally sheets and then shuffled away in the direction of the garrison's canteen, pausing every so often to gasp for breath and wipe the perspiration from his brow.

With the fishing boat securely moored and Anna busy with Nils and Gustav unloading the supplies, Erik and Olof slipped away in the direction of the stony track that led up to the field of long grass and the forest trail that wound its way to Jacob's cabin.

Locating the hidden track between the trees, the two brothers picked their way along the twisting trail suddenly pulling up at the sound of someone chopping wood from a clearing a short distance ahead. Inching forward, they followed the sound, quickly coming to a halt as a voice hollered out, "I know you're there. Come out now and show yourselves."

Peering through the branches, Erik nudged Olof, grinning at the picture of Jacob staring at the trees and raising his axe menacingly.

Smiling, they moved out into the open.

"We weren't spying on you Jacob, far from it," said Erik, offering him his outstretched hand.

"Ha, good to see you back," said Jacob, picking up a full basket of logs. "And good to see you too Olof, my old friend. Come on back to the cabin and see my two long staying guests, they'll be pleased to see you Erik and to hear the news you've brought."

Jacques and Pierre looked up in surprise as Jacob showed Erik and Olof into the cabin. Pleased to see them, they quickly cleared the table while Jacob opened a flagon of ale. Swilling out five mugs, he indicated to Pierre to pull up the old sea chest for someone to sit on, there only being four chairs set round the table. Toasting each other with the ale, Erik cleared his throat,

"You're probably wondering why Olof is here with me," he said, looking at each in turn. "Well, for a long time now we've been waiting for the chance to take up arms against the British, so we're both here to offer you our help when the invasion begins. But before I go into that, let me give you General Bonard's answer to your plan that I put to him. The meeting Pascale and I had with the General and Commandant Joubert went very well. After listening to what I had to say, they spent some time discussing it and then agreed to implement it into the overall planning of the invasion. Magnus, you are to return to Danzig with me in three days with detailed information of the strength of the British naval garrison. Per, you are to remain here with Jacob as you had planned. Now, listen carefully and I will relate the exact instructions that General Bonard has asked me to convey to you."

When Erik had finished, Jacob looked towards Pierre,

"You and Pascale must wait with the marines aboard their ship until we have lit the beacons on the cove. Only then can you bring them in. We can't light the beacons until we have somehow disabled the British longboat that patrols the coast there. We've established the times it passes the cove, so now we must think of a way of immobilising it."

"Gentlemen," interrupted Erik. "That sounds like a job for Olof and me!"

"Yes of course," said Jacob, nodding. "That would answer a nagging question that has been on my mind for several days. An idea is already forming in my mind."

"We would need to see the cove first, Jacob," said Olof, looking towards his brother.

"Fine," replied Jacob. "How about now. The weather's good and it's not even mid-morning yet. We can all go, and while we're there we'll show you the cave and the entrance to the tunnel."

"One last thing before we leave," said Erik. "Have any of you heard of Captain James Carey based here at the British naval garrison? He commands one of the British warships, a frigate I believe."

"He's the captain who interrogated Pascale and arranged for him to be shot," said Jacob. "Pascale told us all about him."

"Yes, that's him," said Pierre. "I also saw him through the little window of the fisherman's hut on the quay, the morning Jacob and I crept around the back of the hut to listen to him questioning Pascale. In fact, Pascale mentioned his name on one occasion during the questioning."

"Well, they obviously didn't execute Pascale," said Erik. "Did he talk?"

"No," said Jacob, "we rescued him before he could tell them anything."

"Well, he didn't mention that at our meeting with General Bonard," commented Erik. "So, this Captain Carey seems to be quite an important voice in the affairs of the British garrison."

"Absolutely," said Jacob, "and highly thought of by the commander of the garrison, Commodore Percival."

"Interesting," muttered Erik, thinking of his conversation with Anna.

Erik and Olof followed Jacob and the two French spies through the forest and down under the overhanging foliage until they reached the narrow pathway that twisted its way towards the row of sheer granite cliffs and the pebbly cove lying beneath it.

Standing near the water's edge Erik studied the lie of jagged rocks stretching far along the coastline. "This seems to be the only opening for any small craft wishing to land on this part of the island. There's no possibility of any vessel coming ashore to a point further along."

"Definitely looks like it," said Olof, looking towards Jacob and the two French spies. "So, this is where the three of you saw the British longboat stop on the nights you were keeping watch here?"

"Yes," answered Jacob. "They approached the cove from about six metres out to sea, avoiding the clusters of dangerous rocks submerged back there. There's a clear straight line from here out to sea where there are no rocks lying under the water."

"We'll do it, Jacob," said Erik, grinning. "Just before the hour of ten on the night of the invasion, we'll be waiting for it, just off here in the dark. As soon as we see the lights of their lanterns we'll drop sail, and with a good wind head straight for them. I can see from here that the seabed is shelving, so six metres offshore will be fine for our vessel. They won't know what hit them."

"Any survivors will obviously swim for the cove," said Jacob. "But we'll be waiting for them. We'll finish them off as they stagger up over the shingle.

Then, we'll light the beacons."

"We'll wait onboard the fishing boat after sinking the British longboat," continued Erik. "When the marines have landed on the cove, Magnus can use one of their boats to row out and pick up Olof and me. Nils and Gustav will remain on the boat. Olof and I want to be part of the attack."

"We'll be going through the tunnel by then," said Jacob, "but use the narrow path that runs along the side of the shoreline and up through the forest. You know the one, Magnus. At the top where the track joins the main forest path wait for us there. Once we're through the tunnel and assembled we shouldn't be long behind you."

"Just signal us with three shades of your lantern and I'll row out and get you," said Pierre.

"Good, but now we must be going," said Erik. "My daughter and our two crew members will be wondering where we are. Magnus, in three days, be ready to depart for Danzig. Jacob knows the rendezvous point. Olof and I will return on the day the supplies are due, a week today. It will be one week before the invasion, so it would be a good idea for us to meet up in your cabin, Jacob. Then, we can discuss anything we may have forgotten to talk about today."

"Good idea," said Jacob, "we'll be waiting for you."

Anna saw him standing a little way past the mooring where Erik's boat bobbed up and down on a gentle swell. Coming out of the quartermaster's storehouse her heart jumped as she watched him looking up and down the quay. Dressed in his uniform of a ship's captain but without a hat, he cut a dashing figure standing alone in the mid-morning sunshine, a small kit bag slung over his shoulder. She wanted to run to him, to throw her arms around him, but controlling her impulses she steadied herself and began to walk over to where he was waiting.

"James," she called, a jubilant smile spreading across her face as she saw him raise his arm to give her a wave. Not caring who might be watching, she took a deep breath then picking up her skirts she ran joyously towards him, her heart jumping again as she saw him sprinting along the quay towards her.

"Well," he said laughing as they came together. "I've never had a greeting as lovely as that. It's so good to see you again, Anna."

"I've never run to greet anyone like that before," said Anna. "You're quite privileged Captain Carey. I guess it's because I've been longing for this moment. I'm so happy."

"Come on," he said, "up there on the highest point is where we can be alone.

I've brought some food and wine, and as it's a beautiful day the view from up there will be exceptional."

Laughing and chatting happily with each other, they left the quay making their way towards the stony path that led up to the island's highest point. Finding themselves alone on the steep ascent, James took Anna's hand, the intimate encircling of their hands sending them private messages of their deep longing for each other. Halfway up he stopped, and with a bird's eye view of the scene below he pointed out the miniature outline of his ship anchored outside the mouth of the harbour.

Anna gazed at the spectacle below, the expanse of sea glistening far out to the horizon. She felt James' hand slip out of hers and as she turned, he took her in his arms. Trembling, she closed her eyes as their lips finally met, the kiss they had both yearned for since their brief encounter on that fateful day at sea. Not wanting to break the magic of the moment she held him close, breathing heavily with the emotion she was feeling. It was then she realised he had captured her heart. As they gazed at each other tenderly, she knew there could never be another to replace him. Joining hands once again, they continued their climb up the rough hilly track, silently relishing the blissful elation they were both feeling.

Keeping well-away from the heavy guns placed to overlook the harbour, James found a quiet spot next to a cluster of windswept trees, high up on the northern end of the peak. Dropping his kit bag on a patch of grass next to a heap of boulders, they scrambled up to the top of the highest one. Bracing themselves against the wind, James wrapped an arm around Anna, gently pulling her in close. Scrunching up his eyes, he pointed out the craggy silhouette of the Swedish coast lying far away over the water.

"If you look really closely and squint your eyes," he said, pointing out over the water to the dark coastline, "you can see the harbour at Nogersund. There, right opposite us, that little inlet."

Anna screwed up her eyes following the direction of James' pointing finger.

"I can't see it," she said, squinting harder. "There are lots of little inlets along the coast. How do you know that one is Nogersund?"

"Ah," said James, smiling, "I've looked at it a thousand times from here and from my ship, picturing you over there in my mind's eye. I know that little inlet so well."

With the wind blowing through her long auburn hair, she turned and wrapping her arms around him she drew him in close finding his tongue with hers and kissing him with all the passion that was welling up inside her. They held each other close, bewitched by the moment and accepting that fate was the tailor of it all.

"James," she said softly, releasing her hold, "am I your first love? Tell me all about yourself. I want to know from the time you were a boy to now."

"I will Anna," he said, stroking her hair, "but first, come and eat the lunch I have brought."

They climbed down from the top of the windswept peak to the bottom of the row of boulders and seeing a sheltered spot, they dropped down onto the soft grass growing beneath them. Giggling, Anna pushed James onto his back and straddling him she began to kiss him passionately. Holding her, he responded to her kisses, his hands moving slowly up under her gown to explore the softness of her thighs.

"Oh James," she whispered, her breath coming in shortened pants. "Not yet, please."

James smiled at her, stroking the side of her cheek. "Of course, Anna," he said softly. "Now, let me up and I'll unpack the food. Oh, and I've got something for you."

Sitting up and smoothing her gown, Anna watched him retrieve the kit bag he had left under one of the boulders, her heart jumping as she saw him look back over his shoulder to give her a special smile. Kneeling opposite her, he opened the strings taking out a freshly baked loaf and a small side of ham. Next came a bottle of wine and two crystal glasses.

"My!" said Anna, showing her surprise, "I am truly honoured captain! Now you are really spoiling me. Crystal glasses from the captain's table no doubt."

"Yes, nothing but the best for you my dearest," he said, leaning over and kissing her softly.

"Is that it?" she said, her eyebrows raised questioningly.

"Yes, why?" said James, chuckling.

"Now, I do have something for you Anna," he said, reaching inside the bag and gently extracting a single red rose. Looking into her eyes he smiled and handing her the rose he kissed her outstretched hand. "A rose that grows only in the early spring. A symbol of eternal love, Anna."

Anna took the rose from his hand. Enraptured by his words, she held the rose closely to her breast, her eyes radiating the love she was feeling for him.

"And now you're going to tell me all about your boyhood and the following years that eventually led you here," she said, dropping her head to smell the rose.

"But first we eat and drink," said James, handing her one of the crystal glasses. "Then I'll tell my story. And yes, Anna Gunnarsson, you are my first and only love. Now tell me what you think of this wine."

Anna listened as James recounted the events of his life, from his school years to his passing out from The Royal Naval Academy in Portsmouth and his first commission aboard HMS Leviathan. As he talked about his home life in England and his adventures at sea, Anna was spellbound, her love for him growing ever stronger. His good looks and courteous manners showed him to be a gentleman and as he came to an end, she flung her arms around him, kissing him and holding him close to her.

"I feel I've known you forever, James," she said. "I'm sure we are soulmates, rediscovered after an absence in time."

"We certainly are," said James, looking lovingly at her. "The moment our eyes locked that day out at sea, I knew. Since that time, there hasn't been a day I haven't thought of you."

"When can we meet again, James? I can't stand the thought of not being with you. But there is one problem, and I don't know how to get over it."

James listened as Anna told him about her father and his hatred of the British. He nodded understandingly when she told him about her grandmother being the reason for her father's sympathetic leanings towards the French. But his ears pricked up when she mentioned the time he had recently spent away from home, returning from Danzig in the early hours of that morning. He began to wonder why her father had been in a city governed by the French, when it suddenly occurred to him that the two elusive deck hands on her father's fishing vessel were the French spies who had sprung Andre Pascale. Her father had to be the link in transporting them to the island. He wondered who the other link on the island could be.

"Anna," he said, taking her hand, "it's going to take some time before your father accepts us and I'm not going to lose you, not for anything. We're building up our defences in the harbour and increasing our schedules of patrolling the sea lanes. My ship has another liberty in three days as we are out at sea tomorrow for two days and nights. So, could we meet three days from now. But not here, I'll come to Nogersund. Shall we say early, at the hour of nine on the quay? I'll wear civilian clothing then."

"I'll be there," said Anna. "We can have the whole day. Now, the sun looks as though it has moved very much towards the west. I should be going James. My father and uncle are meeting with some fishermen on the island and should be returning to our fishing boat soon. I don't want them to find me not there."

They made their way back to the harbour, stopping in the shadows of a thicket of trees at the bottom of the steep stony track. Taking her in his arms, he kissed her gently while she repeated her love for him. Holding her close, he whispered her name again and again, confirming his love for her.

He watched her from the cover of the trees, making her way along the quay to her father's fishing vessel. As she stepped onto the ramp she turned, and gazing back towards where he stood, she kissed the rose in her hand and with a wave disappeared onto the boat. James stepped back into the shadows of the overhanging clump of trees thinking deeply about what he had realised about her father. It was all beginning to make sense. He was the courier of messages leaving the island for the French in Danzig, his fishing boat being the means of relaying spies to the island. If Andre Pascale was still on the island, then it would be Anna's father who would take him off, together with the spies. The cove and the tunnel in the cave had to be central to a French invasion, but when would it happen? Without any evidence he could not arrest Anna's father, but should he be found with Pascale and the two French spies he could then be apprehended. He would discuss this with Commodore Percival and urge a surveillance on Gunnarsson's next visit to the island.

Hopefully, the Swede would then lead them to the island's resident spy master. In the meantime, the British would keep up their search for Pascale and the two French spies.

Leaving the cover of the trees, James hurried along the quay towards the berth that accommodated Commodore Percival's ship of the line. He stopped to look across the quay for a sign of Anna on the Gunnarsson's fishing boat but seeing no sign of her on deck he guessed she had to be down in the hold. He was about to move on when the sight of two heavily - built men stopping at the vessel's gangplank drew his attention.

Erik and Olaf stopped at the side of the fishing vessel pleased to see that Nils and Gustav had made it ready for departure. Erik could see no sign of Anna onboard and hoped she was busying herself down in the hold, but angry thoughts of her disregarding his wishes and flippantly enjoying herself with her Englishman somewhere on the island, flashed through his mind.

As they approached the gangplank his eyes picked out the figure of an English naval captain standing on the opposite quay scrutinising his boat. He was without a hat with a kit bag slung nonchalantly over his shoulder. A deep frown quickly spread across Erik's features. Standing rigidly still and gritting his teeth in enmity he stared over at the figure on the opposite quay, knowing he was looking into the eyes of his daughter's lover, the English naval captain, James Carey.

For a minute, the two men stared across the harbour at each other until Erik turned and made his way over to a wooden post holding the fishing boat's mooring rope. Unhitching it he threw the length onto the vessel's stern, then swinging round he glared over in James' direction, drawing a finger slowly across his throat.

Ignoring the gesture, James gave a grimace of disdain, knowing there could never be any amicable relationship between the two of them. He watched the fishing boat snake away from its mooring, anxious that Anna would not incur any of her father's anger. His eyes followed the vessel until it slipped out of the mouth of the harbour, its sail catching a stiff wind and setting it firmly onto its course towards the distant inlet of Nogersund.

24

Jean-Luc reached for the brandy decanter on the finely polished side table next to his desk. Refilling Henri Joubert's glass, he sat back and, raising his glass, looked across at the commander of Danzig's naval personnel.

"To a successful invasion, Henri," he said, smiling at his colleague. "I trust you are well-prepared?"

"Yes, to a successful invasion Jean-Luc," replied Henri, knocking back the brandy in one mouthful. "The invasion fleet is ready, and a detachment of marines are standing by waiting for instructions of when to go ashore before the main frontal attack on the harbour begins. On your orders," he said, smiling at Jean-Luc, "Lieutenant Pascale has been attached to them, as Lieutenant Renaud will be on his return."

"We'll have a full report from Lieutenant Renaud regarding the British strength on the island," said Jean-Luc. "My guess is that the British will have concentrated all their power around the harbour and left the southern part of the island undefended. When our marines exit the tunnel Gunnarsson told us about and capture their big cannons, victory will be quick. Without control of their guns, it will be impossible for the British to ward off our frontal attack and with Admiral von Krassow's flotilla supporting our windward formation, British resistance will be over swiftly."

"Our last intelligence showed them to have a handful of frigates and two sloops-of war," said Henri, "and there is their ship of the line."

"I doubt if they have the manpower to use that one," said Jean-Luc. "As to their small flotilla of warships, we'll wait for Lieutenant Renaud to bring us up to date. Whatever they throw at us it won't be enough, we'll sweep them aside in the blink of an eye."

"Our invasion plans are set for two weeks," said Henri. "I think some form of reconnaissance would benefit. Just to see if the British have placed any form of defence out at sea. If they have, then I doubt Lieutenant Renaud would know about it."

"You could be right, Henri," said Jean-Luc. "The British navy is good at setting traps like that. If they have, then I expect they'll have placed a frigate or two at settings southeast and southwest of the harbour. They know we'll be coming up from the south, so a couple of warships lying in wait for us could inflict some damage. They'll very likely be patrolling that area now. I'll order two of our corvettes to reconnoitre immediately. They'll cover an area where I am sure they'll find something."

Henri reached for his brandy, thinking seriously about Jean-Luc's suggestion.

"All very well Jean-Luc," said Henri, "but what if they spy a frigate or two and the British engage them?"

"Our ships will be on reconnaissance Henri, with orders not to engage. Should they see a British warship from a distance, then they record its position and get the hell out of it. We only want to know where they are and the numbers in their flotilla. Now, if you just sit back and enjoy another glass of this excellent cognac, I'll arrange for the two ships to depart immediately."

Christina Gunnarsson sat listening to her husband's account of his conversation with Anna as he breakfasted before leaving for a day's fishing with his crew. Shaking her head in disbelief at Erik's suggestion of their daughter's treachery in disregarding the family's feelings towards the British, she listened with surprise as Erik told her of Anna's total infatuation with the English captain.

"Anna would never betray our trust in her," she said, sternly. "I know our daughter would always put her family first."

"She thinks she's in love, Christina," he said, looking anxiously at his wife.

"Perhaps she is," said Christina, trying to see the situation through her daughter's eyes. "It was bound to happen sooner or later. She's twenty-one and a beautiful young woman."

"But not to an Englishman," said Erik. "Remember what they did to my mother."

"Yes, and we can never forget that. But I doubt if this English captain was even there then. Anna's not a senseless person, Erik. She's our daughter, and it seems she has found love with this English captain. Living here in Nogersund she hasn't had the chance of meeting anyone who could be worthy of her. Uneducated fishermen have surrounded her since she was a teenager and, thank God, she never showed any interest in them."

"Bah!" uttered Erik. "I know I can never accept him; however hard Anna may try. I saw him yesterday, watching us from the other quay as we were about to leave Hanö. He'd been with Anna for most of the day, I know that."

"Did he say anything?" asked Christina.

"No, we just glared at each other for a while until I untied the mooring rope and then we sailed."

"It's early now and she's sleeping," said Christina, "but when she awakes, I'm going to take her out. As we walk, I'll encourage her to tell me all about him. I'll listen and make no comment. She'll open up to me, I'm sure."

"Try and get her to tell you anything that he may have mentioned about the British defences of the harbour, and the numbers of marines manning their defensive positions."

"I shall not Erik. I would never break the trust between us."

"In two days, Olof and I have an important task," said Erik, looking up from his breakfast. "We'll be away for the day and night. You remember those two Frenchmen I brought here nearly two weeks ago?"

"Yes, French agents bound for Hanö," said Christina, looking seriously at her husband.

"Shush," hissed Erik, "Anna doesn't know about them being agents and I want to keep it that way. Well, their time is up on the island, or rather one of them, and Olof and I are contracted to take him back to Danzig in two days."

"What about the other one?" asked Christina.

"He's staying there with Jacob, you remember Jacob Forsberg, don't you?"

"That old rascal!" said Christina. "Is he still spying on the British for the French?"

"He is," said Erik. "Now, what I'm about to tell you Christina must go no further than these walls. Do you promise me?"

"Of course," said Christina, looking at him curiously.

"The French are going to invade Hanö in two weeks' time."

"You mean there will be a battle for the island?"

"Yes," said Erik. "The French are almost ready with their preparations and are waiting for vital information of the British defences from the one we're going to return."

"When will the invasion take place?" asked Christina, uneasily.

"You must not tell anyone of this Christina," said Erik, seriously.

"When is it, Erik?" pressed Christina.

"March 31st at midnight," said Erik.

Christina sat staring at her husband as he got up to go.

"Remember, not a word Christina, not a word. Now I must go. We should be back all being well, late afternoon. You can tell me how you fared with Anna later this evening."

"Erik, you're not going to involve yourself with this invasion," said Christina.

"The time has come Christina," said Erik, letting himself out of the backdoor.

Christina rose from the table, a frown creasing her features. She was sure that he and Olof would involve themselves in the attack against the British as vengeance for the murder of their mother. Clearing the breakfast plates away from the table and with her thoughts centred on the news she'd just heard from Erik; she was completely unaware of her daughter standing out of sight in the hallway listening to everything that had been said.

Creeping silently back up the stairs, Anna slipped back into her bedroom, closing the door gently behind her, her mind full of what she had overheard. Her first thought was to inform James of the date of the invasion. She knew he would be in the thick of the action when it came, and if she told him, then he would be well prepared.

Frightful fears began to creep into her mind.

I can't lose him, she thought. *I could never live without him. But if I tell him, and papa finds out that I'd been listening to what he told mama about the invasion, then I dread what he'd do.*

"Anna, wake up," a call came from outside her bedroom.

"It's a lovely morning and I thought we could go for an early walk; just the two of us."

Pulling herself together, Anna called to her mother, "Yes mama, I'm awake. Ok."

Tiny droplets of dew, balanced precariously on the leaves of the bushes that lined the rough track leading from their house to the harbour below, glistened in the early morning sun. Anna stopped halfway down the track to shade her eyes. Focussing on the open sea beneath her, she squinted across its wide expanse, hoping to see signs of a British frigate. Nothing came to sight except for a small dot on the horizon suggesting a ship making its way to some distant point. Anna wondered if it could be HMS Hector, but a call from her mother below compelled her to hurry on down the track.

"I know of a good spot," said Christina, pointing to a narrow pathway leading away from the harbour. "Come on."

The path led them up a narrow incline bordered on each side by lines of silver birches, the long slender trees ascending rigidly like rows of white lances. At the top of the path, they stopped to admire the panorama. A rich landscape of rolling green pastures stretched before them, like a great patchwork hemmed together by rows of towering birch trees. Flocks of sheep grazed peacefully on the sloping meadows, while high up in a clear blue-sky a wedge of cranes flew closely together bound for their mass gatherings at the great lake of Hornborga in Västergotland. Looking out over the pastures, Christina pointed towards the top of a grassy hill rising steeply from behind a row of trees.

"Come on, let's climb that knoll. There's a wooden bench at the top for walkers like us."

Breathing heavily from their climb, they settled themselves on the bench that afforded a sweeping view over the lush countryside below.

"Anna, I want to ask you about your English captain," said Christina, looking at her daughter tenderly, "will you talk to me about him?"

Anna didn't respond. Her mind was flitting from what she had overheard earlier to whether she could confide her feelings about James to her mother. She supposed that whatever she told her would be reported back to her father later, the two of them trying their hardest to dissuade her from any future with her Englishman. But, if she could feel that she could genuinely trust her mother's sincerity in understanding how she felt, then she would gladly open her heart to her.

"Before you say anything Anna, let me tell you about the problems I had with my parents when I first met your father."

Anna listened with surprise as her mother recounted the strict upbringing she'd had as a young girl, and of the marriage her father had planned for her.

"Your father came on the scene one Sunday, after I had attended chapel with my parents. We lived in Karlskrona then, and it being a sunny morning my mother suggested we take a ride in our carriage along the promenade by the harbour. There were several carriages like ours trundling along by the sea when the right wheel of our carriage suddenly came loose and decided to go its separate way. I can remember the terrible grating sound as our carriage hit the ground on its right side. My father was desperately trying to rein in the horse when I felt myself tumbling out of the carriage and landing awkwardly in the dirt. I had lost my bonnet and my skirts were up over my head, I must have looked a sight! Well, before I could get myself up, I sensed strong arms lifting me to my feet and when I looked around, I found myself gazing into the smiling face of your father. Something triggered an emotion in me as I stared at his handsome features. I noticed he was looking at me in a similar way. Much later, we both said that it had felt like time had stopped for a moment, to allow fate to play its hand."

Anna smiled at her mother and taking her hand she looked into her eyes. "That's exactly the feeling I had mama when I chanced to look up from papa's fishing boat on the crossing over to Hanö and saw James looking down at me from his ship, as we passed. I felt it again when I saw him in our warehouse, the time he and his lieutenant came looking for papa."

"Well," said Christina, "do you want me to finish my story?"

"Oh, please mama. You've never mentioned this to me or Lars. In fact, you've never spoken about our grandparents."

"Your father retrieved the wheel to our carriage and offered to repair it there and then," continued Christina. "My father was happy to go along with his offer and we waited while your father went to fetch his tools and some extra help. He returned with his brother, your uncle Olof, and the two of them lifted the carriage, one holding it up while the other slid the wheel back on. They must have been super strong to have managed it. But fix it, they did. When they had finished, your father came to me and we chatted in a relaxed way, both of us laughing when he reminded me of how I had looked when he had helped me up. It was then that the trouble started."

"Do you mean with your father?" asked Anna.

"Yes, with both of them," said Christina looking away from Anna. "My father and my mother."

"What happened mama?"

"My father didn't like the way I was laughing and chatting with your father. He said it was sinful to laugh with a strange man, as it would encourage him to have improper thoughts. I was told to get back into the carriage, and without a word of thanks to your father or uncle, my father flicked the reins, and the horse pulled us away. I was so embarrassed and angry, although I was too frightened of my father to express it. But I remember your father was on my mind all the way back home. While we'd been chatting, he told me he and his brother were fishermen from Nogersund, and they would be returning to Karlskrona in a few days. I made up my mind there and then that I would go back to the harbour when they returned and see him again, regardless of what my father thought."

Christina giggled to herself over her last comment.

"It was the best thing I did," she said, smiling at her daughter. "I went back, and he was there. Every time they returned to Karlskrona I was there at the harbour. We had fallen in love, Anna. But the time was coming when I had to make a choice. My father would never agree to our relationship. He had arranged for me to marry the assistant pastor of the chapel. He was about ten years older than me and had bad breath. Ugh, I could never have married him."

Anna chuckled at her mother's grimace of abhorrence.

"Well," said Christina, "after an awful argument one afternoon with my father, he told me that either I marry the pastor or leave home. So, I left home."

"But that was terrible, mama. What about your mother?" asked Anna. "Didn't she try to understand you?"

"My mother was a cold-blinkered woman, who obeyed my father in every way. She told me I was a sinful harlot for loving your father and wanted nothing more to do with me. I tried to get her to understand how I felt, but it was impossible."

"So, what did you do when you left home, mama?"

"I left with nothing, only the clothes I had on. Your father was waiting for me at the harbour, and we sailed away to Nogersund. The rest you know."

Anna smiled at her mother and looking directly into her eyes she told her how fate had opened its doors for her and how James was everything she would ever want.

"You know your father will take a long time to accept him, Anna," said Christina. "But whatever happens we will never tell you to leave home. I fully understand your feelings, it's the same that I felt for your father all those years ago. Your father and your uncle Olof have very bitter feelings for the British. I know that James had nothing to do with the death of your grandmother, but he wears the uniform of those who did, and that's all they can see. It will take time Anna."

"Maybe we won't have time," said Anna, looking far away over the treetops.

"What do you mean?" asked Christina, warily.

Not wanting her mother to know that she knew about the planned French invasion of Hanö, she quickly side-stepped her mother's question.

"Well, we may not have that much time together because he could be sent back to England at any time," she said. "Navy life, mama."

"I'll speak to your father and try to soften his thoughts," said Christina.

"But be careful what you may say about James' movements when your father is present."

Anna knew exactly what her mother meant. What she had overheard that morning meant only one thing, her father was a spy and a courier for the French. When the attack on the island came, he and Olof would be there, looking to kill as many British as they could.

Her mind was made up. In two days she would let James know everything she had overheard.

25

James flicked open his telescope sweeping it an arc over the choppy waters surrounding HMS Hector. The frigate continued to plough its way further south in its quest to engage and destroy any French vessel probing the area.

With orders to follow a bearing south by southeast for twenty miles and patrol the area for two days and nights until relieved at midnight on the second night, HMS Hector had left harbour the day before. An accompanying frigate was to patrol an area ten miles southwest of Hector's zone. Commodore Percival was creating a constant surveillance of the path he believed the French fleet would take in the forthcoming attack on the island. Prior to the fleet arriving in these waters, he knew the French would send ships to reconnoitre the area. Orders were to destroy and sink any French surveillance vessel seen in their zone. Should the French fleet come into sight then they were to make speed back to harbour with news of the impending attack, and not engage any part of the fleet on their own.

The previous day had been uneventful with no sightings of any vessels. Four battle drills were played out, with emphasis on constant improvement of speed and precision firing from the gun crews. Each rehearsal had been more than satisfactory.

Closing his scope, James gazed out to sea as recollections of the day he and Anna had spent together filled his mind. A feeling of utter joy overwhelmed him at the thought of the intimate time they had expressed their love for each other. He knew there could never be anyone but her. A sudden melancholy, like a dark cloud blotting out the sun, flashed before him. The image of her father staring at him across the quay and drawing a finger across his throat, reminded him of the adversity they had for each other. He hated to think that should the animosity between them deepen, Anna would find herself in a situation where she would have to choose between the two of them. The dark cloud quickly passed with thoughts of a well-earned liberty with Anna the following day. Hector would be relieved at midnight and with a fair wind they would anchor back outside the harbour by two in the morning. A good sleep and then off to Nogersund the following morning.

"Sail, on the portside bow!" yelled the lookout, high up on the top sail yard.

The clanging of the frigate's bell snapped James out of his thoughts.

"Mr. Sutherland, Mr. Devonshire," he yelled, turning his attention to the forecastle. "To the quarterdeck gentlemen."

"Two ships captain," said Dan joining James, with Richard Devonshire following behind.

"Yes Dan, you're right," said James, looking through his telescope. "About a mile off our position, I'd say. Observations Mr. Devonshire."

"They're French sir," said Richard, his scope to his right eye. "Two corvettes fully rigged. Twenty guns a piece. They're watching us to see if we'll engage."

"Of that we will," said James, snapping shut his telescope. "Our orders are to sink any Frenchie we see in this zone. Two points to port Mr. Sturrock. Full sail now Mr. Nark. Call to battle stations Mr. Sutherland. Mr. Piper, prepare all guns."

"They're turning captain," said Richard. Looks like they're going to make a run for it."

James flipped open his telescope training it on the two French ships.

"They might be nippy little sloops," he said, "but they won't outrun our Hector."

"Permission to leave the quarterdeck and prepare the sick bay, captain," said Edmund Kirkland.

"Granted Mr. Kirkland," replied James. "Hopefully, there'll be few casualties on our part."

"Captain, we're gaining on them," said Richard, closing his scope and turning towards James.

"Shall we fire a warning shot, captain," suggested Dan. "They might surrender as they can see we're gaining on them."

"No," replied James. "This is the path the French fleet will take. They're surveillance ships, looking to see our strength and under orders to get back to their base immediately, should they be threatened. We'll engage and sink them, gentlemen."

"What about survivors, sir?" asked Dan.

"No prisoners gentlemen, on board or in the sea. My orders are clear."

"They're separating, sir," called Richard.

James flipped open his scope, levelling it on the two corvettes.

"A clever ploy," he muttered. "Separate, and while we engage one, the other slips away. Mr. Sutherland, focus on the one that's just turned away from the other, on the starboard side. How low in the water is she?"

Dan squinted through his telescope. "She's travelling light sir. Her waterline is almost clearly visible. She must be carrying only powder with a minimum of shot."

"Thank you, Mr. Sutherland," said James, grinning. "Mr. Sturrock, steer a course for the stern of the Frenchie on our starboard side. Take us right up her arse, then when I say, make a swift turn to starboard."

"Aye, aye, right up her arse, captain" chuckled Davey Sturrock.

"Mr. Piper, to the quarterdeck," yelled James to his master gunner.

"Captain?" said Thomas Piper, arriving on the quarterdeck.

"The Frenchie that's just pulled away from the other on their starboard side, study her," said James, handing Thomas Piper his telescope. "Can you see her waterline?"

"Aye sir, she couldn't be carrying much in her armoury," replied Thomas.

"When we come within a sniff of her stern," said James, "we'll make a quick turn to starboard. With this wind we'll overtake her in seconds and as we broadside, give her all your shot. Not the masts Thomas, her belly. She's carrying twenty guns so the magazine below her waterline will be holding powder. Focus on her waterline. No ship of war leaves harbour with an empty powder magazine. Her captain will likely have orders not to engage, so her guns will not have been primed. Blow her out of the water Thomas."

"Aye, captain, that we will."

"Sir, we're gaining on her rapidly," said Richard Devonshire.

"Mr. Sutherland, monitor the other Frenchie, keep your eye on her even when we're firing our guns."

"She won't leave my sight captain," answered Dan, focussing his telescope on the other corvette.

"One hundred yards from her stern, captain," yelled Davey Sturrock.

"Hold her steady," called James. "Mr. Piper stand by, and on my command."

"Aye, aye, captain, standing by," yelled Thomas Piper.

"Fifty yards, captain," shouted Davey Sturrock.

James scanned the deck, satisfied his crew were ready for the approaching action. The wind whistling through the ratlines and the surging crash of the sea's swell against the ship's bow were the only sounds that carried around the deck.

"Twenty yards, captain," yelled Hector's helmsman.

"Now, Mr. Sturrock!" hollered James.

Davey Sturrock spun the ship's wheel, the crew standing fast as Hector lurched to the right in its turn. The French corvette loomed before them, parting to the left as Hector rode close to its broadside.

"Fire portside guns, Mr. Piper," bellowed James.

One after the other thirteen cannons opened fire on the corvette's starboard side, all aiming for the belly of the ship, the waterline bobbing above the choppy swell. In a flash Hector had passed the corvette, the wind filling its sails and driving it ahead of the French vessel. The sound of two explosions coming from the corvette brought a cheer from Hector's crew, but then an almighty blast from the corvette's magazine saw a curtain of fire envelop the doomed ship. Through the smoke they watched as the first of Jean-Luc's surveillance ships quickly disappeared beneath the sea's swell.

"Mr. Sutherland, have you the other Frenchie in sight," yelled James.

"I have sir," responded Dan. "She's pulled up ahead and assessing us. She's turning in our direction, captain, and making for our portside."

"She knows she can't outrun us," said James, flicking open his scope and training it on the remaining corvette. "She's not striking her colours, she intends to engage, contrary to what I thought. Mr. Piper, make ready portside. Mr. Sturrock, hold us steady. Prepare battle stations Mr. Sutherland."

"Mr. Nark," yelled Dan, "prepare for engagement."

"Aye, aye, sir," came the shout from Hector's boatswain. A series of shrill alerts from Bill Nark's whistle saw the crew draw cutlasses and prime muskets in readiness for the oncoming action.

"She's a hundred yards and coming at us with speed, captain. She intends broadside action," called Dan.

"And that's what she'll have," cried James, the adrenaline coursing through his veins. Hold her steady, Mr. Sturrock. On my command, Mr. Piper."

"Aye sir, ready for your command, captain," shouted Thomas Piper.

James squinted towards the French corvette amazed at its speed at such a short distance from commencing broadside action.

"Fifty yards, captain, and she's not manoeuvring for a raking position," said Dan.

"She's going to blast us for all she's worth," said James. "Her captain's in a fit of rage. Mr. Piper let her have it. Fire guns one, two, three and four. Shoot to kill, not their masts."

The two ships passed each other broadside with a crescendo of point-blank fire from their cannons. Twelve pounder cannon balls zipped over Hector's deck, narrowly missing all three masts. The intensive fire practice James had ordered from his gun-crew throughout their daily patrols quickly paid off.

Hector fired faster and more accurately than the French corvette, her eighteen-pounder cannon balls hammering the corvette's hull and screaming across her quarterdeck, killing her captain, and mortally wounding several officers. As Hector passed the stricken corvette, James yelled to Davey Sturrock.

"Turn her around, Mr. Sturrock, we're going back broadside again."

As the smoke cleared from the battle area it was clear that Hector had severely damaged the French corvette. Coming alongside, James viewed the devastation Hector had dealt upon the sloop. Wreckage from the corvette's deck lay dangling over her side while a mass of tangled rigging and broken pieces of mast covered the deck. A deathly creaking sound of wood and metal scraping together saw the ship's stern hanging limply over the water and swinging wildly in the wind.

"Bring us closer Mr. Sturrock," ordered James. "We're going to board her gentlemen. Dan, arrange to lash our ship to the corvette and then drop the boarding ramp. Mr. Hatchet I want a boarding party of twenty men with you, and twenty with me, all armed. Mr. Sturrock, you'll assist Mr. Hatchet. There may be some resistance to us on board the corvette."

"Aye, aye, captain," cried Ned Hatchet, grinning at Davey Sturrock.

To the sounds of the boarding ramp crashing down onto the side of the French ship, James drew his sword and with a pistol in his other hand he turned to his two lieutenants. "With me Dan, and you Mr. Devonshire."

Leading his men across the ramp, James was the first onto the corvette's deck.

Scanning the devastation that met him, his eyes flashed towards the ship's quarterdeck. There were no officers in sight and only half of what used to be the quarterdeck remained. Through the smoke hovering over the deck, he made out a score of bodies lying amongst a scattering of severed limbs. Muffled cries and groans came from a few of the bodies, while the rest lay crumpled and twisted from where they had fallen.

The sound of a musket shot coming from the bow, followed by a loud bellowing in French quickly alerted James and his men. Looking through the smoke they made out a large group of armed men gathered by what was left of the foremast, gesticulating, and brandishing their weapons. They were obviously waiting for the best moment to launch an attack on the British boarding party. Glancing over his shoulder, James saw the last of Ned Hatchet's men appearing on the deck. Ned rounded them up and singled to James they were ready and waiting for him to give the order.

"With me," cried James, looking around at his men. "Mr. Sutherland, to my right. Mr. Devonshire, to my left."

The boarding party of British sailors raced across the deck towards the French, hollering their battle cry.

"For Hector," they yelled, raising their weapons, and crashing into their enemy.

The sound of cutlasses swishing through the air as they sliced into the flesh of the defiant French, filled the air. The crack of an occasional pistol shot going off, lost in the din of battle.

A swarthy looking Frenchman with his cutlass raised high rushed at James.

Turning to avoid the downward slash, James slipped on a pool of blood, falling face down onto the deck. Grinning, the French sailor positioned himself intent on taking James' head, when to his surprise, the end of a British officer's sword came shooting out from the front of his tunic. With his blood spurting in an arc, the Frenchman lurched forward, his eyes staring out in shock as he crumpled to the deck.

"Grab my hand, captain," said Richard Devonshire, holding out his hand.

James took the young lieutenant's hand, and as Richard pulled him up the figure of a huge French sailor, brandishing a thick wooden club, zoomed before them. In an instant James raised the pistol he was still clutching and, pointing it at the club wielding sailor pulled the trigger blowing half the Frenchman's face away. "I guess that makes us equal, Mr. Devonshire!"

"Indeed, it does sir," replied Richard with a grateful grin.

Looking around at the fight intensifying, James yelled to his men. "Don't spare any quarter. No prisoners."

Dan ran his sword through a young-looking sailor with a pigtail. Fighting off two Frenchmen who came at him with axes, he sliced the throat of one of them, then parrying the thrust of the other's axe he pivoted, swiftly running him through with the practised move of a fencing master.

Ned Hatchet was toppling bodies right, left and centre. With Davey Sturrock at his side, they wielded their cutlasses like scythes, chopping and dismembering any Frenchman who cared to take them on. James watched as Ned decapitated a dark-skinned Arab who came running at him swinging a scimitar. Then, as quickly as it had started, it was over. Apart from the groans of the wounded and dying, silence quickly descended over the corvette's deck.

Breathing heavily, James caught sight of Dan wiping streams of blood from his sword.

"Lieutenant Sutherland," he called. "How do you fare?"

"Just a scratch across one cheek, captain."

"Find Ned Hatchet and bring him to me."

"Aye, captain," replied Dan.

"Captain," said Richard, appearing at James' side. "Looks like we killed most of them sir. There are five over there who surrendered at the end."

James looked across the deck at the five survivors of the fight.

He knew what he'd have to do with them.

"Bring one of them to me," he said.

"Captain," said Ned Hatchet, coming alongside James. "We lost six of our men in the fight, sir."

"Instruct some of the men to recover their bodies, Ned. We'll take them back onboard Hector and give them a proper burial. When that's done, get back here."

Turning, James saw Richard returning with one of the French survivors, two of Hector's crew firmly holding the sailor's arms.

"This one speaks a little English, captain," said Richard.

James looked at the French sailor.

"Where are your officers?" he asked.

"Our captain is dead," said the sailor. "Killed by one of your cannon balls that destroyed our quarterdeck."

"And your other officers?"

The Frenchman shrugged his shoulders in the carefree way of the French.

"I saw our lieutenant being carried below after the quarterdeck was hit. We have no more officers, only the boatswain and helmsman who you have just killed in the fight. We have a surgeon, he's probably below with the wounded and dying."

"Very well," said James, turning to Richard. "Take him back to the other survivors and bind them together, then return to me."

"We have the bodies, captain," said Ned Hatchet, appearing at James' side.

"Have them taken aboard Hector now," said James. "Instruct whoever takes them to inform Mr. Kirkland that I have said they must lie in the sick quarters until we arrange the burial for them."

"Aye, aye, captain," said Ned, turning away.

"And Ned, get back here quickly when that's done."

"Captain," said Dan, coming alongside James. "The wounded and dying sir?"

"There is nothing we can do, Dan," said James looking around the deck at the dead and wounded. "They'll go down with their ship."

Dan looked at James seriously, knowing that this was a captain's dilemma after winning a battle at sea. This time, HMS Hector would not accommodate the wounded.

"And those prisoners, sir?"

"That is what I am trying to decide," said James. "We're not taking any prisoners with us. Now, accompany me below. I want to see the ship's surgeon and see if their lieutenant is still alive."

Sea water was slowly rising in the deck below. Although there was a gaping hole in the stern it was above sea level, but with the lapping of the sea outside, water was slurping its way through the hole and spreading at a rate throughout the lower deck. James and Dan squelched through the blood-red water, the screams, and cries of the wounded echoing around them.

Through an open door they saw whom they believed had to be the ship's surgeon, bending over a blood-stained table while sewing up a sailor's deep cut. Half a dozen wounded men lay in cots next to the table, moaning in their agony.

"I know you are there," said the surgeon in English, without looking up. "These men must be taken off this ship and attended to if they are to have any chance of living."

"I am Captain James Carey of His Majesty's Frigate HMS Hector," said James, looking at the surgeon. "Your ship is disabled and sinking. I am asking for your surrender and to accompany me to the upper deck."

"Can't you see I am busy, Captain?" said the surgeon.

"This is war sir," said James, looking at the surgeon angrily, "and you have lost your ship. You will accompany me, NOW."

Looking up at James, the surgeon sighed and cutting the thread he nodded. Reaching for his jacket he followed James and Dan out of the stinking bilge and back to the upper deck.

Ned Hatchet had finished organising the transfer of the six dead British sailors to the frigate and was waiting on deck for his captain.

"Mr. Hatchet," said James, appearing with Dan and the French surgeon. Take this prisoner over to where the other five are standing and bind him.

"But captain," said the surgeon, looking at James. "I am an officer and a gentleman, and should be acknowledged as so."

Turning to face him, James quelled the anger rising in him. "That may be so," he said, sternly, "but you are now my prisoner sir, and you will do as I say. Now, where is your lieutenant?"

"He died from his wounds," replied the surgeon.

"Carry on, Mr. Hatchet," said James, turning towards Ned. "Mr. Devonshire, when the prisoners are secure you will escort them onto the deck of our ship and leave them there securely bound."

"Aye, aye, captain," said Richard, raising an eyebrow in curiosity.

"Dan, gather our men and return to the ship. I want to be away from here."

"And their wounded, sir?" asked Dan.

"Leave them where they are, lieutenant. That's an order."

With dusk slowly setting over the choppy waters, James stood alone on Hector's quarterdeck staring out at the wreck of the French corvette. Cries from the French wounded drifted hauntingly over the sea, a ghostly silence creeping over the British frigate.

"Mr Sturrock," he called, "take us out fifty yards, hold her steady opposite the corvette. Portside, Mr. Sturrock."

"Aye, aye, captain," replied Davey Sturrock.

"Mr. Piper, load portside guns one, two, three and four. On my command you will sink that French ship. Is that clear?"

"Aye, captain. That is clear sir,"

Davey Sturrock brought the British frigate fifty yards from the doomed corvette, her portside guns primed and ready. Silence reigned across the frigate's deck: all eyes focused on the French ship. Above the sound of the sea breaking against Hector's side, a desperate cry for help drifted across the water.

"Fire all guns, Mr. Piper," commanded James.

Hector's four cannons fired at point-blank range into the side of the ill-fated ship, sending it with the bodies of the dead and wounded to the bottom of the sea.

"Mr. Nark," yelled James. "Prepare one of the longboats for winching down. Place six canisters of water in her. Mr. Hatchet, bring me the prisoners."

The five French sailors and the surgeon stood looking at James, disbelief written all over their faces. "You know that we will have a very slim chance of being found," said the surgeon.

"At least you will have that chance," said James, acknowledging Bill Nark's signal that the longboat was ready. "Escort the prisoners to the longboat Mr. Hatchet."

All eyes aboard the British warship watched the Frenchmen scramble into the longboat, the surgeon eying James with contempt.

"Winch them down, Mr. Nark," ordered James.

The screeching sound of the longboat being winched down grated out over the water, two of the prisoners reluctantly picking up the oars.

James watched them pulling away until they disappeared into the dusky light now forming over the water. Turning to his helmsman, he yelled out an order.

"Mr. Sturrock, three points to starboard. Continue on a northerly bearing, north by northwest. Full sail Mr. Nark, we have an important rendezvous in a few hours and six burials to carry out before we leave this damned zone."

26

A timber-built jetty, artfully concealed between the rocks on the eastern side of the island, poked its way out to sea beneath the sheer cliffs that rose to meet the dense forest that topped its high ground. Sitting on a rock next to the wooden pier, Jacob and Pierre stared at the swells of water lapping against the thick underside supports.

"You see that narrow goat's path snaking its way up the side of that cliff face," said Jacob, turning and pointing to a thin line twisting up the side of a cliff. "That's where I led the search party that chased me across those rocks. They followed me to the very top and then into the densest part of the forest. I set a few false trails for them and then led them down a dead-end path until they were hopelessly lost. They were lucky to find their way out."

Pierre squinted over at the cliff face, his eyes moving slowly up the narrow track, picturing Jacob scrambling up the dusty incline with the British hollering and gesticulating behind him.

"I never understood why you did it, Jacob," said Pierre, his eyes still focussing on the precipitous side of the cliff.

"To tempt the search party away from finding a trail to my cabin. I'm not saying they would have discovered us if I hadn't led them away, but there's always a risk that someone will stumble on it. To prevent that happening I had to do something, and very nearly killed myself in the effort."

Pierre turned to look at Jacob, "What happened?" he said, his eyes wide open in surprise.

Jacob began to tell Pierre of how he had led the British search party down the side of the cliff face and how he had almost fallen over its sheer side when Eric's fishing boat suddenly came into sight, rounding the southern tip of the island.

They watched as the wind caught its sail, zipping it through the choppy swells until it turned in towards the jetty.

"Come on," said Jacob, "Erik won't wait around while this wind is up."

Half-way along they saw the fishing boat coast up to the end of the pier, the sight of Gustav leaping off to wrap a thick mooring rope around a sea-battered post, spurring them on. Erik stood at the end of the jetty looking anxious to get away, while Olof held the vessel steady as the choppy swell rocked the boat to and fro.

"Jump onboard Magnus," called Erik. "With this wind we'll be in Danzig quicker than I hoped. Olof's skippering us for half the way, then I'll take over. I hope you've got all the information General Bonard needs."

"It's all up here Erik," said Pierre, tapping his head and jumping onboard.

"Good, then we'll be away Jacob," said Erik, smiling at his friend. "We'll be back here in four days with the usual supplies, one week before the invasion. Let's hope it will be the last business we do with the British. We'll meet you in your cabin, mid-morning."

"And I'll see you Magnus, on the cove with the detachment of marines," said Jacob. "Now I must join Per down there, he's starting to build the beacons."

Jacob unhitched the mooring rope, throwing it to Gustav who was waiting on board. As the boat drifted away from the jetty, the strong wind quickly filled its sail, setting it firmly on its course for the French controlled port of Danzig. Jacob stood watching the fishing vessel until it became a shadowy outline ploughing through the wide expanse of sea off the island's southern-most point. Willing it a safe passage, he made his way off the jetty, mindful that the oncoming invasion was now only a matter of days away.

James grasped the rudder of the little skiff as it bounced its way over the sea's choppy swells. A strong wind was blowing off the sea with rain clouds building up over the horizon, but today was his day of liberty, a day he had been looking forward to since his last day out with Anna. The daunting images of her father running a finger across his throat, and the screams of the wounded on the doomed French corvette had constantly played on his mind, but he had decided to try and keep them from Anna.

His spirits cheered, as the walls of Nogersund harbour came into sight knowing she would be waiting for him somewhere on the wharf. Guiding the skiff through the mouth of the harbour, he brought it up to a mooring at the far end of the quay. Furling the sail he glanced around the harbour, noting there was little activity going on, but then his heart jumped as he saw her coming out of the warehouse, a smile breaking across her features as she saw him on the quay looking her way. With a wave, she picked up her skirts and calling out his name with joy, she raced towards him, leaping into his arms without a care of who may have been watching. Holding her closely he kissed her longingly on her lips, feeling her shudder as their tongues met.

"I've missed you," she said, hugging him tightly.

"Hello," he said, lifting her face towards his. "It's been a long time my darling."

"Three long days," she said, smiling up at him.

"Too long," he said, kissing the end of her nose.

"We're going out into the countryside," she said, "and this time I've prepared our picnic. I hope you like lobster. The crew caught some the other day, and I prepared one especially for us."

"You are spoiling me Anna," he said, stroking her cheek. "How clever of you! I adore lobster."

"My father and uncle Olof are out at sea for the next few days, so there's no need to worry about them. Lars, my brother, will look after the warehouse while they're away. And I have," she said, looking at James and giggling, "as your navy says, liberty!"

"Well, let's make the most of it," said James, reaching for her hand, "lead on my darling."

"Yes, but first we must go to the warehouse and pick up our lobster lunch. Come on."

Anna followed the pathway she and her mother had taken two days before, stopping at the point where the view afforded a look at the steep knoll that accommodated a wooden bench at its summit.

"We're going up there," said Anna, smiling.

At the top, James unslung the lunch bag he'd been carrying over his shoulder and putting an arm around Anna, he gazed across at the lush countryside below.

"Look James," she said. "Over those treetops is our house,

peeping out over those pine trees at the top of that hill. And if you squint far out to sea, you'll see the outline of Hanö Island, over there to the left."

From the corner of her eye Anna could see that James was not looking to where she was pointing. Turning towards him, she saw that his gaze was centred solely on her. Reaching for her, he pulled her gently towards him.

"You are all I want to look at, my darling," he whispered, tenderly.

Before she could respond, he kissed her lovingly on her lips, feeling her mouth open to his. Holding him tightly, Anna looked deeply into his eyes,

"You fill my heart, James. I just wish this moment could last forever, but there's something important I need to tell you. Let's look for a sheltered spot, there's a strong wind blowing up here, and look at those rain clouds coming in from over the sea. There's an old shepherd's shack over there in the next meadow, I think we could make it before the rain sets in."

As the first drops of rain pitter-pattered on the shack's weather-worn roof, James pushed at the badly fitting door, opening it just enough for them to slip through. Layers of straw covered the wooden floor while a blackened fireplace glared over at them from the far end of the room. Beside the fireplace a pile of bone-dry logs lay neatly stacked, evidence that at some time a shepherd had warmed himself while sheltering from bad weather. Clinging to a stone wall, a roughly put together table and two chairs stared out across the room.

"Is it likely the shepherd will be back here today?" asked James, looking over his shoulder as a gust of wind slammed the door shut.

"I very much doubt it," said Anna. "The old shepherd who used to use it died a few months ago. Nobody has been here since. The sheep you saw grazing in the meadows belong to a farm further up the path. The farmer rents the fields from a landowner we never see. So, until the weather out there improves, we have this all to ourselves. I think the lobster's calling to us James, are you hungry?"

Taking a kerchief from his jacket pocket, James rubbed a covering of dust from the top of the table, then wiping the seats of the two chairs he stood back as Anna took the lobster from the bag and placed it on the table. She had already separated the head from the tail and an abundance of mouth-watering leg and claw meat was deliciously spread around the shells. A fresh loaf of bread and a wedge of what looked like home-made butter completed the scrumptious looking display.

"James, at the bottom of the bag is a bottle of wine and two mugs. I'm afraid they're not crystal cut glasses like we had on the island a few days ago, but there again, I'm not the captain of a ship!"

"Ha," said James, chuckling, "the wine will taste the same whether drunk from your mugs or crystal glasses."

Opening the bottle of wine, he filled the two mugs and then taking a fork he scooped up a generous helping of the delicious white meat, closing his eyes with pleasure as the exquisite flavour erupted in his mouth, his taste buds screaming out for more.

At the end of their meal, they sat quietly sipping their wine and savouring the lingering flavours of the lobster.

"By the sound of it, a storm's brewing out there," said Anna, jumping at the sound of the wind howling its way through the cracks in the door.

"I'll make a fire," said James, getting up from the table. "There are enough logs here to last us all day. It'll be nice and snug."

Anna smiled back at him, her eyes following him around the dusky corners of the shack while he rummaged for what would act as kindling. Using a spark from his tinderbox, he soon had the bits of dry wood and straw he'd collected flickering with a flame. Then, adding pieces of dried bark that he broke off from the logs, the look of a cosy fire soon began to take shape. Stacking a few of the logs onto the pile he stood back listening to the hiss of the timber as the flames started to lick their way through the seasoned wood.

A loud crack of thunder from outside, followed by a continuous drumming of rain on the rooftop, brought Anna hurrying over to the fireplace. Taking his jacket off, James spread it over the rough floor in front of the fire. Then, using the kit bag that Anna had packed their picnic in, he stuffed it with the cloths she had used to wrap around the lobster. It would do as a cushion to lay their heads.

They watched the flames in the fireplace dancing their way up through the blazing logs, gyrating their way upwards as they spread their warmth around the shack. A sudden flash of lightning followed by an ear shattering boom of thunder, caused Anna to fling her arms around James in fright. James held her closely, kissing her tenderly then gently guiding her down onto the long-tail jacket he had spread over the floor in front of the fire. Content with just being with each other they lay silently, their eyes staring into the fire as the glowing logs conjured up mesmeric pictures of red pathways leading into caves of orange splendour. Reaching out, James grasped two more logs, placing them on top of those already burning brightly, the flames quickly enveloping them. Through the glow of the fire Anna traced a finger gently over James' features, her finger moving across his forehead and down the shape of his nose until finally resting in the cleft of his chin.

"Civilian clothes suit you my darling," she said, running her finger down the sleeves of his shirt. "But I must say, you cut a dashing figure in your captain's uniform!"

"Wearing these gives me a break from what I do," he said. "I need to sometimes clear my mind of the terrible things war can make us do."

Anna watched him gaze thoughtfully into the fire, his brow creasing with a saddened frown.

"Do you want to tell me about it, darling?" she said softly, propping herself up on an elbow.

Nodding slowly, he told her of the sinking of the two French surveillance ships, his voice trembling with emotion as he described his decision to sink the second corvette. Staring into the fire, he heard again the cries of the wounded lingering over the water as the ill-fated ship disappeared into the dark depths of the sea.

Anna gently put an arm around him, kissing his cheek and smoothing the deep frown lines creasing his forehead. She didn't speak, for there was nothing she could say, only knowing that she would be there to comfort him at moments when such daunting recollections of war overwhelmed him. Turning, he looked sorrowfully into her eyes. "This is a private moment Anna," he said. "I could never afford my men to see me in such a state. To them, I am the epitome of a stonewall commander."

"Then let it be my darling," she said, "let them continue to think that. Is it enough that only I know the real Captain Carey?"

"It is Anna, and I love you for that," he said, tenderly.

James kissed her, his arms encircling her as she lay back on the warmth of his jacket.

"James, I want you," she whispered, untying the strings in the front of her gown.

In the glow of the fire, they made love, James moving gently inside her while her body moved in unison with his. Closing her eyes, she imagined they were in some faraway place of pleasure where her body was free to enjoy the thrill of her man. It was a feeling she had never experienced until now. Enjoying the blissful feeling surging inside her she smiled up at him, whispering her love for him over and again as her body moved with his.

Breathless, they lay back gazing into the glow of the fire. A single log, not yet burnt down, shimmered in the yellow flames, defiant and resistant to its inevitable end. James stretched his hand over to the stack of logs grabbing a couple and placing them on the fire's lucent remains, pushing them in further around the single defiant log. Anna reached a hand over to him tugging him back to where she lay, her head nestling on his left arm.

They lay together with their arms around each other, fulfilled and happy whilst wishing the magic of this beautiful moment would last forever.

"Before we ran for the shack, back on the knoll where the bench is," said James, stroking her hair. "You told me you had something important to tell me."

Anna stared into the fire. "Two days ago," she said, taking his hand and placing it next to her cheek, "I overheard my father telling my mother something that shocked and distressed me. Before I tell you James, promise me that you won't reveal that it was me who told you this, please my darling."

"Of course," said James, "I promise you."

"I awoke early that morning," began Anna, "and feeling thirsty I made my way down to the kitchen…."

James listened without interrupting, as Anna told him what she had heard her father telling her mother. He nodded when she mentioned the two French spies her father had brought over to the island. When she told him the name of the Swedish agent acting for the French on the island, he smiled with pleasure, knowing he had now discovered the island's spymaster.

"Anna, this proves that your father and uncle are in league with our enemy, the French," he said, looking at her seriously.

"They're doing it out of revenge for their mother, James. When the British killed their mother in the bombardment of Copenhagen, they swore they would not rest until they'd had their revenge. They hate anything British, and more so the English. I told you this when we had our day out on the island."

James took her hand and holding it in his, he kissed her gently on her cheek wiping away the tears that now trickled down it. He knew he would have to investigate this further and inform Commodore Percival that his suspicions about Erik Gunnarsson were sound. But he couldn't prove it without disclosing the source, and that he had just promised not to do.

"But that is not all, James," said Anna, looking at him desperately. "I expect you know the French are planning to attack the island, don't you?"

"We know there will be an attack soon," he said, "but we don't know when."

"I heard my father tell my mother, James," she said, looking at the sudden change in his expression.

"You mean, he knows when it will be?"

"Yes, and I'm telling you this is because I'm worried that he'll take part in it with my uncle. Now that you know, it would be better for him to be taken by the British before the action takes place, than to be killed by them in the forthcoming battle.

"When will it be, Anna?" asked James.

"March the thirty-first, at midnight," she said, softly. "Please do something to stop my father. I beg you, James."

James nodded, his mind thinking quickly, "I will try, but you are my first concern. You must stay safe and well-away from the island from that day onwards. There is no way your father will know you have told me this."

"We have a delivery to make on the island in four days," said Anna. "That will be one week before the invasion. Please do something, James."

James took her in his arms, his mind searching for a veritable plan to put to Commodore Percival. With a deep sigh Anna took his hand, pressing it against her breast.

"I know you'll do your best James," she said, looking at him, "but my heart is fretting for you, my love. There's going to be a battle and I know you'll be in the thick of it, whether at sea or on the island. Please be careful and come through it, I can't think of what I'd do without you."

"My darling Anna," he said, kissing her forehead," I will come through it for you. When it's over, I want you to come back to England with me. My ship will be due to return then."

Anna suddenly stiffened. An unexplainable stab of sadness pricking at her heart. Dismissing it, she put her arms around him kissing him intently.

"I'll come to England with you James, I couldn't bear to be without you," she said, smiling at him. "Now, tell me about where we're going to live. Will we live in a big house near the sea?"

Chuckling, James nestled her in his arms and began by describing the town in Devon where he lived."

They made love again, their passion intense and wild.

As the fire dwindled and evening began to draw in, they left the shack arm in arm, stopping for a moment at the bench above the steep knoll where they looked out over the treetops at the darkening outline of Hanö island far out to sea. The storm that had raged earlier had blown away and as they reached the top of the rough track that led to the Gunnarsson's house, James took her in his arms not caring who might be watching through the duskiness of the late evening.

They kissed each other passionately, not wanting their day of love to end.

"Until four days my darling. I'll be waiting for you on the quay."

"I'll be there, James," she said, not wanting to let him go.

She watched him walk away down the track, her heart crying out at his leaving. At the bottom he stopped, and turning he gave her a wave before walking away into the shadows that had already enveloped the little twilit harbour of Nogersund.

27

A grave frown creasing his forehead, John Percival listened as James detailed the information Anna had given him concerning the date and time of the invasion. Not disclosing the source of his information, James sat back watching Hanö's military commander pondering on the intelligence he had just heard.

"March the thirty first," said the commodore, looking seriously at James. "That's only ten days away from now. We've known for some time that there would be every likelihood of an attack on the island. I sent an urgent request to Admiral Saumarez for reinforcements well over a month ago, and another with the sloop that sailed for England with the French prisoners. It now seems that the letter I entrusted with the commander of the sloop will be too late. I only hope that Admiral Saumarez has received the first request by now and understands the seriousness of our situation.

"With all due respect sir," said James, "I'm not that confident aid will arrive in time."

"My God!" said the commodore. "Things look grim. Now, what are your thoughts on the size of the French attack force?"

"That, we can't be sure of, sir," said James. "But it's my guess there will be around a dozen ships, each carrying up to thirty marines. Two of their ships will likely break away from the fleet to offload their marines on the cove."

"We have a longboat that patrols that area during the night," said the commodore.

"Best to give orders to cancel all patrols of longboats that night, sir. We know the French will be coming, those men in the longboats will be needed here."

"Yes, I'll do that," agreed the commodore. "The French fleet will be in for an awesome pounding from our heavy guns when we have them in our sights."

"But not if the French marines have taken them over," replied James. "They'll train those cannons down onto us, and all but destroy us before their fleet enters the mouth of the harbour. We need to think of a plan to prevent them capturing our heavy guns, and how to cripple as many of their ships as we can."

"Precisely," said the commodore. "Now, I've thought of a plan, and I want you to listen to it carefully. If it fails, then we lose the island, and Napoleon will have carte blanche over the entire Baltic. We must stop him at all costs. Nothing must deter us from winning this battle."

James sat back, looking at the commodore.

"We have little hope of defeating the French fleet at sea with our handful of ships," the commodore began, "although we can give them a bloody nose with a concerted effort. But by doing that we'll lose our ships, and nothing will be gained. However, with careful planning we can defeat them here on the island, and this is what I propose. I'll discuss my plan with you first, as a matter of priority. I'll welcome your comments and then we'll arrange a meeting with all officers and commanders for them to consider what I'm about to tell you."

James nodded, keen to hear what the commodore would say, and to the plausibility of his plan.

"We must assume that the French spy, Pascale, has managed to get away from the island and has delivered Napoleon's ultimatum to the Swedish naval commanders in league with the French. So, we can expect them to support the invasion with a flotilla. I doubt their ships will have marines on board but nevertheless, their flotilla will increase the force of the French fleet's attack on the harbour."

"I agree with that," said James. "Please continue, sir."

"Without naval reinforcements we cannot defeat such a force with our handful of warships. What I propose to do is to draw them into the harbour, on the pretence that our frigates will cut and run after a brief engagement with their fleet. Two of our frigates will be waiting for them outside the mouth of the harbour. On sighting them they will advance through the darkness, firing on the leading ships with all their cannons. The French will undoubtedly respond and manoeuvre into action formations to engage. Surprised they will be, when our two frigates turn and make headway back towards the harbour, only to disappear into the darkness. Hopefully, their fleet will pursue thinking they have broken our defence and now have an open route to attack the harbour and deposit their marines. Our other three frigates and the sloop-of-war will be waiting for the two frigates to join them in the darkness, a mile east of the harbour. We'll have set up beacons along the harbour wall and around the quay, and as the enemy fleet enters the mouth of the harbour the beacons will be lit. In the light of the flaming balefires our cannons up on the heights will open fire, raining down a constant bombardment that will pulverise their ships, so letting them know that their special force of marines has failed in their mission to take over our guns."

"Good, but what is the plan to stop that special force?" asked James.

"I'm coming to that now," replied the commodore. "HMS Hector will be one of the frigates to advance through the darkness on the French fleet when it's first sighted. It will later lead our other warships in the attack on what's left of their fleet after our three heavy cannons have ceased their bombardment. Lieutenant Sutherland will be quite capable of commanding Hector, while you James and a selected number of your crew ambush their special force of marines coming out of the tunnel. No prisoners James, we'll defeat this invasion once and for all. With victory in our hands, I doubt they'll venture near us again. The French fleet will be expecting our heavy guns to rain down fire on us in their belief that their marines have taken them over. But when the beacons around the harbour are lit, they will be in for one hell of a surprise. Hector and our other warships will pounce when our cannons stop firing, coming up behind those enemy ships that may have survived the bombardment and giving them hell. Our two platoons of marines, under cover on the island, will then come out of their positions and advance on any of the French who may have managed to get ashore."

"What about your ship of the line, sir, during all that bombardment?"

"We'll have anchored her well-away from the harbour," said the commodore.

"Yes, it could work," said James, nodding. "But what if a sizable number of their marines manage to get ashore. We only have two platoons of marines comprising sixty-eight men, we'll be completely outnumbered."

"Then we'll have one hell of a battle on our hands, James, one that we must win. With this plan I can see no other way of saving the island."

James nodded, a plan of how he was going to ambush the French marines coming up through the tunnel, already forming in his mind.

"I'll call a meeting of all ships' captains and marine commanders to take place in the officer's mess after dinner this evening," said the commodore. "Now, concerning our supplier of fish and vegetables, Erik Gunnarsson. You say he'll be coming here with a supply in three days' time. That will be exactly one week before the invasion. Brief me again, as to his part in all this."

"The information I have, sir, is that he is the link between the French spymaster here on the island, and Napoleon's commanders in Danzig. The invasion force will be launched from Danzig, probably joining up with the Swedish flotilla at a coordinate not far off the harbour. We don't have the actual settings of this rendezvous, but it's my guess it will be in the zone where we sank their two surveillance corvettes. Erik Gunnarsson will likely know. I'm sure he's planning to meet up with this agent on his next delivery to us."

"And where did you uncover all this information?" asked the commodore, looking questioningly at his captain.

"That I can't say at this moment sir, but all will be revealed after we have crushed the invasion."

"I trust you to be right," said the commodore. "So, if we put Gunnarsson under surveillance on his next visit to us, you're hoping he'll lead us to the spymaster here on the island?"

"I am sir," said James. "We know his name is Jacob Forsberg, a local here on the island. I'm now sure it was him who masterminded Pascale's escape from us. He's obviously been hiding the two French agents brought here by Gunnarsson. Forsberg, in all probability, will be the one who leads the French marines up through the tunnel to attack our heavy cannons from the rear."

"Then it's imperative we catch him," replied the commodore. "Yes, you organise the surveillance on Gunnarsson, and I just hope your hunch that the French will use that tunnel on the night of the invasion turns out to be right."

"They will sir, of that I'm sure," affirmed James.

"That'll be all captain," said the commodore standing up. "We'll meet after dinner this evening. Oh, and make sure Lieutenant Sutherland joins us."

"Aye, aye, sir," replied James, "that I will."

The clock on the wall in Jean-Luc Bonard's office ticked away monotonously as Pierre sat waiting for Napoleon's First Secretary General to finish the document he was scrutinising. Turning to glance up at the clock, Jean-Luc grunted, then closing the document he looked over to where Pierre was sitting upright and rigidly still.

"No need to sit at attention, lieutenant," he said. "You can relax now. Lieutenant Pascale should be here shortly."

Pierre sat back rehearsing in his mind his report on the state of the British defences on the island. A single commanding knock broke the silence.

"Enter," Jean-Luc commanded.

Andre Pascale, finely suited in the uniform of a naval lieutenant, stepped into the room, closing the door quietly behind him.

"Sir," he said, coming to attention in front of Danzig's supreme commander.

Jean Luc nodded, "be seated," he said. "You are here Lieutenant Pascale to listen to the report Lieutenant Renaud will give on the current strength of the British defences on Hanö Island. The planned invasion of the island is now only ten days away and should Lieutenant Renaud's report prove favourable, then I will be ready to give the order for it to go ahead. In our last meeting Lieutenant Pascale, I informed you that you would be part of the detachment of marines landing on the cove with Lieutenant Renaud. I want you both to lead this mission. You will have full command over the detachment of marines chosen for this task, a task that you will complete successfully. I need not remind you that a speedy victory in our invasion will depend on us taking over those cannons. You may begin Lieutenant Renaud."

Pierre began by explaining the benefit of using the tunnel through the cliffs to get the detachment of marines safely and quickly up to the main path through the forest. Looking intently at the French General, he emphasised the importance of the main fleet waiting before manoeuvring towards the harbour, so allowing the detachment of marines to land safely on the cove and giving them time to move up through the tunnel to finally surprise the British gun crews.

"I remind you Lieutenant," interrupted Jean-Luc. "Our naval commanders have orders to begin the main frontal attack on the harbour at midnight. Prior to that the Swedish flotilla, under rear-Admiral Hastfer, will have linked up with our fleet. So, you will have one hour to take over those British cannons.Have you any questions, Lieutenant Pascale?"

"No sir," replied Pascale, "it is clear."

"Good," continued Jean-Luc, "then you can now proceed with your report on the British defences, Lieutenant Renaud."

Jean-Luc listened without interrupting as Pierre gave details of the layout of the harbour and the number of warships the British had anchored there at one time, specifying the frequency of the warships' movements in and out of the harbour. Staring intently at his young lieutenant, he listened closely to Pierre's facts concerning the two platoons of British marines stationed there, raising an eyebrow thoughtfully at the depiction of the gun crews manning the heavy guns that overlooked the harbour.

"Approximately how many marines would you think make up their platoons, lieutenant?" he asked.

"What we observed, sir, over the two weeks of being there," replied Pierre, "I'd say between sixty and seventy men."

Jean-Luc nodded, deep in thought.

"Would you say that one hour would be enough for our special force to get up to the island's highest point and take out the British gun crews?"

"The southern part of the island is completely undefended, sir," answered Pierre. "The British assume that because of the vast number of rocks and boulders covering the coastline, there will be no threat of any invasion along that section of the island. So, they have concentrated all their power in defending the harbour. We will see no resistance when we land on the cove. Moving the marines up through the tunnel will be quick, as we know the route through it. In daytime it's colonised by bats, but at night they are out hunting and existing nocturnally. Yes, I believe an hour will be enough, sir."

At this point Pierre refrained from mentioning Jacob's belief that the British had discovered the tunnel, afraid that Jean-Luc might cancel using it as a precaution against the mission failing. But as Jacob had pointed out, how could the British monitor it with their limited manpower, not even knowing the date and time when the

French may even use it. Pierre was certain that should Jacob be right in his assumptions, then the plan to use it for this mission should go ahead. He would say nothing about it.

Jean-Luc sat quietly, his mind absorbing the facts of Pierre's report.

"Thank you, lieutenant," he said, getting up from his chair and walking across to the large bay window. Looking down onto the courtyard below he considered the information Pierre had reported, his mind assessing the probability of a successful invasion. *Our invading fleet will obviously outnumber the British ships stationed in the harbour,* he thought. *Our marines aboard each ship will be more than enough to defeat the two British platoons of Royal Marines. The key to guaranteeing a successful invasion will be to take over the three heavy cannons overlooking the harbour, and with the secrecy of the invasion date still very covert, a swift victory over the British looks a certainty. Once those cannons are in our hands, victory will be assured.*

Turning, he walked slowly back to his desk. "Gentlemen," he said looking at his two officers. "Prepare for the invasion. We go on 31st March."

Dismissing his two lieutenants, Jean-Luc walked back to the window. Lighting a cheroot, he gazed down at the bustling activity in the courtyard below. Something was beginning to trouble him. It was then that he thought of the two surveillance corvettes he had ordered to make a reconnaissance three days before. No reports of them returning had been conveyed to him. *Could they have come across British warships and been unable to get away?* he thought. He would wait to see if they returned over the next few days, hopefully they would have something to report.

Calling for his secretary, he reached for a bottle of cognac next to his desk. Pouring a good measure, he sat back dismissing the nagging thoughts of uncertainty playing on his mind.

"General?" said the middle-aged officer entering the room.

"Inform Commandant Joubert I want to see him now," ordered Jean-Luc.

"Sir," replied the secretary, saluting and leaving the room.

Staring at the glass of cognac in front of him, visions of the two corvettes being blown out of the water by the British flashed before his eyes. A commanding knock on his door brought him back to the present.

"Ah, Henri," he said, looking up and smiling. "Take a seat and a glass of cognac."

As Henri settled himself, Jean-Luc raised his glass. "It's on Henri. We're going ahead. I trust you are ready and prepared."

"I take it that this is the green light for 31st March?" said Henri, grinning.

"That it is Henri," affirmed Jean-Luc.

"Well in that case," said Henri, raising his glass with a jubilant look, "to your good health, Mon General. To a successful and triumphant offensive. Vive La France."

28

Anna eased herself out of bed to the sound of her father's voice rising from the kitchen below her bedroom. Slipping into her robe, she made her way through the darkness, gently opening the door and stepping out onto the upstairs hallway. Candlelit lanterns, placed above and below the stairs, threw up freakish shadows that danced over the walls of the stairwell as she tiptoed warily down.

Moonlight, streaming through a glass window at the end of the lower hallway, lit up the face of a small carriage clock staring out sleepily from the top of a corner table. Anna noted the time, fifteen minutes to eleven.

A sliver of candlelight breaking through a gap in the kitchen door caught her eye. Gingerly inching her way towards it, she stopped a few feet from its source. Controlling her breathing, she listened to the voices coming from inside the kitchen.

"I've asked you to keep your voice down, Erik," she heard her mother say. "I don't want Anna to know anything about this."

"She's asleep, she won't know what we're telling you, Christina," the voice of her uncle Olof sounded through the slightly open door.

"I'll tell you once again Lars," she heard her father shout, "you will not take part in this invasion. You will remain here to protect your mother and sister should the French decide to invade the mainland. Only your uncle Olof and I will be involved in the attack on the island. And that is that!"

"Shush, please Erik," begged her mother.

"Yes, yes Christina," replied Erik irritably. "Now, Gustav and

Nils have been waiting here patiently, so it's time to brief them for the part Olof and I want them to play."

Keeping in the shadows, Anna stepped towards the door and bending forward she peered through the gap. From the view she had, she could see the two brothers Nils and Gustav sitting alongside Lars at the side of the kitchen table, all three looking expectantly towards what had to be her father at the far end. The angle of the gap in the door prevented her from seeing him, as it did from seeing her mother and uncle.

"There's a British longboat that regularly patrols the coastline at night, passing the cove at around the hour of eleven," she heard her father say. "If the British marines in that longboat see the flaming beacons and the French longboats approaching, they'll row like hell back to the harbour and raise the alarm. Our job will be for our vessel to wait off the cove in the cover of darkness. When we see the British patrol boat, we'll drop sail and ram it to kingdom come. Any of their marines who manage to swim ashore will be taken out by Jacob and Per. Once we've sunk the British patrol boat Olof and I will be picked up in a longboat by Magnus and then rowed to the cove where we'll make our way to join up with Jacob and the special force of French marines."

Anna heard her father pause, obviously allowing Nils and Gustav to digest the information. Several seconds passed before his voice sounded again.

"You two will stay on the fishing boat, keeping it in position just off the cove in case we need to make a quick exit from the island, should things go badly."

Anna thrust a hand over her mouth to quell a gasp of horror as she listened to her father explaining the part he and her uncle would play in the forthcoming invasion. She knew it was pointless for her mother to try and dissuade them, their minds were made up and she was very much aware of the stubbornness that flowed through their veins. Now that they were intent on joining the battle for the island, the probability of them coming face to face with James seemed inevitable. They would kill him, of that, she was sure. She had to think of a way of stopping them but as much as she racked her brains for a means, nothing came to mind. Her only option was to inform James of what she had overheard and hope he would find a way of preventing them from joining the others in the forest. He'd be waiting for her on the island in three days' time when the next delivery of supplies to the British garrison were due, she'd tell him then. She hoped her father and uncle had business elsewhere on the island, if not she knew it would present a problem with her plan to meet James.

Peering through the gap she noticed the looks of excitement breaking over the faces of Gustav and Nils.

"So," said Erik, his voice sounding from the end of the table. "How do you feel about the plan of taking out the British longboat, and then waiting off the cove in the vessel should we need to make a quick exit?"

"We're with you," said Gustav, nodding eagerly.

"Yes, Erik," said his brother Nils. "We're with you all the way."

"Good," her father's voice boomed.

From where she stood, Anna could picture the smile of gratitude spreading across her mother's face when Erik once again told Lars he would not be part of the operation.

"Now, be away," continued Erik. "We're all up early tomorrow to catch the fish that will be part of our last delivery to the British garrison in three days' time. But wait, before you go, one last word. On that delivery day, Olof and I will meet up with Jacob and Per in their hideaway for a final briefing, we'll return to the harbour later in the afternoon."

Hearing her father's words, Anna let out a sigh of relief.

"Lars, you and the two brothers will help Anna with the dispersal of supplies, then remain with the vessel until Olof and I return. Make sure Anna stays on board when her job is done."

Anna saw the disheartened look that had spread over her brother's face and the pleading look he gave his father.

She'd have to think of a plan to get away to meet James, it wouldn't be difficult with the way Lars was feeling now. Her father's last words brought the meeting to a close and, at the sound of chairs being hastily pushed back, she crept quietly away, tiptoeing back up the stairs and silently closing her bedroom door.

In a quiet corner of the officers' mess that overlooked Commodore Percival's ship of the line, the English ships' captains and the two officers commanding the Royal Marine platoons, listened to the commodore's detailed explanation of the plan to defeat the French attack on the island. Sitting next to James, Dan concentrated on every word delivered by the commodore. Earlier, James had informed him of the decision to appoint him temporary commander of HMS Hector, and the part he would be expected to play when the French fleet was sighted.

Captain Rupert Crisp, commander of the two Royal Marine platoons, sat erect, his lieutenant sitting stoically next to him. Raising an arm, he cleared his throat, "Commodore if you please, I have a point to raise."

With a nod in his direction, Commodore Percival gave him permission to speak.

"I have a feeling that the dozen or so ships in the French fleet may not all follow our two frigates into the mouth of the harbour. Also, some may escape the bombardment by our three heavy cannons and offload their marines into longboats. By rowing close to the harbour wall these longboats could escape the bombardment and find their way into the harbour without being spotted. With their ships containing an average of thirty marines, my platoons would be heavily outnumbered. I propose you allocate thirty men from the crews of each of our warships to bolster the numbers of my platoons. I can then use this force as an effective means of defending the harbour, should their marines manage to get through."

"Gentlemen, Captain Crisp has a point," said Commodore Percival. "Hand to hand fighting will happen only on the island, should their marines manage to get ashore. Boarding any of their ships after a successful engagement is out of the question, your orders are to sink those that will have avoided our bombardment. Therefore, I'm sure you can spare these men."

It didn't take long for the ships' captains to agree to Rupert Crisp's request. Turning to the marine captain, they nodded their approval. With a grateful nod towards them, Captain Crisp sat back in his chair, relieved at their decision.

"Captain Carey," continued the commodore, turning to look at each of the commanders. "I'd like you to advise us about the surveillance plan you have suggested to me, concerning a certain treacherous Swedish supplier!"

Eyebrows raised in shocked surprise, they waited for James to respond.

Nodding to the commodore, James turned to face each of the commanders.

"Gentlemen, I've recently uncovered a nest of spies that have been operating here on the island. You may remember the French brig that my crew and I captured some time ago, and the French lieutenant who escaped our custody before our sloop sailed for England with their crew as prisoners. The lieutenant was a spy, bound for the Swedish port of Karlskrona to enlist the support of a treacherous group of Swedish aristocratic naval commanders sympathetic to Napoleon. His escape was masterminded by an agent of the French here on the island, by the name of Jacob Forsberg. Forsberg has also been sheltering two additional French agents somewhere, we are sure, in his cabin in the forest.

"I now have reason to believe that these two agents were brought to the island in the disguise of Swedish fishermen aboard Erik Gunnarsson's fishing vessel and that he, along with his brother Olof, are in the employ of the French in Danzig. They act as couriers, ferrying information from Forsberg on our military strength here on the island. I also believe they are complicit in transferring French agents to various destinations ordered by the Danzig commanders. Erik Gunnarsson is our garrison's supplier of fresh fish and vegetables, and Forsberg is his link here on the island. Several searches inside the forest have proven negative in finding any trace of him, but I feel that in three days' time when Gunnarsson delivers a fresh supply to our garrison, he and his brother Olof will pay a visit to Forsberg and the two French agents. They'll very likely draw up last minute plans in their role of rendezvousing with the French on the cove. I'll arrange to have him followed, and hopefully he'll lead us to Forsberg's hideout."

"Why can't we just pick him up when he sails into the harbour, captain?" asked the marine lieutenant.

"Because we have no proof, lieutenant," answered James. "There's nothing we can charge him with. But if we catch him and his brother in company with Forsberg and the two French agents, then it's a different matter."

"And where did you get this information on him, James?" asked one of the ships' captains.

"That I cannot divulge yet, Robert," answered James, "but I can assure you my source of information is beyond question."

"Gentlemen, I will remind you that this has been a secret and confidential meeting," said the commodore, getting to his feet. "What we have discussed this evening must not be repeated anywhere outside these walls. Our success over the French in ten days' time will depend on the total surprise we'll give them, so prepare for the action we must take to save the course of history. Should Napoleon take this island, the Swedish mainland will undoubtedly be next, and with the French controlling the Baltic, freedom as we know it will be finished. There'll be a final briefing at midday on the thirtieth. Tomorrow, we'll continue our patrols as normal. Captain Crisp, I leave it to you to nominate those of your marines who'll be responsible for lighting the beacons on the harbour wall. Give me the plan of action at our final briefing. And lieutenant," he said, turning to the marine lieutenant. "Regarding the night of the invasion, I want you to cancel the longboats patrolling along the shoreline. We know the French are coming, so you and your marines would be better deployed here with the rest of the platoon. That is all gentlemen, thank you. Captain Carey and Lieutenant Sutherland, please wait behind."

"Well James, have you decided on how you'll tail Gunnarsson?" asked the commodore, as the last of the ships' captains made their way out.

"I have sir. Gunnarsson will arrive here early, as he usually does. It's my guess he'll leave the unloading of his supplies to his daughter and crew while he slips away with Olof to find Forsberg. Lieutenant Devonshire and Ned Hatchet will be waiting discreetly on the quay for the fishing vessel to arrive. When Gunnarsson and his brother leave the boat, they'll follow them, staying well out of sight, particularly if they go through the field of long grass on their way to the forest. When they see them reach what looks to be a hideout or a well-hidden shack it will be Forsberg's. Hopefully, he and the two French agents will be inside. As soon as Gunnarsson and his brother enter the hideout, one of our men will remain there maintaining surveillance while the other makes his way back to the harbour to report to me. He will then lead Lieutenant Sutherland and me, together with a detachment of our crew, back to Forsberg's hideout. I'm confident we'll be able to get all five of them, commodore."

"Indeed, Captain. I hope your confidence plays out. But why are you sending your second lieutenant instead of Lieutenant Sutherland or yourself?"

James looked across at Dan. "Because if by some chance Gunnarsson sees us on the quay he'll recognise us, sir. He saw us once before when we stopped and searched his vessel at sea.

Lieutenant Sutherland was the officer I sent to check out his boat and crew. While Hector was alongside his vessel, he happened to look up to our starboard side as I was looking down on the operation. Our eyes met and I knew at once he'd remember me."

James was not going to reveal the moment when they had locked eyes onto each other down on the quay, and the threatening gesture Gunnarsson had given him.

"Hector is out on patrol tomorrow, sir," said James. "I'll brief lieutenant Devonshire and our master-at-arms. I'm sure they'll execute the proper surveillance. The two Gunnarsson brothers, Forsberg, and the French agents, will be in our custody before the day is out."

"I trust it to be so," said the commodore. "Now, as it's getting late, I'll bid you both a good night. Remember our final briefing here on the thirtieth."

"That I will. Goodnight, sir," replied James.

29

Anna looked out onto the British garrison's harbour as Erik guided his fishing boat up to a mooring post at the end of the quay. Her father's words of three nights' before, describing how the French would turn the heavy British cannons down onto the harbour, killing and destroying everything, played on her mind. She trembled at the thought of James being caught up in the middle of the devastation.

Her eyes searched the quay, seeking out her English captain, but apart from various groups of red-coated marines going about their business, there was no sign of him. She'd recognised his ship anchored outside the harbour, and presuming he was still onboard she knew it wouldn't be long before he'd be there, waiting on the quay for her.

Unseen in the shadows of a row of quayside huts, Richard Devonshire and Ned Hatchet watched the vessel they'd been following brush up against the side of the quay. Keeping well out of sight, they watched a crew member sling a length of rope onto the quay, then jumping off the boat he wrapped it around a mooring-post securing it with a double fisherman's knot.

"That's Gunnarsson's boat," whispered Richard. "We'll wait until he and his brother leave and then we'll follow them. Make certain we keep our distance, we mustn't let them know they're being followed."

They watched the boat's ramp crash down onto the quay, the sound alerting someone from the harbour master's cabin as the door to the wooden workstation was suddenly thrown open and an overweight official wobbled out, peering around for the new arrival.

Sweating profusely while fanning his face with a wad of papers, he scuttled off down the quay towards Erik's boat, stopping every so often to catch his breath.

"That lump of lard is Quigley," whispered Ned. "He's what they call, "The Reckoner". It's his job to reckon up what supplies are on the boat and tally them with the order sheets he's fanning himself with. He won't let any of them off until he's checked that everything's in order. He then examines their papers, even though he knows exactly who they are. He's about as fast as a pregnant snail, so we'll have a bit of a wait until they start to offload the supplies."

Richard smiled, chuckling at the comical sight of Quigley.

"That must be Gunnarsson's daughter standing at the top of the ramp," he said quietly, seeing an attractive auburn - haired young woman looking out over the quay.

"That's right, sir," replied Ned. "She's probably looking around to rope a few marines into carrying the supplies."

"Well, she's not our target," said Richard. "Look, seems like Quigley's started his reckoning."

The minutes ticked by as Richard and Ned waited patiently for signs that Quigley was coming to the end of his inspection when a shout from the quartermaster hurrying along the quay, broke the sluggish progress of the inspection.

"Quigley, hurry it up man," shouted the quartermaster, "I haven't got all day and I need that fish inside the cold room, tout suite."

Looking over his shoulder as he scanned the crews' identity papers, Quigley scowled. He enjoyed making people wait, even more so those who weren't attached to the garrison. He felt a sense of power over those he compelled to wait.

"Very well," he said with a sigh, turning to Erik. "All in order, you can unload and then leave the ship. Report to the office as usual before leaving the harbour."

Richard and Ned watched the corpulent Reckoner waddle off down the quay in the direction of the canteen, while Anna began the task of organising the offloading of the supplies.

"Looks like we're in business sir," whispered Ned, seeing Erik and Olof make their way down the ramp.

The two navy men slunk back into the shadows, keeping Erik and his brother firmly in their sights.

"Ok," said Richard pulling the front of his cloth cap down just above his eyes, "let's go."

Mingling in with a group of marines dragging a heavy tarpaulin along the quay, they followed the two Gunnarsson brothers until they saw them stop outside the last hut in the row. Keeping them partially in sight, they pretended to be busy helping the marines. In a matter of seconds, the two brothers suddenly disappeared round the corner of the hut. Hurrying after them, Richard and Ned stopped at the corner.

"They're going up the stony track that leads to the top of the island," whispered Richard. "I'll wager they're making for the field of long grass. Come on, I don't want to lose them."

"Best if we keep in single file, sir," said Ned. "I'll follow you."

Under the cover of a clump of trees at the bottom of the track, they looked up to see the brothers entering the field.

"Looks like the captain was right," said Richard, "they're making for the forest."

Erik and Olof came to a halt at the edge of the forest. "We're being followed," said Olof, looking back across the field.

"I know," said Erik. "Saw them make a dash into those trees down at the bottom of the track. Looks like our cover's blown, but how? They're probably following us to see if we lead them to Jacob's shack."

"You make your way there," said Olof. "I'll lead them off through the forest and down to the rocky shoreline. I'll lose them down there, then make my way back up here. I remember the trail to Jacob's cabin. Go on, I'll wait here and let them catch up a bit."

Erik nodded and, grinning at his brother, leapt over a few scattered boulders to disappear into the trees.

With the two brothers in their sights, Richard and Ned sneaked through the long grass, keeping to the rough animal trail that led to the fringes of the forest. Half-way along they saw the brothers stop.

"Duck," whispered Richard, "they're not far away. Did you see them?"

"I did sir," replied Ned crouching down out of sight.

Slowly, Richard eased himself up to look over the long green shoots.

"One just jumped over some boulders and disappeared into the forest," he whispered. "But the other's still standing there with his back to where we are."

"Let me have a look, sir" whispered Ned.

Ned inched himself up to look over to where Olof stood with his back to them, his legs slightly apart.

"He's having a piss sir!"

Olof stood looking at the trees in front of him, chuckling at the deception he was making. He could hear the soft shuffling of the grass as the two stalkers edged their way closer towards him. Knowing their eyes were fixed on him, he feigned the act of finishing his leak, then with a grunt he turned, and leaping over the stones vanished into the murky shadows.

James stood on the quay, his eyes examining Erik Gunnarsson's fishing boat moored at the end of the jetty. He watched two of the crew members swabbing down the deck, while another busied himself with checking the boat's mast and yard arm. There was no sign of Gunnarsson or his brother Olof.

He knew they were on their way to Jacob Forsberg's hideaway, when later in the day he and a detachment from his ship would storm the hideout taking the nest of spies into custody. With Erik and his brother Olof locked away, Anna would feel more at ease knowing they would be out of danger when the invasion started.

He had confided in Dan about his affair with Anna and the vital information she was now providing. Dan had listened thoughtfully, his expression telling James he was pleased for him in his newly found love, and the way the two of them were collaborating. James entrusted him to keep it from the commodore as he would divulge everything after they had defeated the French.

Moving away from the quay, he slipped into a shady space between two wooden huts overlooking the quartermaster's stockroom. It would not be sensible for those on Gunnarsson's fishing boat to see him meet with Anna.

He'd catch her attention as she came out of the stockroom and then take her to a quiet spot away from the harbour. He knew he'd have to be back well in time to meet up with either Richard or Ned, who'd have news of the whereabouts of Forsberg's hideaway.

From where he was, he had a partial view of the activity going on around him.

A sloop-of-war glided gracefully into the harbour, neatly positioning itself behind the commodore's ship of the line. James watched as several sailors leapt off to wrap thick ropes around several of the wooden mooring posts that stood erect along the quay.

Looking around at the sudden sound of the stockroom door being slammed shut, he saw Anna standing in front of the door, her eyes searching every inch of the quay for a sign of her captain. Peering through the gap, he nodded, knowing the crew on Gunnarsson's fishing vessel would have easily picked them out had he stayed there to meet her. He knew it wouldn't be long before she moved towards the quay, he'd surprise her as she walked past.

Anna's spirits dropped when she saw there was no sign of him.

Where is he? she thought. *The tallying of the supplies took a little longer than I expected, but he should be there waiting on the quay as we'd arranged. Oh James, where are you?*

A deep frown spread across her forehead as she slowly walked towards the quay, her eyes darting over every possible place he could be. Passing a row of wooden huts, she jumped in surprise as a hand shot out from the shadows firmly grasping her arm and gently pulling her into a shady gap between two wooden huts. Shocked and bewildered, she felt strong arms tenderly encircle her. Her eyes had not yet become accustomed to the dim light of the narrow passageway, but the way the arms enveloped her she knew it was him.

"Shush, don't speak," he said, gently kissing her lips. "Over there, right in front of these huts are three of your father's crew working on the fishing boat. They're going about their chores, but their eyes are taking in everything going on around the quay. I had no other option, Anna; they would have seen us."

"I hope this is the last time we have to meet like this!" she whispered.

Looking at her he grinned, "Well, you never know, maybe I'll have to steal you away onto my ship one-day."

"You'll never have to steal me away," she said, folding her arms around his neck, "I'll follow you willingly! Four days has been too long, James," she said, breaking away from him. "I can't be away from you for that long."

"Nor me for you," he said, stroking her cheek. "But after everything is over and we've defeated the French, you're coming to England with me. My ship will be recalled after the invasion."

"I will James," she said, knowing that this was what she truly wanted. Smiling she looked into his eyes. "But now I must give you some important news."

"Not here," said James, taking her hand. "Come with me, I know a quiet spot away from the harbour."

"I can't be away too long. My brother Lars is supervising the boat until my father gets back. I told him that I was going to pay a visit to Ulf's daughter. Ulf's the owner of the store just outside the harbour and over the years of coming here I've got to know his daughter Ulla. It's a good excuse to be away with you."

"Then, we'd better get you back in time," he said smiling. "It's a good excuse, but not if your brother decides to come looking for you in Ulf's store!"

They left at the back of the dark passageway and seeing a pathway leading away from the harbour they headed along its rough surface. The path led them past rows of trees, where huge round boulders nestled comfortably alongside tightly grouped conifers. On their left, open views of the sea shimmering under a deep blue sky stretched as far as they could see. It wasn't long before James took her hand and led her off the stony track. They dropped down onto a narrow stretch of shingle where large scabrous rocks stretched far along the coastline.

"Over there," said James, "a flat rock we can sit on."

They crunched across the shingle, settling themselves on top of the flat rock. Taking James' hand, Anna looked at him seriously.

"I need to tell you James that three nights ago I overheard my father and uncle briefing two of our crew and my brother Lars about the invasion."

"What did you hear, Anna?" he asked.

For a moment Anna was quiet, her eyes gazing far out to sea.

"I'm telling you this," she said, turning to look at him, "so you can think of a way to keep them away from the oncoming action. They're planning to assist the French in the invasion next week."

"Go on," said James.

"My father and my uncle Olof are now meeting with Jacob Forsberg and the one remaining spy at Forsberg's hideaway, somewhere on the island."

"What do you mean, one remaining spy?" asked James.

"There's only one here now, the other must have been taken off the island some time ago. I heard my father say that he was coming back with another spy, by the name of Andre Pascale."

"What?" cried James. "Andre Pascale?"

"Yes," said Anna. "They'll be accompanying the French marines who are going to land on the cove in longboats one hour before their main fleet attacks the harbour. Jacob Forsberg and the other spy, called Per, will light beacons on the cove to guide them in. Their fleet will then unload longboats carrying more marines who will engage the British in the harbour. My father thinks it won't take them long before the island is theirs."

"I know of this, Anna. You told me some of it before. But what I didn't know was that Andre Pascale would be accompanying them."

"But that's not all James. Forsberg knows you have a longboat patrolling the coastline and passing the cove at about eleven o'clock at night. He needs to take that boat out and my father has stupidly offered to do that for him. He and his crew will wait for the longboat to appear and then with the wind in his sails he'll ram it, killing every British marine onboard. Those who can swim to the shore will be killed by Forsberg and the French spy."

"Anna," said James caressing her hand. "We've cancelled the longboat's patrolling schedule for that night, so your father will be in for a surprise. At this very moment, two of my crew are following your father and uncle to Forsberg's hideout. When they find out where it is, one of them will return to the harbour to inform me. Lieutenant Sutherland and a detachment of heavily armed sailors from my crew will then accompany me to where the hideaway is located. We'll then storm it and take your father and the rest of them into custody, but should they put up a fight I can't guarantee their safety."

James could see the worried look stamped over her face. "We'll keep your father and uncle securely locked up Anna. They won't be able to get out when the serious fighting begins. But I want you to promise me that you'll stay at home and not come anywhere near the island."

"James, you must promise me you won't take any risks in this forthcoming battle and come through it, for my sake."

"I will, Anna," said James, "for your sake and our future in England."

Anna threw her arms around him suddenly stiffening as an unexpected stab of sadness pricked at her heart. Trying to dismiss it she looked at him tenderly.

"I love you, James Carey."

"And I love you too, Miss Anna Gunnarsson," he said, kissing her cheek. "I'll come for you when everything is over. Three days after the invasion just before dusk, meet me on the bench at the bottom of the hill where the track leads up to your house. I'm taking you to my ship and then to England the following day. Tell your parents we'll return some day, with their grandchildren."

"I will James, ten days after tomorrow on the bench where I fell in love with you."

James smiled at the memory. "Come now, we'd better be getting back. My two crewmen will be returning soon with news of Forsberg's hideaway. Lieutenant Sutherland will be waiting for me, and you don't want your brother to be looking for you in Ulf's store!"

They walked away over the shingle and back along the dusty pathway that led to the harbour. Standing well back, in the cover of the row of huts that overlooked her father's fishing boat, she watched him walk away unable to understand the sudden feeling of sadness that was again biting at her heart.

30

Richard and Ned scrambled over the loose stones and boulders that lay scattered in front of a wide gap in the trees. They had seen the two brothers enter the forest from this point and, not wanting to lose their trail, they hastened in after them.

Erik had disappeared through the pines, following a narrow animal track that zigzagged its way beneath the thickness of the trees until ending before a dense thicket of undergrowth. Finding a gap, he pushed his way through and coming out onto a grassy clearing he brushed himself down before striding towards the well-hidden shack that served as Jacob's hideaway.

Olof sauntered off down the forest path, slowly turning to see if the two stalkers had come through the gap in the trees. Squinting through the half-light there was no-one to be seen, but he knew they were there. Turning back, he searched ahead for the fork in the path and the trail that led down to the rocky shoreline. The sudden sound of a twig breaking from under someone's foot made him spin round again. With a grin towards the sound of the breaking twig, he sped away down the path and, rounding a bend, came to the fork and the trail leading down to the shoreline.

When they come round the bend and see me, I'll take that trail, he thought. He listened for their footsteps but there was nothing, only silence. He'd wait until they came into view.

Hidden behind a thicket of bushes, Richard and Ned watched Olof turn round, listen, and then race off down the path to disappear round a bend.

"Look sir," said Ned, "up there behind those trees, there's a track running parallel with the forest path. If we follow it, we'll be out of sight but still able to see where he goes."

"Yes, you're right," said Richard, "no point blundering after him round that bend."

Shielded by the closeness of the trees, they set off on the narrow trail, keeping sight of the main pathway below them. Ned suddenly came to a halt, indicating to his lieutenant to sidestep away from the trail.

"Down there, sir," he whispered, "he's there, standing at the fork and looking back up the path."

"Looks like he's waiting for something. Do you think he knows he's being followed?"

"I don't think so, sir," said Ned, quietly. "Maybe he's looking for a sign that his brother came this way. I remember that fork, it's the fork where we stopped when we were searching for the French prisoner who escaped. That trail leading off it drops down to the coastline."

"We'll wait and see what he does next," said Richard.

Olof listened for a sign that his pursuers were following, but all was quiet and nothing stirred at the bend. He knew they had to be watching him from somewhere near, or even looking down on him. Casually he looked up,

That's where they are, he thought. *Let's see how close they can get before I lose them.*

Turning, he made off down the trail, looking back occasionally to make sure they were following.

"Come on," said Richard, "he's going down to the shoreline. His brother must be down there already. Forsberg's hideout must be hidden down by the shore."

They slithered down the grassy trail, ducking to avoid overhanging branches until the track levelled out. Gaps between the trees afforded them glimpses of the sea and, stopping to get their bearings, they stood absorbing the peace and solitude before them. Looking down, Ned noticed a narrow shingly inlet set between rows of rocks. "He wouldn't have gone there, sir, he must have headed further along the track. You can see it twisting along through the trees there. I guess it follows the shoreline for as far as the forest goes."

"Probably to the southernmost tip of the island," said Richard.

"Come on, we'll continue along this track. Hopefully, it'll take us to Forsberg's hideout."

Pausing between the trees further up the path, Olof heard the voices of his pursuers drifting towards him. He'd have to lose them, and soon.

I'll lead them to the cove where the French longboats will arrive, he thought. *But instead of going down onto the cove I'll hide away in the trees where this track ends. They're bound to go down onto the cove, thinking that's the way I went. When they're clambering over the rocks looking for me, I'll double back to the main forest path and then onto Jacob's cabin. I could kill them both as they pass me, but that would cause one hell of a hue and cry. Better just to lose them, but I'll be looking for that one with the eyepatch when the action starts. Now, I'll let them get a glimpse of me.*

Ned suddenly grabbed Richard's arm, pulling him off the track and into the cover of the trees.

"It's him sir, far up the track. He's having another piss!"

Olof grinned to himself as he feigned the last act of his deception. Now was the time to lose them.

"I have no idea who they were," said Erik, looking seriously at Jacob. "They followed us into the field of long grass from the harbour. It's my guess they're looking for you Jacob. As they somehow know that Olof and I are associated with you, they think by following us, we'll lead them to you."

"Let's just hope that Olof manages to lose them," said Jacob.

"Do you think they know about the invasion," said Jacques, looking concerned.

"I'm now sure those navy men who passed me down on the quay found the tunnel through the cliffs," said Jacob. "But I very much doubt they know our exact plans for the invasion. Unless of course either of you two have turned traitor!"

"What! Don't be ridiculous, Jacob," said Erik, glaring at his friend. "Why on earth would we do that?"

"Someone's in league with the British, of that I'm now certain," replied Jacob.

"It's too late to find out who it is, so everything we now plan to do is not to be spoken of outside our circle."

"Agreed," said Erik, pleased to see Jacques nodding his agreement.

"It's a good thing you won't be coming across to the island with further supplies," said Jacob, smiling across the table at Erik. "The British may have heard of something happening next week, they'll be suspicious of everything entering the harbour, even you Erik!"

The sudden noise of the front door bursting open made them all look up in alarm.

"Ah, always on time for a drink, Olof!" beamed Jacob, opening his sea chest for a bottle.

"Couldn't have timed it better," said Olof, striding into the room.

"Well," said Erik, staring at his brother. "Did you lose them?"

"You know I did, Erik!" he replied, sitting at the table.

"I led them down to the cove, hid in some trees on the pathway while they clambered over the rocks down there, and then made my way back up here.

They never saw me, apart from when I wanted them to."

"Did you get a good look at them, Olof?" asked Jacques.

"Not up close," replied Olof, "but I could swear they were British navy men. I could see from a distance one of them wearing a bandana around his head. He was about your size Erik and had an eyepatch over one eye. I've marked him for when the action starts."

"They are the British Royal Navy," said Jacob. "From what you've just said, the big one with the bandana and eye patch was in the group of sailors I saw leaving the harbour with lanterns a few days ago."

"Well, they're on to something," said Olof. "And they've obviously connected it to you and us."

"We think they've got wind of some type of armed attack on the harbour," added Jacques. "How they've connected this to you and Jacob we don't know. But we're certain they have no idea of when it's going to take place."

"The invasion goes ahead on the thirty-first as planned," said Jacob, opening the bottle of brandy and filling the four glasses he had placed on the table.

"I'll drink to that," said Erik raising his glass.

"So, to recap," said Jacob looking at each of them. "Erik and Olof will wait off the cove on their fishing boat until they see the light of the British longboat approach. Best to have your boat in complete darkness Erik, we don't want them to see you waiting there." Erik nodded in agreement. "Per and I will be waiting on the cove to finish off any who manage to swim to the shore. Once that's taken care of, we'll light the beacons. You and Olof wait on your vessel until Magnus rows out to you in one of the French marines' longboats to pick you both up. We'll have moved off into the tunnel by then but will meet you where the coastal track meets the fork up on the main forest path. We should have no problem getting up to the point where the three heavy guns are positioned. Then gentlemen, the action begins!"

"Skol," bellowed Olof, raising his glass. "Skol!" they all cried, raising their glasses.

Sitting quietly, Jacques looked condescendingly at the three Swedes toasting each other in their premature triumph.

Fools, he thought. *They don't know we're just using them. This island will never be returned to them. Mainland Sweden will be our next prize, but first, we will turn this island into a fortress, our fortress. Yes, it will be our triumph.*

Looking at his three confederates he smiled patronisingly, then raising his glass he muttered quietly under his breath, "so, here's to a French victory gentlemen and, to Hanö Island becoming our fortress in the Baltic. Vive la France."

31

From her bedroom window, Anna looked out across the wide expanse of sea, picturing the French fleet lining up at midnight to begin their assault on the British held island garrison. Feeling utterly helpless, she sighed despairingly at the thought of the danger that would ensue. She had to find a way of stopping her father and uncle from getting involved. James' plan to storm Forsberg's hideaway the week before and apprehend her father and uncle, along with Forsberg and the other French spy, had failed badly.

The sound of a bedroom door slamming shut somewhere along the landing caused her to quickly move away from the window, her eyes darting around the room. Gathering herself, she stood a little shakily, her mind racing with a multitude of thoughts, then looking towards the door she smiled as an idea flashed through her mind. Smoothing down her skirt, she left her bedroom quietly, the idea swiftly turning into a daring plan of action.

Lars was angry, angry at being left out of the plan to sink the British patrol boat off the cove that night. He couldn't understand why his father had strictly opposed his son's wish to be part of the operation.

Why should the two Lundberg brothers be part of my father's plan? he thought bitterly, *when I'm quite capable of taking charge of the fishing boat. I can't conceive why he refuses to let me be at his side when the action starts. I'm eighteen on my next birthday, even if it's in ten months' time, but I'm fit and strong and well-used to looking after myself when fights break out down on the quay at night. Stay home and look after your mother and sister in case the French decide to attack the mainland, he said. That's rubbish, the French won't come anywhere near Nogersund, it's Hanö Island they want.*

Frustrated, he picked up a book lying at the end of his bed and hurled it across his room, watching it hit the wall and fall to the floor. A gentle knock on his door, and Anna's voice whispering to him, caused him to look round.

"Lars, it's me, Anna. Let me in. I've got something to tell you."

Hesitating, he wondered what she wanted, then frowning at being disturbed he crossed the room, partially opening the door to peer out through the gap.

"I'm not in the mood, Anna. Leave me alone for a while, will you?"

"No Lars, this can't wait. I've had an idea of us sneaking over to Hanö island tonight. Let me in."

Lars had always looked up to his sister. Being a few years older than him, she had kept a watchful eye on him when they were younger, and as they had grown up together a special bond had developed between them. Opening the door, he let her in.

"What d'you mean, us sneaking over to Hanö Island tonight?" he asked, looking at her curiously.

"Shush, I don't want to wake father, but just listen to what I've got to say."

"Ok, I'm listening," he replied. Come and sit next me and we'll keep our voices down."

Seating themselves on the side of the bed, Anna looked seriously at her brother. "I want to go over to the island tonight before the French fleet attack. If you come with me, we may be able to prevent father and uncle Olof from being killed. How, I'm not sure at this moment, but by us turning up before the action starts, we may be able to influence them to leave the island before it gets too dangerous. I'm going Lars, with or without you."

"That's crazy Anna," said Lars, staring at his sister. "Even if we found them, father would explode with anger at us. We'd be in deep trouble with him for ages afterwards. I wouldn't want to think how Uncle Olof would react!"

"There may not be any afterwards if we don't do something," said Anna.

"Anyway, how do you know about this invasion and how do you know father and Uncle Olof are involved?" queried Lars. "We've never discussed it with you."

"If you listen, Lars, I'll tell you more about how I am involved in all of this and why I need to go to the island tonight. Don't interrupt me."

Lars listened as Anna told him of her affair with the English captain and how she had overheard their father talking to their mother about their father's secret operations with the French. She confessed to listening outside the kitchen door the week before when her father had given information to the Lundberg brothers of how he and their uncle were going to sink the British patrol boat. Lars listened wide eyed, hardly believing what she was telling him. At this point, not sure whether Lars would go along with her idea, she said nothing about the British longboat's schedule being cancelled that night. When she'd finished, Lars sat staring at her, unsure of whether she had betrayed her family or what she was proposing could ultimately save her father and uncle.

"Anna, if father got to know you'd been feeding this British captain with information of the invasion, he'd throw you out and disown you. You know how our family feels about the British."

"Do you hate them as much as father and Uncle Olof do?" she replied.

"They killed our grandmother, Anna. What do you expect?" he cried.

"Shush Lars, keep your voice down. But that doesn't mean all of them killed her. Unfortunately, she was in the wrong place at the wrong time. We can't blame every Englishman for that."

"But father and Uncle Olof do," he said, frowning. "Anyway, what's the name of your English captain?"

"James Carey," replied Anna, "he's only been on the island for a few months. He was made captain of the frigate HMS Hector in the New Year."

"Ok," said Lars wanting to know more about Anna's idea, "but If I were to go with you, how would we cross over without father knowing?"

"James is another reason why I must go," she said, looking intently at her brother. "I have a feeling he'll be in great danger and that he'll come face to face with father when the fighting starts. If we can't do something to prevent this from happening, then I'm fearful one will kill the other. You've got to help me, Lars. My idea is to leave here tonight after father and his crew have left. The British know they're coming and will be waiting for them. There are several skiffs moored down at the harbour, we can take one and sail it across to Hanö's southern point. You know how to sail those small skiffs. We'll put in somewhere near the cove and watch and wait for them to come ashore."

"As long as we don't get wrecked on the rocks that lie submerged all along the coastline," said Lars.

"We'll have to take that chance," said Anna, desperately.

"There's only one thing that you've forgotten," said Lars. "Father and his crew will be waiting offshore in the dark for a British longboat to come past. They're going to ram it and make sure it sinks with all the crew. Any who make it to shore will be killed by Jacob Forsberg and the other French spy who'll be waiting on the cove. We don't want to be caught up in that."

Again, Anna refrained from telling her brother that the British would not be patrolling the area in their longboat, fearful that by some chance he may inform their father before he left that night.

"We won't be," said Anna. "We'll keep well-away from where father's fishing boat will be waiting. I know you know that part of the island Lars, you often talked about it when you started fishing with father."

"I do," agreed Lars. "I could take you there blindfolded; I know it so well. I think I know where the cove is that they've been talking about, and if I'm not mistaken, there's a very narrow inlet just past it where we could put in."

"Perfect," said Anna.

Lars was warming to Anna's plan. This was his chance to get involved. When his father found out it would be too late, he'd take the consequences then.

"There's only a quarter of a moon tonight," he said, "and there'll be a fair amount of cloud around but there's a good breeze up now, which hopefully will stay with us tonight."

"I think it best if we leave around an hour after father has gone," said Anna.

"He'll be gone by eight tonight, I'm sure."

"We'll sail directly towards Hanö's harbour," said Lars, "turning well-away before we're sighted. The British won't be expecting anything before midnight as you've said, but they'll be on the lookout. I have an idea where father will place the fishing boat, so we'll keep a good distance from there. It'll be dark and should he see us in the distance, he'll think we're only a couple of fishermen out checking our pots. I remember he told us at our last meeting that the British patrol boat comes past the cove at about eleven, so we'd better be well past him by then."

"Don't forget that the French fleet will be arriving around then," said Anna.

"I know," replied Lars. "But they'll be a good distance from us and father. It's a big risk though Anna, but if we're careful we should make it."

"Not a word about this to anyone, Lars," said Anna looking seriously at her brother. "Father will be up soon, so let's get through the day as though we're complying with everything, he's told us. When he's gone, we'll tell mother we've got some work to do down in the warehouse."

James stood on the quarterdeck of HMS Hector, looking far out to sea at the horizon where dawn was breaking. Anchored just outside the mouth of the garrison's harbour, Hector's deck was already abuzz with the crew going about their early morning duties. His thoughts were of Anna and the new home they would build together in Devon after they had returned to England, but these were quickly interrupted with recollections of Anna pleading with him to keep her father and uncle away from the oncoming battle. He would have had them locked away, had it not been for his second lieutenant and master-at-arms losing them in the forest a week before. There was now every likelihood her father and uncle would be killed in the ambush. He dreaded the thought of having to inform her. He wondered how he'd face Andre Pascale if it came to it, and if it did, would he kill him immediately. He would have preferred to capture the French lieutenant again, but strict orders from the commodore clearly stated no prisoners.

A polite cough behind him announced his two lieutenants waiting to come onto the quarterdeck.

"Please gentlemen, join me," acknowledged James.

"Good morning captain," they said in unison.

"I trust all the crew are about their duties," said James, turning once again to look out to sea.

"Aye sir," said Dan, "under the supervision of Mr. Nark."

"Good," replied James, "so, let us now select forty of the crew to be with me tonight."

"My apologies again captain, for losing the Gunnarsson brothers in the forest," said Richard, standing to attention and staring out to sea in the direction James was looking."

Turning, James regarded his second lieutenant.

"Apology accepted for a third time lieutenant but let me say that had my order to you been directed towards an operation at sea and was botched in the same way as was done last week, then you sir, would not be standing on this quarterdeck now."

"Yes sir," said Richard, red in the face.

"We'll forget it now, Mr. Devonshire, and put it down to experience, but in future I demand one hundred percent commitment in carrying out my orders and to achieving a successful mission. Is that clear, lieutenant?"

"It is clear captain, Thank you sir."

"Now, Mr. Sutherland, I want you and Mr. Devonshire to select forty good men from the crew to be with me in the forest tonight. The men must be used to skirmishing, and not reluctant to kill the enemy. Mr. Devonshire you'll be with me as first officer. Include Ned Hatchet in the list. When that's done, we'll go over the plans for tonight's action."

"Aye, aye, captain," they called, as James left the quarterdeck.

"Captain's giving you a second chance by choosing you to be with him tonight," said Dan, smiling at Richard.

"He'll want you by his side when the fighting starts. He obviously rates Ned Hatchet highly too. I think you can forget the fiasco of last week."

Richard, still smarting from his dressing down, grinned at his fellow officer.

James sat at his table, mulling over the plan of action he had drawn up with Commodore Percival at their meeting the previous evening. He and his detachment of forty crewmen, together with Richard Devonshire and Ned Hatchet, would leave the harbour at nightfall, crossing through the field of long grass and into the forest. He had already selected a position where they would make their ambush as he and Dan had scouted the main pathway two days before, looking for the most suitable hideaway. A line of dense shrubbery, just before the fork on the main forest path, afforded the perfect place. The line stretched from the fork and finished a good hundred yards back along the path. Holes within the thick bushes, made by burrowing forest animals, were ideal for his men to hide in while still having the advantage of a good view of who would come down the pathway. Nightfall would begin at around nine o'clock that night, ample time for them to leave the harbour and be in position before the French marines arrived on the cove in their longboats.

A gentle knock on his cabin door told him his two lieutenants were ready with the list. "Enter," he called.

Richard stood rigidly to attention as Dan presented James with the list of the forty crewmembers who'd make up the ambush party later that night. James scanned the list noticing the names of Clifford Williams and Richard Davis. Pleased at their inclusion, he nodded to Dan.

"One hour after leaving my cabin here, I want you both to inform each of the crewmembers on this list that there'll be a briefing in the enlisted men's mess at midday. I'll preside, where they'll learn of the mission they'll be on tonight. Mr. Devonshire, you will attend and stand alongside me at the briefing together with our master-at-arms. I trust you to inform Mr. Hatchet."

"Captain," acknowledged Richard.

"Mr. Sutherland, while our briefing is taking place, you will gather the rest of the crew on deck and inform them that you will be taking temporary command of the ship tonight. There must be no mention to the crew of our planned ambush in the forest. It will be enough for them to know that there'll be action against the invading French fleet. When that is done, dismiss the men but keep back the warrant officers and petty officers. Brief them as to why you are taking temporary command of the ship tonight, and of the plan we have decided on without mentioning the ambush in the forest.

This afternoon will be spent here at anchor, drilling the calls to action stations. Speed to the call will be practised again and again, until I am happy the exercises are hitting perfection. Have you any questions gentlemen?"

"No captain," they said in unison.

"Good. Mr. Devonshire, please leave us while I go through Mr. Sutherland's plan of action for tonight's mission. Midday, Mr. Devonshire."

"Aye, aye, captain," replied Richard, saluting his captain, and leaving the cabin.

It didn't take long for James to content himself with Dan's thorough understanding of what he had to do that night as temporary commander of HMS Hector. The captains of the other five warships and the two marine officers, had been briefed the night before. It was now only a matter of preparing for the oncoming battle and waiting for darkness to fall.

32

Jean-Luc Bonard walked briskly along the west quay of the French controlled port of Danzig, his eyes taking in the bustling activity going on around him. Rows of warships moored up along the port's quays were undergoing final preparations, their crews busily readying the decks for the forthcoming offensive. Lines of cranes worked ceaselessly in loading the ships, winching up boxes of ammunition and the heavy cannonballs that would rip into the British defences protecting Hanö's small harbour. He nodded in appreciation at the zealous commitment each of the ships' crews were showing to their duties. Stopping at the end of the quay he gazed at the last ship moored along the row, a third-rate ship of the line carrying seventy guns on its lower deck. A hive of activity was taking place on board. Sailors clambering up the ratlines swung agilely across to the yardarms, checking the shrouds that held the furled sails. Pigtailed crew members scurried back and forth across the upper deck, carrying boxes of munitions being winched aboard. Groups of marines lolled around the deck, cleaning items of their weaponry and watching the hubbub of activity.

Jean-Luc's eyes settled on a group of officers standing on the quarterdeck engrossed in a map being held by the ship's captain. With a grin, he hastened along the ramp, stopping at the end to await recognition. An abrupt shrill whistle from the boatswain's pipe brought the crew on deck to a sudden standstill. All eyes turned to the figure standing at the end of the ramp.

"Officer wishing permission to come aboard, captain," roared the boatswain.

The group of officers spun round at the sudden interruption to see Napoleon's First Secretary General to the city-state of Danzig attired in his uniform of an army general, standing at the end of the ramp. Snapping to attention they saluted him stiffly.

"I am General Jean-Luc Bonard. Permission to come aboard captain."

"Absolutely. Permission to come aboard General," replied the captain.

Stepping onto the deck of the flagship that would lead the attack on the island, Jean-Luc turned to salute those of the crew who had come to attention at his presence.

"For what do we deserve the honour of your visit, general?" asked the captain.

"I've come to wish you Godspeed captain, and to confer with the two lieutenants briefing you on the island's defences."

"Ah, yes of course, Lieutenants Renaud and Pascale," replied the captain, turning towards the quarterdeck and indicating to the two officers concerned.

"Please accompany us below, general. A good claret awaits."

Removing his bicorn hat, Jean-Luc glanced around the captain's spacious cabin. As a rated ship of the line, the accommodation had been designed to offer maximum comfort to its captain, in addition to being well-equipped for the social engagements a ship's captain would be expected to perform. Selecting a bottle of claret from a corner drinks cabinet, Captain Hugo Charbonnier pulled the cork, half-filling four of six haughty looking crystal glasses he took from a section of the cabinet.

"A special toast to our esteemed visitor," he said, raising his glass. "A votre sante, general."

"Sante," chorused Lieutenants Renaud and Pascale, raising their glasses.

"I trust you have been briefed well, captain," said Jean-Luc, appreciating the fine claret.

"We are ready, general," replied Charbonnier. "Lieutenants Renaud and Pascale will be leaving the flag ship shortly to embark on one of the fleet's frigates. This frigate together with another, will disengage from the fleet on sighting the island and move closer to the southernmost tip where they'll each offload two longboats loaded with our marines. Our two lieutenants will be aboard a longboat each, directing all four of them towards the selected cove where two of your agents will be waiting. I've been informed there'll be beacons lit to guide them in."

"That is correct," said Jean-Luc, "and once your two frigates have offloaded the longboats and marines, they will then re-join the fleet."

"That is so, general," replied Charbonnier, "in time for us to meet up with rear-Admiral Hastfer's Swedish flotilla before the hour of midnight."

"Excellent, captain," beamed Jean-Luc. "Now, you two," he said, turning towards Pierre Renaud and Andre Pascale. "Have you any questions for me before you depart?"

"No sir," they said in unison. "We're well-prepared, general," said Pierre, looking confidently at Jean-Luc.

"I will again stress the importance of this mission. Its success will depend on you taking over the British heavy cannons located on the island's highest point. I have every confidence our fleet will then succeed in sinking their puny force of warships and release the rest of our marines to wipe out any resistance the British may put up. Defeating the British and taking over this island will determine complete victory for us in the Baltic."

Smiling, Captain Charbonnier refilled their glasses and, raising them up, they toasted Jean-Luc's words of inspiration, confident that by daybreak the following day, Hanö Island would finally be in their hands.

From the upper deck Captain Charbonnier and the two lieutenants stood to attention as Jean-Luc left the flag ship. Turning round at the end of the ramp, the highly decorated general stood to attention, then saluting the flag ship he about-faced and walked swiftly away.

"The loading is complete, messieurs," said Charbonnier, turning to the two lieutenants. "I suggest you report to the captain of the frigate you'll be sailing on. There's a good wind up for our passage. We set sail on the tide at midday, in just over an hour."

Pierre and Andre came to attention, saluting the captain as he hurried away to the quarterdeck where his officers were lined up and waiting for his final instructions before receiving the order to cast off and set sail.

Leaving the flag ship, the two lieutenants hurried along the quay, searching the ships moored along its long walkway for the frigate they were expected to join. Half-way along, Andre pointed it out.

"There she is," he said, nodding towards a sturdy fifth-rate frigate bobbing up and down on the harbour's swell. "Look up there, painted on her bow side - Esprit De La France - that's our ship!"

Hurrying up the ship's ramp, they waited for permission to go onboard, their eyes taking in the bustling activity going on around the ship's single deck. The ship's crew were busy in preparing the ship for departure while groups of marines sat around the deck on boxes, going over their plans for when they reached the island. Pierre picked out the captain on the quarterdeck, who, surrounded by his officers, seemed busy in studying a series of charts spread before him. Noticing them waiting, a young lieutenant whispered in the captain's ear, promptly leaving the quarterdeck to make his way over to the two spies.

"Captain has granted permission to come aboard, messieurs. We are ready to depart and are only waiting for orders to set sail. I'm Lieutenant Philippe Laval, marine platoon commander. We've been expecting you. The captain knows you've been briefing Captain Charbonnier on our flag ship. It's good to finally meet up with you both as I'll be with you when we attack the British heavy guns. Please follow me, the captain is waiting."

Pierre and Andre followed Philippe to the quarterdeck where Captain Louis Marchand looked up as they approached.

"Welcome aboard our frigate, messieurs," he said. "We'll be setting sail in under an hour when we receive the signal from our flag ship. Until then, please use this time to acquaint yourselves with Lieutenant Laval. Use the time to go over your plans for when we release you into the longboats. There'll also be plenty of time for this when we're underway."

"Thank you, captain," they said, turning to follow the marine commander.

"This way," said Philippe, leading them away from the quarterdeck, "we'll find somewhere in the stern to talk."

Spotting a space at the rear of the frigate, Philippe guided them past a group of marines cleaning and checking their weapons.

"They're part of my group," he said, "fifteen marines. They'll be with me and you Pierre, in the longboat. Over there is your group, Andre," he said pointing to another group milling around the frigate's midships. "Remy Moreau, the giant standing in the middle of the group, is the sergeant in charge of that group, although he'll answer to you. There are fifteen in the group, including Remy."

"What about the other frigate?" asked Pierre.

"The same numbers," said Philippe. "Two groups of fifteen marines each. When our longboats have been winched down, we'll be first to row away. The marines on the other frigate will wait in their longboats until they see us pulling away from our frigate and then follow us to the cove. We'll have a couple of lanterns onboard and won't be too far ahead of them, but I understand that two of your colleagues on the cove will light beacons to guide us in."

"That's right," said Andre. "I assume you've been briefed about the tunnel?"

"Yes, and I just hope it's free of bats when we go through," said Philippe.

"There won't be any there then," said Pierre with a shudder, "they're nocturnal and only use the cave and tunnel during daylight. We'll be met on the cove by Jacob Forsberg and my colleague Jacques Petit. They'll lead you up through the tunnel with Andre, but I won't be with you as I'm using one of the longboats to row out to pick up a Swedish skipper and his brother from their fishing boat just offshore. They are loyal to us and will have taken care of a British longboat that has a schedule of patrolling past the island at the hour of eleven every night. In collaboration with this skipper, we've planned for him and his crew to wait for the patrol boat to come within sight and then ram it and sink it. There'll be no survivors to worry about. These two Swedes are anxious to help us in defeating the British and want to be part of our attack on the British heavy cannons. For their role in sinking the British patrol boat we've agreed for them to be with us when the action starts. When we come ashore onto the cove, we'll take the narrow coastal path up to the forest and meet up with you on the main pathway. From there it should be an easy route up to the highest point of the island where we'll attack the British controlling the heavy guns."

"Their cannons will be manned with the usual number of artillery gunners?" asked Philippe. "Would I be right in saying four to each cannon?"

"I would say so," said Pierre. When I was up there with Jacob and Jacques, I counted two guards for each cannon. Jacob confirmed that there'd be four gunners to fire each cannon when action commenced plus the two guards to defend them."

"So, eighteen in all on the night we attack," said Philippe. "We'll take them out in one hit and then turn the fire power down onto the

British, destroying their ships in and out of the harbour. Your intelligence counted two platoons of British marines, numbering no more than seventy men, a meagre number to resist the full force of our marines when they're put ashore. With the size of our fleet and our superior numbers of marines it won't take long before the island is completely in our hands."

"I think we're moving," said Andre, feeling the ship shudder.

"That we are," replied Philippe looking over the portside bulwark. Glancing back at Pierre and Andre he grinned, "Now messieurs, the invasion begins."

33

The sound of desperate pleading from Christina, trying to dissuade Erik from joining the French invasion of the island, rose from the kitchen to where Anna stood listening on the landing outside her bedroom.

"It's not for you to get involved Erik," she heard her mother say. "You have a family here who need you. Please don't go. I dread the worst."

"I'm going to avenge my mother, Christina. They murdered her in that bombardment. Now Olof and I have an opportunity to pay back those who wear the uniform of her killers. No matter what you say Christina, Olof and I are going. Now come here and give me a hug, you know I'll return."

Anna imagined her mother gripping her father tightly in their embrace. Seconds later, the sound of the kitchen door closing confirmed he had left to join the French. Hurrying down the stairs, she made her way to the kitchen where her mother sat at the table holding her head in her hands.

"I couldn't make him stay, Anna," she said, looking around at her daughter.

"I heard, mama," said Anna, putting an arm around her mother.

"You know, don't you?" asked her mother.

"Yes, I do mama," said Anna. "I know everything that papa and Uncle Olof have planned. I overheard most of what has been said here."

"I tried to keep this from you, Anna," said Christina, tears filling her eyes.

"I knew you'd be worrying about your English captain and the battle that's going to take place. But now it seems unavoidable. Your father won't listen to me. He's got this idea fixed in his head that he and Olof must have revenge for the killing of their mother. So, they're going to join the French in the fight to take over the heavy guns on the island after sinking a British longboat that patrols the island's southern coast. Thank God Lars is not going with them."

"Come mama," said Anna, taking Christina's hand. "I'll light a fire in the parlour, you'll be comfortable there. Drink a glass of schnapps, it'll calm you."

"Thank you, Anna," said Christina, rising from the chair.

Anna guided her mother into the parlour where a fire had already been laid. Lighting a taper, she held it under the kindling, watching the flames shoot up around the thin sticks that filled the wide grate. A stack of logs lay next to the fireplace and, selecting a few, Anna placed them onto the reddening embers of the kindling, the flames quickly taking hold. Stepping back, she took a bottle of schnapps from a sideboard and filling a small glass with the fiery liquid took it over to her mother, gently placing it in her hand. Christina sat gazing into the fire, the worry of Erik going off to war clearly stamped across her features.

"Drink this mama, it'll help you to relax," said Anna, tenderly.

Christina looked at the glass and in one swift action swallowed the contents.

With a slight shiver she held out the glass for a refill.

"It's just past the hour of eight, mama," said Anna, filling the glass with schnapps. "Lars and I have to go to the warehouse to make sure everything is locked," she lied. "I need to work on some invoices that are outstanding, and Lars has rolls of nets hanging outside the warehouse he needs to put away inside. If we're not back by the time you retire, we'll see you in the morning."

Anna handed her mother the glass of schnapps, hating the lie she had spun.

"Yes, thank you Anna," replied Christina. "I think I'll retire early. I need to sleep to blot out the worrying thoughts of your father and uncle. By the morning it should all be over, and he'll come back home safely."

"God willing, mama," said Anna, stooping to kiss her mother's forehead.

Leaving her mother with the glass of schnapps and the warmth of a roaring fire, she hurried back upstairs knocking softly on Lars' bedroom door.

"Lars, it's me," she whispered. "Papa's left, and mama's going to retire early. She's sitting in the parlour now but will probably go up to bed soon. Are you ready, we can leave now?"

Lars' bedroom door opened slowly, "I'm ready," he said peering through the gap. "Are you?"

"I'll just get my cloak and put on some warmer clothes. Give me a minute"

Anna rushed into her room pulling out from a cupboard some extra warm woollen tops which she hurriedly struggled into. Next, she grabbed her cloak and, wrapping it around her, she left her bedroom, quietly closing the door behind her.

"Lars, I'm ready," she whispered, outside his room.

Lars came out dressed as though he was going out for a day's fishing at sea, a thick woolly hat closely pulled down just above his eyes.

Silently, they tiptoed down the stairs quietly opening the front door so as not to disturb their mother. Stepping out onto the front steps, Lars gently closed the door behind them and with a look of apprehension followed his sister down the steep track that led to the harbour.

Darkness was beginning to set in, casting deep shadows over the mooring where Erik usually secured his fishing boat. Approaching the end of the quay they stopped, their eyes fixed on the empty space alongside the mooring regularly used by their father. Lars nudged Anna, pointing towards a dark shape bobbing up and down on the harbour's gentle swell.

"There's our skiff," he said, "all alone and waiting for us. There's a good breeze, so it won't take us long to get out of the harbour."

"I wonder who it belongs to?" asked Anna. "When this is over, we must get it back to whoever owns it."

"No problem," said Lars, "we'll just sail it back here tomorrow morning and leave it as we found it."

Don't think it's going to be as easy as that, thought Anna.

Looking around to make sure no-one was watching, they slipped the mooring rope from its post and boarded the skiff. Unfurling the sail, Lars pushed against the wooden sides of the quay and grasping the tiller guided the little boat towards the mouth of the harbour.

"Take this and light that lantern swinging from the side of the mast," said Lars, handing a tinder box to Anna. "Quickly, before we're out of the harbour."

Anna struck a flame in the tinder box lighting the candle in the lantern as a stiff breeze suddenly filled the skiff's sail, sending it zipping over the dark choppy swells. With the wind blowing through her hair, Anna stared out at the darkening sea, wondering how they could keep their father and uncle from joining the French and the oncoming battle. She thought of James, and how she could keep him from coming face to face in a bloody fight with her father. It was all a long shot, she knew. But at least she'd be there.

"There's a sea mist coming up," said Lars, squinting out over the dark waters.

"And it's going to get worse."

"How far have we gone?" asked Anna.

"About half-way," replied Lars. "Don't worry, I could get us there with my eyes closed. I've steered this course hundreds of times in papa's boat. If it weren't for this damn mist coming up, we'd be able to make out the shoreline of the island soon. My guess is that another half hour should see us at the mouth of the harbour. But we don't want to go anywhere near there, so in twenty minutes I'll bear the skiff hard to starboard, and hopefully we'll be able to make out land on our left side. That little inlet I told you about will be along that coastline, just past the cove where the French marines will land. Papa will be waiting somewhere along there in his fishing boat for the British patrol boat to come by. We're too small for him to mistake us for the patrol boat. Should he see us, he'll think we're a small fishing boat checking our nets."

Anna said nothing. *I just hope you're right Lars,* she thought.

Dusk had descended over the island of Hanö, bringing with it a slow-moving blanket of cloud. Heading along an animal track that twisted its way through the forest thicket, Jacques looked up at the sky through a gap in the trees.

"Look at those clouds, Jacob," he said, pointing upwards, "does it look like rain to you?"

Jacob stopped and, peering up through the dimming light, paused before answering. "Night's drawing in fast," he said, "but I doubt it'll rain here. Those clouds may linger around all night. They'll blot out the moon and stars which will be good for us when we're making our way up to the three heavy cannons. Good for the fleet too when they approach the harbour. Don't worry, even if it rains the beacons on the cove won't get wet, they're well covered. Come on, it's getting dark, and I want us to make sure those four pyres are ready for us to light."

Quickening their pace, they hastened along the track coming out onto the main forest pathway at the fork where they descended the narrow grassy trail that led down to the shoreline. Both carried a bag slung over a shoulder containing a small amount of dried grass and bracken, some kindling sticks, two candles and an axe. Jacob had included his telescope, while a leather scabbard holding a sword hung from his side. Jacques carried the lantern he had used on the cove when a little crab had crawled up the inside of his trouser leg, nearly ruining the vigil he had been keeping on the British longboat.

Turning a bend, they came to the cove where deep shadows caused by the fading light were enveloping the surrounding rocks, giving the scene before them a creepy spectacle. The squawking of a lone seagull calling out for its mate echoed along the darkening shoreline. Four beacons, shrouded in blankets and embraced by the descending darkness, stood in the middle of the cove like four ghostly wraiths.

Smiling at the wary look on Jacque's face, Jacob jumped down onto the shingle making his way over to the four pyres.

"Come on Per," he called, whipping off the blankets covering the four bonfires. Everything's dry so they'll burn well when I light them from my new tinder box. We'll start by packing in the kindling."

Shrugging off a nagging feeling of gloom that had overwhelmed him back on the forest trail, Jacques made his way over to where Jacob was packing his supply of kindling around the bottom of two of the beacons. Following suit, he stacked his kindling under the mounds of dry sticks and logs that made up the other two pyres.

"Now we're ready," said Jacob, looking at his pocket watch. It's approaching the half hour of nine. We should be seeing the lights from Erik Gunnarsson's fishing boat soon. When they're sure we're here, they'll extinguish their lanterns and wait in the darkness offshore for the lights of the British longboat. The patrol boat should be coming past any time between the hour of ten and eleven, hopefully before the French warships come into sight. Once Gunnarsson's boat has rammed it, we'll wait down at the shoreline to finish off any of the British crew who manage to swim ashore. Then we'll light the beacons, as it will be close on the hour of eleven. So, all we must do now is to wait."

"I'll light the lantern I brought with us," said Jacques.

"Yes, do that," said Jacob, "we can sit over there by those rocks."

"Ha, not me!" said Jacques with a smirk. "Not after what I went through when a little crab wandered up my leg to nestle in the warmth of my crotch. I'll stay standing, Jacob."

"Ha, suit yourself," said Jacob, grinning. "I doubt that little crab recovered after being stuck in your crotch for all that time. As soon as you shook it out, it probably collapsed and died from all the noxious air it had to breathe!"

Jacques smiled, taking out a candle from his bag and placing it inside the lantern. Chuckling, Jacob took the lantern from Jacques and striking a flame from his tinder box he lit the wick of the candle putting the lantern onto a rock beside him, then settling back onto the blankets he had spread out over a flat rock, he stretched out with a yawn.

"Don't worry Per," he said, "I'm just resting my eyes for a while. You keep a good watch out there for the lights of Gunnarsson's fishing boat. When you see them, tell me, I won't be asleep."

Jacques scanned the murky waters in front of him, his eyes peering deep into the darkness. There was nothing out there, only the silence of the sea at night and the sound of the waves gently lapping over the pebbly shoreline.

"Jacob," he whispered, not certain whether he was awake.

"What?" came the reply.

"You never told us why you hate the British so much. Is it because of what they did to the Gunnarsson's mother?"

There was silence. Jacob lay on his back with his eyes closed. A minute passed without any response from him and as Jacques turned his head to look out over the dark waters, Jacob spoke.

"No, nothing to do with their mother," he began. "My father was a Danish fisherman. He married my Swedish mother after a whirlwind courtship when his fishing boat docked in Karlskrona. They had twin sons, my brother and me.

As we grew up together, we became very close, always sticking up for each other and supporting each other when times were good and bad.

"Well, my father wanted us to be fishermen and eventually take over his business of fishing the waters of the Baltic. I joined him and learnt the trade, eventually taking over from him when he had to give up the sea due to chronic back problems. He didn't last long after that and died a year later. My brother didn't want the life of being a fisherman and joined the Danish navy. He had no problem in that as our father had always kept his Danish nationality. My brother did well in the navy, rising to able-seaman first class.

"Now, just before the British bombarded the city of Copenhagen in 1807, my brother was part of the crew of a Danish frigate, "The Friderichsvaern", that was ordered to sail to Norway on the 12thAugust of that year. At that time there was a pact between the Danish and Norwegian navies. Denmark had not declared war on Great Britain then but had been under great pressure from the French to join Napoleon's Continental Embargo against the British.

"Anyway, for some reason the British suspected the Danish frigate my brother was on of carrying a secret document to the Norwegian navy, requesting a joint action against the British. No evidence of any kind was presented to verify this claim. However, the British sent a frigate to pursue the Friderichsvaern. An engagement took place resulting in the captain of the Danish frigate striking its colours and surrendering the ship. The British boarded it, demanding the Danish captain hand over the secret document. He refused, as there never was a secret document. So, the British hanged him from a yardarm, along with five other crewmen, one of them being my twin.

"This, Per, is why I hate the British. I will never stop hating them nor wanting revenge for what they did to my brother. What they did wasn't even an act of war. They murdered him."

A gradual bobbing of lights from out at sea made Jacques suddenly whip round. Squinting into the darkness, he made out two lights shimmering at a short distance from each other.

"Jacob, there are two lights out there. It must be Erik's fishing boat. Looks like a nasty sea mist is forming."

Jacob bolted upright. Jumping to his feet he grabbed his bag, searching for his telescope. Finding it, he flicked it open, trying to focus on the two lights wobbling to and fro out in the misty darkness.

"Can't see very well owing to this mist. But it's them," he said. "Looks like they've fixed lanterns to their bow and stern. Give them a signal, Per."

Jacques held up the lantern and, snatching a blanket from the rock, covered the lantern with the blanket for five seconds. This he repeated several times.

"That's it," said Jacob, "they're signalling back. They know we're here.

"How is the hour, Jacob?" asked Jacques, holding up the lantern.

Taking out his pocket watch, Jacob held it in front of the light.

"Near to the hour of ten. The British patrol boat will be approaching soon.

Erik will see the lights in their longboat through the mist, no doubt of that."

Jacques blew into the lantern, extinguishing the flame from the candle. As he did so the two lights aboard the Gunnarsson's fishing boat suddenly went out.

"Keep your eyes peeled," whispered Jacob, "because the next light you see will be from the British longboat. When Erik sees their light, he'll drop sail and ram their boat to the bottom of the sea. There's a good breeze up now."

Sliding his sword out from its scabbard, he turned to Jacques,

"Get an axe from your bag and take out the skinning knife. You'll need them for any of the British who make it to the shore. No survivors, we'll kill them all."

Through the thickening mist, Lars suddenly pointed out the dark shape of land ahead. A pocket had opened in the mist, allowing them to see the mouth of the harbour a short way ahead.

"Now," he yelled, grabbing the tiller, and turning the little skiff hard to starboard. Anna gripped the sides of the boat as the wind caught the skiff's sail, turning it sharply away from the mouth of the harbour.

"Look to your left Anna," shouted Lars, "that's the island's coastline. Now we're heading south and should be passing the cove shortly. Damn, we're into the mist again. Anna, take the tiller and keep her steady while I furl the sail a little. We've got to cut our speed."

Anna grasped the tiller, keeping the skiff steady as their speed quickly decreased. The mist had enveloped everything around them, blotting out the view of the island's coastline and their range of vision from the skiff's bow. Anna grasped the sides of the skiff, anxious whether Lars would be able to find the narrow inlet. The mist was now engulfing the inside of their little vessel, blanketing everything within arms' reach. Nothing could be seen, just the twinkling glow of their lantern swinging to and fro against the mast.

34

James held up his hand at the entrance to the forest, bringing the forty selected men from his crew to a halt. Holding his finger to his lips he gathered them round.

"From here on," he said, quietly, "there's to be absolute silence while we're moving down the main forest path. We'll come to a fork in the pathway where we'll hide until we spring the ambush. Unfortunately, dark clouds are blotting out light from the moon and stars, plus there's a thick mist rising from the sea below. Mr. Devonshire, hold up the lantern you're carrying."

Richard raised the lantern for James to peer at his pocket watch.

"It's just past the half hour of nine. We'll get to our hiding place in about fifteen minutes. Four of you to each space. Lieutenant Devonshire and Mr. Hatchet will direct you. Once there, wait for the order to attack, even when you see and hear the French coming along the path. Wait for my order. I'll fire the first shot which will be my signal for you to go. We'll hit them hard and fast. None of them must get past us. Our job is to stop them getting to the heights and our heavy guns. We're not taking any prisoners, is that clear?"

Holding up the lantern, he saw the nods of agreement ripple around his men.

"Able seamen Williams and Davis, you'll be up front with me and Lieutenant Devonshire. Mr. Hatchet will position himself at the rear. If that's all clear, we'll continue into the forest. Mr. Hatchet, advance the men in twos, after me."

"Aye, aye, Captain," called Ned Hatchet.

The light from the lantern didn't give much visibility over the rough forest pathway as Richard, up front with James, held it outstretched to warn of any tree roots or boulders that may hinder their passing. An occasional yelp of pain followed by a blasphemous expletive from someone tripping over or banging a toe against a sharp stone or boulder, brought an irate command for silence from Ned Hatchet. Pitch blackness had enveloped the forest, slowing down their progress. Nothing moved around them, save the sound of forest animals scurrying away into the undergrowth. Rounding a bend, James brought the men to a halt.

"I'm sure the fork is up there on the right," he said, turning to face Richard. "Give me the lantern Mr. Devonshire, I'll go and look. Keep the men here in silence."

Richard handed James the lantern watching him walk slowly up the forest path. Swinging the lantern to his right, James nodded approvingly at a thick row of shrubbery running along behind the trees. A little further on he swept the light in an arc, glimpsing the fork at only a stone's throw from where he stood. It wasn't long before Richard saw the light bobbing back down the pathway.

"It's just up there," said James, handing the lantern back to his lieutenant.

"We'll move on and halt at the fork, and then you and Mr. Hatchet disperse the men into the line of shrubbery behind the trees. There are natural gaps in the bushes, wide enough to take a group of men. Place them four to a gap and ten yards apart. That'll cover the hundred yards of the thicket's length. Mr. Hatchet, you will join the four in the end gap. You, Mr. Devonshire, will be hiding at the fork with me, together with Williams and Davis."

"Aye, aye, Captain," responded Richard and Ned in unison.

"And lieutenant," added James, "some of the men have pistols and muskets, make sure they're primed and ready for firing when they hear the order to attack. Cutlasses and knives must be unsheathed once the men are in their hiding."

By the light of the two lanterns, James watched Richard and Ned allocating the men into their hiding places, the pathway quickly becoming empty and silent. Slowly walking up the forest path, he checked his men were in position, nodding with approval as each group of four answered his softened call. An eerie silence was descending over the darkened scene.

Ready and in position, James turned to his second lieutenant.

"Extinguish the lantern, Mr. Devonshire. It won't be long now."

As they waited in the darkness a deep frown spread across James' forehead. Erik Gunnarsson and Andre Pascale would be part of the French force about to come down the pathway, both intent on turning the heavy cannons on Hanö's heights down onto the British positions. Tightening the grip on his pistol, he knew there would be no alternative but to kill them both.

Erik squinted through the thick mist for signs of a light moving through the water. The mist had engulfed everything around them and even with a moderate breeze blowing across the sea, the mist still hung in thick patches along the island's southern coastline. The fishing boat bobbed up and down in the darkness, its sail furled but ready to be dropped at Erik's command. Olof gripped the boat's wheel, keeping the boat steady and pointing the bow north along the coastline where he was sure the British longboat would eventually appear on its nightly patrol.

"Can't see much further than the bow," said Erik, joining his brother at the helm. "I've told Gustav and Nils to keep a constant look out for signs of a light out there. They know it'll be the British patrol boat. If Jacob's reckonings are correct, it'll be coming past soon. It's just past the hour of ten now."

"If we can't see the boat through this mist," said Olof, "we'll certainly see the light from its lantern."

"And it's then that we'll drop sail," replied Erik. "And with this breeze, we'll ram the fucker to kingdom come."

"If the breeze strengthens it should clear the mist," said Olof. "There are already pockets of clear space out there. It seems the mist is thicker closer to the coastline."

"Another hour should see the French frigates arriving with the marines," said Erik, peering out over the bow. "Jacob will then light the beacons on the cove and with a bit of luck the mist will have dropped by then, especially if this breeze moves closer to shore."

"How was Christina when you left home this evening?" asked Olof.

"She begged me not to go," replied Erik. "She said, the French invasion of Hanö Island wasn't my fight. She seems to have softened her feelings towards the British, probably because of Anna's newly found relationship with that British captain on the island. I'll look for the bastard when the action starts. I have a feeling he'll come my way."

"Yes, and I've already marked that big one with an eye patch whom I led on a merry chase with his partner through the forest," said Olof. "I'll be looking out for him when the fighting starts. D'you think the French will let us have the island back once we've kicked the British off?"

"Well, that's the plan," replied Erik. This island belongs to Sweden and the Swedes who live on it. I'm certainly not fighting for another foreign power to take it over. Why do you ask?"

"I don't really trust the French," said Olof. "If you think of it, the island would be a great stepping-stone for them should they think about invading our mainland. It would also serve as another garrison port for Napoleon's navy, and a good naval base for protecting his ships in the Baltic. It's served the British well over the last two years."

"Bah, it's too small for Napoleon's ambitions. No, we'll take it back for us Swedes, and that'll be that!"

I Just hope you're right, brother, thought Olof.

"ERIK!" came a shout from one of the brothers standing up in the bow. "A light, and it's bobbing about through the mist on our starboard bow."

"Get ready Olof, this could be it," said Erik, leaving the helm and moving up to the front of the vessel.

"Where did you see it?" he asked, joining Gustav, and peering closely into the mist.

"At about one o'clock on the clock's face, directly off our bow." replied Gustav. It was moving slowly, just off the coastline. Look there it is again."

"You're right," said Erik, seeing the light from a lantern wobbling around a few hundred yards from where they were. It's them, the British patrol boat. Quick, get ready to drop the sail when I say."

Gustav and Nils rushed to the mast grasping the ropes that would release the fishing vessel's sail. Erik made his way back to the helm where Olof was peering out through the darkness.

"I've seen it, Olof," said Erik, excitedly. Look over there to your right, just off the bow. There it is, can you see it?"

Olof nodded, his eyes picking out a dim light moving slowly through the mist.

"Looks like they're not far off the rocky shoreline," said Olof. "The water shelves deeply here so we'll be alright." Gripping the vessel's wheel, he grinned at his brother. "Give the order to drop sail now. There's a good breeze springing up."

Erik turned around, his eyes fastening onto the mast where the two brothers stood waiting for him to give the order.

"Now," yelled Erik, "drop that fucking sail."

Lars felt the breeze pick up as the skiff's half-furled sail drove them further through the misty darkness. He knew the rocky shoreline was not far off their portside, and if he kept the boat on its present course, they'd avoid the rocks jutting out to sea. He sensed the narrow little inlet was not far away, but unless a clear pocket of air opened for him to see where it was, he'd have to guess its location and hope his intuition was right.

Anna sat grasping the sides of the skiff peering out into the darkness, willing the mist to rise so they could see where to come ashore.

"It's not far Anna," yelled Lars. "If we don't hit a clear pocket in this mist, then I'll try to take us in from memory. I'm pretty sure I'll be able to do it. When I say, you furl the sail and lash the holding ropes around the hook in the middle of the mast, just below the lantern. I'll turn the skiff into the inlet when we cut our speed, just keep your fingers crossed we make it."

Anna nodded, focusing on the lantern swinging back and forth on the mast.

"Okay," yelled Lars, "now, pull up the sail."

Anna jumped up to the mast grasping the holding ropes that raised and lowered the sail. Suddenly she gasped, her eyes widening in horror. For a moment she thought they were heading into the side of a steep cliff as a dark shape suddenly loomed off their bow.

"What the hell is that?" hollered Lars. "It's coming straight for us. Oh my God it's going to hit us."

Through the mist, Anna recognised the shape of her father's fishing boat. A picture of her standing outside the kitchen door at home suddenly flashing through her mind as her father described his plans to sink the British longboat.

"Oh my God," she screamed, "he thinks we're the British patrol boat."

In an instant, Anna felt herself being catapulted backwards, her shoulder crashing into the arm of the tiller as Erik's vessel struck the bow of the little skiff. In a daze she managed to stagger to her feet, slipping and sliding over the boat's saturated bottom. She heard herself call out for Lars, but he was nowhere near her. In her dazed shock she heard the splintering of wood and the roar of water as the little boat disintegrated. Choking and gasping for breath as water filled her nose and ears, she felt herself sinking down into the depths of the blackened sea until darkness enveloped her and there was nothing.

Erik stared over the side of the fishing boat. "Turn her round, Olof," he yelled. "We'll go back and see if there's anyone in the water. I couldn't see through the mist, but I heard their boat disintegrate as we hit it."

Olof spun the wheel, the fishing boat gliding back to the point where they believed they had sunk the British longboat.

Wreckage floated on the sea's swell, the little skiff's mast and sail slowly sinking under the choppy water.

"Nothing but debris," shouted Nils, holding a lantern over the side of their vessel.

"Can you see any bodies?" asked Erik, scouring the murky swell.

"Nothing," replied Nils.

"What about you, Gustav?" yelled Erik. "Any bodies floating around back there off the stern?"

"No, nothing apart from bits of wood," came the reply.

"Then they must've all drowned," said Olof. "Any who may have surfaced and swam ashore will be seen off by Jacob and Per."

"Look," shouted Nils. "They've lit the beacons on the cove."

"Back to our waiting position, Olof," said Erik. "The French frigates must have arrived. Those beacons will guide their marines onto the cove. We'll wait for Magnus to row out and pick us up."

Turning to his brother, Olof grinned, "That was the first part of our revenge, Erik. Now for the second part!"

35

A searing pain as if her hair were being pulled out by the roots, snapped Anna out of the darkness she had slipped into. Half-conscious, she was mildly aware of being hauled out of her watery tomb, a nauseous feeling to vomit overwhelming her as she felt something being forced down her throat. Giving way to the urge, she spewed up the volume of sea water that had filled her stomach, coughing, and gasping for breath. Opening her eyes, she saw Lars perched on a rock in front of her, one hand holding onto her while he withdrew the fingers of his other hand from inside her throat.

"Thought I'd lost you for a moment," she heard him say as she felt her stomach heave again to spew out the last drops of sea water. Spluttering, she looked up.

"What happened, Lars?" she asked, weakly.

"I'll tell you later," she heard him say. "We can't stay here. There are two men over there on that cove. They've just lit beacons, and I think they're looking for us. One's carrying a sword and the other's wielding an axe. They seem to be scouring the rocks intent on killing us. The mist has risen, and I've seen a nook between two big rocks over there which will keep us hidden. Come on, I'll help you up."

Gripping his sister round her waist, he pulled her up. Through the dim light coming from the beacons, he focused on the dark nook between two scabrous boulders, a stone's throw from where they were. The two men searching the shoreline had dropped out of sight, giving Lars and Anna the opportunity to stagger over to the dark cranny that would act as a shelter and hideaway. The little nook gave a good outlook to the shingly inlet, and with the mist now lifted they had a perfect view across the cove to the sheer cliffs that rose on the other side. The two men Lars had seen stood at the bottom of the cove, gazing out over the darkened sea.

"They're waiting for the longboats carrying the French marines," said Anna, beginning to shiver with cold. "The frigates carrying the French marines must have arrived, so it won't be long before those longboats come ashore onto the cove."

"Papa and Uncle Olof must be waiting offshore somewhere," said Lars. "Why did he think we were the British patrol boat?"

"Because he didn't know it had been cancelled," answered Anna.

"And you did?" queried Lars, looking surprised.

"Yes, I knew," said Anna. "James told me the British command had given orders for no coastal patrols tonight because they knew the French were coming. I didn't tell you Lars because I wasn't sure whether you'd tell papa before he left. If you had it would've ruined James' plans and papa would've known the British had found out about the French marines landing on the cove. He would've told the French somehow, and they would've changed their plans of attack, putting James into greater danger. I didn't know papa would mistake us for the British patrol boat in all that mist."

"But Anna," said Lars, "don't you think that papa is now in great danger. The British know they'll be coming through the forest, so it doesn't take much to realise they'll be waiting to ambush them. Somehow, we've got to warn papa and uncle Olof."

"Yes, I agree," said Anna. "But think, Lars. We can't afford for papa to see us here. If he sees us, he'll be so furious that he'll get someone to ferry us back to his fishing boat. He'll never listen to us. No, we'll have to follow them up into the forest and see if we can single them out before the British attack them."

Lars suddenly stiffened. Squinting out over the rocks he nudged Anna. "Look, out there, just off the coast, the French longboats are coming. It won't be long before they're ashore."

Shivering, Anna peered towards the shoreline watching the two men with weapons light a torch each from a flaming beacon, then running down to the shoreline they waved their fiery lights back and forth, signalling the marines to make haste to the shore.

Jacob ran to the first of the longboats as it slipped between the rocks to surge onto the shingle. Holding his torch above his head he rushed over to help the marines heave their boat further up the cove, while a second longboat made ready to pull in directly behind them. Jacques recognised Pierre leaping out of the first vessel and, with a shout he hurried over to him, clasping him in a brotherly hug.

"Come on," said Pierre, looking over Jacque's shoulder, "the second longboat looks stuck in the shingle, Andre's in that one. You help drag it up, while I take this one back out to sea. I've got to row out to get Erik and Olof. I've just seen them signalling from their vessel."

With the help of three of the French marines, Pierre pushed the longboat down to the shoreline. Scrambling in, he picked up the oars and as the three marines pushed him out to sea, he began to row towards the light signalling from Erik's fishing boat.

Philippe Laval quickly called his marines to gather around him, the giant Remy Moreau coming to his side.

"We're going up through the cave now," he said. "It's quicker than going up the narrow path that leads to the forest. Once we're up there we'll follow Jacob and Lieutenant Petit through the forest until we reach the British heavy guns. Wait for my order to take out the British gunners and their guards. When we've taken the cannons, redirect them down onto the British positions, then wait for the order to open fire."

Looking over at Jacob he nodded. "Ok, we're ready to go."

Jacob looked at Jacques, a grin forming around the edges of his mouth.

"Ready Per?" he said, "this is what we've been planning for. Let's go."

Andre Pascale appeared at their side as they clambered over the rocks towards the entrance to the cave, the French marines and Philippe Laval following closely after them.

Anna and Lars watched the last of the marines disappear over the rocks, the beacons still aflame on the now empty cove. They had seen a lone Frenchman detach himself from the group to scramble into a longboat and then row out into the darkness towards a flashing light. They both knew it was their father's boat sending the blinking signal, it wouldn't be long before he and their uncle appeared as the longboat returned to the cove. They waited, peering out over the cove into the darkened sea for a sign that the longboat was returning. Anna shut her eyes, praying her father and uncle had decided not to come and had sailed away, back to the small harbour of Nogersund.

From the cramped dark cranny, Anna and Lars watched the longboat come ashore onto the cove, her father and uncle leaping out onto the wet crunchy surface like two giant Vikings come to pillage and plunder.

Pulling the longboat up onto the shingle the two of them watched Pierre light one of the several birch-wick torches left behind by Jacob. Beckoning them to follow him they trudged across the cove and up towards the track that would lead them up through the forest to the fork on the main forest pathway.

"Come on Lars," said Anna, "the path I heard papa mention when he was giving you all the final instructions that night in our kitchen, is up there. It will lead to the fork where they'll meet up with the marines. We'll follow the light of the torch they're carrying and hopefully find a way to waylay them."

The hoot of an owl from somewhere deep in the forest echoed through the trees to where James and his men lay hidden. Peering out from the gap of his hideaway he noticed the mist had finally lifted.

"Thank God for that," he thought. "We'll have a better view of when they come round that bend. Shouldn't be long now."

"Captain," whispered Richard, turning his ear towards the gap. "Did you hear that? It's coming up from down there."

James thrust his head out of the gap, listening for any unusual sound. Nothing but silence filled the pathway before him. Concentrating, he listened again. The muffled sound of voices slowly rising from below led him to look round at the narrow track leading off from the fork and down to the shoreline.

"Someone's out there," he whispered, "and their voices are coming up from the track to the right of us. I'm going out."

Wriggling out through the gap he took a step towards the fork, stopping at the top of the track. It was too dark for him to see anyone, but the sound of voices coming from somewhere beneath him was now becoming clearer.

He listened, trying to distinguish the language he was hearing. And then something in the tone of the voice's inflection caused him to grasp the pistol in his belt. It was English he was hearing but spoken in the accent of the Swedes. Another voice speaking English drifted up through the darkness, this time with a French accent. The sudden sight of a flaming torch wavering between the trees warned him they were getting closer. Turning, he hurried back to the hideaway.

Squeezing back through the gap he held his finger to his lips,

"It's not the main force," he whispered, "they'll be coming round that bend any moment now. Coming up the trail that leads down to the shoreline are two Swedes and a Frenchman. It's my guess they'll be meeting up with the marines at the fork. I know who the Swedes are, but at this moment all you need to know is that they're here to help the French take over our heavy guns and to kill as many of us as they can, so treat them as the enemy. If you can, leave the one with the long grey beard to me. Just wait for my command. It won't be long now and remember: no prisoners."

The sound of heavy footsteps tramping up to the top of the narrow trail brought a stillness to the men hiding in the long line of shrubbery. Regulating their breathing, they listened intently to the fresh voices coming from the main pathway.

Pierre held the birch-wick torch at arm's length peering up and down the main forest path, hoping it wouldn't be long before Jacob and Jacques came jogging round the bend with the marines. Coughing up a wad of phlegm, Olof spat it into the darkness. "I need a piss," he said, walking through the darkness to the thick bush where James and the three navy men lay hidden.

Not daring to blink, they listened as Olof shuffled his way into the bush. Gritting their teeth, they waited for the rush of urine to come gushing through the tiny twigs that surrounded them. For some reason they remained untouched from the soaking that drenched a good part of their bushy hideout.

Erik suddenly became alert as Olof made his way back from the thick row of shrubbery. "Listen, can you hear that?" he said, turning to look back down the main path to the bend. "It's boots stomping along the path. They're coming."

Olof quickly drew the pistol he'd been carrying from under his belt, checking it was primed and ready to fire. Erik pulled out a long skinning knife that he knew would take a man's arm off with one swipe. With his free hand, Pierre gently extracted his officer's sword from its scabbard.

Carefully watching their movements, James tightened his grip on the pistol he was holding in one hand, while the other clasped the sword that had seen him through various battles and skirmishes at sea. Taking a quick look at the two able seamen next to him, he nodded with approval at the sight of their readiness. Richard looked ready enough, a determined look chiselled into his features, his sword firmly grasped in his right hand while his left clenched the handle of a vicious looking dagger.

The ground-thumping sound of a column of men approaching the bend grew louder, and as a shaft of light suddenly lit up the pathway Eric grinned to see Jacob and Jacques turn the corner, followed by the heavily armed platoon of French marines. The silence that had shrouded the forest was quickly stifled as a giant of a sergeant brought them to an abrupt halt.

"We'll take five minutes," said Lieutenant Laval to his men.

James watched the front leaders converse with the two Swedes, the light from their torches showing up the resolute looks on the fishermen's faces. He thought of Anna as he pushed himself out of the hideaway. There was nothing he could do now to save her father.

From the deep shadows of where he stood, he looked along the dark line of bushes knowing his crew were ready and waiting for his order. Taking a deep breath, he raised his pistol, "Charge," he bellowed, levelling the pistol at the group of marines, and pulling the trigger.

Jacob spun round at the sudden roar of armed men spilling out from a line of bushes in the dark recesses of the trees. A volley of pistol and musket balls came zinging through the air, finding their targets amongst Lieutenant Laval's men. Drawing his sword, he looked on in shock at the bewilderment and confusion now ripping through the special force of French marines. Turning to Jacques he screamed, "What the hell, how did they know we were coming?"

But Jacques never answered, a sweeping slash from Ned Hatchet's cutlass severed Jacques' head cleanly from its shoulders.

Pierre stared at Jacques' head lying in a pool of blood on the pathway. Shock at what he had seen froze him to where he stood, leaving him defenceless to the battle going on around him. He didn't see the two able seamen rushing towards him or feel the wrench as one of them pulled his head back by his hair, while the other sliced his throat with the sharp end of a bayonet.

James ducked as a marine made a swipe at his head, the swish of the sword zinging as it cut through thin air. As quick as a flash he lunged at the belly of the Frenchman, feeling his sword sink into the soft flesh, a gurgling cry coming from his assailant as he toppled over. A score of marines had fallen to the initial volley of musket and pistol fire, but the platoon quickly rallied to the shouts and commands of their lieutenant and were now fighting back with a fury to survive. As James cut down a marine charging towards him, he saw from the corner of his eye that Richard was in trouble. The giant of the marine sergeant had him on the ground by his throat, raising what looked like a short sword to stab through his eye. Pushing his way through the melee, James ran his sword through the back of the giant's neck, pulling it free as a powerful jet of blood gushed upwards like a forceful spurt from a geyser. Offering his second lieutenant his hand, he hauled him to his feet, "Now Mr. Devonshire, we're more than quits I believe!"

Richard smiled back at his captain and with a nod of acknowledgement dived back into the action, slashing the throat of a French marine with the dagger in his left hand.

The sound of a familiar voice angrily addressing him from behind brought James to an abrupt standstill.

"And now you are finally mine, Captain," sneered Andre Pascale as James turned slowly round to see a pistol pointing directly at him.

For a moment time seemed to stand still, the shouts and screams of the battle becoming a distant echo as James watched Pascale's finger pull back slowly on the trigger. A picture of Anna flashed into his mind, her voice soft and soothing as she whispered her love for him. Something heavy suddenly bowled him over, the sound of the shot from the pistol ringing in his ears. Shaking his head, he looked up to see Clifford Williams quickly pick himself up and level the bayonet attached to his musket at a trembling Andre Pascale.

"Williams," yelled James, "leave him to me." Turning at the sound of James' command, Clifford Williams was too late to avoid the sword Pascale lunged into his back. With a look of surprised disappointment spreading over his face he toppled over, his musket falling from his grasp. Gritting his teeth in anger, James picked up the musket from his fallen crewman and, facing Pascale, he screamed in rage: "You bastard Pascale, you didn't have to do that."

Pascale ran at James, his sword ready to slice down on James' head. As he made the downward swipe, James blocked the cut, bringing the musket up to parry the lethal blow, the sound of steel on metal ringing across the pathway.

Then bringing up his booted foot, he kicked the Frenchman firmly between his legs, sending him sprawling backwards, the sword slipping from his hand. With a look of horror, Pascale felt the searing pain of the bayonet rip through his ribs and then nothing as James sliced it upwards to bury it deep into his heart.

"Captain," a voice called. James turned to see Ned Hatchet standing next to him, his bandana stained with blood and his one eye darting from the dead Frenchman to the body of Clifford Williams. "It's nearly over, most of them are dead. It seems there's a core of them up the pathway fighting our men with a determined passion to win.

"How does it go with our men, Ned?" asked James.

"Williams' mate Richard Davis took a pistol ball through his throat. He didn't last long. Fought well though, sir. Don't know the number of our dead but it's minimal compared to their loss. Come on sir, we need you up the pathway."

Scattered over the pathway, torches still burned brightly as James followed his master-at-arms over the dead bodies of the fallen French marines. Through the light of the torches, he saw his men battling what was left of the French special force. As he and Ned approached the fighting, a body of marines suddenly broke away, running towards the trees where they disappeared into the darkness.

"Look sir," yelled Ned. "Up there, next to those burning torches. It's the two Swedes, with two others. Looks like they're about to leg it up the pathway."

"You're right Ned," said James, seeing Erik and Olof about to run.

"Mr. Devonshire," called James, seeing his second lieutenant. "Stay here and wait for our return. We've won this battle but send half a dozen of our men into those trees to find the handful of French who ran off into the woods. No prisoners, Mr. Devonshire. Come on Ned, we'll follow those four who've legged it up the pathway. I've a feeling they'll try and take over one of the heavy cannons. We've got to stop them."

Standing in the shadows of the trees that lined the edge of the trail leading off the fork, Anna and Lars looked on in horror at the slaughter taking place before them. Her heart jumped with relief as she saw James suddenly appear with a giant of a man wearing a bloodied bandana and an eye patch. Her eyes scanned the scene before her, searching for her father and uncle amongst those left standing and those lying lifeless along the pathway. The sudden movement of a group of marines running away into the darkness of the trees gave room for her to recognize the figures of her father and uncle standing with what looked like the two sole survivors of the invading French special force. She was about to call out to them when Lars quickly placed a hand over her mouth, shaking his head as a warning for her to keep silent. They watched the giant with the bandana point at the group of four, James then turning to yell an instruction to a young naval officer wiping clean a bloodied dagger. No sooner had James finished his instruction than they saw the group of four running hell–for–leather up the pathway and disappearing into the darkness of the surrounding trees. In an instant, James and the giant took off after them.

Anna stood in the cover of the shadows wondering what to do. There was no way now that she and Lars could pursue her father and James. With a heavy heart she looked at her brother, not knowing whether she would ever see the two men she loved most in her life again. With a deep sigh she took Lars' hand, suddenly sensing the familiar feeling of sorrow that had now begun to haunt her. Walking out of the cover of the trees they made their way towards the young British officer, who seeing them approach, laid down the bloodied sword and dagger he'd been calmy cleaning.

36

Jacob brought his three comrades to a halt at the end of the field of long grass. Standing near the track that led to the island's highest point, he squinted through the darkness listening for any sign that they were being followed.

"Anyone out there?" asked Olof, panting for breath.

"Can't hear anything," said Jacob. "The British guns are placed up there at the top of that stony track, about twenty yards apart from each other. Listen, they're silent now but when they sight the French fleet they'll open up like hell's fury. Each of the cannons has four gunners with two marines guarding it. In this darkness I'm sure we can take over one of their guns. The British marines manning the other cannons won't even see us as long as we're quiet. We'll have the element of surprise, so slitting their throats shouldn't be that difficult. Once we've dispatched them, we'll sight the cannon down onto the British positions around the harbour, blowing as many of them as we can to kingdom come.

"What are we waiting for then?" said Erik, moving out onto the track and starting the uphill climb.

Coming out of the forest James and Ned paused in the field of long grass. Darkness covered the way in front of them and, as they had no means of lighting up their way through the field, they knew they'd have to rely on their night vision.

"They must have come this way," said James. "If they're heading for our guns then this is the only way to the track that leads up to the highest point of the island. Come on Ned, I can't see any signs of them carrying a light in front of us, so they're in the same situation as we are, relying on their night vision."

Ned followed closely behind James as they picked their way along the narrow animal trail that twisted its way through the long grass, their night vision allowing no more than a few yards ahead. A blanket of cloud covered the moon and stars, plunging everything around them into pitch blackness.

"You ok Ned?" asked James in a whisper, hoping his master-at-arms was keeping up with him.

"Aye, aye, captain. I'm right behind you," came Ned's hushed reply.

James knew it wouldn't be long before the two platoons of British marines made their way up to the field to wait for the attack on the harbour to begin.

"I think we're coming to the end," he whispered, the long grassy stems suddenly dwindling around them.

"Look sir, to your right. Up there, torches," said Ned pointing.

James looked up to where Ned had indicated seeing the glimmer of torch light shimmering through the darkness.

"That's where our guns are placed," he said. "The gunners are waiting for our beacons down on the harbour wall to be lit. The flaming beacons will be their signal to open fire on the French fleet moving towards the harbour. The French ships will get one hell of a shock when they realise their marines have failed in their mission to take over the guns!"

"As our boys will, sir!" exclaimed Ned, "if we don't stop those four ahead of us from taking over one of the cannons."

"You're right Ned," said James, making out the rough stony track leading up to the summit. "We've made it through the field to the track here, so let's just hope we're in time to stop them. Come on."

Jacob slowly withdrew the sword he was carrying from its scabbard, his eyes fixed on one of the heavy guns pointing out over the dark void from its position on the edge of the island's highest point. From the cover of darkness, they could see four British gunners loading the barrel of the huge cannon, three flaming torches placed around the site to shed enough light to see by. Two marines acting as guards stood a few yards behind chatting together nonchalantly, oblivious to the danger watching them. Philippe clutched the handle of his navy issue dagger, waiting for the signal from Jacob to go.

"Look," whispered Jacob, nudging Philippe, "they're even loading it for us!"

"You, Erik, and Olof wait until we've taken care of the two guards. Once that's done come over and join us. But keep silent. We'll creep up on the gunners and cut their throats before they see us. Come on Philippe, the two guards have just turned their backs on us."

Enjoying a joke about their sergeant major, the two guards never got to the punch line of their story, rough hands clamping over their mouths and a sharp stab of pain were the last feelings they had, the cold steel of two finely sharpened weapons suddenly appearing out of the darkness and slicing across their throats.

Silently, Erik and Olof joined Jacob and Philippe, nodding as Jacob indicated which of the four gunners each of them would tackle. Spreading out, they crept towards the four unsuspecting artillery men, unaware of James and Ned coming off the stony track and stealing quietly up behind them.

Corporal Sidney Luscombe, a hardened regular of the British army, now in charge of number one cannon on the heights, was the first to whip round at the deep throated yell that broke the silence behind him.

"LOOK OUT, LOOK OUT BEHIND YOU," he heard a voice bellow in the darkness.

Years of army drilling quickly prompted him to respond to the warning. Stopping his men from loading the cannon, he barked out an order.

"Grab muskets men," he yelled, "we're under attack, turn and level bayonets."

In an instant his men turned, levelling the bayoneted ends of their muskets at the four silhouetted figures looming up at them from the shadows. Knocking away the musket held by the youngest gunner, Jacob ran his sword through the lad's red-coated chest, wrenching it back out amidst a jet stream of blood.

Lunging at Corporal Luscombe, Philippe Laval slipped on a dewy clump of bracken, tumbling forwards onto the wheel of the cannon. In a flash the British corporal drove his bayonet into the side of the Frenchman, quickly wrenching it out and then thrusting it again with all his force deep into his armpit.

James and Ned raced to the skirmish, James knocking Erik off his feet, so saving a young artillery soldier from having his throat cut.

Recognising him immediately, Erik yelled an obscenity at James, but in struggling to get to his feet his left shoulder took the full force of a bayonet from one of the artillery men. Coming to his brother's aid, Olof sliced at the marine with the dagger he had picked up from Philippe Laval's dead body. Stepping back, he yanked the bloodied dagger from the neck of the marine, watching his brother stagger to his feet.

"Captain," yelled Ned, "behind you."

Too late to sidestep the swipe of Jacob's sword, James felt the searing pain of the sharpened edge tear into his left arm. With blood spurting from the deep wound, he turned to see the island's spy master raising the sword to finish him. The look on Jacob's face, as the tip of a bayonet came pummelling out from the front of his chest, was one of total shock and bewilderment. As he toppled to the ground in a sea of blood, Corporal Luscombe pulled the bayonet from the bloodied back, and with a nod towards James wiped it clean on the side of the dead Swede's jacket.

Loud voices coming through the darkness meant the gunners and guards from the other two cannons had heard the ruckus and were on their way to help their comrades. Hearing the voices, Erik and Olof knew they would soon be outnumbered and seeing Jacob and Philippe lying dead in pools of blood they turned and fled.

"Captain," yelled Ned, "they're getting away."

"Come on, after them," shouted James, his left arm hanging limply at his side.

"They've headed for the rocks up there," said Ned, "that's where I saw them disappearing into the darkness."

"Corporal," shouted James, looking back at Sidney Luscombe. "I owe you. But send those men back to their cannons, the beacons will be lit soon."

"Sir," yelled Corporal Luscombe, pointing his comrades back to their heavy guns.

Leaning on his brother, Erik hobbled over the loose stones and bracken, his shoulder still pumping blood from the deep gash. He was already feeling weaker due to the extreme loss of blood and knew that unless the bleeding stopped, he would soon be in serious trouble. A shout from behind told them they were being followed, so quickening their pace they hurried on towards the silhouette of a towering row of boulders. Reaching its safety, they paused to catch their breath, then scrambling up to the top of the craggy columns they searched for a nook or cranny that could act as a hideaway. With a cry, Erik suddenly stopped in agony, his shoulder burning with the pain of his wound.

Olof caught him as he staggered towards the edge of the rock, pulling him away from the void that dropped sharply away into a chasm of darkness, the sound of the sea echoing far below.

"There's a narrow goat's trail around here somewhere," he shouted, through the wind. "We'll make our way down to the shoreline, and if the tide's right we'll pick our way round the tip of the island to where Nils and Gustav should still be waiting in the boat. This part of the coast is facing north, opposite to where the French fleet will attack the harbour. We should be safer down there."

"Olof, I need to rest," said Erik, gasping for breath.

With the wind whipping around them, Olof noticed a split in the rock offering a narrow cranny just wide enough for them to shelter. Easing their way down, he held onto his brother, gasping at the ashen look that was spreading over Erik's face. A sticky wetness was beginning to saturate the sleeve of Erik's jacket, the deep hole where the bayonet had been driven in, oozing with a flow of dark blood. Finding the gap between two huge boulders, they squeezed their way in and stretching out they lay perfectly still, listening for any sound above the wind that would alert them to the danger of their British pursuers whom they knew were not that far behind.

Erik moaned as he tried to take the weight off his shoulder, and as Olof helped him move, he howled in agony at his brother's touch. Lying back listening to the wind and Erik's heavy breathing, Olof suddenly jumped in shock. Bolting upright, his hands covering his ears, he turned to look at his brother. The booming sound of the British heavy cannons thundering out their salvo through the darkness, was a signal that the invasion had started.

"It's begun Erik," he said, "the fleet must be attacking the harbour. Wonder what they thought when they realised those cannons were being fired by the British, and not us?"

"Bastards," uttered Erik, grimacing with the pain throbbing in his shoulder.

"I'm going out to look for that trail," said Olof. "We can't stay here for much longer."

Erik nodded, trying to force a smile but a sudden pang of pain made him wince. "Be careful," he muttered, "that English captain who's trying to take Anna away is out there. It's him who's following us."

"Hold onto this," said Olof, slipping his brother's skinning knife from its scabbard and placing it in his hand. "Just in case. I won't be long."

Erik watched him slide out of the narrow little nook, the sound of his footsteps fading in the cacophony of wind and cannon fire resonating around them.

James and Ned stood on the top of the row of high boulders, listening to the sound of their heavy cannons sending the French fleet a message that the British were not about to surrender their hold on this island in the Baltic. Steadying themselves against the wind they peered into the darkness.

"My night vision is still good captain," yelled Ned. "I think I saw two silhouetted figures ease their way off these rocks from just up there and drop down onto the grassy area below."

Cupping his hands over his mouth, James yelled back. "We'll go and see. Erik's wounded badly so they won't get far. They must be holed up here somewhere."

Inching their way along the top of the rock and steadying themselves against the force of the wind, Ned suddenly stopped. "Look captain, one of them's making an escape. It must be Olof."

James squinted in the direction Ned was pointing, seeing the dark outline of a figure appear from a gap and scramble over the rocks until disappearing into the night.

"Yes, it's him," shouted James, "his brother must be down in that gap."

"You go after Olof, Ned. I'll find Erik."

Erik lay back thinking of Christina and how right she might have been in trying to stop him from taking part in the catastrophic failure he was now in. He would never forgive his daughter, if it had been her who had given away the secret of the French mission to take out the British heavy guns. He was disappointed he hadn't been able to kill his daughter's lover, but his chance would come again, of that, he was sure.

Wriggling his way out of the gap he cried out in anguish, uttering a blasphemous oath as he knocked his shoulder against the side of the rock. Struggling to his feet, he inched his way up the dark face of the rock, gritting his teeth with determination and howling out in agony at the increasing burning sensation the wound was giving.

James had lost all feeling in his left arm, being only aware of it hanging limply at his side. He could still use the sword in his right hand but hoped for Anna's sake he could talk her father into surrendering when he found him. Ned had jumped down from the rock they had been walking along, disappearing into the darkness in his search for Olof. He was certain Ned would find him, and not bother to offer him the chance to surrender.

Step by step, James moved along the top of the huge rock, his head bent against the wind as he scoured the dark crevices below where Ned had seen Olof suddenly appear. He knew Erik would be languishing in the shelter of a cranny somewhere, seriously wounded but armed and dangerous.

A desperate cry of agony and a mumbling of words shouted out in anger, brought James to a sudden halt. Listening intently to the sound being carried up on the wind, he was certain Erik was nearby. He tightened his grip on the sword in his right hand, turning his head so his ear pointed towards the rising sound, he heard it again. It was stronger this time, desperate and breathless. And then through the darkness before him, he made out the towering frame of Erik, hauling himself up onto the top of the rock. The two men in Anna's life stood facing each other.

"I'll kill you for two reasons, Englishman," screamed Erik, shuffling closer towards James. "First as revenge for my mother, and second for daring to take my daughter away from her family."

"I love your daughter, Erik, and she loves me." James yelled. "And I'm not responsible for the tragedy that killed your mother."

"But you wear the uniform of those who did!" he bellowed, taking a step forward. "And that's enough for me."

James saw him raise the long skinning knife in his right hand, his left arm hanging limply by his side. Levelling the sword in his right-hand, James braced himself for the lunging attack he was sure would come. But Erik didn't move, he'd stopped a few feet from where James stood, tottering against the full force of the wind. The ringing sound of metal knocking against hard rock echoed around them as the skinning knife fell from Erik's grasp, plunging over the side of the rock to disappear into the darkness of the void. With his empty hand Erik clasped his shoulder, screaming out in pain as a stream of fresh blood cascaded down his sleeve. James dropped his sword taking two quick steps over to where Erik stood bent and crying out in agony. He'd help him, but only for Anna's sake.

"Get away from me, you bastard Englishman," screamed Erik,

lunging out with his free hand.

James stepped back as Erik's right hand caught the sleeve of his jacket, pulling him nearer to the side of the rock. With his good hand James grabbed Erik's collar, dragging him close to where they both stood teetering on the edge of the sheer drop, the sound of the sea roaring far below them. James felt himself careering backwards as Erik tried to grasp him round his throat, his fingers grappling for a hold around James' neck. Still grasping Erik's collar with his right hand, James willed up a superhuman effort to raise his damaged left arm to knock Erik's hand from his throat. With a roar of anger, Erik put all his weight into pushing James further backwards, the look on his face contorted with pain and rancour. Feeling the power in Erik's driving force, James tightened his grip on Erik's collar dragging him with him but unable to stop the momentum of them both going over the edge. With a despairing cry he felt his legs suddenly give way as he slipped backwards over the sheer drop. His arms flailed out desperately trying to grab at something, but there was nothing except the sound of the wind rushing past him as he plunged down through the dark void. Looking up he saw Erik tumbling after him, his legs paddling thin air, the echo of his scream reverberating off the cold damp sides of the cliff face.

And then everything changed into a peaceful slow-motion.

The rush of wind coming up through the void seemed to calm the inevitable end, spiriting him back to the quarterdeck of HMS Hector. He was finally at one with the ship he loved, breathing in again the salty air that whipped around him as Hector ploughed through the white crested swells that surged against its bow. Looking up, he smiled with admiration at the majestic sight of Hector's sails, the wind swelling them with the power to finally carry him home.

He would wait for Anna until her time came, he'd know when. Together, they would be inseparable in his beloved Devon, strolling in the sweetly scented lanes where peace and tranquillity would be theirs for all eternity.

37

Captain Hugo Charbonnier stood on the quarterdeck of the French fleet's flagship, waiting to be informed that Admiral Hastfer's Swedish flotilla had been signalled to join his column and await orders to proceed. The fog that had persisted in blotting out the French ships manoeuvring into formation alongside their flagship had now lifted, but the thick cloud that covered the moon and stars still prevented a night of clear visibility.

"Admiral Hastfer's flotilla are in position and ready, captain" his first lieutenant reported.

"Very well," replied Charbonnier, "signal the fleet and the flotilla to proceed as planned. There's a good wind to carry us forward. Give the order to open all gun ports. Crew to battle stations and officers on the quarterdeck with me. Proceed lieutenant."

Fifteen French warships each containing a score of French marines, together with eight Swedish frigates, dropped their sails to ease their way into formation for the short stretch towards the small harbour of Hanö, confident of victory and a successful end to the British base on the Swedish island. Captain Charbonnier nodded with satisfaction, feeling his task would not be that difficult, the secret being in the taking over of the British cannons positioned on Hanö's highest point.

With a smile he flicked open his telescope, focussing it on the distant lights flickering around the compound housing the meagre number of British sailors and marines detailed to defend their garrison from the might of Napoleon's navy. Tonight, would be acclaimed as his, and a first-class accolade to follow. Snapping the scope shut he yelled the order to reduce sail and load all starboard guns. Peering out through the darkness he saw the outline of the harbour drawing closer, knowing it would not be long before the few British frigates protecting the island would be sent out to engage his fleet. His leading ships would deal with them quickly, and then he'd wait for the captured British heavy cannons to begin their fusillade onto the British positions below. When they opened fire, he'd give the command for his ships to begin their bombardment, supporting the barrage of fire raining down on the British from above. Finally, he'd release the marines aboard his ships to complete the take-over. Now, all he needed to do was to wait.

Dan looked across the starboard side of HMS Hector seeing his accompanying frigate waiting in the darkness, ready to drop sail the moment he gave the order. Thomas Piper nodded towards Dan, his gunners ready and waiting. Dan's instructions were for Hector to make a head on assault on the fleet, making a sharp right angle turn to starboard when a hundred yards away from the leading ships. As they sailed past, they were to release only one salvo from their cannons, tempting the leading French ships to give chase. The accompanying British frigate sailing directly behind Hector was to complete the same manoeuvre, firing all portside guns on its turn. But before commencing their mission all lights aboard both frigates were to be extinguished, leaving the two British warships in total darkness.

The British plan expected the leading French ships to give chase with the remainder of the fleet following, as Hector and her sister ship sped away towards the harbour. Under cover of darkness the two British frigates would then disappear to link up with the four other British warships waiting alongside Commodore Percival's ship of the line, a mile east of the harbour. Hector was to fire one of her cannons as a signal that the French fleet were in proximity of the harbour, prompting the British marines on the harbour wall to light the beacons. The British gunners waiting for the beacons to shed their light would then rain down their salvos onto the invading French ships. When the barrage ceased, HMS Hector and the five other British warships waiting in the darkness were to set sail, coming up behind the fleet to finish off those who had managed to escape the blitz. The two platoons of British marines undercover in the field of long grass, would then rush the harbour to engage any of the fleet's marines who had managed to get ashore.

Hector's crew waited patiently outside the mouth of the harbour, sensing the imminent order to drop sail. Dan stood on the quarterdeck listening to the wind rattling through the ship's rigging, hoping all had gone well with the ambush in the forest. Looking up at its dark outline, he wondered how many of Hector's crew had survived the fight, praying they had stopped them from getting to the heavy cannons.

"Sir, lieutenant sir," a voice called from behind the quarterdeck.

Turning, Dan saw Bill Nark the boatswain calling him.

"Sir, the lookout has sighted the fleet. A column of dark shapes about a mile off our bow."

"Signal our sister ship, Mr. Nark. We move now, full sail."

With the wind billowing her sails, Hector leapt through the dark swells crashing against her sides. Davey Sturrock grasped the ship's wheel keeping her on course towards the French fleet, now less than a mile off her bow. Dan glanced back over his shoulder at the dark shape of Hector's sister ship following just off the wake of their stern. He knew the French commander would be expecting British frigates to engage him and would be scouring the dark waters for signs of lights approaching.

Attacking in the darkness with no lights on board would surely create an element of surprise, the French having no warning they were coming. With luck they would inflict some damage on the leading ships, so convincing their commander to give chase immediately.

"Sharp turn to starboard at a hundred yards, Mr. Sturrock."

"Aye, aye, lieutenant," replied Hector's helmsman. "Two hundred yards and approaching."

"Mr. Piper," yelled Dan through the wind. "Prime all portside guns. Get ready for my order."

"Aye, lieutenant," responded Thomas Piper.

"One hundred and fifty yards and approaching, lieutenant," called Davey Sturrock."

"Reduce sails, Mr Nark," yelled Dan.

The sudden reduction of Hector's speed coincided with Davey Sturrock's call, "One hundred yards, lieutenant."

"Now, Mr Sturrock," hollered Dan, "sharp turn to starboard. Fire all portside guns Mr. Piper."

A crescendo of noise filled the silence around the darkened sea, the booming sound of Hector's thirteen portside cannons firing simultaneously bringing shocked alarm to the French fleet. Within minutes a second salvo reverberated as Hector's sister ship made her turn, releasing her eighteen pounder cannon balls into the leading French ships.

Hector sped away with her sister ship following, the wind carrying the sound of alarm bells ringing aboard the French ships. Dan peered through the darkness trying to discern whether the two salvos had caused any damage, but with the darkness enveloping everything behind him it was impossible to make out the effect they'd had.

"Mr. Nark," he yelled, "what sees the lookout astern?"

He listened as Bill Nark yelled up to the main top yardarm.

"Ships are breaking away from the fleet and following us, lieutenant," he yelled back.

"Full sail, Mr. Nark," ordered Dan. "Their hell awaits, let them follow us."

Captain Charbonnier gasped at the outline of a British frigate suddenly appearing out of the darkness, no more than a hundred yards from where he stood on the quarterdeck of his flagship. He watched it turn, yelling out an order to sound the ship's alarm bell as Hector's portside cannons opened with a deafening salvo. Eighteen pounder cannon balls whistled through the air above him as they found their targets in the ships around him. Masts and rigging toppled from two of the leading ships next to his flagship, the screams of their crew being carried towards him on the wind. His anger quickly rose on seeing a second frigate emerge from the darkness, its cannons sending another salvo into the ships surrounding him. Turning to his first lieutenant he yelled, "Why weren't those two British frigates spotted?"

"They are showing no lights, captain," came the reply. "It was impossible for us to see them."

"They're not turning to engage us," raged Charbonnier peering through his telescope. "They're making a run for it, signal the fleet to make sail. They'll be heading back to the harbour, so we'll follow and sink them before they get near their base."

"They've fallen for it Mr. Nark," yelled Dan looking over the stern, "they're following. Reduce sail so they close the gap. I want them close to the harbour before hoisting full sail again. Mr. Sturrock, when I give that order turn us two points to port and follow the coordinates Captain Carey gave you to link up with our other ships."

"Aye, aye lieutenant," called Davey Sturrock.

"Mr. Piper," bellowed Dan. "Load number one portside cannon. On my order, fire out to sea, it's our signal for our marines to light the beacons on the harbour walls."

"Aye, aye lieutenant," shouted the master gunner.

The captain of Hector's sister ship had duly followed Dan's strategy, shouting an instruction to redeploy full sail the instant Hector did. He knew Dan was about to make a turn deeper into the darkness to join their sister ships.

The dark shapes of the harbour walls suddenly loomed on Hector's starboard side, the sound of cannons firing from the French ships behind testing the range between them and the two British frigates. It wouldn't be long until the French closed the gap enough for them to have gained the right range to target Hector and her sister ship.

"Now Mr. Nark, full sail," hollered Dan. "Mr. Sturrock, two points to port. Fire cannon number one, Mr. Piper."

Hector turned smoothly in the wind, the boom of her number one portside cannon firing into the darkness. As the wind filled her sails, Davey Sturrock turned her gracefully onto the coordinates James had previously given him, a loud cheer resounding around the deck as Hector's crew hailed the flares of light that suddenly burst along the harbour walls. Umpteen beacons erupted into flaming torches, illuminating everything within a few hundred yards out to sea, the twenty-three combined warships of the French and Swedish navies standing out like the black pieces on a chess board.

Dan looked up at the dark heights overlooking the harbour, praying the imminent salvos from the heavy cannons were to be those aimed by the British gunners and not by the French special force. He wondered again how James had fared and how many of Hector's selected crew had survived the battle with the French marines.

"Lieutenant sir," yelled Davey Sturrock, "two hundred yards and we're at our rendezvous."

"Reduce sail Mr. Nark," shouted Dan. "Steady as she goes Mr. Sturrock, I can see the outline of our ships ahead."

Hector coasted through the darkness coming up next to Commodore Percival's ship of the line, the four other British warships bobbing steadily up and down on the dark swells. Dan stood alone on Hector's quarterdeck staring at the glare of the beacons across the sea, knowing that the silence that had descended around them would soon be shattered by a fusillade of cannon fire raining down from Hanö's highest point.

Corporal Sidney Luscombe nodded at the sudden illumination coming from the harbour below, the columns of French warships clearly in his sights. The flaming beacons along the harbour's walls were the signals he and the other gunners had been waiting for. With the remaining gunner from his previous team of four and with the assistance of a young marine from one of the other guns, he barked out the order for them to load the cannon. The young gunner acting as the sponge man rammed a bag of gunpowder down the barrel of the cannon. He waited for his comrade to insert the heavy cannon ball, then drove it down the barrel, wedging it tightly behind the bag of powder. Standing at the rear of the cannon Corporal Luscombe inserted a thin spike into a small vent on top of the rear section of the cannon's barrel. Then piercing a bag of gunpowder next to him, he filled the vent with a charge of powder. By the light of the torches set around the two other cannons, he saw their gunners were waiting for his signal to fire. Peering down the top of the barrel at the

French fleet below, he smiled, satisfied with the cannon's angle.

"Stand back," he yelled at the two gunners, his left arm raised in the air. "Fire," he bellowed, bringing his arm down and lighting the powder charge with a slow burning taper held in his right hand.

The sizzling sound of the charge of powder sparking its way down the vent and igniting the bag of gunpowder in the barrel, quickly gave way to a deafening boom as the heavy cannon ball jettisoned out of the barrel, the cannon jolting in an upward jerk, like the bucking action of a stubborn mule. The two other cannons followed suit, the sound of their cannons firing simultaneously echoing far across the island.

With smoke billowing out of the end of the barrel, the young gunner dipped the sponge end of the pole into a bucket of water and yanking it out thrust it deep inside the barrel of the cannon, swishing it alongside the hot metal amidst clouds of steam and smoke.

"Load," hollered Corporal Luscombe standing at the back of the cannon.

The firing of the heavy cannons continued without interruption, the thunderous sound of them discharging their missiles down onto the French fleet reverberating far into the night. When the last cannon ball had been fired, Corporal Luscombe stood back mopping the sweat from his brow. Peering down at the scene in front of the harbour, he shouted to his two gunners. "Come and look lads, looks like we've had a good night!"

Dan was quickly alert as silence took over from the sudden ending of the deafening barrage. Looking to his left, he saw the captains of Hector's sister frigates dropping sail as they prepared to advance on what had to be a depleted French fleet. To his right, the sloop-of-war stood ready and waiting for his signal to go.

"Mr. Nark," he called, "are the crew at battle stations?"

"Aye, aye lieutenant. That they are sir," came the reply.

"Signal our sister ships to move in attack formation with us."

"Signalling now, sir," replied Bill Nark.

"Mr. Sturrock, two degrees to starboard," shouted Dan, "then dead ahead towards the French fleet, or what's left of them. Mr. Piper, load all starboard and portside guns. We're going to finish off any Frenchie that may have survived that deadly cannonade. Full sail Mr. Nark."

38

Captain Charbonnier smiled, as three flashes from Hano's heights flared through the darkness to be quickly followed by a set of thunderous booms reverberating over the harbour. The British heavy guns had opened fire as if on cue for his arrival. His smile quickly changed into a look of horror as the sound of whistling cannonballs zipping through the night air overshot the harbour to find their targets on two of his fleet's ships. As the screams of injured and dying men reached him, three more flashes burst from the darkened heights, quickly followed by a deafening salvo as the heavy guns roared in the darkness.

"Mon Dieu!" he yelled, "What has happened? Is that our special force up there? The idiots are firing down at us."

His words were drowned out as two twenty-four pounder cannon balls ripped through the flagship's decking, toppling the main and fore masts in an ear-splitting explosion, the armoury on its lower deck suddenly detonating as another cannon ball tore through an already gaping hole in the upper deck. The captains of the surrounding ships looked on in dismayed horror as their flagship and crew were blown to smithereens, chaos spreading amongst the fleet as they looked to see who would now take over command. Several of the fleet's leading ships found it unable to turn, due to ships incurring direct hits from the cannon fire raining down on them.

From the field of long grass where they were waiting to storm the harbour, the two platoons of British marines and the designated sailors from the six British warships, watched the devastation being inflicted on the French ships, the beacons along the harbour wall still burning furiously as they lit up the carnage before them. Cheers and whistles could be heard from between the long shoots of grass as the British looked on at the death of Napoleon's invading fleet, and still the deafening fusillade continued. A few of the French ships managed to fire their cannons, their cannonballs missing the harbour and falling away somewhere into the darkness over the island.

Admiral Hastfer, standing on the quarterdeck of the Swedish flagship, watched in alarm at the chaotic scene before him. Being at the rear of the fleet, his ships were yet untouched by the lethal bombardment going on.

"Signal our flotilla to make an about turn," he commanded his first officer. "We're leaving."

Without firing a shot or giving the doomed French ships another thought, the eight Swedish warships turned about and slunk away under the cover of darkness.

Captain Rupert Crisp, commander of the two platoons of British marines watched the scene through his telescope, focussing on three frigates that had managed to break away from the devastation and manoeuvre up to the harbour wall. By the light of the beacons, he watched as grappling irons tied to the ends of ropes were slung up onto the walls, the silhouettes of French marines scrambling up the ropes causing him to turn quickly to his lieutenant.

"My God, they're scaling the harbour walls. Three of their ships have released their marines. Bring the men to attention, we're going to see some action after all. On my command we go."

The heavy cannons suddenly ceased firing, allowing a strange silence to settle over the harbour. Captain Crisp flicked open his telescope, sweeping it over the devastation below. He tallied eight ships half-submerged, their masts and rigging hanging over their sterns like thick splinters of wood and hemp. Shreds of torn material that had once billowed proudly in the wind, hung limply over crumpled bulwarks, while the rising swells of the sea greedily swallowed the scores of bodies that drifted aimlessly around the wrecks. He counted six ships still afloat, including the three that had deposited their marines on the harbour wall, slightly damaged but still seaworthy and capable of putting up a fight, the marines on board a dangerous threat should they find their way ashore. Scanning the scene, he looked for their flagship but there was no sign. He searched again focussing on the half-submerged ships, their bows bent deep under the sea while their sterns stuck up out of the water like ostriches burying their heads in the sand. None of them resembled a ship of the line. It was then that he realised the heavy cannons up on the heights had hit the bull's-eye and destroyed the fleet's command ship and crew, blowing them literally to kingdom come. Snapping his scope shut he drew his sword.

"We take no prisoners men!" he hollered, "After me, charge!"

Standing on the quarterdeck of his ship of the line, Commodore Percival watched HMS Hector and the sloop-of-war sail away at the head of an arrow formation, the other four frigates sailing behind them. As commander, he would stay with his ship, confident that the heavy guns had inflicted crippling damage on the French fleet. It was now up to the six British warships to finish the job at sea. He knew the captain of the two marine platoons would be securing the harbour from inland, finding and destroying any of their marines who had made it ashore.

Dan flicked open his telescope sweeping it over the scene of devastation before him. He was quick to pinpoint six French ships, still seaworthy and manoeuvring away from the stricken remains of their fleet.

"Mr. Nark," he yelled, "signal our ships to break away from formation and select a Frenchie from any of those six manoeuvring away from the destruction. Orders are to sink them before they can regroup."

"Aye, aye sir," responded Hector's boatswain.

Turning to his helmsman, he pointed towards Hector's bow.

"Mr. Sturrock, there's a Frenchie dead ahead, about to make a turn off our starboard bow. She's ours."

"Mr. Piper. Load the five carronades on the forecastle with heavy shot. Fire at her stern when we're a hundred yards. Once we turn to portside, give her all our starboard guns. I want her sunk, Mr. Piper."

"Aye, aye sir, that she will be, lieutenant."

"Mr. Nark, reduce sail when I order."

"Aye, aye lieutenant. Sister ships signalled sir. They're ready and have chosen their targets."

"Very good Mr. Nark. Mr. Sturrock, count us in."

"Aye, aye sir. Three hundred yards and approaching fast."

Dan flicked open his telescope appreciating the flaming light from two of the French ships on fire, the captain of the French frigate Dan had set his sights on being totally unaware of the danger converging on his stern.

"Two hundred yards, lieutenant," yelled Davey Sturrock.

Dan swept his telescope in an arc, seeing the sloop-of-war and two of Hector's sister frigates engaging the French ships they had selected, their cannons booming out over the night-capped sea. Turning to face Bill Nark, he yelled out his order, "Reduce sail now, Mr. Nark."

"One hundred yards, lieutenant. She's dead ahead, sir," yelled Davey Sturrock.

"Fire carronades, Mr. Piper," ordered Dan.

The sound of Hector's carronades releasing their heavy shot echoed across the sea, the smoke from the small cannons wisping across the deck like some ethereal entity. Dan had only a few seconds to see the shot tear into the stern of the French ship before giving the order to turn to portside.

"Now Mr. Sturrock. Sharp turn to port. Mr. Piper, give her all our starboard cannons. Fire now."

Hector's timbers shook with the force of all her starboard cannons firing, the smoke from the cannons blotting out the view of her target.

"Bring her round, Mr. Sturrock," yelled Dan, as Hector sailed past the doomed French frigate.

As the smoke cleared, Hector turned back to view what remained of the French ship. Dan smiled at the cheers from his crew, his eyes ranging over the damage Hector's guns had caused. The stern of the French frigate had been blown away leaving a gaping hole that was quickly filling with seawater. Masts and rigging lay scattered over the sea, while two great holes stretched along her portside from midships to bow.

"Mr. Piper, to the quarterdeck," called Dan.

"How fare our other ships, Thomas?" he asked.

"From what I could make out, they scored well, sir. Of the six Frenchies we spied manoeuvring away, five have been sunk, the other losing her mizzen in a broadside with our sloop. She's managed to limp away."

"The sole survivor," said Dan. "We'll leave her to carry back the news of their defeat. Mr. Nark, signal our ships to return to Commodore Percival's ship of the line, we'll all link up there. Looks like we did it, Thomas. Captain Carey's ambush was obviously successful in stopping their special force from taking over our heavy guns. Thanks to the accuracy of those cannons, it's safe to say the invasion's over. Come the dawn, we'll know for sure when Captain Crisp reports the island safe from their marines. Mr. Sturrock, take us back to our command ship, we've got good news for the Commodore. Full sail Mr. Nark, it's been a long night."

Ned Hatchet stopped on the edge of the cliff making out a narrow goat's trail leading down through the darkness to the rocky coastline below. He was certain Olof had found his way down this trail to check out a route back along the shoreline or to hide out until dawn. Only a matter of minutes had passed since he had seen the outline of him emerging from under the rock not far from where he and James had been standing. Ned knew there was no other escape route for him to follow.

Gingerly he took a few footsteps down the murky trail holding onto a row of small bushes sprouting along its side, the sound of the sea raging far below. The darkness was blotting out everything around him, but concentrating on his night vision he managed to make it half-way down to where the trail took a sharp turning. Stopping to catch his breath he suddenly heard it, the sound of a terrifying scream echoing on the wind. It had come from up on the boulders behind him and meant only one thing, James had found Erik. The despairing cry had come from one of them; overcome with the urge to rush back and help his captain, he stood still, focussing on the trail and convincing himself that the scream had come from Erik. Gripping the handle of his cutlass, he hastened on down the steep incline.

The trail finished at the bottom of the cliff, levelling out onto a short stretch of shingle where rows of rocks loomed up along the coastline, the sound of the heavy cannons above still pounding down onto the French fleet. Scouring the scene before him he grinned, pleased to see the mist and cloud slowly disappearing as light from the moon began to shed its glow over the rocky shoreline. Taking a few steps forward he crunched over the shingle towards the cluster of rocks when instinct made him suddenly stop, his intuition warning him of danger.

A sudden movement to his right made him draw his cutlass. Turning, he automatically ducked, as the dark outline of Olof sprang at him from the shadows, the swishing sound of steel slicing through the air passing above his head. Olof stood in front of him, the long-bladed dagger he had rescued from Philippe Laval raised and ready to strike again.

"You're one of the two who followed my brother and me into the forest some days ago," he sneered. "I'm going to gut you from crotch to gullet for what your kind did to my mother."

"That I very much doubt, Swede," said Ned, swinging the cutlass in his right hand.

"But before I do," continued Olof, "just tell me. How did you know we were coming through the forest with the French marines?"

"Well, I'm not sure I should let you know, it being confidential like," said Ned, enjoying the questioning look spreading over Olof's face.

"But you are going to tell me aren't you, Englishman?"

Now's my chance, thought Ned, *this'll off balance him.*

Ned tightened his grip on his cutlass. "I overheard our captain telling our first lieutenant that it was your niece, Erik's daughter Anna. She's in love with the captain, and she told him everything."

For a moment there was silence as Ned's words sunk in. Squinting towards Olof, Ned waited for the moment when the Swede would drop his guard.

"You lie," screamed Olof, "no member of the Gunnarsson family would be so treacherous."

"Her information led to the failure of your mission, and that's a fact," bellowed Ned, waiting for the moment.

Olof dropped the hand he had raised with the dagger and in his fury charged at Ned. In one nimble movement Ned sidestepped but cried out as his footing slipped on a lump of wet seaweed. In an instant Olof was on him forcing him down onto the damp shingle. Still clutching his cutlass in his right hand, Ned raised his left hand, locking it onto Olof's wrist to press the dagger away from his own throat. His eyes red with fury and spittle dribbling from his mouth, Olof pressed the dagger back down towards Ned, the muscles in his right arm bulging with power. For a moment Ned thought it was all over and then a vision of him fighting with his captain and crew in one of their many sea battles flashed before his eyes. Pride and fealty to his ship and comrades suddenly surged through him, giving him an added will to survive. Summoning up an almighty effort he brought up his right hand holding the cutlass and, smashing the hilt into the side of Olof's head, he roared with rage, kicking away the dagger from Olof's hand and slicing his head cleanly from his shoulders. Panting, he watched the incoming tide slowly claim Olof's severed head, the pounding of the British cannons still thundering from the top of Hanö's heights.

Reflecting on the scream he'd heard from the top of the cliff he knew he'd have to get back to his captain and, with a carefree glance at Olof's headless body now half submerged in a pool of water, he trudged across the pebbly shoreline towards the goat's trail. Something lying on the top of a row of rocks a stone's throw from where he was standing suddenly caught his eye. Peering through the dim light, he froze.

"No, it can't be," he cried.

Tearing across the shingle, he scrambled over the rocks, slipping and sliding over their wet tops until he came to what he had been dreading to find. Broken and grossly twisted, yet entwined like sleeping lovers, were the bodies of James and Erik. Under the moonlight, Ned gazed down at them; part of Erik's face was set in a look of determination, one cold eye staring closely into the face of his daughter's lover as though he were still telling him that it had all been in the name of revenge, revenge for his mother's death at the hands of the British Royal Navy; with his eyes open and staring into the disfigured face of Anna's father, James lay in a peaceful repose, a hint of a faint smile showing across the corners of his mouth.

Ned dropped to one knee, and taking his captain's hand placed it reverently against the side of his cheek. Silently he prayed for his soul, telling him of the respect and admiration he'd had for him.

Looking up at the peak of the sheer cliff before him, he tried to imagine James' last moments and the terror he must have felt. He'd fetch help immediately to move the bodies before the tide swept over the rocks to claim them.

Hastening back over the shingle, he stopped at the start of the goat's trail. Looking back over the rocks, he bowed his head at the sight of the two bodies lying together in the moonlight. Then with a deep sigh, he hurried up the narrow track, noting that the sound of the bombardment from the heavy cannons had finally ceased.

39

Sitting on the bench at the bottom of the rough track that led up to her house, Anna stared out across the sea at the distant outline of Hanö Island. Dusk was beginning to set in, the sky already aflame with the red and orange hues of a setting sun. This was the time James had promised to come for her. A night on his ship and then the start of the voyage to England the following day.

Her mother had wept uncontrollably, when Dan and the young lieutenant had come to give them the news the day after the invasion. As she had listened to Dan's sorrowful account of the discovery of the two bodies, she had reflected sadly on the irony of James and her father being found wrapped closely together, as though they had finally accepted each other in their last moments.

It had taken a while for the tragic news to sink in, and when it had she had shut herself away in her room, grieving desperately for the loss of her one and only love. She knew she would carry James in her heart forever.

Before he had left, Dan had promised to come for her in the morning when they were to bury James and the fourteen others who had lost their lives in defending the island. He would stay with her during the funeral service, being her support, as her captain was laid to rest in one of the fifteen graves dug on the island's heights.

HMS Hector was to return to England later that day, with Dan acting as temporary captain until his promotion was approved by the Admiralty. Anna would spend a few days on the island with her friend Ulla until Lars came to fetch her.

Her father's body had been buried that morning in the small cemetery next to the church in Nogersund. There had been no news of her uncle Olof, his body never found.

A pretty lace kerchief lay on the bench next to her, the sides of the fabric turned inwards to protect the cherished treasure she had placed there. Reaching out she picked it up and, putting it to her lips, she kissed it gently before opening it. For a long while she gazed at the red rose petals spread around the centre of the lace, remembering the beautiful words he had spoken to her when he had given her the single rose. Tears filled her eyes as she pictured him in her mind's eye, pointing out the tiny inlet of Nogersund as they stood holding each other on the rock that overlooked the sea on Hanö's highest point. Closing her eyes, she visualised herself back on the island's stony track when he had held her hand in his, while pointing down at his ship anchored at the mouth of the harbour far below.

Forcing her eyes open she gave way to the tears that flooded down her cheeks, her body quaking with the deep sobs that were breaking her heart. She saw him then, standing by the corner, his arm raised in a wave, his smile telling her he was fine.

"James," she cried, rushing to the corner where she could see him waiting.

But he wasn't there.

Beside herself with grief she stood at the corner, her sobs heavy and unending. She was sure it had been him. She had seen him, and he had looked as he had when she had last seen him.

Walking back to the bench she bent to pick up the kerchief and petals that lay where she had left them. Looking back out to sea, she watched the silhouette of a three-masted ship sailing towards the horizon, the outline of Hanö Island deeply set in the shadows of the setting sun.

With her heart aching she made her way back up the hill to her house. She would wait there until morning when Dan came to take her back to the island, and the agonising finality of the last farewells.

A brisk breeze fanned the little skiff's sails, driving it further towards the British garrison on the island of Hanö. Anna sat in the stern watching the walls of the harbour draw nearer. Dan guided the boat past the wrecks of the French warships, bringing it smoothly up to a mooring at the end of the quay. As she stood waiting for him to furl the sail, her eyes wandered over the deserted harbour stopping at the building that served as the quartermaster's store. She saw herself closing the door behind her as she hurried out, her eyes searching the quay for him. She saw him in her mind's eye standing where she was now waiting, and how she had gasped with joy on seeing him. Her eyes welled with tears as she remembered how she had lifted her skirts and ran to him, leaping into his arms as he stood smiling towards her.

"Everyone's up on the heights," said Dan coming up next to her. "They're waiting for you before the service begins. Word has got around of the part you played in giving James the information that saved the island, and of the future you had planned together. I am sure he'd want them to show you their thanks for what you did for us all."

Together they walked up the stony track, Anna stopping halfway. Turning, she looked down at the harbour, closing her eyes for a moment's private reflection.

"Thank you, Dan," she said, smiling at him, "I'm ready."

The crews of the six British warships, together with the two platoons of Royal Marines, lined the wide grassy area of Hanö's uppermost point. Hector's chaplain, Sebastian Pomeroy, stood beside the fifteen coffins ready to begin the service. Each of the coffins lay next to a freshly dug grave. A respectful applause greeted Anna as she walked sedately alongside Dan towards the first coffin in the row. Opposite, the crew of HMS Hector stood rigidly to attention, each member silently grieving the loss of their esteemed captain and fellow sailors.

James' name and rank had been engraved onto his coffin as were the names of the fourteen other servicemen. Clifford Williams and Richard Davis, two prominent able seamen from HMS Hector, lay next to James.

Sebastian Pomeroy spoke well of each of the deceased, paying tribute to the young captain of HMS Hector who through his skilful captaincy at sea had regularly brought his ship and crew through many dangerous engagements, his final triumph leading to the defeat of the French invasion. As the coffins were committed, Anna gripped Dan's arm, fearful of breaking down with the painful emotion that was tearing at her heart.

At the end of the service each of Hector's commissioned and non-commissioned officers took turns to stand in front of their captain's grave for a moment of private contemplation. Seven servicemen, one sailor from each of the warships and one marine, gave a three-volley musket salute that was duly followed by a twenty-one-gun salute from the three heavy cannons.

As the servicemen left the area, Commodore Percival approached Anna, letting her know his regard for James and how he would be recommending him for a posthumous gallantry award.

Thanking him, she turned to Dan, "I'd like a few moments here alone, Dan," she said.

"Of course," Dan replied, "I'll wait for you at the top of the stony track."

"Oh and Dan. Was it from up there that James and my father fell?" she asked, pointing towards a group of boulders nestling on the peak.

"Yes, Anna," said Dan. "They fell from there."

Standing alone at James' grave, Anna looked down at his coffin.

"Goodbye my darling," she said softly. "I know you're home and at peace, and that you are fine. You told me so yesterday when you came to me on the corner. I'll wait for you to come to me when it is my time, you'll know when. When Dan sails for England later today, I'll come back here to be alone with you. There's something I need to tell you."

Reaching into a deep pocket of her gown, she took out the lace kerchief that she'd had on the bench the previous day. Turning her back to the wind, she gently drew back the sides picking out three of the blood red petals, leaving the other three safely within the lace. Standing over the grave, she opened her hand watching them flutter down to rest on top of the coffin.

"Goodbye my love," she whispered.

As late afternoon brought a fresh wind to the sails of HMS Hector, Anna stood alone next to James' grave, gazing out over the sea far below her. Looking out over the wide expanse, her heart jumped as the frigate that had once been the pride of her captain sailed into view, a dot in a wide ocean.

On board, Dan Sutherland breathed in the salty air whipping before him, relishing being back on the open sea. Looking around the deck he smiled with admiration at his crew's vigour to their duties. Up on the topsail yard the lookout scanned the horizon for any sign of unfriendly vessels, while Davey Sturrock waited for

Dan's order to set Hector on her course.

With the wind ballooning the frigate's sails, Dan turned round to take a last look at the island that had very nearly fallen into the hands of the French.

"Farewell James my friend," he called into the wind. "Rest in peace captain."

Turning back, he yelled the order to Hector's helmsman,

"Mr. Sturrock, set the course I gave you. We're going home."

Anna watched the frigate sail into the sunset knowing she would have been there with her captain had things turned out differently. With a deep sigh she turned to the grave, her hands resting over the new life growing inside her.

"I'm here my darling," she said, softly. "Now, there's something I want to tell you."

The End

ABOUT THE AUTHOR

Chris Thorndyke was born in Totnes in South Devon and lived in what he describes as the most beautiful resort in Britain, Torbay. For many years he taught English to foreign students until moving to Sweden where he continued to teach in an International School in Lund. Now retired he spends his time writing and enjoying Sweden's forested and lakeside walks with his wife Anki and their two pet dogs. A father of three grown-up sons and six grandchildren he and his wife regularly visit the UK to spend time in their favourite haunts and to catch up with family and friends.

Ingram Content Group UK Ltd.
Milton Keynes UK
UKHW040846190623
423681UK00004B/312